Hope Nicely's Lessons for Life

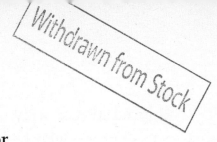

Praise for

Hope Nicely's Lessons for Life

'I can't even find words to say how much I adore
Hope Nicely's Lessons for Life! A heart-bursting
book, full of tears, laughter and hope. Gorgeously
written with an incredible protagonist . . . I cannot
recommend it enough. It's FABULOUS'
Jessica Ryn

'A sunburst of a story, full of love, kindness and
one of the sweetest, most engaging central
characters you're likely to meet. I was drawn in
from the very first page by Caroline Day's sensitive
portrayal of Hope Nicely's inner voice; as I
followed Hope on her mission to make sense of
the present, to uncover the past and to write her
book, I found myself sharing in her triumphs and
frustrations, her laughter and tears. It's a touching,
tender story, but Hope Nicely's wonderful humour
and delicious honesty mean that it's never
sentimental. An absolute joy'
Sarah Haywood

Hope Nicely's Lessons for Life

About the Author

CAROLINE DAY is a freelance journalist and consultant editor, from Crouch End, North London, where she lives with her husband, children (when one's not away at university and the other out with friends) and two dogs. She is an alumna of the Curtis Brown Creative novel-writing course and has written extensively for national media, with a focus on the human side of health and family issues. She first started writing *Hope Nicely's Lessons for Life* as part of National Novel Writing Month (NaNoWriMo), and successfully completed her 50,000-word target in the space of a month (although she has since edited it a lot). Caroline is in close contact with the charity FASD Awareness and is grateful for all their help, input and encouragement. She does have some personal experience which gave her both the seed of the idea for her novel ('where Hope comes from' as she describes it) and huge respect for those living neuro-diverse lives.

Hope Nicely's Lessons for Life

Caroline Day

ZAFFRE

First published in the UK in 2021 by
ZAFFRE
An imprint of Bonnier Books UK
80–81 Wimpole St, London W1G 9RE
Owned by Bonnier Books
Sveavägen 56, Stockholm, Sweden

A CIP catalogue record for this book is
available from the British Library.

Hardback ISBN: 978–1–83877–271–0
Export ISBN: 978–1–83877–272–7

Also available as an ebook and an audiobook

1 3 5 7 9 10 8 6 4 2

Typeset by Palimpsest Book Production Limited, Falkirk, Stirlingshire
Printed and bound in Great Britain by Clays Ltd, Elcograf S.p.A.

Zaffre is an imprint of Bonnier Books UK
www.bonnierbooks.co.uk

For Ben, who has been Hope's champion from the first page – and who has always been mine.

Contents page

1

INTRODUCTIONS
AND OPENINGS . . .

Prologue

My name is Hope Nicely. Hope as in hope. And Nicely like nicely.

Why I am writing this book? That's easy. This book is going to change my life. I have never even been in a group like this one before. I never thought I would ever try to write an actual *book*. Not a real one anyway. I mean, flip a pancake, most of my teachers would have told you I'm the last person who could ever do *that*. They would say there's not much chance I'll see it through. Not likely, Hope Nicely. Not if the book is more than one page long. My brain is a bit of a jumble sale, you see – that's what they always told me, the teachers at school. They said it was a right old jumble sale, with all the jumble piled up high so you don't know what's in there, just all the clothes and the curtains and the toys, all in one big pile. It's not a *real* jumble sale, of course – not like the one at the church, which is every summer,

3

and you have to pay 50p to go in, and maybe there's a Nike hoodie or a yellow teapot or an ice cream maker and it's still in its box. It's not a real-in-the-world jumble sale. Because that would be impossible. It's just my brain that's a bit of a muddle.

My boss says it too. Karen, my boss. That's why I have to do my walks with her. Never just me with the dogs. I'd forget which dogs were out walking with me otherwise. If I was on my own, I'd take the wrong dogs home and leave my ones running around alone in the woods. Because I've never been very good at remembering. And maybe that will make writing this book, my book, a bit difficult. And I'm not very good at – what's the word – flip a pancake, it will come to me, I'm sure . . . I'm very easily distracted, that's what they always said when I was at school. Flitty. Like a flitty thing. Flit, flit flittery flit. A flitty sieve. My mind wanders and my memory – well, maybe the less said about that . . .

Persevering! See, I knew the word would come. That's what words do. My mum says words can be like puppies who bring you a ball, and when you reach for it they run away with it, but really they just want to play and if you turn your back they will rush back and drop the ball at your feet. Teasing you. My brain is just like that. *Persevering.* That's what I'm not very good at. That's what people have always said. All my teachers. And Karen. That's my boss. And I do have a little problem about getting confused. Just when there's too much to think about. And also I . . .

I talk too much. Everybody says this to me. I don't know what to say and what to keep back. And some of this I'm saying out loud. And some of it is in my head. I'm never quite sure which is which. And it's worse when I'm nervous, my mum, Jenny Nicely, says, or when I'm excited. Or when I haven't slept enough. Or when it's just a day when my mouth feels like it has a lot to talk about. And so what I do – what I'm doing now – is I sit on my hands, and I tell myself: Hope Nicely, you need to count to three. And I count. One. Two. Three.

Now, it's true that my counting isn't good and when it's bigger numbers they can float out of my head like balloons into the sky. But one, two, three is as easy as blinking my eyes. Even I can't let one, two, three slip through my fingers like balloon strings. I've done it with my mum, that's Jenny Nicely, a hundred times. A million. Practising. Sit on my hands. One, two, three. And I talk my brain back down. Calm. Slow. Count. Don't go telling everyone everything that's in my head. Think about other people, when they're listening to you, and try not to just talk and talk and talk and talk.

And so here I am – see – my hands are flat on the chair beneath my bottom. And I'm looking at the big round table and the people sitting at it. And I take a nice deep breath and I count to three again. And then I count the people sitting at the table – not big and round, did I say round? Flip a pancake. That's not what I meant at all. Oval. You see, that shape word, dropped by a puppy. Big *oval* table. Not round. Oval. And there are one – two – three – four – five – six – seven – eight – nine – ten people around the *oval* table. And because the numbers have come to me kindly and have not hidden in the wrong bits of my head, I'm feeling calm now and my brain is clear. And I start again. From the beginning . . .

1

My name is Hope Nicely. Hope as in hope. And
Nicely like nicely. I am twenty-five years old. I have
a real job as a dog walker and I live with my mother,
Jenny, in the close by the station. Station Close. I am
here because I'm going to write a book. It's not a
historical book – like the woman with the glasses on
a chain around her neck, who just told us hers is set
during the revolution in France, or a detective one,
like the man on my left – no, my right – with a
watch that is ginormous and very gold. No, it is my
left. Because, look, if I bring my hands out from
under my bottom, with my fingers pointing up and
making a corner with my thumbs, there's an L
between my finger and my thumb on this side, and
that's how you know. Because of L being for left. My
book is going to be – I look for the words and they're
right there, because my brain is all clear and kind
– *non-fiction*. That means real. Not *fiction*. Not a

make-it-up story. It's called a memoir. Or an autobiography. About my life.

And I want to say a lot of other things: about how this book is very important. This is the book that is going to find out who my birth mother is and why she gave me away, even if it was all for the best, actually. This is the book that is going to give me the word I can't remember at this precise moment but is a bit like closing time. And my mum, Jenny Nicely, says it's a very good thing to write this book. It will be a Big Achievement. But I know I should stop talking now, because the writer, our teacher – Marnie Shale, who has written four novels and been shortlisted for an award whose name I can't quite remember but I think it's like a cup of coffee – is leaning forward in her seat, on the opposite side of the round table. And she is smiling at me and holding out her hands towards me. Oval table. *Oval.* And I know – because I have role played this with my mum, Jenny – that this is a cue that she's about to talk. And I want to tell her lots of other things about my book and why it is so important that I write it, I am bursting to tell her more, but I am sitting on my hands again and I am breathing in deeply and I am telling myself that it is her time to speak now and that we have to take turns. This is how a conversation works, and that means everyone has their chance, not just one person talking, talking, talking. I am leaning towards her, too – this is called mirroring – and I am telling myself I have to stop talking. I have to listen now.

It is hard to be quiet. There is a buzz in my head and I want to shout. I want to tell her, listen to me, listen to what I have to say about my book. But I count inside my mind. One, two, three. One, two, three. One. Two. Three.

And I stop. Because now is my turn to listen.

'Hello, Hope.' This is Marnie Shale, and her hair bounces as she speaks. Her voice is low and warm and I think she might be Scottish because when she talks it's a bit like music that I've heard before. I'm not very good at accents, actually, but I don't think she can be from Harpenden because she doesn't sound like me and she doesn't sound like Jenny Nicely, my mum, and she doesn't sound like Karen or the people in the shops near us. There are so many accents. Scottish and Irish and American and the accent from Cornwall where we went last summer and Kingston in . . . I can't remember where . . . but which is where someone comes from. Someone I know. But I can't think who.

'I am particularly delighted to have you participating in our writing class.' Marnie Shale is smiling at me and then she is looking around at the other people in the room and she is telling them about the course scholarship that she offered, and how it's me who won it and how important stories can be for all of us, and how vital it is that the voices that are heard are not the same ones that have been telling the stories for the past ex-hundred – that's what she says, 'ex-hundred' – years, like the letter X, or ex like ex-husband. And when she speaks she uses her hands and her arms to make big gestures. And she says that for centuries women couldn't write unless they pretended to be men, and even after that, it was only the privileged minority who could do it at all. 'A woman must have money and a room of her own if she is to write fiction,' she says. And pauses. There is lots of nodding. And lots of the other people in the room have notebooks open and they are writing in them. And some have laptops instead. And one of them has her phone, and she's holding it up, like maybe she's videoing Marnie Shale while she's talking – like maybe Marnie Shale is famous and she wants to put it on Twitter or Facebook, maybe.

I have my hand in the air and I'm humming with my lips pressed together, because my brain has forgotten that I'm not back in school – and that's what you had to do, even though I usually forgot, because otherwise it's called interrupting. And I wait, until Marnie Shale smiles and raises her eyebrows towards me. 'Yes, Hope?'

'I'm *not* writing fiction. I'm writing *non-fiction*. It's an autobiography. My book is real and it's about me and it's going to help me find my mother and it's going to make her come and . . . and I do have money of my own. Because I have a real job. And I have my own bedroom, too. But it's not *fiction*, it's *non-fiction*. It's real and it's very important because my birth mother is going to—'

'Good point, Hope.' It's not rude, even though she's interrupting me, because she has put her hand towards me, with the palm facing out – that's a cue, actually, that it's still her turn to talk – and because she's the teacher. The teacher is allowed to talk when you're talking already and you shouldn't shout or bang your head on the table if they do it, because it's not really interrupting. It is allowed because they are there to teach you. And she is smiling to show that she's not cross. So I smile back at her, too.

'Absolutely, Hope. Good point. And the essay in which Virginia Woolf made this very point was also non-fiction. But her message is more that we can't see creativity as a gift that will flourish in a vacuum.'

It's a bit confusing, actually, because I'm not sure why she's talking about a vacuum, which is like a Dyson, or a Hoover, or one from Lidl and it's red, which is the one my mum, Jenny, has. But I'm not going to interrupt. Because of it not being my turn to talk. I'm going to keep on listening very hard.

'Only certain lucky, wealthy, privileged individuals . . .' This is Marnie Shale with her up-and-down Scottish accent.

It's Jamaica. That's where Kingston is. And the person who comes from Kingston in Jamaica is Julie Clarke who is my social worker, although not really anymore because really now she is retired, actually. But she still comes round every Thursday evening to see how I am. And that is the accent that she has which is not very much like Marnie Shale's. It's more like every word she's saying is stretching out slowly. And as I remember I want to shout it out – Jamaica – but I don't shout. It's really not very loud at all. Almost like silent thinking it. Almost like not even saying it at all. I don't think anybody's heard me, except maybe the man with the shiny scarf with the knot at his neck who is beside Marnie Shale. I think maybe he did because he turns and looks right at me and he makes a noise which is a tut and then a sigh. Like: 'Tuh-huhh.'

He is the man who was in the lift when I came

in today. He was talking to the woman in the glasses on the chain, and I asked which floor for the writing class and he took a long time before he answered me – third floor. And then he turned his back, so he was only looking at her again. And although he said it like a whisper, I heard what he said. 'Here was I thinking I'd signed up for literary classes, but now I'm rather wondering whether they might be *literacy* classes.'

I thought how he was going to find it difficult to write a whole book if he doesn't even know what class he's going to.

Marnie Shale glances at him when he does his tut-sigh, but she is still talking about how it may only be a tiny drop in the ocean of inequality but that she hopes our society, and the publishing industry in particular, is finally beginning not only to tolerate but to listen to and embrace the voices of the unheard. '. . . because this is how we move on from ignorance. It is time we swung the balance away from all those centuries in which the only narrative has been from a white, heterosexual, middle-class, able-bodied, neurotypical' (she lifts up her hands to by her ears and wiggles two fingers on each of her hands here. I've seen people doing this before and it's saying something, not just pretending to have little rabbit ears, I just can't remember quite what) 'focus, and lacking in all fluidity. For too long, those from the BAME and LGBT communities, let alone those with . . .'

I can't really listen properly anymore because I'm a bit confused by the wiggling fingers and also now I'm trying to put these letters together in my head to see what words they make. B-A-M-E. *Bame?* What does bame mean? And *lgbt?* That doesn't even sound like a real word. It's like ligbert but without the long sounds, just l-g-b-t, really fast. Maybe they are places. You call it a community when people come from places. So maybe these are countries. Bame and Lgbt. Maybe they're in Russia or somewhere with different sounds.

And I'm trying to work out what the teacher is talking about and if they are real countries or if she's spelt them wrong or if I've remembered the wrong letters, when I realise she has said my name again. And she's looking at me with her head bent over to one side. She wants to check that I'm still happy for the group to know about *it* and that I don't mind her telling them. When she says *it* she means *me*, and why my brain is a bit unique. She means about my birth mother making my brain damaged because of drinking alcohol when I was in her tummy and being developed. It's called Foetal Alcohol Spectrum Disorder. And it's also called

FASD. And I say no, because I don't mind, and anyway, because she's already asked my mum, Jenny. They've had a long conversation on the telephone about me doing this course and if I will be able to persevere enough, and if other people should know about *it*, and Mum has said that it's always best to tell people because I have nothing to be ashamed about and that way they will know and understand. Not that there will be any outbursts, Mum said on the phone. She was laughing.

She and Marnie Shale know each other a little bit. Because my mum, Jenny Nicely, is a poet. But being a poet doesn't pay billions of pounds, more's the pity, so she also works in the bookshop. The one near the station. And when Marnie Shale wrote a new book a few years ago, the book was sold in the shop and Marnie came in and did a talk, so that she could sign her book and people could buy it. And Marnie and my mum talked about poetry and bookshops and ideas and life. And afterwards they stayed in touch a little bit. On Twitter and Facebook and the telephone sometimes.

Marnie is talking about hurdles and challenges and milestones and triumphs. She is looking at me while she talks. And she's smiling a lot.

'. . . only saying this because Hope has asked me to raise it with you, as she feels both she and you will be more relaxed if everybody is aware of the issues she has faced. And, while I'm sure none of you would have been anything but perfectly understanding, I think you'll all agree that it is testimony to her resilience that . . .'

'Labels don't matter.' I forget to put up my hand in my sudden need to tell everybody this in case they don't know already. 'It's only people that matter, actually. I have a real job. And I can read and write. I'm blue, maybe. Or maybe a little bit indigo. But not red or orange or . . .' I try to remember what colour comes next. Something about a battle. But I can't think which one it is. So instead I say, 'And I've never jumped out of a car or been in prison.' Because otherwise all these people might not realise that I'm one of the ones who are on the lucky side of the rainbow. And that even if I forget things and have a head that's a bit of a jumble sale – not a real jumble sale with a yellow teapot or an ice cream maker in the box, of course, but just a brain that's a bit of a muddle – and even if I sometimes have to shout a little bit, I'm . . .

I don't mean rainbow. That's just for Mum and me. That's our word. I mean the other word, of course. I mean . . . I mean . . .

There's a bit of silence now, because I'm trying to remember my word, except now I'm thinking about the rainbow, and everybody else is looking at me, like they're waiting, except for one man who has a bit of a cough. He's not the one with the detective story, or the one from the lift. He's a different one in a T-shirt that says 'The Clash'. But I can't remember the word and Marnie smiles – she's always doing that – and says, anyway, good for you, Hope Nicely. Now, let's hear about some more of the group and what you all hope to achieve from these classes and then we'll do a little exercise.

For a moment, I think she means an exercise like in school when it was PE and before gymnastics or netball because of needing to be warmed up. And I almost want to shout it out – because that would not be helping us to write a book, not a press-up or touching our toes or running on the spot. But then I do a little laugh, because I'm so silly to think that's what she's talking about. She means a writing exercise. Of course. My mum – she's called Jenny Nicely – has told me that we will probably do some exercises in this class. And I thought the same thing – about touching my toes – and Mum said, no, she meant writing exercises – like making up scenes or people or imagining things – so it really is very silly of me to think it again now. But I don't laugh very loud so it's not really interrupting, and I don't think anybody even notices very much. Or maybe just the man with the knot in his scarf, because he does look at me quite hard.

He's not even talking at this moment. That's Danny Flynn, who is on the seat to his left – finger, thumb, yes, left – who has hair that is light brown but a bit orange and curly and quite long for a man, except on the front of his forehead where there's not so much hair. He's told us his name and now he's talking about his book which is set in a future world where there is not enough clean air left for all the babies that are born, so only the babies of the very rich people are allowed to live in the normal world, that's called Up-world, and the poor babies have to go into caves where they work collecting water to use for energy, and they also have to make it clean for the Up-world people to drink.

And Marnie Shale is asking him whether he thinks this book is different enough to all of those other class-based post-apocalyptic novels, and – she's not being critical, but – if his plot doesn't feel just a little bit well trodden. That is the word she uses – 'trodden' – like he's writing the book with his feet. Like he's treading all over his story while he's writing it. Like all the books that have already been written have been covered in the footprints of their writers. And the man – Danny – takes a moment to reply. My mum always says I'm not always very good at reading people's faces, but his mouth is quite straight and his cheeks are redder than they were a moment ago, and I wonder if maybe he is counting to three so that he doesn't shout or bang his head on the table. And I'm thinking how horrible it would be to have to collect water in buckets under the ground all day, and I'm wondering whether having a mum who is a poet and a bookshop seller would give me enough money to be a baby living in Up-world, even if it doesn't make billions, more's the pity.

And Danny is talking now about the dystopian literature canon – this is confusing because of a cannon being a big gun pirates use that shoots out balls, like bowling balls but grey. And I haven't read any of the books by the writers that he is talking about – 'influences': Margaret Atwood and Aldous Huxley and Philip K. Dick. (I sit on my hands when he says that name and press my lips tight together because it's rude to laugh when someone else is talking, even though I really do want to laugh because dick is another word for penis and I don't know if Danny Flynn even realises that, so it's really very funny.) Marnie's questions are like music rising up and down with her accent. His answers are flatter. I don't think he has an accent at all, actually.

Marnie Shale says his book sounds well thought through, but he will have to make a targeted effort to keep it different if anybody is going to actually want to read it. She is saying that he must be careful that his novel doesn't feel too *generic*. I don't know that word, but I don't put up my hand because I'm busy thinking. There is another word that means having a jumble in your brain or like being in a wheelchair or having lungs that don't work well, when it's the way you were made in the mother's tummy. And it's when it's not the mother's fault at all and there's nothing they can do about it. It's only because of things that are already in their body and then go into your body because you're inside them, and those are the things that they can't help. Not like the way that my birth mother made me. That wasn't *generic*. She did it to me all by herself, with her wine and her beer.

And now I realise – flip a pancake – that it wouldn't make any difference to me: even if being a baby whose mother was a poet and a bookshop seller made you rich enough to stay in Up-world and breathe the air and not go down to the caves and spend all your life putting water in buckets. That wouldn't help me. Because Jenny Nicely wasn't my mother when I was born. She didn't even know me then. And my mother when I was born didn't want me in normal not-up-or-down world, so she definitely wouldn't have cared about having enough money for me to grow up in the clean air and the sunshine instead of underground. I would have been in the caves. Definitely. And I would never have been adopted by Jenny Nicely at all. It wouldn't have been all for the best. I'd just have been stuck in Down-world with my bucket. And it would have been dark and wet. And probably cold. And the air would be dirty. That's where I'd be now.

I'm humming but now it's not because I'm trying not to laugh about Mr Dick. It's because I'm trying not to cry about being a poor baby in a cave who has to collect up the water for all the rich babies whose mummies didn't throw them away.

The man with the knot is giving me a look again. I think it's because I'm humming, and I really want to bang my head but I mustn't. So I sit on my hands and I count to three, and then I do it again. One-two-three. I'm humming louder and louder and I'm counting so hard I can feel it bulging in my head. But then, just when I think I'm going to have to yell out and the tears are going to come, I have a good idea and take a big, deep breath and I open my notebook – it's blue and it's got a hard cover and it opens right to left like a real book, not top to bottom like the ones with wire rings at the top. And it's quite big. Lots of the other people in the room are writing things in their notebooks, so – I've taken my hands out from under my bottom, of course, otherwise I wouldn't have been able to open it, unless I did it with my mouth – I get my special pen and I do some writing too. My letters are quite neat. Much neater than they used to be. They aren't joined-up though. I used to do them joined-up, but they weren't so neat.

My special pen is really very special, actually. It is gold at the top and black at the bottom, which is like my mum, Jenny Nicely's, special writing pen. It's exactly the same, actually, because of her buying it for me, because of being so proud of me. But mine has a special grip, too. It is blue, which matches my notebook. It's squidgy and plastic and it's where I hold the pen with my fingers, to make it feel nice.

Writing Group. I write this at the top and I underline it, and then I put my name. *Hope Nicely.* And I put the day in – *Wednesday* – remembering the d, because it sounds like Wensday but that's the wrong way to write it, although people will still understand maybe but they'll just think I'm stupid. I want to put in the date, because you're meant to do that too, but I can't remember what it is right now, so I leave it out.

This week is all about introductions, I remembered that! Marnie Shale said it right at the start and I knew it was important – to ourselves and to approaches to writing, which is what Marnie Shale said – so I write *Introductions* and then the names of the people who have already spoken in our class. The woman who talked about her book first, who is the one with her glasses on a chain, was called Susan. I remember that because I had a teaching assistant called Susan when I was in junior school. And her last name is Ford, and that's easy as anything to remember because we have a car that's called Ford too. So I write down both her names. The name of her book is – I'm thinking hard and it works because it comes back into my brain – *The Lady and the Lock* – so I write that too. Then, on the next line down, I write *Malcolm* because that's the name of the man doing the detective story. He has hair which stands up a bit like my hairbrush and a big square ring on his finger, and the watch which is very big and very gold, and he has a face which is a bit of a surprising colour, actually, like the colour of a tangerine or an orange, or maybe a Fanta, except by his ears where it's more like the colour of my skin. I can't remember what his last name is – it's certainly not a car – so I don't write that. The name of his book is right there, though. *Costa Del Death.*

Next, I write my name – because I was the next person to introduce myself and my notes have to be in order. But I haven't really thought about my book needing a name, and I'm a little bit sad because I should have done that. I just write *My Book* instead of a real name. And I don't have time to think about it anymore right now anyway, because I have to write *Danny Flynn* and *Down-World*. And I write it very quickly without letting my brain think about the babies in the caves. And there's no time anyway because we're already on to the next introduction person.

Veronica Ptitsky. I don't have to spell it myself because the woman does that herself – it's a Russian name, she says. I don't know if she has an accent – maybe a little bit – but she has very red lipstick and her hair is frizzy and she is making Marnie Shale laugh by telling her about what she's writing.

'Priceless. So, Jilly Cooper for the LGBT community?' That's Marnie saying this.

The woman with the lips is laughing too. And now I know I must have been right about Lgbt being in Russia, so I put that in brackets (*Veronica Ptitsky from Lgbt, Russia*).

'Precisely,' she's saying – Veronica Ptitsky. 'Jodhpurs and whips and all. Straw in hair and very mucky mucking out. Different sort of steamy.' Everybody else is laughing apart from me, because I don't know much about horses. 'Hopefully it will make me as much as *Fifty Shades.* Working title of *Champing.*'

I'm starting to write it like *Champion* because I don't know the other word, and *Champion* sounds like a good name for her book, until Marnie Shale says: 'Well, I'm sure we're all *champing* to read your excerpts. Right, who's next . . .'

And now she's looking towards the man with the neck scarf with the big knot and he's stretching back in his seat with his arms across his chest. 'I can't claim to be one of the worthy under-represented, I'm sorry to say,' he says, 'since I have to confess to being twice published already. To some acclaim, actually, if only on a limited scale.'

He puts his hands behind his head, as if he's sitting on a deck chair in the sunshine. 'So. Me? Ludovic Philip Sawyer, PhD. Lecturer in classics and, along with all the normal volumes of academia, I've written two books for a wider readership about domestic law-keeping in the Roman and Byzantine Empire. Both still in print. Now embarking on my debut novel, incorporating aspects of the mythical and the thriller into the history of Constantine the First and his assassination of his wife Fausta. Let's call it Dan Brown meets *I, Claudius*. My first foray into fiction, hence my enrolment in these classes. I *was* hoping they might be of benefit.'

He's saying this and his eyes are looking at me, but out of the side of his eyes, not straight on, like he doesn't want to turn his whole head. And there is something about the way he talks that is making the inside of my head buzz like it has wasps inside it. I'm glad when Marnie Shale turns to the next person. And even though my brain is feeling a bit tired, I try to keep my letters neat in my notebook.

Simon Taylor. Road trip in America. Sort of rock and roll memoir – except called grunge because of the 1990s. Soul Caravan. *Working title.*

Simon Taylor is the one who made a funny noise when I was talking about my book. He's the one with the T-shirt that says 'The Clash'. And it was him doing a bit more coughing later, too. Probably he has a tickly throat and needs some Tixylix.

Jamal Ali. Personal trainer who is a vampire. This is the plot. Not real. Jamal is a cook. Real job. Jamal not vampire. Joke. Book called Sharp.

When he first said his name, I thought it was Jam Al, two different names. Like my mum, Jenny, has a friend who is called Ella Jane. So I thought his whole name was Jam Al Ali. And I thought it was funny to have a first name which was Jam, like strawberry jam, or plum jam. But then Marnie Shale said about Jamal's book sounding fun, and I realised that – silly me – his name was just one word, actually. Not Jam Al, just Jamal. But his joke was still very funny, the one about not being a real vampire, only a cook. It made me laugh. But I have to stop laughing now, because of having more people to write in my notebook.

Kelly Perkins. War. Time. Factory. Book is called Belles of the Shells.

She's the one with the longest hair ever, down to nearly her bottom.

Peter Potter. Peter Potter.

I only notice that I've written Peter Potter's name twice as I'm realising that I've forgotten to listen to him talking. I've just been thinking how much I like his name. It feels nice in my ears. He's quite old with white hair and big white eyebrows. And he has an accent that I like because it's like in *Coronation Street*. But it's too late to ask him more about his book, which is lots of short stories, actually, not just one long one like most books are, because now it's time to exercise.

2

'OK, guys. What is the number one rule of writing?' Marnie Shale asks. And she is looking around at all of us. I am already writing: *Number 1 rule*, because rules are important, like keeping our feet and hands to ourselves and not running into the road in front of the cars, and not rubbing our fanny when there are other people with you. I have a book for writing golden rules in. It's a very important book. Mostly it was for when I was little and my mum, Jenny Nicely, wrote all the important rules for me to remember, and with little pictures sometimes, too. We'd read it before I went to bed, or when we needed to do a bit of extra remembering. And even though I'm grown up now, and I have a real job, actually, sometimes I do like to look at it still. Because rules are very important.

So I'm holding my pen and I'm waiting: *Number 1 rule* . . . Danny Flynn says: 'Keep the wifi turned off or you'll get nothing done,' and people laugh so I think it's a joke.

Veronica Ptitsky says: 'Show, don't tell?' and Marnie Shale says: 'Bingo.'

I have been to the bingo once, with my boss Karen. She said what a fun evening we would have, but in fact I didn't have a very fun time because the numbers were read out too quickly and I couldn't keep up, so I didn't know if I was winning or not. I had a pen called a dabber for putting green spots on the numbers when they were called, but each time I put a spot, there were too many new numbers for me to move my hand or my brain in time, and the nachos were greasy and they smelt like bad breath. And the lights were very bright, and there were lots of colours going flash, flash, flash, and I didn't like that very much. Karen and her sister drank quite a lot of glasses of wine and it was so noisy that in the end I had to go away, and then I couldn't find my way home until my mum, that's Jenny, and Karen told the police to come and find me. I was in the children's playground, hiding under the slide, and they drove me to my house and it was very late.

But I don't think this is a real game of bingo, because there are no numbers and because then Marnie Shale says, 'Exactly that. The golden rule of all writing.' And now I'm thinking that bingo was just like her saying, that's right, or yes, that is the number one rule of writing. And everybody else is noting in their books, so I write it down too. *Show. Don't tell.* Even though I don't really understand. Because books do tell. It's pictures that show, and this is a writing group not a drawing group. So, I'm worrying that it's the other way round and that Marnie Shale has got a little bit confused, and that really the first rule of writing is *tell, don't show.*

I don't really mean to say it but it comes out, maybe a bit loud, and Marnie Shale is looking at me and she's saying: 'Yes, Hope, you're right. Pictures are to show. And that is exactly why this rule is so important – and it's also true for non-fiction, especially narrative non-fiction like you are writing. Because if you just tell the reader something, then they are passive. There is no investment for them. It brings your story alive no more than a technical manual. But if you can create a picture for them, if you use your words to paint the picture, as Hope says, well, then the reader becomes active, because then they are involved in interpreting this *written picture*, to unveil . . .'

And I'm a little bit confused but I tell myself to listen hard to what Marnie is saying. And I don't put my hands under my legs because I need to have my pen ready for writing. Because if it is a rule then it is very important, so I also write down <u>rule</u> again and I underline it twice, so that I remember and don't forget.

Marnie is telling our group that *show, don't tell* is what will make our writing unique and define the space between writer and reader. She says that if she tells us Bob is angry, then all she has done is impart information. We are no closer to Bob. We do not know anything more about him and whether his anger is of the sad type, or the sinister type, or the murderous or pathetic or catastrophic type. We do not know whether we should like him or pity him or fear him or detest him. And we do not know if Bob is young or old or kind or evil; whether he is a medieval knight or a time-travelling chimpanzee. And what's more, if the writer continues to do nothing but tell and not show, we won't care. No relationship is established by just telling. 'To make the reader care about Bob and what happens to him,' Marnie is saying, 'you have to use your craft in the *showing*. Let's see Bob snarling. Show us the curl of his lip and the flash of hatred in his eyes. Let's see his anger in the balling of his fist and the tread of his feet.'

I write *tread, feet, anger*, in case it is important. Because I'm remembering Danny Flynn's book being well trodden. I'm not quite sure why that is showing not telling, but I'm not surprised the babies in the caves are angry with their treading.

'Don't merely tell me Bob is sad. Let me see the tears that he's struggling to contain. And not all at once. Tempt me. Show me just enough to engage me in uncovering the whole. Bring me in. Make me care.

'Don't *tell* me the underworld is wet and cold. Let me see the water dripping from stalactites and the shivering babies gnawing on raw tree roots.' She nods at Danny Flynn.

'And I don't want to read that these women are working their fingers to the bone to fill the weapons they are making. I want to feel the calluses on their hands and smell the sulphur and the gunpowder. I want to hear the bravado hum of gossip above the clatter of metal and the whirr of the factory machines.' She's looking at the one with the long hair, who I think is Shelley. No, it's Kelly, I think, actually. Not Shelley. But she is writing about shells maybe. And bells too. Kelly Shell-y Bell-y.

Marnie Shale turns to look at Veronica Ptitsky. 'And when I come to read *Champing* – which I'm looking forward to very much – I don't just want to be told Helena and Lucy were having marvellous sex in the hay barn. I want first to glimpse a discarded rider's hat on the stone floor and, a few feet from that, a crumpled jacket. Make me wait a moment longer before I see the silky underwear, and let me hear indistinct moans and smell the odour of sweat and saddle leather. And I don't just want to be *told* about romping on straw bales, I want to feel the prickle of the straw against bare skin, I want to feel the burn of it. I need to be *shown* all of this, in a cleverly crafted manner of course, and not just *told* that it's happening.'

I'm feeling uncomfortable and a bit confused – in my head – now because part of me wants to laugh about sex in a barn, because it's a little bit rude and also quite shocking that a teacher would talk about this. But I don't like anything scratchy, and straw on your bottom would be very, very scratchy. So, part of me wants to laugh and part of me wants to put my hand under my trousers to rub my bottom better and make the itch from the straw go away. I'm relieved when Marnie Shale isn't talking about naked skin and sweaty leather and barn sex anymore, because she's handing round printouts to have a look at.

There are extracts from classic openings, and Marnie Shale is asking us to read and to think about how the author is employing *show, not tell* from their very first sentences. And the first one is by Charles Dickens, called *The Old Curiosity Shop*, and it's about a man who likes to walk but only when it's dark.

But there are words that make my brain do a shrink thing, like *roam* and *seldom*. And also it's making me think about walking, too. And I'm looking at the words on the paper, but in my head I'm forgetting that I'm reading this and instead, in my head, actually, I'm walking as well. Not in a real, definite place – like not in the same woods where I was this morning with Scrappy the bearded collie and Suzie and Sallie who are whippets and Henry the beagle and Tinie Tempah who is an I-don't-know-what.

I'm too busy walking in my head and I forget to read the next extracts, the one called *Lolita* and the one called *Norwegian Wood*, and I'm not even listening. The voices are in my ears, but not like words that you understand and think about. More like when you've forgotten the television is on but it's like it doesn't even exist for a little while. But then, flip a pancake, I remember that I have to be listening, because this is very important. Except it's too late, so I am just going to have to leave a gap in my notebook – and I'm going to try extra hard on my exercise.

None of us will have to read out what we've written. Not unless we want to – but Marnie Shale wants us all to have a go. She wants us to think about where our books start. She wants us to use a scene or a character, something important to our story, and to write an opening where we are only showing and not telling.

'Think about engaging your reader. Give them a part of the picture but not everything. Don't *tell* them who or where or when. *Show* them enough that they just *have* to read on.'

She takes off her watch and puts it on the table in front of her. 'Right, group. Fifteen minutes.'

I'm not very good at minutes – sometimes I think just a few have gone past but then I realise the whole day has gone away and I've forgotten to go to the library, or maybe the whole of *Coronation Street* has already been on ITV at 7.30 and now I'll have to watch it on ITV+1 and so now I'm going to have to think about when it's on now, and now I'll have to remember to not forget again. But everybody else is writing away – their pens are moving quickly or their fingers are tapping on their laptops (the computers, not the tops of their legs), or else they're looking in a way like they're thinking hard, but not like they're humming or wandering in the woods in their heads. I'm still looking at the lines on my notebook and there are no words on them. I'm thinking now I must put some words on them.

I count to three and I write: *My book by Hope Nicely.* And then I write, in brackets: *Working Title.* And then I write: *Opening.* And then: *Show, don't tell.*

And now it really is time to be doing the exercise and I try to remember what Marnie said. I know I have to start at the beginning and with my important character. And in my book that is me, because of it being an autobiography.

So I start writing: *My name is Hope Nicely and I was left . . .*

But I cross that out. That's telling who I am and what happened to me. So instead I write: *I was left on Christmas . . .* Crossing out again.

This is not easy as anything. Not even a bit easy. Because how can I say what happened without telling it? How can I paint a picture with my words? Marnie Shale said I can't say when or what or who. I'm thinking about humming but then it comes to me.

There were Christmas trees in the windows of the houses. I write: *because it was Christmas.* Then I cross out those last words because you only have Christmas trees at Christmas. So that is how I have shown it. And I'm very pleased with myself. I can feel myself smiling, which is nice. Because I have avoided doing the telling and I have *shown* the Christmas trees, which is the number one rule of writing. Bingo.

There were Christmas trees in the windows of the houses. And there was a cardboard box and it was on the doorstep of the church. And when the vicar who was

36

called Anne Bentley came to the church in the morning, she wondered if Father Christmas had brought her a present in the night. Because of the cardboard box.

I nearly cross out about the vicar being called Anne Bentley, because that's telling, but I can't think how I can show a name. So I keep it in for now and I carry on.

Anne the vicar smiled in a way that looked like she might be a bit surprised by the box but happy about Father Christmas leaving presents for her on the doorstep of the church. So she opened the box and in it was a . . .

And I stop. Because I mustn't tell what was in the box. I must show it instead. So I cross out a few words and I think very hard with my brain.

She started to open the box but before she made it completely open, there was a noise. It was crying. Like a little cat or a . . .

Can I write *baby* or is that telling? How can I show a baby without telling a baby?

Like a little cat. But in the box was not a baby cat. Not a cat animal at all but a different type. A . . .

And I don't need to think for very long even though the word isn't right there. But I find it so quickly. Maybe because exercises make us stronger. Because the word – *human* – is there now. Even bigger bingo.

A very little human animal with eyes that were brown and hair that was black and skin that was . . .

How do you show and not tell skin? When people say they are black or white it doesn't really *show*. It's not a very good showing even when they say it because they're not really painting a picture with their words. It's not even very good *telling*. Because black and white are like words on a page in a book and people don't really look like that. And some of us don't know where our skin comes from. Anyway, it doesn't matter. It's an . . . I can't remember the word, it's an irreli-thing, but it doesn't matter because we are all unique. That's what my mum, Jenny, says. And how do I show-not-tell what the baby-me looked like when I don't know anyway? I'm thinking hard in my brain about what people say when they see babies – like on *Coronation Street* or *Call the Midwife*, maybe, or when Pepper the puggle's owner had a baby who was called Meg and also Meggie-Moo.

My brain is thinking so hard because it is doing the exercise and it's important. And the rule is important too. It's golden. It's the number one rule.

A very little human animal with eyes that were brown and hair that was black and skin that was unique, but a bit like the colour of a peach yoghurt. Or maybe more like an apricot one. And she had ten perfect fingers and ten perfect toes. And they were tiny. And she looked like a perfect baby with nothing wrong at all. She was wrapped in a pink blanket and she stopped crying when Anne the vicar picked her up. And the baby from the box fell asleep like just any other baby. She didn't look like a baby with a brain that was damaged by being filled with vodka and beer and wine in her birth mother's tummy.

I've stopped writing. Because this is all I know. The vodka and the wine and the beer. But even this is not really knowing. Because maybe it was whisky or rum. Or . . . or . . . those drinks that come in funny colours with umbrellas in them and circles of orange. Cocktails. I don't know much about those drinks. And I don't know if she was drinking them in glasses or gigantic bottles. Or if it was in a house or a flat or a field or on a railway station bench or in a pub. I don't know if it was in the morning or late at night, or if she was on her own or with a whole party of people drinking their drinks too. Marnie Shale says you can't just tell *when* and *who* and *where*. You have to show. But I can't show it either. I don't know anything. How can you *show* if you don't *know?*

And I hear my name and I look up and everyone is looking at me. Staring right at me. And it takes me a moment to realise that I have been humming and banging my head. Not hitting it on the table, thank goodness, but just a little bit. Up and down.

And now I should take a deep breath. And I should sit on my hands. And I should count to three. I should be quiet and calm down.

But I don't feel like doing that.

3

'Hope?'

She knows where I am because she's bending down and looking at me.

First she went to the stairs and looked out to see if I was there. I could see her legs and some of her body. And she looked at the lift too. And she checked in the corridor and looked in the women's loo. But now she's looking under the desk in the reception and she's found me because that's where I am, with my knees under my chin.

'Are you all right under there? I didn't know where you'd gone.'

'I'm sorry.' I'm crying only just a little bit now. 'I didn't mean to be interrupting during the exercise. And I didn't mean to go away without saying excuse me. It was an . . .' I'm looking for the word and I nearly say *accident* but that is not the right word so I don't say anything.

Marnie Shale is kneeling down on the floor now, and she's talking to me with her accent. 'You don't have to be sorry, Hope. If the exercises are upsetting, or if they're too difficult, just tell me. I don't want to make you do anything—'

'It's not because of the exercise.' I'm interrupting a little bit but I've put my hand up in front of me like a cue and I don't think Marnie Shale is cross. I'm not humming or shouting. 'It's because of my mother. Not Jenny Nicely. My birth mother. Because I can't *tell* her and I can't *show* her. In my book. But it's not my fault that I can't do it – it's *her* fault. For leaving me. Even if it was for the best. I can't *anything* her because I don't know anything.'

'But you're writing this book about her?'

'About *me*. But this book will find her. And then she can tell me *why*. Why she did what she did and made me like I am.'

'You think your birth mother is going to read your book?'

I'm shrugging now – with my shoulders – because I don't know exactly quite how. Like I don't know the name of my book. Yet. Only a working title. But I know my book will help. I don't know how. I just know that it will. My memory, well, the less said about that . . . My brain is a big old jumble sale, with all the jumpers and books and saucepans muddled in one huge pile up to the ceiling. So it's all a bit of a flitty old mess and I can't explain *what* this book will do. But it will do something.

'If I write it, it will help me.'

'I get that. A bit of closure at the very least, I should imagine?'

That's the word, the one that is like closing time. My brain feels a bit better. And Marnie Shale is holding out a hand. 'I have to get back to the group. You don't have to, if you'd rather . . .' She's the one shrugging now, like I could stay here under the desk for the rest of the class. But I take her hand and say I'll come back.

At the end of the class, all the other people are taking ages picking up their notebooks and their laptops and putting on their coats, and they're asking each other if anybody might fancy a drink but a bit quietly and like nobody wants to say it out loud. Somebody asks Marnie Shale and she says unfortunately she can't. Nobody asks me but that's good anyway because I don't like pubs with their noise and their football on the telly and their smelling of beer, and because my mum, Jenny Nicely, is coming to meet me and she made me promise that I wouldn't forget and go off without her.

I'm the first person out of the room – and I'm not dawdling because I really need a wee and I don't want to queue up because there are only two cubicles in the Ladies (I know this because I went before the class) so if all the women wanted a wee at once, some would have to wait. It's good though because I'm the first one in there and nobody else comes in and, when I come out, the rest of the group are still walking through the reception to where the lift is and I'm a little bit behind them.

Their voices are all muffled because they're talking together but not very loud, except for the one voice that I can hear and that is the man with the knot whose name is . . . I can't remember right now, but his voice still makes my head buzz a bit. And he's saying: '. . . have sympathy of course, but *seriously*, the rest of us have paid good money to be here and is it really appropriate to . . .' Then he doesn't say anything more because Peter Potter with the nice name and white hair and white eyebrows and the *Coronation Street* accent speaks louder than him and it's because he's saying: 'Hello, Hope, love. Didn't see you there.'

I say hello Peter Potter. I don't say *love* like he did, because I don't know him, and then everybody is a little bit quiet. I don't like waiting. I'm thinking we won't all get in even when the lift comes and then maybe I'll have to stand here and do even more waiting because I'm at the back. I'm at the back for the lift even though I was at the front for the wee in the Ladies because of hurrying. And I know where the stairs are. So I go.

I'm nearly at the bottom of the first lot of stairs, just before the bend, when he catches up with me. Not Peter Potter, but the cave babies man called Danny Flynn. He says: hey Hope. He says not to worry about any rubbish I heard *him* say, but I don't know what *him* he's talking about.

'Nothing, forget it,' Danny Flynn says when I ask him what rubbish I shouldn't worry about. And he starts saying that he likes the sound of my autobiography. He tells me that his little brother is on the spectrum and I'm a bit excited to hear this, because that is the right word for my rainbow, of course. The one which I couldn't remember earlier, except for FASD, which is Foetal Alcohol Spectrum Disorder, because of course I know that. Rainbow is only for my mum, Jenny Nicely, and me. Like the red and yellow, except that I'm only blue. Or maybe a little bit indigo.

My mum, Jenny, wrote a poem about a rainbow, actually, and it was very clever because it was a little bit about me, too. In her poem she said about the sun making a rainbow when it's raining and there are millions and zillions of raindrops in the sky. But most of the drops are just ordinary and the sun goes through them because they are just clear, like glass. It's only light, with no colour, just like the air. But there are some drops that are not just ordinary. They are the rainbow drops. The sun chooses them because they are the ones that make the colours. Like red and yellow, and blue and indigo. And that is a rainbow. And it's also a spectrum.

My mum's poem was called 'Extraordinary Drop of Light'.

I ask Danny Flynn if his brother's spectrum is the same spectrum as mine.

'Oh, no, actually. Connor has Asperger,' he tells me.

And I don't tell him that actually that's a vegetable that you can dip into eggs, like toast soldiers. Because maybe that's how his family like to talk about their spectrum. Like my rainbow. Because everyone's unique. Maybe, instead, they have potatoes and carrots and peas, and aspergers. I don't tell him, because that would be rude, and instead of asking about his brother's spectrum, I ask if Danny Flynn is going to the pub now, and he says no, he's worked all day and he's tired. He says didn't I say I lived near the station, because that's his way. Unless, of course, I'm going to the pub . . . ?

'Not likely,' I tell him – but with my voice, actually, I'm saying no way at all. *No way Jose.* We're at the bottom of the stairs now, coming out through the library which is on the ground floor, three floors down from the writing group room, except that the library is shut now, and the caretaker is near the door with the key in his hand. And I can already see my mum, Jenny Nicely, through the glass. I always know it's her even if she isn't looking towards me because of her clothes which are always happy and bright. It's because she lived a little bit everywhere when she was little, because of her parents being hippies with itchy feet – that's not their real feet, just a thing to say because of them living in lots of different places. And, when she was little, they went to so many countries, like Ibiza, which is an island in the clear blue sea, and to the US of A, which is also called America, in the place which is the song with flowers in your hair, and Goa, which is somewhere else, and also mainly to the Caribbean and other places too which I can't remember, but mostly places where people aren't afraid of colours that sing and clothes that smile. And she always smells lovely, my mum, Jenny Nicely, like just-peeled oranges and warm clothes from the washing machine, and lavender and bread.

'Hello my Hope.' That's her talking to me and she has her arms open for a big hug, with her bracelets going jingle and jangle. Sometimes I don't like to be hugged but tonight I do. 'Good writing group?'

I tell her it was good. I'm trying to remember the bad bit to tell her too but I can't remember it right now. And she asks if I've learned anything and I say no telling. Danny Flynn says: 'We've been talking about show, not tell.' And Mum says hello and nice to meet him, and she's laughing when she says good of Hope to introduce them, and he says his name is Danny Flynn. She says hers is Jenny Nicely and they shake hands.

Danny Flynn walks with us and I'm not talking as much as I usually do because my head is very tired. I think I will sleep well tonight. But he is talking and my mum is talking too so it doesn't matter that I don't have my chatty head on. They're talking about science fiction books and poetry and libraries. Danny Flynn works in a library but not the library where the writing group is, a different one. My mum knows his library and he knows her bookshop. And now they are talking about his mum and my mum and about their health. My mum, Jenny Nicely, loves to talk about poetry and bookshops and her health. Now she's saying about all the pills she has to take and how she shouldn't have so much butter and salt and sugar but we all need our little pleasures. Danny Flynn says, yes, and his mum has the blood pressure too and also the cholesterol and that she finds it annoying – Danny Flynn's mum – because she's always been one for a cream bun. And my mum laughs and says yes, she too is one for a cream bun, more's the pity. And they laugh.

Our road comes first so we stop and we say, well. And Danny Flynn says nice to meet you, Ms Nicely. This is to my mum. And he says which number house are we, he'll bring round the book he was telling her about, that's science fiction by a woman who she's not read, and he says that he's going to read a book of her poetry, too. My mum says that's very kind. Then Danny Flynn says nice to meet me too – the other Ms Nicely, he calls me – and see me next week. As we're walking back to our home, Mum says what a nice young man and asks me what the other people at the class were like but I can't remember because I'm a bit tired now and my head doesn't feel like talking.

Inside our house – that's number 23a Station Close – we both have a sit-down and a cup of tea. And Mum is breathing quite loudly like a cat who's purring, like she always does when she needs a cuppa. She's telling me how proud she is of me to have my scholarship and be going to a writers' group. And she's sure that I will persevere.

After dinner, I go off to beddy-byes. I think maybe my mum has a conversation on the telephone with Marnie Shale. Or maybe it was on Twitter because, after a little bit, she opens my door. She sits on the side of my bed and she touches my hair and says: 'Hope Nicely, did you hide under a desk during your writing class?'

And I have to think about it because my brain is a bit cloudy now. I think I did hide but I can't quite remember why. So I shrug with my shoulders and say maybe.

My mum asks me if everything was all right. She pauses and asks if anyone was mean to me. And I say no, they were all very nice. And then I wonder if she's going to say something more but she doesn't. She just kisses me on the forehead and says: 'Night then, Hope Nicely. Sweet dreams.'

2

CHARACTER AND DIALOGUE

4

This is a bit of an exercise but not my exercise. It's by Veronica Ptitsky and she gives me full copy write. That means it's OK to copy it even though I didn't write it.

> *In life, you meet many people. Some you like, some you don't. Some you can talk to for hours without time seeming to pass; others you find a minute in their company drags and embarrasses. Some you admire, some you wish you'd never met. Few make you think: 'When I woke up this morning I didn't imagine that I would meet somebody like you.' When you do, it's rather like taking a step and finding gravity has relaxed . . .*

It's a funny thing, because when Veronica Ptitsky is reading, I don't even know who her exercise is about. I only know that it is about the first person who comes to her mind who is someone she doesn't know very well. It's not from her book, the champion one, just from her head. But who it is about is a gigantic mystery, actually, because of her not saying. So I don't know who her person is.

It's not only Veronica Ptitsky who has done the exercise. It's me too. But I'm not telling about my exercise straight away. I'm showing not telling what we are doing first. This is called setting the scene. So I'm not going to *say* that we are at the writing class. But there is a table. It is not a round one. It is an *oval* one and there are lots of legs below it and there are arms on it, some are crossed, and elbows too, and notebooks and laptops, although not for me. But in my fingers is my gold and black pen with the blue grip. And there is a voice. It's an accent which is going up and down. And it's saying, this week, the topic is *character*. This is before the exercises. This is just the scene which is being set.

Marnie Shale says that character is of utmost importance. Even if our story is the most exciting, most gripping or – looking towards Veronica Ptitsky from Bglt – sexy story the world has ever seen, without amazing characters, it is not a book that people will like to read. It will be flat.

'Characters need not be likeable.' That is Marnie Shale talking. 'We don't need perfect heroes who are nice to their mothers and raise money for charity. Often the antihero is the more interesting protagonist, be they loathsome or weak or mean. They can be as vile or spiteful or psychopathic as you care to make them. But we must believe in them.'

She asks us to think of which flawed characters compel us. Danny Flynn says Winston Smith, and Veronica Ptitsky says Humbert Humbert. (I do laugh a little bit because that is a funny name, because of the twice thing, like Peter Potter but if Peter Potter was called Peter Peter or Potter Potter.) The man with the scarf, with pink dots today but still with a knot, says Richard the Third, but first he does the tut-sigh and he's looking at me. I think maybe it's because I'm laughing at Humbert Humbert's name so I sit on my hands and I make myself quiet.

'The evil Count Dra-cu-la.' This is Jamal Ali, who is a personal trainer, or maybe just in his book. Maybe not a real one, actually. He must really like vampires because that is what Count Dracula is and it is what he is writing about too. And he says it in an accent, but not his own accent. And he's making his eyebrows go low and showing his teeth with his lips up, a bit like Tinie Tempah when he's growling at another dog. It's really very funny and I can't help laughing again, even though I just made myself quiet.

Marnie Shale says good, and what do all these

characters have in common? I can't think about that because I don't know these characters, only their names. I'm trying to think about my favourite characters who aren't nice but it is hard because I haven't read as many books actually.

Everyone is talking about depth and credibility when I remember my character, and I'm so happy to have found it in my head that I shout it out even if it's a little bit interrupting: 'Miss Trunchbull.' Scarf-knot man makes a noise like t-*shh* and another person laughs but I'm not sure who. But Marnie Shale smiles and says Miss Trunchbull is an extremely good example, certainly flawed and exactly what she was trying to say about a character, even if they are the villain of the piece, being compelling to the reader so long as we glimpse their motivations. So with Miss Trunchbull her motivations are . . . ? And she's looking at me and I'm looking at her and I'm trying to think what motivations means. And I think about Miss Trunchbull who is called Agatha, which is not a nice name, and how she is a horrible person even if she's not real, and Marnie Shale is still looking at me with her expecting eyes, and so I say: 'She hates children.'

And I'm not sure if it's the right answer but Marnie Shale says 'Exactly' as if I've been very clever. 'A headmistress who hates children. What could be more intriguing? What happened to make her deny ever having been a child herself? But Dahl shows her fears, along with the hatefulness and, bingo, a fully formed, three-dimensional baddie.'

My cheeks are a little bit warm. When I was little my mum, Jenny Nicely, did star charts on the fridge door and it made me try so hard to do the things that the stars were for. Like not shouting or going away from the class when the teacher was talking, or banging my head or pushing Shanya into the wall because she called me Fanny Wanker. I liked the silver stars best. Even better than the gold stars. Sometimes my mum, Jenny, gave me stars just for trying, even if I'd forgotten the right rule (except for bashing Shanya's head – she never gave me a star on that day, not even a red one). And now I'm feeling a little bit like Marnie Shale has given me a silver star and I want to try really hard in our exercise, which is about character.

'Malcolm Bradbury said,' this is Marnie Shale talking now – and this is called quotes – 'that plot is no more than footprints left in the snow after your characters have run on to incredible destinations.' I'm a little bit confused by this – because she's talking about feet again. Maybe this is why I choose the character that I do.

'For this exercise,' this is what Marnie is saying, 'I want you to describe a character but solely through your own feelings. Don't choose a key figure from your book or your life, but someone you don't know well and who is the first person that comes into your mind when I say: they have done something to surprise you.'

And the first person that comes into my mind – maybe because of the footprints, and them making me think about walking – is actually a dog. And maybe it's because of Humbert Humbert's name, but the dog that I think about for my exercise is Humpty. He's a good person for this exercise because I don't know him very well. He's not been coming for walks for very long, which is why I haven't ever walked him in the snow and seen his footprints, even though I have walked some of them in the snow, like Tinie Tempah, which was very funny because there was a snowman by the gate to the wood and he did a wee on it, which made it all yellow at the bottom. He doesn't come every day – I mean Humpty now, because Tinie Tempah is there every day – which is Monday and Tuesday and another day and I think actually it is Wednesday, because of working three days and because of it being Wednesday today, and having been working. Some weeks I work on different days, too, if there are more dogs coming than usual or if Karen, my boss, wants me to. But most weeks it's just three days.

And Humpty has surprised me, because he looks very fluffy and you think he won't be very fast or very – flip a pancake, what is the word? But then, the other day, there was a squirrel and it was on a log on the side of the frog pond and Humpty ran so fast that he caught it and he came running back and there was all this blood on his face and in his mouth there was this dead squirrel with its tail still all bushy and sticking out. Luckily Karen was with me, because I don't do my walks on my own, and luckily she's not . . . she's not . . . Anyway, it was all for the best because she managed to take the squirrel out of his mouth, even though he – Humpty – growled a bit. And I was shouting and crying because it made me sad about the squirrel, but Karen said I should be brave and she buried the squirrel under a bit of mud, or otherwise the foxes would have taken it and eaten it.

So this is why – and the foot thing – I decide to write my exercise about Humpty. Marnie Shale says remember, show, not tell. She says that we must not feel inhibited and to experiment because nobody is judging us and she's not going to force anybody to read their exercises out loud unless they want.

'So, *show* me something of your character through your attitude to them. OK guys . . .'

Marnie Shale takes off her watch and puts it on

the oval table. And it is a very good day because the word comes to me: *ferocious* – pop, like a balloon just floating into the right place, like a bingo balloon – but I am trying so hard that I don't shout it out, not even a little bit. And my cheeks are warm again, like I'm giving myself a silver star. So this is a good moment to start writing and I don't say that Humpty is a dog, or even a Tibetan terrier, because that's telling. I want to show:

Humpty has four paws and a tail and he is furry all over, like a teddy bear. If it was me who was his owner, I think I would have called him Teddy, because of the furriness and also because his face is a little bit like a bear. He is very friendly with the other dogs and with the humans like me too. Humpty does not look like he is very ferocious – I'm smiling writing this because the right word came to me and I didn't even shout it. I didn't even need to sit on my hands or count because today is a very good day – *so until you know him better you do not know. Humpty is a killer. Not with a gun and not with a knife and not with a bomb.*

I am very happy with this because Marnie Shale said that it is good to bring our readers in with a bit of mystery. I am going to read it to my mum, Jenny Nicely, when I go home. *Humpty is a teeth killer. Humpty is not very big but he is like Jaws except with paws instead of a fin on his back and much more fur.*

And now I am so happy with myself – big gold star for me – because of the Jaws thing which is a comparison and another word which I learned in English and which my mum has said to me, but it's not in my head and I don't think it's going to pop into it. But I am still so happy with myself – it's called chuffed – and, when Marnie Shale puts her watch back on and asks if anybody wishes to read what they've written, I have my hand right up, like a stretch to the ceiling, and I'm not quite shouting but nearly shouting, maybe a little bit shouting: 'Me.'

Marnie Shale says she likes what I've written very much, which makes me feel like a million dollars – which are like pounds but not quite so big and only in America where I've never been, and a few other countries with accents. She says she loved the Jaws analogy. I do shout 'analogy' a little bit because – bingo – that's the word that I thought I would never remember. Now I write it in my notebook, under my exercise – *analogy* – so that I will remember it next time. And really, the million dollars – like me feeling like a million dollars – that is an analogy too. Because I don't really feel like money. I don't think a human can feel like a big pile of money, even if it's showing not telling. But feeling a million dollars is like having warm, pink cheeks and a silver star on a star chart.

So now I'm very chuffed. The spotty scarf-knot man was shaking his head a bit while I was reading and it made me think he wanted to read his exercise next. But he doesn't put up his hand after me – that's Veronica Ptitsky. I don't know who her exercise is about – it's the one about meeting lots of different people but not expecting to meet somebody like this person – but she doesn't say who the person is and it's a gigantic mystery. And that is very good, I think, because of Marnie Shale telling us about mystery pulling in readers, so Veronica Ptitsky's done it very well. And it makes me a little bit less chuffed because her exercise sounds like a real book and part of me wishes I'd written that instead, even if Marnie Shale loved my analogy. But this is still a good day, and I don't even sit on my hands because I'm still very happy.

5

'Oh, for heaven's sake.'

Marnie Shale should be the one talking because she's the teacher – but this is scarf-knot man. Maybe he's saying it because my answer was wrong – well, not answer, because of there being no question. And probably I shouldn't have shouted. But it was because of Marnie Shale saying about one of the greatest influences on the writing world and about it reaching far beyond the horror genre – and then me remembering about not liking horror, especially when it's on telly by accident, because of being in a show called *50 Best Ever Trick or Treats* and the show being mostly funny bits of films like ET Phone Home with his sheet over his head and his funny little walk, and then Snoopy's friends who are children and the Great Pumpkin which is going to come, but hasn't come yet, actually, and them still waiting, but then the horrible, horrible mask making me scream and the huge knife, and my mum, Jenny Nicely, saying oh crikey, let's turn this rubbish over. And maybe it was a bit interrupting for me to tell Marnie Shale about not liking it and not wanting to talk about it, but it's worse for him to interrupt because he's not even on the rainbow. He should know better.

But Marnie Shale is smiling and she's not even saying anything to him. 'No, Hope, not *Halloween*, though I see where you're coming from. And you're right, it is *pretty* gruesome. No, King wrote *The Shining*, *Carrie*, *It* and *Misery* – but not *Halloween*. I don't know who wrote that, actually. But, to return to the quotes on the printouts, these are Stephen King talking about the craft of writing, across *all* genres, and as I was saying, every writer should be aware of what Stephen King has to say about dialogue . . .'

Dialogue is a conversation. I know this because I've been listening really hard to what Marnie Shale has been saying. So I know that if someone is having dialogue angrily you don't say 'angrily'. You can show that with them punching a wall. We don't need to say our characters are uttering or exclaiming. We just need to say they *say*. And dialogue is very, very important, because it can show our characters and what their motives are.

Now it's another exercise and this time I'm not

going to write about a dog that I don't know very well. Because we have to write a dialogue between ourselves and one of our main characters but not say said or yelled or cried or whispered. Just the words. And the dialogue needs to be us asking them questions. And even before Marnie Shale has put her watch on the oval table I am writing.

'Did you know that one day I would write a book and that you would read it?'

'What do you think I'm going to say?'

'Did you always hope it, that you would see my book one day?'

'What do you think I'm going to say?'

'Did you always think that one day you would tell me about why you put me in the box?'

'What do you think I'm going to say?'

'Was it to give me to a lovely mum, like Jenny Nicely? Was it all for the best?'

'What do you think I'm going to say?'

'Did you know you were making me like this?'

'What do you think I'm going to say?'

'Did you know about the vodka and the beer and the wine and the drinks in your tummy? Did you know you were hurting my brain? Did you ever think a little bit about my brain when I was in your tummy? Did you ever think maybe it would be better if . . .'

I'm looking at the pen in my hand, the gold and black one, and my blue notebook is open but my hand has stopped writing, and there are more and more questions in my head. They're buzzing and shouting but only in my head. I'm looking at my pen, with its blue grip in my fingers, and it isn't moving.

'Why did you keep your bottles of beer and wine and vodka and why did you throw away your baby?'

The pen has a bit to press on the top to make the writing bit go in and out. Where the ink comes out of it. But the ink isn't coming out. The question is only in my head.

'Did you never think about throwing away the beer and the wine and the vodka instead? Did you never think that if you threw away the beer and the wine and the vodka instead you could make a baby that was . . . ?'

The pen is tapping on the paper in my notebook. The word I'm thinking of is *'better'*.

'Did you know you had made me like this? When I was born out of your tummy – did you know it then?'

Marnie Shale is talking but her voice is a very long way away and I'm staring at the tapping pen. I'm trying to pull myself out of my dreamy head.

'Is that why you did what you did? Did you put me in a cardboard box because you knew what you'd done to me? Did you want a better baby?'

'. . . fifteen minutes. So, does anybody want to read out what they've written?'

'Or did you throw me away just because you didn't want the baby even if it had a brain that was just like every other baby's brain? If it was a different baby, would you have put it in the box anyway – or was it because the baby was me?'

And I'm seeing that some of the people have their hands in the air, like Danny Flynn and the dotty knotty scarf-knot man who said for heaven's sake. I don't want to read out my questions. I'm looking at my notebook and the tapping pen that is in my fingers, and I'm not even sure why I'm writing this book. Because if she threw me away in a cardboard box, maybe she didn't want me to ever find her and she just wanted me to go away. And maybe she will not even want to read the book. Maybe she will not want to make a dialogue at all. Maybe she will just say, go away, I didn't want to be your mother, not even when you were a little bean in my tummy. Maybe she will say, actually, I wanted to make your brain bad with my vodka and my wine and my beer and I didn't even care and then I wanted to throw you away for ever and not ever, ever, ever see you. Maybe she will say she does not care about my closing time or who I am or what my name is and she wishes I'd never written the book – which is the book that

I haven't written yet. And now I'm thinking how much I want my mum – not that mum, my real *Mum*-mum, Jenny Nicely.

I'm not shouting and I'm not banging my head or humming. I'm not crying, not even very quietly. I don't want to go away. It's not buzzing like wasps in my brain. I'm just inside my head, in a quiet bit, not listening, even though Danny Flynn is talking, and I want a cuddle from my mum. And I'm not very good at knowing what my feelings are called but I'm better than I used to be, because of talking about it a lot until it's easier to know them. I'm not anxious and I'm not angry. I don't think I am anyway. Marnie Shale looks at me and asks if I'm OK and I say I am, because that is the polite thing to say. But I'm not really OK. I think the thing that I am is sad.

6

At the end of the class I don't hurry to the loo to be first, even though I do want a wee. And it's because I want to be in the lift first, and I want to be down at the bottom of the building, because I want to see my mum, my real mum, not the one who threw me away in the cardboard box. It is my mum, Jenny Nicely, who will be there waiting for me, waiting outside. She will be in all her colours and she will give me her big, happy hug with her jangling bracelets, and all the sad feelings in my head will turn to different feelings because of how happy I am to see her.

And there is not enough space in the lift for everyone to go in together, but the man with the scarf says ladies first. And Peter Potter says he will wait for the next lift, with his *Coronation Street* accent and his big, white eyebrows. And the other man does too whose name I can't remember, but maybe it's

Simon, the one with the not-quite beard, and then the woman who is called Susan, but I can't remember what her last name is. I do know it, but I can't find it in my head right now. She has her glasses around her neck, except now they are on her face. Danny Flynn is in the lift with me, and Veronica Ptitsky too. Danny Flynn says some of them are going to the pub and why don't I come with them, and Veronica Ptitsky says yes, because we've worked hard and we deserve a drink. I say I don't like pubs and, anyway, I'm going home now because my mum, Jenny, is coming to meet me.

But now I'm coming out of the lift and I'm looking through the glass doors and I can see the shapes of the bench outside, with streetlights above and cars behind, but I can't see her. And even when I'm outside and I'm looking up the road and down the road, and I'm shouting it – 'Mum' – in case she can hear me, because maybe she's somewhere where she can see me but I can't see her yet, there is no reply. And there are lots of cars in the road, because this is a main road called the high street, and lots of lights from the cars, because it's dark now, and it's like: flash – there's a car, flash – there's another car, flash, flash, flash, and I wonder if my mum is on the other side of the road and hidden by all the cars, because of how busy it is. I'm thinking I should go and see but then I can't because my coat is pulled really hard to bring me back onto the pavement and I nearly fall over because of being grabbed so quickly. And I can hear my name: Hope, and that's Danny Flynn and it's him who is pulling my coat and there is a big BEEP, and the driver is shouting out of the window. What he shouts is 'Fucking lunatic.' I think probably it is at me he is shouting it.

'Christ, Hope.' It's very noisy because of Danny Flynn shouting and me screaming and the man in the car shouting, and his horn and the horn of the car behind that one too. And Danny Flynn says Christ again and he's shaking his head and he says I can't just run into the road or I'll get myself killed. And he's right because the cars are going very fast, except now that there aren't any cars for a little bit because the traffic lights have made them stop, I can see that my mum, Jenny, isn't on the other side of the road. She isn't on this side and she isn't on that side and she isn't here at all.

'It's all right, Hope. I'm sure she's just got held up. She'll be here any moment. Please don't worry.' That's Veronica Ptitsky. And she has her arm around my shoulder. I don't like people hugging me when I don't know them but part of me does want Veronica Ptitsky to do it. She says don't I have a telephone to see if my mum's sent me a message or to send her a message and then I will know where she is. And of course I should have thought of this. Because I do have a phone, because that is important when you have a real job in case your boss has to tell you about anything, like it's raining too much to take the dogs out or the woods are closed because it's too windy, so we're going to walk in the park instead, or Sallie the whippet has to stay on the lead because she's in heat, which isn't about being a bit hot, but which means boy dogs will want to make puppies so they can't come and mate on her. And also a phone is important in an emergency. So this is a really good idea, but not so good when I take my phone out of my pocket because the screen is all dark, and that is because of my light bulb. Well, it's because of show, not tell, too, actually. And also it's because of my golden notebook, where I write all the golden rules.

And it's because, last night, my mum, Jenny, said have I remembered to charge my phone. She said it when I was trying to go to sleep and she was going to bed too, and I said yes, because I had, and she even came in and looked to make sure about it. And she said goodnight, Hope Nicely, and sweet dreams. And I was going to sleep, except in my head I was also doing some exercises, not touching my toes of course, but my writing exercises. I was thinking about how I would show not tell myself being in bed and going to sleep – because of show, not tell being the number one rule of writing. I was thinking about not saying that I was about to be snoring, but to hear my breath being noisier, and to maybe feel the breath being ticklier on my lips, too.

But then I thought that, really, I should have written 'Show Not Tell' in my golden rules notebook, actually. Because of it being the number one rule of writing. And so I thought that I should do that.

But when I pressed the switch to turn on my light my light did not go light. And – flip a pancake – this is when I realised that my light bulb was gone, like not gone away but broken gone. And I was going to tell my mum, Jenny, that she should come and change it but I could hear her snoring from her bedroom that is next to my bedroom. It was noisier breaths and probably ticklier on her lips, and I thought it would not be nice to wake her up, because she's been very tired all week. And I have a light on the table by my bed, too – my mum, Jenny Nicely, sometimes calls this light a lamp, not just the ceiling one, but when I couldn't turn on that light, because of my mobile phone, because of it being plugged in instead. So I took the plug for my phone out from the socket and put in the other plug that was for the light so that I could write down the number one rule with all my other golden rules. And that's what I did.

I wrote *Show, don't tell*. But when I had written in my notebook I turned off the light but I didn't put the plug back out and the phone one back in. Because I forgot.

'Don't cry.' This is Veronica Ptitsky again and she's holding up her own phone which is a colour like pink but it's gold all at the same time, and it has a clear jacket on it that is see-through except that there is glitter in it and I wish I had one on my telephone except my telephone is smaller anyway. 'I'll call her for you. What's her number?'

But I don't know her number. I don't know any telephone numbers because they are too long for me to remember, and I don't write them down because they are in my phone, but there is no charge in my phone. Because of the light bulb and the golden rule.

Other people are here now, from the class, coming out from the library and saying what is wrong with Hope. There's Kelly Bell-y Shell-y, saying can she help and what has happened. And Veronica Ptitsky is saying nothing, don't worry, and why don't they head on to the pub and she'll be there in a minute, when we've found out where Hope's mum is, and yes please, G&T please, lovely. And her arm is around my shoulder still and she's making nice sounds with her words and she's saying it's all right, she's sure my mum will be here any minute. And

Danny Flynn is asking if I want him to walk me back to my home, but I don't even know if my mum will be there. And he says, OK, so why doesn't he run there now and he can see if she's there and I can . . .

But then Marnie Shale is hurrying out of the glass door and she's holding up her mobile phone and running fast and saying thank goodness I'm still here, my mum is on the phone and she's holding it out to me. It's black, not pink and gold with glitter like Veronica Ptitsky's. And it really is my mum, because I know her voice, even though it sounds a little quiet. She says hello Hope, and she's been trying to get hold of me. I say where are you, you weren't here, and my mum says she's sorry, she says she sent me a text to say she's in the hospital, no need to worry though. And she says she had a little scare, because in the bookshop she was a bit dizzy and nearly fainted in the crime fiction section. But everything's all right and the doctors are going to let her come home just as soon as she's spoken to the registrar, which is very soon.

And I tell her about the light bulb in my bedroom and she says she thought it would be something like that because she sent me the message two and a half hours ago. Karen my boss had already brought me to the library for my writing lesson then. And my mum, Jenny, says she sent another message, too, about being late to pick me up, because she's ended up being longer than she expected. She does a bit of a sigh and tells me she's tried me lots of times. Marnie's phone was off too, until now, because of Marnie teaching, and so it's lucky she managed to find me. Mum asks me if I am all right. I tell her I didn't know where she was and she says she's sorry and she was worried about me, too.

I say will she come and she says soon, as soon as the registrar's come, and she asks if there's somewhere I can wait. And I look up from the telephone and Marnie says is everything OK, and I say I have to wait for my mum. She says do I want to come back upstairs to wait because she's having a one-to-one tutorial with Jamal about his book, which is the vampire one, so she has to go back there now and I can wait in reception. But Veronica Ptitsky is saying why doesn't Hope come with her and Danny to the pub, that will be nicer than sitting on my own. The pub is called the White Hart – and when she says it, I think it's the White Heart, like a heart in your body which my mum has some pills for, but Veronica is pointing up the road and saying look, it's just there. There is a picture of an animal a bit like a horse or a deer, and it's a hart and it's white.

Danny is saying he can always see me home if that is easier. But my mum knows where the White

Hart is, and she's getting a taxi and will be coming past on the way from the hospital anyway. I'm going to say that I don't go to pubs, because they are loud and they smell and I don't like vodka or wine or beer. But I don't really want to sit outside the writing group room. And what I do want is a wee, because of being in such a hurry for the lift. And now I am having to remember about it being a rule to not put our hands on our fanny when there are other people there. I say: 'Is there a loo in the pub?'

'You're in a rush.' Veronica Ptitsky is trying to push her hand under my arm, like the film on television that my mum, Jenny, watched at the weekend, which was about Pride and something else, too, when the women with their long dresses walk together and talk about making good marriages, and I'm making my arm be hard to my body so she can't do it. We're coming into the pub and she's pointing to the toilets – 'Over there in the corner.' And she's asking what I want to drink, she's saying: 'G&T?'

I say what's that? And she tells me – gin and tonic. I say isn't gin like vodka and she says yes, a little bit. And I say is tonic like vodka and she says no, more like lemonade or soda water. So I say just tonic. And then I say I mean T, because that is what Veronica Ptitsky said. I say it quickly because I'm running now. I don't even say please. I'm pushing the door with both of my hands, not just one hand. And, flip a pancake, inside the door is another door and the door is shut. So I'm jumping a little bit and banging on the door a little bit. And I'm counting – not in my head, in my actual mouth – one-two-three. I'm jumping more and I'm saying – not in my mouth in my head – to the wee to stay in my tummy. Because of the rule.

And a woman comes out of the door and I knock her with my shoulder as I'm hurrying in and she says something that I think is swearing, but I don't even say sorry because of the worrying about an accident. I am pushing the door shut with two hands, and the lock is a bit tricky but thank goodness it goes in first time, and I'm pulling at my jogging bottoms and my knickers. In my head it is a bit like a race and it is because of remembering all about school and all about the singing. And the singing was about Hope smells like granny's knickers and pissy pants. I have my hand over my ears because of the singing in my head and because of the noisy pub, but I can still hear the sound of my wee and that is good – it's fan-tanty-tastic – because it is going in the toilet and it is not an accident, except for just a little bit, but only in my pants, so I take them off and put them in my bag, and then I put my jogging bottoms back on after.

But now I've forgotten about my drink. So when Veronica Ptitsky gives me a glass and says there is my T, I say it doesn't look like tea, it looks more like a lemonade and she says no, silly, *T*, remember. *T* without the *G*. And she puts her hand through my arm like the ladies in the long dresses.

I take out my purse from my bag, being careful not to take out my pants which are on top and are just a bit damp. I have some money in my purse, like a five-pound note, or a ten-pound, but Veronica Ptitsky says just buy her one another time. She sees me looking around and she says, not the world's best pub but she's been in worse.

There is football on a television which is up on the wall and it's a blue team playing against a red team but the noise is turned off so you can't hear all the yelling and the people talking about kicking and goals and the other words to do with football, which I don't like, but it's still a bit noisy because of all the people and most of them are talking so it's hard to hear anything else. It smells like beer and crisps, cheese and onion mostly but like all the flavours are mixed together. And it smells a bit like when one time I put my clothes in the washing machine, because of being independent, but I forgot they were in there and when my mum, Jenny, found them, they smelt a bit like wet towels or maybe cheese. So that is what I'm thinking, about how the pub smells a bit cheesy.

'Been here before?' That's Veronica Ptitsky.

I say: 'I don't go to pubs.'

She laughs. 'Wish I could say the same. What do you do to have fun with your friends then?'

'I don't have any friends,' I tell her. 'Or only dog ones, because they don't make you do bad things. I don't want any human friends, actually. It's for the best.'

She opens her mouth, like she's going to say something else, but then she closes it again and takes a sip of her drink. I sip mine, too. It is a strange drink because it's like I'm not tasting it in my mouth but in my nose. Maybe I make a funny face, because Veronica Ptitsky starts laughing.

'I only have it for the gin. Don't drink it if you don't want it.'

But I take another taste. Not a big one with my whole mouth, just a little one in the front. It's sort of horrible but your mouth wants to try it again. I have another taste and it makes me press my mouth up towards my nose, like doing a pig nose.

'Hope, you're hilarious.'

I don't say anything because I don't know what to say.

'And have you never drunk alcohol?' Veronica Ptitsky is looking at me very hard and I forget about the rule about personal things and telling everything that's in your head.

'When I was at school I drank vodka because the boys gave it to me.' They gave it to me in the school canteen and in the park after school. They said it was because they were my friends and it would be fun. Those were the only times they asked me to sit with them on the same tables or to walk with them, to the little children's playground or the benches by the big tree. And my brain is remembering this but I'm forgetting to talk, because I'm stuck in my head and it's a bit like something you don't want to look at, but you can't look away.

'You didn't like it?'

I can't remember what she's asking me.

'The vodka?'

'It made me do not good things.'

She's laughing again. 'That's a feeling I know. What not good things?'

My head forgets to tell my mouth about not saying everything that's personal. 'Like shouting at teachers or letting other people put their hands under my clothes. And like banging Shanya's head on the wall. And there were other things.' I'm trying to remember. And then I do remember. 'I ran under a car. And I tried to kill myself.'

'Oh my God, Hope. I'm so sorry. But please, don't ever do that. We'd miss you.'

In my head there is another thing I'm trying to remember, and Veronica Ptitsky is rubbing my arm like I'm a dog who wants to be stroked, and saying poor Hope. I'm thinking that I don't want to talk about this anymore and so I ask her what it's like in Russia – this is called changing the subject and I've role played it with my mum, Jenny – and she says she's never been to Russia.

'But in Lg . . . bgt . . .' I can't remember the name. 'Where your community is.' And she says her name is Russian but she was born in Rhode Island, in America. But she's lived here since she was fourteen. So, she guesses her community is right here in Harpenden.

And this is a bit confusing because of her and Marnie Shale saying the different thing before, in last week's group, but I don't say this because that's correcting people and it's not polite. Veronica Ptitsky says how interesting my book sounds and how brave to be writing an autobiography. She even remembers what I said about changing my life and finding my birth mother because she says she's really interested to know how my book is going to do that. And I'm thinking about how to make an answer to this. And I'm thinking maybe Veronica Ptitsky is not all that clever, and maybe I'm not the only person with a jumble brain if she says she's from Russia and then she forgets she's even said it, and if she can't see how this book is going to change my life. Because books go in bookshops and people read them and they think about them and they talk about them – like Harry Potter and the other one about children killing each other with arrows. And then maybe my birth mother will think: that must be my baby, and then she will want to come and tell me and say she's never stopped thinking about me and even though she threw me away in a cardboard box, she is very proud of me now I have persevered and achieved a book. But I don't say this to Veronica Ptitsky.

'I liked what you wrote in your exercise.' This is me. It is a compliment. I think I did it very well because Veronica Ptitsky is smiling.

'I'm glad you liked it. I was worried you might be offended.'

This is a bit confusing because offended is a bit like sad, and a bit like anxious, like when people call you Fanny Wanker or Hope Headbanger or Pissy Pants, but I don't even understand why I might be offended by someone else's exercise. And Veronica

Ptitsky is looking at me and she's asking if I know who she was writing about. And I say no, because she didn't tell us. And she's stopped stroking my arm but now she puts her hand back and she says: 'Didn't you realise, Hope? I was writing about *you*.'

This is a big surprise and I think Veronica Ptitsky can see that, maybe, because she laughs, and says would I like to have it. Her exercise. And I say yes. And it's very lucky because she wrote it in a notebook, instead of on her laptop or on her phone, so she can tear out the page. And so I'm reading it in the pub, and it's very funny, because of now thinking that it's about me, actually, and not a ginormous mystery at all.

In life, you meet many people. Some you like, some you don't. Some you can talk to for hours without time seeming to pass; others you find a minute in their company drags and embarrasses. Some you admire, some you wish you'd never met. Few make you think: 'When I woke up this morning I didn't imagine that I would meet somebody like you.' When you do, it's rather like taking a step and finding gravity has relaxed.

This person is a little like that. There is something of the Mary Poppins about her and I feel a strange desire to watch her constantly, in case she pulls an umbrella from a carpet bag and flies out of the window. Physically, she is – I hope she won't mind me saying – quite tiny. The height of a child with the voice of a little girl. She has eyes that flash sparks at times and stare into the distance at others, but seem to be constantly searching. There is a vulnerability about her that brings out something protective in me, though I'm not the mothering kind, but also a brightness that carries me along. With her chatter and her unpredictability, she reminds me of a baby animal – a bear cub perhaps, on one of those BBC nature programmes – which you watch, not knowing if it will growl or lie on its back and kick its little legs. And those eyes dart around, as if her brain is a butterfly and those eyes are the net that is trying to keep up . . .

'Do you like it?' This is Veronica Ptitsky and I say yes, because I do. And it makes me feel like a big silver star, even though I don't have a carpet bag, really. I did have an umbrella, which was yellow, but I put it down on a bench in the wood when I was picking up a poo from one of the dogs, and then I forgot to remember to take my umbrella again.

Veronica Ptitsky says good, she's glad I like it. And I say can I put it in my book. And Veronica Ptitsky laughs and says yes. This is when she says about the copy write and I can copy it as much as I like.

I'm trying to think what else to say, because maybe this is a thing that I need to say thank you for, but I'm not sure. But then my brain finds another thing to think about, because across the pub, where Danny Flynn is talking to some of the other people, like Peter Potter with his white hair and eyebrows, and Kelly Bell-y Shell-y, with a long plait and a hairband, there's also a dress that is yellow and pink, and in the dress is my mum. And that is why I'm smiling so much and not saying thank you, actually. I say to Veronica Ptitsky: 'I'm going now.'

I can feel the smile on my face and I'm hurrying and I'm looking and listening only towards my mum, like she is the most important person in the pub. And even though it's loud with the talking all around, I can hear what she's saying to Danny Flynn as I'm coming near to them, because I'm looking and listening so hard.

'. . . but I told them there was no way I could stay overnight, so I'll go in again tomorrow for more . . .' And then she sees me. She stops talking to Danny Flynn because she's opening her arms and she's saying, 'Here she is. My Hope.' And it's the best hug ever, because my mum is here now. And even when I was drinking T with Veronica Ptitsky and she was saying the surprising thing, really I was just waiting for my mum to come. Danny Flynn is saying can he get her a drink, and my mum, Jenny, is saying, thank you but the taxi is waiting. And Danny Flynn says, sorry, he still hasn't brought that book round. And then we're in the taxi and putting on our seatbelts because that's important. And I'm telling my mum, Jenny, about how I was crying when she wasn't there after my class. And I'm telling her that she will have to remember to change my light bulb when we get home.

3

RAISING THE STAKES

7

Flip a pancake, this is not a good week. I am looking at my watch and I'm remembering that I am meant to be somewhere. And that is in my writing class. And instead I am here, in the library downstairs, doing research and thinking about this week's topic, which is plotting. I'm putting my hand over my mouth and thinking: flip, flip, flip a flipping pancake. Because it is bad to forget and it is rude and unreliable.

My book of rules helps me to remember the things that are the most important, like about if you're meant to be somewhere, called an appointment, you should always try your very best to be there at the right time, and not to forget and just go away and not be there at all. But even with the rules written down, in my very special book, sometimes I forget anyway and that is what has happened this week, which is not a good week.

My brain is always a bit of a muddled place, like in the woods where there is no path and just trees. But this week it's like there are even more trees and even less path, in my head, and the ground is muddy. It's like a muddy muddle.

When I was at my job yesterday, or the other day which was before yesterday, Sallie the whippet was off her lead and she ran off, like she was chasing a squirrel or maybe another dog, and so I went into the trees to find her and bring her back. I forgot about telling Karen, who is my boss, where I was going, and then I was in the trees in the wood and I couldn't see Sallie and I couldn't see Karen my boss, and I couldn't even hear them when I was shouting and yelling to ask where they were. And it took a very long time, I can't remember how long, but more than an hour and maybe more than two hours, and in the end they were at the café, and Sallie was with Karen and all the other dogs and she said – Karen not Sallie, of course, because Sallie is a dog – where the hell had I been because she was about to call the police. And it was especially bad, it happening on that day – maybe the day that was before yesterday – because of me being late in the morning, which was because my mum, Jenny Nicely, did not wake me up and she was staying in bed and not going to her work at the bookshop because of feeling so tired and sweaty and a bit under the weather.

And Karen my boss said to me that when you have a job, and it's a real job, it's very important to be on time and not to go away, into trees and away from the real path, without saying to anybody where you're going. And I said that I was sorry and that I was going to try really hard to remember. But now I am still down here, in the library, and I have forgotten to remember to go upstairs to my class on time and I am banging my hand on the button for the lift and people are looking at me and asking if I am all right. I don't want to say anything to them. Even when a little boy asks his mum: 'Mummy why is that woman making those noises?' I don't say anything. I just want the lift to hurry up and to take me up the floors to the top floor.

The reason why I am downstairs in the library, with my research and my thinking about plotting, is because of my mum, Jenny Nicely, and her having to go for some blood tests before they go home in the hospital at five o'clock, and because of Karen my boss and Julie Clarke being busy too, actually, so that is why I was here so early and my mum said was I sure I was all right on my own while I was waiting and was I sure I would remember when it was time to go up to my class. And I said I was not stupid, actually, and of course I would be perfectly fine. Because that's what I thought, before the forgetting. And now I remember my phone was ringing in the library and I couldn't even answer it – when I tried to put my finger on it to slide to answer, it kept on ringing and ringing and some people were standing up and looking around to see where the noise was coming from – and even when I said hello, nobody was there on the other end, and – of course – it was because of the alarm that my mum put on my mobile. And now I can see that's why it sounded like a long bell instead of the tune that sounds like it's on a . . . that instrument that's not a piano and not a drum and that you hit it with a stick, and . . .

The lift is here now but even though it's going up, it feels like it's going so slowly that it's not hardly moving, like the lift is being moved by a snail or a very old person. And I'm looking at the floors: 1, 2, 3 – and even I can count those, because it's easy as anything. But I could have counted them ten times, or twelve or maybe a hundred, because it's moving so slowly. And just as the doors open – maybe because of the ping they make – I remember it. The word. It's a *xylophone*. Of course. That's what my phone sounds like. That's the word I couldn't find in my head. When it's not the alarm that's a bell instead, when it's a real person calling because they want to talk to me, it's like a tune on a xylophone.

'Hope!' This is Marnie Shale as I come in the door. I knocked and opened all at the same time, like I am banging on the door as I am walking into the room, so it is a little bit noisy. And I'm a little bit falling into the room because of the pushing and the knocking all at the same time but I don't end up on the floor because of Peter Potter being in the chair by the door and because of me almost landing on him but not quite. And Marnie Shale is looking at me and all the words sort of come out of my mouth about my mum going to the hospital for the blood test and the alarm on my phone and me forgetting what it was, and about the lift and about Sallie running into the woods and it being a bad day today, and all the rest of the group are looking at me and Danny Flynn and Veronica Ptitsky are sort of smiling and sort of looking with mouths like 'O's.

The man with the scarf has a different one this week. This scarf is green with a pattern, like lots of loops. But still with a knot. And he isn't smiling and his mouth isn't an 'O'. It's more of a turned-down mouth but open so I can see his teeth. And I didn't use to be good at faces but I'm getting better because of practising with my mum, Jenny Nicely, all the time. We look at pictures in newspapers and magazines, or on the side of buses, and she says what do I think they are thinking and feeling. And I think maybe the scarf-knot man is a bit sad or maybe a bit anxious or angry. Probably it is angry, not sad. Because his eyes are quite squeezed up and they don't look wet like they want to cry. And Marnie says to me come in and sit down quickly because we are just discussing Ludovic's opening chapter. And the words are still coming out of my mouth but I have to make them stop, because interrupting is rude.

I sit down and I'm looking for my notebook but it is in the bottom of my bag underneath my research, which is in a big folder, and my packet of biscuits for in case I'm hungry. And when I pull out my notebook my knickers come out too, from the almost accident in the pub, so now I'm thinking I must remember to take them out for my mum to wash, and not forget about them being in my bag again. And I push them back in quickly and I don't think anybody has seen them except for maybe Ludovic scarf-knot man because he has a very odd look on his face that I have never seen on the side of a bus.

'If you're ready for me to continue . . . ?' This is him and I think it's because I'm pulling my biscuits out again – silly me. I've only just put them back in, but, flip a pancake, I forgot my pen. But I have it now, my special pen which is gold and black, with my blue grip to make it nice to hold, and I smile at him to say I am ready. He doesn't smile back.

'I hope you had the email with this in it?' Marnie Shale is pushing some printed sheets over the table to me. 'We're talking about the opening of Ludovic's book. Maybe you had a chance to read it at home?'

I nod my head. And it's true. I did have the chance to read it. But what happened is that even though I did have the *chance*, after I'd read the first bit of it, I didn't read the rest, mostly because of not knowing who these people called Flavius and Flavia and Crispus were and it sounding a bit like flavours of crisps, and everybody being Constantine-something and something-ius and because of lots of the other words being words that I didn't know, and also because of it being *Coronation Street* on telly and time for my tea. But I don't say this because I'm thinking it might be a little bit rude, so I just nod and it's not a real lie, actually, because of my having the *chance* to read it even if I only read the tiniest bit. So I'm nodding and it's not fibbing.

Marnie Shale is nodding too and saying that's really good, and just quickly, to recap, when we're talking about each other's work, it's good to be constructive and to offer our honest thoughts and reactions, but can we please also make sure we're being considerate in our criticism. And she looks back towards Ludovic, the man with the scarf and the knot.

'To come back to Susan's point, I agree that your voice is engaging and the world feels very real. I like how you're not overwhelming us with the historical detail and the plot feels timeless. And I can also see how cleverly you are raising the stakes for your characters. It's a fascinating premise – to take these murders that so little is known about – and did anybody else feel that Flavia . . . ?'

I am trying very hard to listen not just with my ears but with my brain, but my brain is in one of its moods, like Sallie the whippet but not so fast, where it doesn't want to be a good dog and walk along with the others. So the words from Susan Ford, which is an easy-peasy name, because it's Susan just like my teaching assistant at school, and also Ford like my car, with her glasses on a chain, and Danny Flynn and Peter Potter, are there in my head, but just floating, not properly going into my brain, and the bit about Ludovic saying no, actually, the character of Claudius is fictional and in terms of the plot . . . that's floating too. In my head, I'm trying hard not to be a dog going away in the woods but the listening thing is a bit difficult. But then the knot-man, Ludovic, says a thing, and I'm not going away anymore, because it is so horrible and so sad, and so shocking. And even if it's interrupting and rude to shout I can't help it, because of the shocking thing. And it's my mouth shouting and my brain shouting too: 'Horrible, horrible, horrible.'

And I really do think the look on his face is angry because it's like a face in an advert in a magazine that my mum, Jenny Nicely, and I looked at when we were practising the thing about expressions. And in the advert, the man is pouring his cereal but his cereal box is empty so no cornflakes are coming out. And in the corner behind him is a woman who is maybe his wife and she has a big bowl and she has a spoon in it. And when I said that the look on the man's face was angry – because of his eyes being all squeezed and his mouth being in a line and there being wrinkles on his forehead – my mum laughed and said, yes, definitely angry. And Ludovic's face is a bit like that but only for a little bit and then it is more normal again and he says: 'Indeed. Boiled alive, poor old Flavia Maxima Fausta. History records *how* she died, despite the *damnatio memoriae* issued by her husband. Not a nice way to go. Suffocated in an overheated bath. But the *how* is not so vital to the plot of my novel, as the *why*.'

I'm sitting on my hands, with my lips tight together, because I don't want to make the knot-man, Ludovic, look angry with more shouting, but I'm counting in my head, too, and it is because I don't like thinking about death. When Anne Bentley, who was the vicar who found the cardboard box which was me, died, because of being very old and having had a good innings, I had to go away, even though it was still in the church, and the other vicar who was still alive was still talking and people were standing up for singing and Anne Bentley was still there in the box, not the cardboard one the coffin one. But I'm telling myself I can't do any going away now, because I've only just come in, and I've done enough interrupting today. So I make myself smile in my mouth, while Ludovic knot-man and Marnie Shale, and some of the others like Peter Potter and Danny Flynn and the man called Malcolm, are talking about the murders and the story still. I think maybe he is even more orange this week, Malcolm is. And he has some sunglasses on his head, even though it isn't sunny in the room.

I keep sitting on my hands and counting in my head, counting really loud, like I'm taking big, loud steps inside my brain – one, two, three – one, two, three – until Marnie Shale says thank you and well done to knot-man Ludovic, and he does a little nod, and she says she'll let us have a quick break in case anybody needs the loo or a glass of water. And then we'll talk about another one of our openings, and it will be Simon Taylor's book this time, and if anybody didn't have a chance to read his extract that she emailed during the week, she has some spare printouts of it here. And even though I had the chance to read this too, I didn't really read it, because of *Coronation Street* and then because of forgetting, so I take one of the pieces of paper so that I can read it a bit now.

Marnie Shale is looking at her phone, not just looking, but touching it because probably she's reading her emails and her messages and things, and she says, excuse me, I'll just be a moment, and she goes outside of our room. And most of the rest of the group are in the room and some are talking, like Susan Ford, with her glasses round her neck, and she's talking to the Ludovic man but with their voices quiet. I can just hear 'antiquity' and 'exhibition' and 'divine'. And some people are looking at their mobiles, like Veronica Ptitsky, or at the printouts, like me. Kelly Bell-y Shell-y is reading a printout too. She has her long hair in two plaits and she's reading it with her mouth moving just a little bit. I don't think I'm moving my mouth. I'm just reading, with my finger on the words. And Simon Taylor's novel is easier to read than Ludovic's was, because of the names being real names, not made-up ones that sound like crisp flavours, and because of it not being about people dying by being boiled in a bath.

Soul Caravan *by Simon Taylor*

Ellie was only nineteen when I met her and to me she shone. Our paths crossed, as was so often the case back then, at a party. I forget whose, but I can still picture the living room: paisley-print throws on the sofas, a striped rag rug on threadbare carpet, one of those round paper lampshades of course, and that poster of the soldier being shot. The Fugees from a two-tape ghetto blaster on the bookshelf in the corner. Sandalwood joss sticks that you could hardly smell beneath the fug of tobacco and weed. I wasn't meant to be there that night. It was a student thing and I was no longer a student. I had graduated that summer, and was signing on whilst waiting for a job to materialise like a holy apparition. I had never been in love but I was meant to be meeting a girl called Jo there. Only I'd come to this place late, after a club, and there was no sign of Jo. This was before mobile phones. I didn't know anybody else so I'd decided to call it a day and I'd gone into the room where I'd left my jacket. The bulb had gone so it was pitch-dark apart from a lava lamp on a desk by the wall and I was fumbling, blindly, through a pile of coats on the bed.

'Leaving already?' The voice was low, female and teasing. It made me jump. I hadn't realised there was anybody else there.

I said I didn't know anyone so there didn't seem much point staying.

'Do you have a cigarette?'

I said I did, but I'd lost my lighter.

And then there was a little flash – just a second – and then a slightly longer one. And I caught a glimpse, behind the flame of a Zippo, of her sitting on the floor, legs crossed. I couldn't make out very much of her, just two eyes watching me. Big dark eyes. Confident. Smiling.

I sat on the floor beside her and shook out two Marlboro Reds from a soft pack. She lit both and passed me one back. For a moment, we sat, silent, apart from the crackle as we inhaled, orange flowers glaring then fading on the tips of our cigarettes. The room smelt of tobacco and patchouli oil and other people's coats.

'I'm Simon,' I told her.

'Eliana. Call me Ellie.'

'Nice to meet you, Ellie.'

'Nice to meet you too, Simon.'

We shook hands in the dark. Her fingers were soft and they stayed around mine after we'd finished shaking.

'Well, Eliana, Ellie, since it seems I'm staying a little longer, can I go and find you a drink?'

'I never drink.'

'What, really?'
Her laughter in the blackness of the room was
like warm syrup. And she passed me a bottle.

Simon Taylor is opposite me – in the writing classroom, at the *oval* table – and I'm looking at him now because I'm thinking he doesn't look like a person who sits in the dark talking to women at parties. And he looks towards me, too, but then he moves his eyes away quickly. And I'm thinking that maybe he is writing non-fiction like me, as his name in the book is Simon too. And I'm thinking how funny it is that he looks so old, with hair that is a bit dark and a bit white, and his beard which is a bit of both too, and not even like someone who would go to a party at all. And I'm thinking that I've never been to a party like this one, or even really a real party – only things like the Christmas evening in my mum Jenny's bookshop and, once, a summer party for a group that was for people with the same rainbow which is Foetal Alcohol Spectrum Disorder, actually, and the group was called FASD Friends – and also the funeral in the church was a bit like a party because of all the people, but that was when I went away, so that doesn't really count.

And it's really especially funny because the girl in the room in Simon Taylor's story, which is maybe an autobiography, was called Ellie and, in fact, I know *two* people already called Ellie, but I think not also called Eliana. And, actually, I don't really know them anymore, because one was in school, but only until Year Nine because then she was excluded, which means she had to go away to another school. And I think it was because of throwing a chair. Or maybe smoking. And the other Ellie was a social worker, with Julie Clarke, when Julie Clarke was my actual social worker and not only a retired one. But she only came once, the one called Ellie, and she was quite nice, because she brought me a teddy bear that was a monkey, but then she didn't come anymore after that, only that one time.

And while I'm thinking this, about the one, two, three Ellies and also about the parties, Marnie Shale comes back into the room and she kneels down and says something very quietly to Danny Flynn and he looks at her and nods and they both look at me. And then Marnie Shale comes to my side of the table and she says: 'I've just spoken to your mum on the phone.'

'My mum?' That's me, and I'm saying it because of being a bit surprised, like why would my mum call Marnie Shale and not me. But I'm taking out my phone from my bag – it's under my knickers but I'm careful not to pull them out – and I see that my mum has been calling me *eleven times* but I pressed the button to make the noise stop, because of the bell ringing when I was in the library and I'd forgotten about it telling me to go to my class.

Marnie Shale is smiling, and she puts her hand on my arm and says: 'Don't worry. Everything's fine, Hope. But Jenny's quite tired after all the blood tests, and she's going home to have a bit of a sit-down. She said for you to walk home with Danny, if that's OK.'

On the other side of the table, the oval one, Danny Flynn is doing a big smile and he's holding up his thumb, which is like him telling me it's OK. I say to Marnie Shale: 'I don't know Danny Flynn very well.' And it's true, because of only seeing him in the writing groups, and it's only two times, and also going to the pub, which was the White Hart, but I was mostly talking to Veronica Ptitsky and not to him even. And it's a bad idea to be alone with people when you don't know them. So I say: 'I don't think I should walk with Danny Flynn. I think my mum should come really. I think that would be for the best. Because I'm meant to walk back with her.'

'But it's OK, isn't it, because it's to help your mum and if she says it's all right?'

I'm thinking really hard. I only have one hand under my bottom, because of Marnie Shale having her hand on my other arm. But it's like in my brain

I'm being pulled in one way and also in another, because of thinking it's a rule about waiting for my mum and we talked about it, when we were practising before I started the writing group, that I should wait for her at the end, but it's confusing because of my mum also being on the phone to Marnie Shale. And I'm looking at Danny Flynn, and I'm thinking about how we walked home last week, or not last week maybe, but the other week before it, and my mum said what a nice young man, so I'm thinking that maybe it is absolutely fine for me to walk back with him, maybe, actually, that is what is for the best, and so now I'm nodding and saying that's OK then.

8

'. . . do find it hard to keep up the momentum. Coming in after work, to then find the energy to sit down and write, when all I want to do is collapse.'

Collapsing can be bad, like one day Karen, my boss, was at the bus stop and an old man just collapsed. That's what she told me. He collapsed. Just like that. And he was dead. But I don't think that is the sort of collapse that Danny Flynn means. I think it is the sort of collapse that my mum wants to do when she's been on her feet all day long and says she's so ready to collapse. And it's also with a cup of tea.

This is Danny Flynn talking about wanting to collapse, and we are walking past the White Hart. Some of the writing group have gone in but not us. It smells of smoking, because of people being outside, with cigarettes, and the vape ones too that make the big fruity clouds, and beers or other drinks. But then we're further up the road and it just smells like autumn again.

'It's establishing the right patterns though, isn't it? This week, I only managed a couple of thousand words. What about you? How much have you written?'

I'm not very good at numbers. That's why it's best for me to not have all my money inside my purse. But I don't want to say this to Danny Flynn because he will think I am not very clever. I don't think he will call me names like Spaz, but I think Danny Flynn is nice, and I don't want him to even think it, so I say thirty-nine thousand because I'm thinking that is a big number, not a Spaz one. I say it like I know it exactly and like I counted all of those words. And then I add, 'And twelve.' I'm not quite sure why.

'Wow. Hope. I'm . . .' and he doesn't finish for a moment. 'That's incredible.'

I'm really happy – with my cheeks feeling warm and my smile there, even without me telling it to be. And even though it's not the real number – and I don't know how many words is the real number, but probably not so many because of having a real job and *Coronation Street* and *X Factor* and not knowing what to write and mostly just thinking very hard, which is called research – even if my number was a bit of a make-it-up one, I'm very pleased with myself for making Danny Flynn so surprised. And I'm nodding like I'm agreeing with him about it being incredible. And he's saying it runs in the family then, the talent, and about how he's been reading some of my mum's poems, in her book of poems called *Life Still*, and how powerful and thought-provoking they are.

'My mum wrote a poem about me in it,' I tell him. And it's true, because it was a poem called 'Matching' and it was about how adopting me was the hardest thing and the best thing she ever did – that's what she tells me. And it was very hard because of her husband being a bad news bear and then being an *ex*-husband, and having to tell everybody that it would still be for the best for her to be my mum, even if it was only her and not any husband, actually, and my mum, Jenny, had to persevere a lot to make them see it was true, but in the end she did. I've read it thousands of times, my mum's poem, or maybe hundreds, and it makes me feel happy, even though I don't really understand all the words, because some of them seem like she's written them a bit muddled, like *my hope baby abstract now my mewling, puking, baby mine*.

But I don't say that to my mum and I don't say it to Danny Flynn now. I just tell him about adopting me being the best thing ever for her and how she tells me she's prouder of me than of all her poems put together, and that if she couldn't have had me, she wouldn't have wanted any other baby. And then I'm telling Danny Flynn about me wanting a puppy – because of talking about adopting and that's what I want to do, but with a dog and not a baby, because of nappies – and I'm telling him about what puppy I'd want, maybe one like Tinie Tempah, even though I don't know what type he is, and not like Sallie because of her going into the trees and because of whippets chasing squirrels, and not a chihuahua because of them being so little and I like bigger dogs. But I'm telling him about how my mum thinks it's not such a good idea, actually, because of babies creating a lot of chaos whether they're human ones or dog ones.

Then it is my house, and I'm a bit tired because of all the talking and I want a wee and my mum, Jenny, is taking a long time to come to the door. When she comes, I run in, but it's all right because I'm remembering to say thank you to Danny Flynn for walking me back, even as I'm hurrying inside. I can hear my mum saying thank you too, and no, not great, to be honest, but she's sure she'll be right as rain again soon, and not to worry about the book, drop it in any time. Honestly, no rush.

When I come out from my wee, Danny Flynn has gone already and my mum is sitting in the big armchair, which is green and corduroy and has a dip in the seat from our bottoms, and that is where she is sitting instead of standing up and chopping and stirring and being by the cooker, which is where she usually is in the kitchen at teatime. And Mum says, Hope, and I say, yes, and she says how about a takeaway for tea because she's not sure she's up to cooking and I say fan-tanty-tastic, because of liking takeaways, especially when they come in boxes like pizzas, or with lids that go click, like Chinese. And especially with prawn crackers. Because those are my favourite. But you can't have prawn crackers and pizza together, and now I can't decide which I want the most. And my mum says it's up to me because she's not hungry actually, so she'll only have a little bit. And I say, can she show me the menus, so that I can think about it. And Jenny, my mum, says can't I please get them and they're right there in the drawer by the fridge, but I can't see them because I don't think it's the right pizza menu – because I think the picture was different on it last time, which was a long time ago, because of it being a special treat and not being allowed to have it all the time.

'Let me have a look.' That's my mum. She says

it as she's standing up, but she only stands up for, like, a tiny moment, like counting only one, two and not even three. Then she sits back down again. And she's making a noise that is a bit like a sigh or like when you've been running. And I say is she OK, and she says yes, yes.

And she stands up again and she is walking towards me, saying, surely that's the same pizza menu, and I'm saying no, because the other one had a picture of a man with a big spoon on the front. And she says but maybe it's the same place just with a different . . . And she stops. And she puts her hand on the corner of the table. It's like she's slapping it, because the noise of her hand on the wood is very loud. She puts her hand onto her neck.

'What are you doing?' This is me.

She looks at me. Her mouth is open but she's not saying anything. And it's like she's trying to tell me something with her eyes.

'Mum?'

She is bending forward, like there's something on the floor she needs to look at more closely. She drops down, onto her knees.

'Mum.' This is me. I am shouting. 'Stand up.'

And then she falls. Like from kneeling, her body goes down to the side. There is a thump.

'Stand up.' That's me. I'm shouting other things

too that are not words but just sounds. And I'm kneeling down and putting my hands around my mum's cheeks to turn her to look at me but her eyes are closed and she doesn't wake up.

9

I'm crying now and I'm rocking and I'm pressing my hands on my mum's shoulders and I'm rubbing my hands on her face.

'Wake up.'

There are thoughts in my head that I do not want to be there. Because I want my mum to open her eyes. I want her to stand up. And I don't even mind if it's not the same pizza. Or even no pizza.

'Please wake up.'

There is a thing. A thing that you are meant to do. If this happens, this – this which is a – I'm trying to think, but in my head there is just shouting and screaming and not wanting my mum to be lying down. And I'm banging my head a bit now, against my mum, on her shoulder – not so hard to hurt her. And still she's not awake. And I'm telling myself it is important that I make my brain work better. But my brain just feels more muddled, like it's a jumble sale in a fog, and I can't even see the pile of things. And I'm crying so hard that my shoulders are shaking. But if my brain doesn't work then I can't make my mum wake up. I hate it. I hate my brain.

And it's like there are two of me – one me who is yelling and screaming and pressing my head on my mum, Jenny Nicely's, chest – and one me who is in my head and shouting because of how rubbish I am. *Rubbish No-Brain Nicely. Stupid.*

There is something. There is a thing. There is the thing I should be doing. I do know it. I know what I should do.

But my head is yelling too loud. My head can't think.

I'm looking at my mum. She's not moving. She's not doing anything. I am the only one who can do the thing. So I stand up. And I punch my hand on the table. And I hit my head on the table. And I'm still shouting. And what I'm shouting is: 'Stop, stop, stop.' Because if I can stop my brain doing this, then maybe the thing will come to me. The right thing. And I want to keep on screaming, but this is important. It is so important. So I sit on a chair. I want to kick and punch. But I sit. I put my hands under my bottom. I can feel the plastic under me and it's cold. And I do a thing with my brain like making it be as strong as it can. And I tell it no more shouting. I tell it stop. I tell it, count. I tell it, stop and count – for your mum.

One-two-three.

I am sitting on my hands and I'm squeezing my eyes so they're shut and I'm telling myself to breathe slowly, even though I want to breathe as fast as I can and to be screaming all at the same time.

One-two-three.

I have to think about the thing. I have to think about the thing that will be for my mum. And make it not be too late.

One, two, three.

If my brain was better, it would remember. But one, two, three – that's so easy even I can remember. And there's another thing . . .

One. Two. Three.

A number. There's a number to ring. In an . . . In an . . .

I can remember. I *can* remember.

Emergency. Bingo!

The word comes to my head. And I do a big breath out. Because – of course – that is the thing. That is the thing I should have thought. That's the thing I was trying so hard to remember. And also an *ambulance.* And both of the words have been dropped in my head at the same time, like twins. It is an emergency. I just have to ring the number for an ambulance. And my bag is still on the table and I open it. There is a little smell of my knickers when I unzip the zip. I take out my phone and I put in the numbers. And they are right there in my head.

It rings. A woman answers. I say hello this is an emergency. I say I need an ambulance. 'Please,' I say. 'Quickly.'

'At the third stroke the time will be seven forty-four and twenty seconds.' She sounds a bit like the Queen. I don't think she's understanding and so I tell her again.

'Send an ambulance for my mum. She's on the floor.'

But she's not listening. Because, flip a pancake, she's still talking about the time. And I'm shouting now, because even if it's rude, it is very, very important. 'I don't care about that. Just the ambulance. It is for my mum, Jenny Nicely.'

'. . . seven forty-five precisely.'

'I don't want the time.' This is me and I'm holding the phone in front of me and I'm yelling as loud as I can. 'I just want you to come and make my mum OK.'

But the woman is stupid. I press the stop button.

And I'm shouting: 'Stupid, stupid, stupid.' And in my lungs, it's like something heavy is pressing on me. I'm crying but it's even hard to cry because of the heavy pressing in my lungs. And I'm making noises like a car when it's squeaking as it stops because of needing oil. And I'm banging on the table.

And then there is another noise. More banging. And I'm looking at my hands, because I'm thinking maybe it's me. But even when I stop hitting the table, the banging is still there. And my brain is a bit confused until it realises that it is the door. Because of our bell being broken but there is still a knocker. It is shaped like a lion.

This is very strange. Because it must be the ambulance. But the woman didn't even ask where our house was. She only told me the time. But I know that I have to hurry and that it is important. And I'm thinking maybe because of me telling her my mum's name, maybe that was how she knew where to send the ambulance. And maybe I shouldn't have shouted at her for being stupid. And I'm hurrying, but my legs are feeling clumsy, and I knock a photograph off the table in the hallway as I run past. And it's the photo of me in my school uniform with clouds and sky behind but they aren't really real, actually. And I hear it smash but there is no time to pick it up.

Now I'm opening the door. I'm saying thank the Lord, and I'm saying it's incredible how fast you came and I'm saying I didn't even think . . .

But it is not an ambulance. It is Danny Flynn and he is holding up a book which is called *The Nightmare Project*. And he is smiling.

'Why are you here?' This is me. I can't help it. I'm shouting. 'I didn't ask for you. I asked for an ambulance.'

And he's saying, I thought I'd run back with the book for your mum, while it was in my mind. He's saying, otherwise I'd only forget again. And he's saying, why are you crying? And what's that about an ambulance? And Hope, are you all right? Hope, what's happened?

And I can almost not say the words from my mouth, because of the crying and because of my chest still having the heavy pressing. But I manage to say it – 'My mum' – but it's like not one word, but four or seven or eight, because of my voice not being right. And Danny Flynn is asking if something has happened to my mum and I'm nodding and crying and he's coming inside. And I shouldn't let people into the house if I don't know them. But I think it must be absolutely fine. Because of him walking me home. And because of the emergency.

When he sees my mum, he runs to her and

kneels down. 'Is she breathing?' he asks. He's bending very close to her face, like he's going to kiss her. And he's lifting up her hand, like he's holding it, but higher than her hand, nearly her arm. 'Shit.' This is Danny Flynn. It's swearing. It's a word we shouldn't say. But I don't tell him. I just stand watching. 'Hope. You said you've called 999 already?'

I'm looking at him. And I'm thinking about what I called. On my telephone. And I'm thinking that I did know that. 999. Of course. Like, *call 999, this is an emergency*. But the number I called was 123. Maybe because of all the counting.

'Hope?' Danny Flynn is moving my mum's head, so that now she's staring up at the ceiling. And he's putting his fingers over her nose, like he's pinching her.

I don't want to tell him about calling the wrong number. Because he will think I'm stupid.

'Hope?' his voice is loud now. Like maybe he's cross. Or scared. 'Have you phoned an ambulance?'

And I say no. And my voice feels very little.

He pulls his phone out from his pocket and he presses the number and he puts it on the floor. And it must be on the loudspeaker because of me being able to hear the ringing. And a man's voice says which service does he require and he says ambulance. And while he's talking, he's also pushing down on my mum, in between her boobs, with her lying on her back now. And he's saying something under his breath that sounds like counting and then there's the woman who says, ambulance, what's the problem, and he's saying, woman unconscious, not breathing and he's saying 23a Station Close, that's right, isn't it, Hope . . . ? And I'm not crying and I'm not shouting and I just say yes, but it's like all my feelings are hiding and I don't know where they've gone.

The woman has an accent, and it's maybe Scottish like Marnie Shale, and she's saying does he know how to administer CPR, and he's saying, yes, he has had first aid training and she's saying, OK, so he knows thirty compressions, then two rescue breaths, and he says yes, that's exactly what he's doing. And in between speaking to the woman, he reaches down to my mum's face with his head and he puts his mouth on her mouth.

I'm thinking that maybe I should shout and push him off, because of keeping our hands to ourselves and not kissing people we don't know or even touching them, but I'm also thinking I've seen this on *Coronation Street*, or maybe that other programme that my mum likes, which is in a hospital and everybody is a doctor or a person in a bed and they're all saving lives and talking about sad things and relationships.

The woman is asking Danny if he can give her the postcode and he looks at me and he says: 'Hope, what's your postcode?' And I don't know it – or, in fact, I think I do know it, but my memory doesn't want to tell me it. But if I say that, then Danny Flynn will think I'm stupid, so I just say some numbers. The numbers that I say are 7-6-9-4-3-20.

Danny Flynn puts his eyebrows close together but he doesn't reply. Instead he says to the phone woman: 'My house is literally around the corner, so only the last letter will be different, and mine is . . .' And he gives her letters, too, not just numbers. Maybe that's why his postcode was better than mine. One of the letters was A – like my flat. Like 23a. I don't know why I didn't say that.

'That's fine. I've found it. And the patient is still unconscious?'

'Yes.'

'How long has she been unconscious for?'

He looks at me. I'm thinking about crying and I want to go away. And I want my mum to be back awake. I don't say anything. I feel like it's all my fault for having a brain that can't answer all these questions.

'It can't be more than five minutes' – this is Danny Flynn – 'because I spoke to her when I dropped Hope off, and I came straight back. Hope, did your mum collapse as soon as I'd left, or was it nearer to when I came back?'

I'm thinking about the pizza and the prawn crackers and the picture being different because of not having the man with the spoon, and I'm thinking about my mum being alive and talking and I don't want this. I. Don't. Want. This.

'Hope? It's important. It could help your mum.'

I put my hands on my head and I pull my hair until it hurts. 'She was coming to see about the pizza. And then she fell down.'

The woman on the phone can hear this because of the loudspeaker thing.

'Patient's name?'

Danny Flynn and I tell her at the same time but I can hear his voice mostly because of mine feeling so small.

'Her age?'

I don't like numbers. Numbers are like a thing I can't hold in my head. But I'm thinking my mum, Jenny Nicely, is fifty-four, because of her having had a birthday not very long ago. Or maybe thirty-four. But I say fifty-four because of it being the first one in my head. And I think it's right.

'Any medical conditions? Is she taking any medication?'

They want me to tell them more things because

of Danny Flynn looking at me again. But my brain is telling me that it has done enough talking. And I'm putting my hands over my mouth and I'm breathing fast and it's noisy because of the air coming out of my nose. Danny's saying, Hope, darling, why don't you sit down. I know this is hard. And he's saying to the woman that my mum has told him she has cholesterol issues and high blood pressure too, and then he says – to me again – perhaps Hope knows where her pills are. I do of course, because they are all in her duck bag in the bathroom. It's a duck bag because of having little ducks all over it. But how can I sit down, like Danny Flynn said to do, and go and get her pills, like he's saying now?

And he's bending over again and giving my mum, Jenny, two more blow kisses. And I want her to open her eyes and give me a big, happy smile, and say: hello my Hope. But she's just lying there, with Danny Flynn pressing on her body and the woman on the phone saying about 'any history of . . . ?'

I'm not very good at knowing what I'm feeling. But this is not like sad or angry, or it's not like anxious. It's like the worst thing that I've ever felt. And I can't find a word, and I can't make my nose stop making the loud noise of breathing on my hand, and it's very fast, like I'm blowing hard too, although not into my mum's mouth, like Danny did, but just into the world. And Danny Flynn is asking, Hope, are you all right, and he's saying, Hope, you really should sit down. But I still don't know about the pills in the duck bag. And I don't even know if my mum is going to wake up. And I don't want the things in my head that are feeling like this. And I . . .

I don't want this.

'Hope, where are you going?' This is Danny Flynn. He's shouting because of me walking to the door. And I can still hear him shouting as I'm out of the door, and the door is still open. And even when I'm two or three houses away, running past the house of Mr Khan, I can hear Danny Flynn shouting my name.

I've never been a good runner, because of being very clumsy, because of being a Stupid No-Brain, but I'm running fast as I can. I'm not even thinking where I'm going, but at the end of Station Close I turn right – or maybe left – but I don't know because of running too fast to put up my hand to see the L thing. But I'm running and running. And a couple of people say am I OK, because of the crying and the loud noise of my breathing. And one car beeps its horn, and that's because of me crossing the road with running and without looking. But I'm still running and when an ambulance goes past, with its lights all blue and loud, I think maybe that it is for my mum and it's going to our postcode, or Danny Flynn's with the letters too. But I'm still running and I don't turn back.

4

FINDING YOUR VOICE

10

My name is Hope Nicely. I am twenty-five years old and my brain is a bit unique because of being made this way. I am sitting behind a bench, between the bench and a wall. The wall is of the café in the park, and it is of the toilets of the café. It smells like stale wee, like my knickers in my bag. But I don't want to move, because of being here, with my knees pulled up to under my chin and my head down on them with my hands on top. And because of it raining and being dark and cold. And because of having already tried to go away from the park one time but not being able to because of the chain on the gates and the big lock.

I wish I had my umbrella. The yellow one. I left it on a bench when I was picking up a dog poo, and I forgot to take it again after. That was quite a long time ago. I do have another umbrella now, but it's not yellow, only black, and I don't have that one here either. And I wish I had my anorak with the hood. But I didn't wear it today, because of it not being rainy then. Usually, when I come home, I take off my anorak and my shoes and I put my slippers on, but I didn't do that today. I didn't take off my anorak because of not wearing it. And I didn't take off my trainers because of hurrying so much for the loo. And my mum, Jenny, didn't ask me why I was wearing my shoes and not my slippers, maybe because of not feeling so well. But maybe it's for the best, actually, because my feet are a little bit wet, but they'd be even wetter if I'd had my slippers on instead of my trainers, probably.

I don't know what the time is and I don't know how long I've been here. And I don't know if my mum, Jenny Nicely, is dead and in a box already. I don't know what I am feeling, because of not being very good at knowing it, but it is a very horrible feeling and I do not want it in my brain at all. And I am shaking, mostly my hands and my arms which are over my head, like they're holding it tight, but they won't stop moving, and my teeth too, which are making a funny noise and I don't know if it is my head or in the real world too.

And what I am thinking about now is how I don't want to be made like this. With this brain that tells me to go away when I should be there with my mum, with a brain that doesn't remember the phone number for an ambulance. Because *everybody* knows 999. But not me. I am thinking what a bad person I am. When I was younger, like sixteen or maybe eighteen or maybe even twenty, I tried to kill myself. It was because of not wanting to be like this. I wanted to not be stuck in my stupid, rubbish brain anymore, but I didn't know how to make myself different. I couldn't think of another way to not be me. But, in fact, I didn't end up dead in a box, because of not being good at tying knots, and because of my mum, Jenny, telling me that she loved me more than anything in the whole entire world and that she wouldn't have wanted to adopt any baby that wasn't me, and certainly not one that was an ordinary drop of light, and that my brain was part of who I am, and that is unique and perfect. But now my mum, Jenny, is maybe dead and in a box all by herself, and I am not even there. I am not feeling unique and perfect. I am feeling a very horrible thing, and if I had a rope and I knew how to make a knot, then I would want to go away even from being alive.

After that time, with the rope that fell off – because of not being very good at tying knots, and because of the rope being scratchy and itchy, and not wanting it to be too tight on my skin – I had to go and see a woman called Camilla da Silva, which was a nice name, actually, because of sounding like silver, and she would ask me lots of questions about my week and how was I feeling. And sometimes I would make up answers, because of not really knowing what the right answer was. Mostly I would say that I was feeling fine and better. And Camilla would say: 'But are you really . . . ?' Or 'So let's talk about that . . .' I didn't like it very much, going to Camilla da Silva, because of normally being a chatterbox but not with her, because of not knowing the answers.

And I saw a doctor, who was a woman too, and she said to take some pills. But I can't remember her name. My mum, that's Jenny Nicely, said that the pills were to help me not be the thing. It will come to me. But she said that the most important thing was to know that I could talk to her about anything in the whole entire world and that I could say anything at all and she would love me just as much. And she wanted to know about what had made me so sad that I would try to do the – I know this word – and that she wanted us to talk about it. And I told her about not wanting my brain the way it was, and that if it was unique and perfect then why did my birth mother throw me away in a cardboard box like rubbish. And I told her, my mum, about not knowing any other way to stop being inside my stupid brain, and about that being the reason for trying to do it.

134

Trying to kill myself. I didn't really want to be dead, actually. I just didn't want to be *me*. And that was why, I think, we went to the thing, like a party, which was called FASD Friends, with other people who all had the same thing as me.

And my mum, Jenny, showed me videos, too, and there were other people, who were maybe a little bit blue or indigo or yellow or one of the other colours, and they were talking and some of them said how they didn't like it too, and some said about being unique, and some said about coping. There were bad things, like drinking and drugs and the touching bodies thing, and about being angry or anxious or forgetting not to run into cars or jump out of windows.

And there was another video, and it was women who had been the mums with the babies in their tummies and who had done the drinking. And some of them had had their babies taken away from them, because of not looking after them. And some of them were very sad and said about it being a disease and not wanting to hurt their babies but not being able to control their thirstiness. That's because of being an alcoholic. And one of them – she had a name but I can't remember it – said nobody told her. She said she did not have the disease but her friend, who already had a baby, said it was OK to have a little glass of wine and she was having a stressful time, and she thought if a little glass was all right then why not two or three or maybe five. And one said she did know about it, and that she would not have had even one glass in the whole entire time of having her baby in her tummy, except that she didn't know about having the baby until her tummy was really fat, and that was why she kept on having the glasses of wine. And that by the time she knew, it was too late for the baby's brain to be made right again. And all of the mums in the video said about being very sorry for making the babies the way they were. And I thought it was sad about them feeling so sorry, because really it wasn't their fault. But it was sad about the babies, too. And one of those babies was me. And even if I was unique and even if I was an extraordinary drop of light, maybe it wasn't all for the best after all.

That was when I started thinking about what my mother – not Jenny Nicely, my mum, but my birth one who made me – about what she would say if she met me. Would she say that she was sorry too? Like the video mums. Or would she say good riddance to bad rubbish in a cardboard box? One day when Camilla da Silva asked me, what feelings do you have towards your biological mother, I said how could I know what I felt if I didn't know why she'd thrown me away. And, it's a bit silly, but I started crying. And Camilla said had I ever tried writing down what was in my head. And that is when I started thinking about my book . . .

And I'm crying a bit now, too, because of being cold and wet and hungry, and it's like my tummy is growling, like a dog, and my legs are starting to hurt from sitting and being bent – and because of maybe my mum, my real mum, Jenny, being dead and alone and I don't know where she is. And I'm pressing my hands onto my head, and I'm rocking a bit. And I'm counting, one, two, three – one, two, three.

But then I hear something. What I hear is like squelching but in a rhythm like walking, like someone is walking in the wet leaves coming nearer to me. And not just that but also talking. And the talking is like angry swearing, like fucking shitty bastard, bastard fucker. And it's not like an accent but it's like a man, and it's not very clear, because of all the words being scratchy and blurred, like a drunk person. And I hold my hands over my head really tight, with my head pressed down on my knees, even though my hands are still shaking. And I'm squeezing my eyes tight shut, even though it's dark and they're pressed against my knees so I can't see anything anyway. And I can hear the footsteps, because of all the leaves, even though they're wet. It's like heavy feet stepping into soggy leaves and making a noise as they do it. And I know it because of hearing the same noise when I'm walking the dogs, except then the noise is my own feet in their Wellington boots, but with my very long socks because otherwise it would be too scratchy, but this is with the talking and the fucking and the shitty and the fucking kill him. And I'm wanting to make a noise with my mouth, like not a real scream because I don't even know if I could make the noise. My whole body is a bit stuck, like squeezing. And it's scared. That is the feeling. Even if I'm not good at knowing my feelings, that is what it is. I am so, so scared.

He is nearly at my bench. I can hear him – the breath that comes out with his angry, slurry words. And I can smell him. He smells like sick. And then the squelching walking stops, but because of his breathing and his angry talking, I can hear that he is just beside my bench. And then another sound, and it is like water from a tap splashing into the sink. And it is very close, onto the wall beside me. And I can smell the wee, so I know what it is. And a couple of splashes hit my cheek, and it's not the rain, because of that coming onto my hands above my head but not onto my face, but this is splashing from the wall right beside me. And I know that it is his wee that is splashing me, because of the smell. My feeling is scared. So scared that my mouth cannot stop the squeak from coming out. And then another squeak. And I'm telling myself, no noise. Stop. But my mouth is squeaking again.

'Is someone there?' This is what I hear, but it sounds like one word – like 'ssomeonethere'. With no silences between the words. And I'm pushing on my head with both my hands and I'm telling myself: not a sound. And I'm pressing my lips together.

'Whosfuckingthere?' The wee has stopped, so there's no more splashing or water noise, but I can still smell it. And the sick smell. 'Whothefuckishthere?'

And then there's no more talking from the man, but I can hear his breathing, and I can hear my breathing too, like the loudest breathing in the world. And I'm thinking he must definitely be able to hear me too. There's a squelch, and another squelch. And he's coming even closer, right up to the bench itself. And it's the hardest thing ever not to do more squeaking. My whole body wants to make itself tiny and go away right now. And the squelching stops. I don't look up. My eyes are still squeezed tight against my knees, but I can feel breath on my hands, and I know he's bending over the bench and he's above me. And I think if I put my arms up straight then I would touch him. And I really want to make a noise. But I'm pressing and pressing my hands onto my head, like I'm trying to make myself really small. And the smell is like fingers pushing into my nose: and it's like sick and wee and sweat when you've forgotten the rule about deodorant under your armpits. And it's making me want to be sick too – and to squeak with being scared at the same time. But I'm telling myself about being silent, because I can still feel the stinky breath on my hand.

Something touches my cheek. And I can't help it. I put up my head and open my eyes. And its scraping on my face. On my cheek. Cold and hard against me. And I nearly scream because of thinking it's a knife. I have to take my hands away from my head and press them over my mouth instead, because otherwise the scream will come. But then it's wooshy and soft. And it smells like the smelliest, sweatiest, sickiest thing ever. And it's smooth and a bit squeaky, like my anorak that I wish I was wearing. It's too dark for me to see properly, but I can feel that it's pressed against me, and that it's coming through the space in the back of the bench, where there are the spaces, between the wood bits. And there is a noise like a zip and now I know what it is, because of working it out in my brain but not knowing the word yet. And it's not a knife, but I'm still scared and I'm still hearing my breathing. And feeling it on my hands too. And there's another zip noise. *Sleeping bag.* That's what is pressing against my face through the bench space. And there's more swearing, but not who the fuck is there, but instead back to just fucking bastard fucker. And I'm listening to my breath, and trying to count in my head, even though I can't sit on my hands because of them being over my mouth still, with my eyes still open and looking at the dark. And I don't know how long I'm there but the swearing stops a bit and then there's snoring instead.

The sleeping bag is pressing just under my nose, and onto my hands, where my mouth is. And I don't like the feel of the sleeping bag. It's scratchy. And it's so stinky. And it's squeaky, like my anorak, except my anorak is softer. The sleeping bag isn't soft. It's itchy. And my skin feels hot and it feels cold too. On my face, and my arms, and everywhere. I'm hungry and my legs are like they're screaming because of wanting to move. My legs hurt and my tummy hurts. It's not growling now, which is good, because maybe it would have woken up the smelly man, but now it's pulling tight inside me to show how empty it is. And I'm trying not to think about the pizza – the one I didn't have – and about the pepperoni on it, because of it making my tummy hurt even more.

And the snoring is carrying on but I'm too scared to try and go away in case of waking up the smelly, swearing man. And I don't want to even be here. But

I'm telling myself how pleased my mum, Jenny Nicely, would be, because of me not trying to go away, because of thinking very carefully about consequences. And that is an important rule. Because of people, like the ones at the party, wanting to do things that are bad, like running into a bus or jumping out of a car or letting a man touch you under your clothes. So I'm thinking that my mum would be proud that I'd remembered it. Except actually not if she's dead, and in a box. Because how can she be proud then? And mostly I'm thinking about how this is the worst night ever, and about not wanting to be here, scared and cold and hungry in the dark, which is wet, but wanting to be with my mum, Jenny, and her be alive, and giving me a big hug, and saying: 'Adopting you was the best thing I ever did.'

And it's harder and harder to be quiet, and I can't help it but I'm humming a bit, to try and stop the squeaking and the screaming and the shouting that I want to do. I have my eyes shut, with the stink of the sleeping bag in my nose, and, if I move, the zip is scratching me. And I hate scratchiness. I *hate* it. It makes me want to scream. It makes me want to shout. And the snoring is so loud, like: ZZZhhhh ZZZhhhh ZZZhhhh. And I'm going to have to scream. I can't help it. I'm humming and I'm counting but I'm going to scream.

But then I hear something else, and it's more squelching footsteps, coming near in the park. And then there's another voice. I don't know if it's a man or a woman, but the voice is calling: 'Hello, is someone here?' And the man on the bench isn't waking up, though, he's just going on ZZZhhhh ZZZhhhh ZZZhhhh and I can smell the wee and the sick and the sweaty smell. And then it's again: 'Hello. Who's there?' And the squelching in the leaves is coming nearer. I open my eyes, just a little tiny bit, and I can see a circle of light, and it's coming towards me. And now I can hear myself humming, because of trying so hard to not be screaming and shouting. And I don't want to even hum but I can't help it.

'Is there someone over there?'

And then the snoring is more like a spluttering, like ZZZhhhh ah SHP ZZhh Shpppp. And then it's a ZZ-ZZhhuckwhafuckinwha . . .

'Hello . . . ?'

I stand up, and I scream, like the biggest scream of my whole life. With my hair in my hands and I'm pulling it while I'm screaming. And the light which is the torch is shining towards me and into my face. I have to put my hand in front of my eyes. But I can still see – though not properly see, because of the light making my eyes be squeezed, and seeing funny shapes that are orange and yellow – the man in the sleeping bag is standing up going: 'Whathefuckinfuck . . . ?' And I still can't see him properly except that his hair is very big and long.

And, with my hand over my eyes, because of the light, I can just see through my fingers that he's nearly falling over in the sleeping bag, but then he's stepping out of it, and he's still swearing but he's starting to run away. Then there's the other voice going: 'Hello, is that . . . ?'

The light is shining at me and I hear this new voice say: 'Stop. Wait there.' But there are loud footsteps going fast, like really running, and squelching because of the leaves, and going fuckfuckingfuckers.

And I want to go away too, running, as fast as the wind, but my legs won't move, because of hurting from staying still so long, and because of them being too scared to do a thing. And I'm screaming, no words just a massive sound and the light in my eyes.

'Hope? Is that Hope?'

I keep on screaming, and in my head, I'm trying to think about how this person with the light even knows my name, but mostly I can't even think about it because all I can think is about this huge fear in every single part of me. And I don't even care if this is a bad person or a good person, I just want to not to have to scream and be so scared anymore.

'Hope, it's OK, I'm a police officer. You don't need to worry. You're safe now.'

I'm still screaming. My brain is listening, just a little bit. But it can't stop straight away.

'Hope. It is you, isn't it? I know this is difficult, but I need to know if you've been harmed in any way.' And then she talks some more, but quieter, and she's saying: 'I've found her, in the park, there was an unknown man with her. He's run away.' And then to me again: 'Can you confirm that you are Hope Nicely?'

And my head manages to tell my mouth to stop screaming, but it's not ready to say yes. I'm just watching her with my mouth open. But I nod. Yes, it's me. It's OK to speak to people in uniforms, like police and nurses and firemen, even if they are people that we don't know. That is a rule because of them being the people who have a job to help us and so we can trust them.

'Hope, sweetheart, my name is Police Constable Nicola O'Brien. I'm sorry to ask you again, but that man . . .'

'He was only sleeping.' This is me. 'And swearing and weeing on the wall. But he didn't know about me being here. He didn't do any touching. Only snoring and swearing. He didn't know about me.'

'That's good.' And then her voice is quieter again

and she says: 'Confirming this is Hope with me. She says she is unharmed.' And it's very dark but my eyes are seeing a bit now, because of her light not shining right at me but now down onto the floor and lighting it around us. And when she is talking quietly she is bending her head to her neck. But really she is talking into a radio, not a phone or just to herself like the sweary man. And she says: 'We're coming out now.' And she holds out a hand towards me and says: 'Come on, sweetheart. Let's get you into the dry.'

It's OK, because of her uniform, even though it's one of the important rules to not go with strangers. So I come out from behind the bench and my legs are still not wanting to move because of having been bent for so long, and I say: 'How did you know about Hope Nicely being my name?'

She says: 'A lot of people have been worried about you. I think half the town has been looking for you.'

11

The gate of the park isn't closed anymore. It's open with the chain taken off and there's another police person, a man, and he's very tall, like his chest where he has his police sign is about where my eyes are, and he's waiting there and he says hello, and that his name is PC Tom Barrington, and that he's very glad that they've finally managed to find me. And in the car I don't talk, because of just looking out of the window, and I have a blanket around my shoulders, except it's not a real blanket because I think it's made out of tin foil, like my mum cooks turkey in, and there isn't anybody on the pavements and not really any cars apart from us.

And I'm thinking that maybe I'm going back to my home, or else maybe to the police station – well, in fact, I'm not really thinking it, not very much, because of my head not having very much in it, just looking, watching, light, light, light – but anyway, that's where I would think we are going, if I was thinking. But when we stop it's not my home and it's not a police station. It's at the hospital, actually – and I know it because of the time when I ran into a car – and the PC, which is a police person, the one called Tom, parks us just next to an ambulance. And Police Nicola says: 'OK, come on then, sweetheart.'

Inside my blanket I'm shaking. Not just because of being cold but because of thinking about the hospital. And I say: 'Is my mum here? Her name is Jenny Nicely.'

And PC Nicola says we're going to find all of that out but that first she thinks I should see a doctor to be checked out, because of being cold and wet. And that she and PC Barrington here will have to take a statement from me, too, which is just procedure, but that can wait, and let's get me inside. And there are lots of people, and some of them are in uniforms like on TV – not police ones, hospital ones – and some are behind glass and asking my name and my date of birth and other questions, and mostly I don't know all the answers. And then I'm going into another room with lots of chairs and some with people in and then I'm hearing a voice that I know. And it's saying, I had a message that Hope Nicely was here. It's Danny Flynn and he's angry, and that is not because of knowing the feeling from his face, it's because of him walking to me, really quickly, and saying: 'Why the fuck did you run off like that? What were you thinking of?' Because of the swearing I know he's angry. And the loud, scratchy voice. And I start crying, which I don't mean to do, but I can't help it. And I say I'm sorry.

He looks at me and he puts his hands on his forehead, like one on top of the other with his head underneath, where there's not so much hair as on the back of his head and right at the top, and he says, oh Hope, he's sorry too, and he didn't mean to shout, but fuck, he's exhausted and do I know how many people have been up all night trying to find me. And I say no. I say I've been in the park and he says that's where Karen told them that I might be but they'd searched it once already. And he's shaking his head and I'm thinking in my head how does he know Karen because I didn't even think that they knew each other. And he says my name again, Hope, and he says he didn't know where I'd gone.

'I even called Marnie.' This is Danny still. 'I woke her up. I'd better ring her back and tell her you're safe. I have lots of people to call. Hope . . .' My name again. 'What were you . . . ?' But he stops. And he does a sigh. And he's shaking his head. He's looking at me and his face looks funny, like it's more creased than last time I saw him, with dark around his eyes, like when you smudge a pencil. 'Thank God you're safe. Look, there's something I need to . . .'

But now there's my name again, and it's a doctor or a nurse, maybe I think a nurse because of the uniform, and he says come with him please and he gives me a . . . like a coat, except it's called a gown and he tells me to go in there please – that's a little room, like a cubicle but without a toilet – and pop it on and there's another one to put over the top of it. And there's a bag for all my wet clothes. And it takes me a long time, because of not really understanding how to do it up, because of there being no buttons on the gown, and only two laces and when I put it on you can see my tummy and even my fanny, because of me having taken all my clothes off like I was told. But when I come out of the cubicle the nurse says, oh my goodness, no it goes the other way round, with the opening at the back, and pop the other one the other way round over the top, so that it covers me up from the back and let's warm me up a bit. It takes me a bit longer to put it on, because of not being able to tie it up behind the back of my neck, but I do it at last and the nurse says, yes much better and come into this other room and here's a blanket and a drink and can I ask you some questions. The drink is tea but with lots of sugar, like my mum likes it, but not me usually.

But I drink it all, even though it's hotter than I normally want it, and I'm really hungry and I wish there was a biscuit too.

The nurse tells me he's going to take my temperature, but it's not with a stick in my mouth, it's with a thing in my ear, and my blood pressure too, round my arm, and it puffs up and squeezes like someone holding me too tight. I don't like it. I'm a bit scared and I reach out to pull it off my arm but the nurse tells me not to worry, because it will only squeeze for a moment. He calls me sweetie. And he listens to my heart, but it's through a tube with a cold metal thing, I can't remember the word, and asks me questions like how long was I in the park, and was I shivering or did I stop shivering and did I sleep at any time or lose conscious.

And a person comes in, opening the door which is really a curtain, and it's a person who is a doctor with a name, but the name goes into my head and out again, because of my head being tired now, and a bit muddled. And the doctor, who is a man, says the PC Nicola told him about the man on the bench and am I absolutely certain he did not touch me in any way. And I say no. He just did his wee and snored and didn't even know about me, actually. And the doctor says, well, that's a big relief to know, and he looks at some papers on a board thing that he's holding, and it's the papers that the nurse has been writing in, the things like from my ear and the squeezing of my arm. And he asks how I'm feeling now. And I say: 'Do you know my mum, Jenny Nicely?'

He looks at me. He has glasses that are not properly circles, just a little bit on the bottom. And it's like he's looking over the top of them at me.

I say: 'Jenny Nicely. She's my mum and she was going in an . . .' But my brain is feeling too tired and muddled. '. . . because of being on the floor in the kitchen. And she . . .'

He does a little movement with his head which is not as big as a nod. 'Your friend is just outside in the corridor.' This is the doctor. 'He said I should check with you if you'd like him to come in?'

I look back at him and my head is just thinking what is he talking about. And I say to him that I don't have any friends. He looks at his papers and he says Daniel Flynn, the gentleman who came into A&E with my mother. And for a moment, I think he's the one with the muddle in his head, but then I think that Daniel Flynn maybe must be Danny Flynn, and when the doctor says again is it all right for Mr Flynn to join us, I say yes that's OK, because of it being Danny Flynn who was the one who called 999 to help my mum, Jenny. And so even if

I don't really know him very well, I think it's all right.

'How are you doing, Hope?' This is Danny Flynn and he's sitting beside me and he puts his hand onto my hand and puts his fingers around mine. And I'm looking hard at both our hands, with my brain not quite understanding, because it is what people who are boyfriends do, or maybe mums. And my brain thinks maybe I should take my hand away, because of the rule about keeping our hands and feet to ourselves, but I don't take it away, because of it feeling nice, actually, and because Danny holding my hand stops it from shaking a bit. I'm crying again now and I don't know why. I open my mouth and I say: 'Is . . . ?' But I can't make any more words come.

'So, Hope.' This is the doctor. I'm thinking why does everyone keep saying my name. Hope. Hope. Hope. But mostly I'm thinking: one, two, three – one, two, three – one, two, three, and I'm telling my breathing and my crying to be quiet. And the doctor is standing up, and I'm sitting down. And the doctor says, so Hope, like maybe he thinks I didn't hear him the first time, and he says do I know what a cardiac arrest is. And I shake my head, because of not having any words in my mouth.

'Well, Hope.' Like he needs to keep telling me

who I am. 'You know how the heart beats, which makes the blood flow around our bodies?'

I do know it, because of having been told in school, which was called biology. And because of not being stupid. Even if I am on the rainbow, I'm only a little bit blue and maybe I need to tell the doctor about this. But I don't say anything. I just hold onto Danny Flynn's hand.

'Well, a cardiac arrest happens when there is a problem, an electrical malfunction which interrupts the beating of the heart and disrupts its beating.'

I'm looking at the doctor, because this is a very strange thing to say. Because electrical is not about biology. It's about light bulbs and televisions. And my mum is not a television or a light bulb. She's a person and she's unique. But I don't say anything because it is rude to interrupt. And also I don't say anything because I can't find any words. I can't say anything. I just hold onto Danny Flynn's hand, very tight, and I look at the doctor and listen to what he's saying now.

'And because the heart stops pumping the blood which carries oxygen to our brain and our lungs, cardiac arrest causes a person to lose consciousness and to stop breathing.'

He pauses. Looking at me over the top of his glasses which are not like real glasses because of being not a full circle but straight on top. And my own heart is beating and pumping so hard that I can feel it inside me, like it's banging to come out, and I can hear it in my ears. There is a question in my head but I don't want to ask it. I don't even know if I can. Because of the words not wanting to come. Because of my head saying no, not yet.

One-two-three, one-two-three, one-two-three.

'Now, the thing about cardiac arrest is that . . .'

'Is my mum dead?' I didn't even know they were coming. The words. Now I want them to have stayed in. And I want to put my hands over my ears. Because of not knowing the answer. Because of not wanting this at all. But I can't. Because of Danny Flynn's hand being in my hand. And I'm holding it so tight that maybe I'm going to make him scream. And maybe I'm going to scream too. Because my mouth is open. But it's not screaming. It's just noisy, noisy, noisy, like crying big sobs but the other way round. Like the sobs are going into my mouth instead of coming out of them. And I'm looking at the doctor and he's looking back, over his not-quite glasses.

He takes them off, the glasses, and holds them in front of him. Like he's tapping them. 'Your mum . . .' One-two-three, one-two-three. My breaths. My heart. My brain. One-two-three. 'Is alive, Hope. She's still alive. The paramedics restarted her heart, however . . .'

I can't listen anymore. His mouth is moving and there are words – *unconscious, coma, cooling, uncertain, lack of oxygen, vital minutes, even if she does regain . . . risk of brain damage* – but I can't let them in. My head won't let them in.

There is humming. The humming is me.

'I wonder if this could wait until tomorrow?' This is Danny Flynn. The doctor puts his glasses back on and he's saying yes, of course, perhaps best in fact, even though I'm listening but not listening. And he's saying about Hope, saying of course and she's been through a lot already and she's been out in the wet and – he's looking at papers again – mild hypothermia and he'd like her to stay in overnight, where the nurses can keep an eye. And there are more nurses, and the thing – the thing in my ear and not my mouth – and a chair with wheels and it's for me, even though I'm a person who can walk on my legs, and a kiss on my cheek, which is Danny Flynn, and him saying try just to sleep and try to not worry and he'll see me tomorrow. There's a bracelet, but I don't think that's the right word, but it's on, with my name and lots of numbers too. There's a lift and corridors that go on and on. And there's a smell like hospital, and it makes me think of ice cream. And there's a bed, but it's not my bed. It has curtains around it. And my head is too tired for humming or shouting or saying I want my bed not this bed. There's a cheese sandwich on a plastic table and a pill in a tiny little cup that's only as big as my little finger. Like a paper cup for a baby. And even though my tummy is sore inside because of being so hungry, I look at the sandwich and I don't want to eat it because of my throat feeling like it is closed and dry from all the crying and the noises and because of not thinking I have enough energy to chew. So just the pill, and the pillow isn't nice and big and soft like my pillow in my house. And I don't have my special blanket either. But my head is too tired to think about it. Nobody says goodnight, Hope Nicely, sweet dreams, just the nurse says pop this on your finger for me darling, and let me check your pressure. And I can't even look, only just hear it – whoooosshh – and feel it going squeezy tight on my arm, because of my eyes being shut now. And even when I tell them to open, they say no. Not right now. Maybe in a moment. And even if this pillow isn't my pillow, it is still good to put my head on it, with my eyes still closed.

12

When I was a little girl, like eight maybe, and for quite a lot of years before, when I was even littler, anyway, but bigger than a baby, nobody knew about my rainbow and about my birth mother and how she made me with all the vodka in her tummy. They just knew about the cardboard box and about me being left in it. But then they – like the teachers, and my mum, Jenny Nicely, and Julie who was the social worker then but isn't really anymore – they noticed about me not being like all the other children, who were in the same year as me, because of me not talking with as many words and wanting to hide under tables or to bang my head on the wall and not to play with them at all. And because of me being so little, with little feet and little hands and with my head being quite small too and me talking more like a baby, with silly baby words. And because of me not remembering things like rules, like, don't hit the other children, or don't shout when other people are talking, or like where I was this morning or how old I am.

That's why my mum, Jenny, used to take me to be measured, not just my height but my cumfrence, which is all the way around my head, and to play games with the doctors like put the dominos together and point to the pictures and remember where the blue squares are. And every time my mum, Jenny, would tell me good girl, and she would say you're doing so well, Hope, and she would say when we've finished we'll go for a nice ice cream. And that's because near the hospital was a very special ice cream shop and I don't even know if it was this same hospital, because of it being dark when I came in, and in a police car, and not in the same way. And it wasn't in this room, because, when I was little, there were pictures of lions and giraffes on the wall and the other ones that go in water and there's a game with them eating balls, but I didn't play it then. And there was the smell of the hospital that was different to the smell in my house or in my school or in the real world outside, and I didn't know the word for the smell. But when I went into the hospital for the measuring and the games, and I smelt the new smell, I thought it smelt of ice cream, because of knowing that if I was a good girl and put the dominoes together, that

I would have a special ice cream on the way home. And the animal was a hippo, like a hungry hippo, but there is another word too, which is longer and it's the real word, and I still can't remember that one.

In the morning, my mum, Jenny Nicely, wakes me always with a big smile and a wakey-wakey hug and a cup of tea. So my head is asking what is going on and where can I possibly be? Because no smile and no mum and no cup. And it's just a noise like zzzhhhppp and zzzhhhppp and lights that are coming through my sleepy eyes and into my sleepy head and mixing with the sleepy thoughts in my head, which are telling stories about hippos and ice cream and dominoes and I don't know what. And I'm not sure about what is happening or even about where I am. I know I should know. But my memory, well, the least said about that . . .

I am not in my bedroom. I am in the smallest bedroom ever, without even a door, and the walls are made out of material because they are moving and not like a real wall. And I know I should remember something. *Something* . . . In my head there is a feeling that I don't want to be there but I still can't remember. And on my wrist, it's a not nice feeling too. There's a thing, like a band, and it's plastic, with too much space at the end that is sticking out with holes. And I'm holding it up and pulling it away from my skin, because of it being a bit scratchy. Or not scratchy, actually, but a bit too *touchy*. And I'm reading what the letters are, and it says my name with lots of numbers. And I am in . . . I am in . . .

Something happened. Something bad. I *should* know. I am in . . .

And then there is a noise, the same noise, zzzhhhhppp, and it is my bedroom wall, which is not a wall and not a bedroom, which is opening. It was a curtain. And it is not my mum, not Jenny Nicely, but it is a woman in a uniform which is blue, and who says good morning but not wakey-wakey or rise and shine, and she's just going to take my temperature. And I say where is my mum. My mum is Jenny Nicely. Where is she. And I say please.

And the woman puts a thing in my ear and she says something back to me but I don't really know what she's saying, because of the thing in my ear and because of the accent and I think it's like an accent, which is maybe Chinese because of her looking a bit like the woman in the takeaway with the best prawn crackers in the whole wide world. And in a bit of my brain, I'm remembering about a takeaway, but I don't really know what I'm remembering. And I'm pulling on the band on my wrist, because of not really liking it there. Because of not really wanting it, actually. And I say again: do you know where my mum, Jenny Nicely is. And she says something again but I still don't understand. And I have a bad feeling. I think like something has happened but when I try to find it in my head, it's like opening the curtains and all you can see is fog. Not even a muddle. Not even a jumble sale. Just a big everywhere fog, that is too grey for anything to be seen even if it's right there in front of you.

'Are you a nurse?' This is me, and it's because of the uniform and the putting the thing in my ear and telling me better – which I know even in the accent – and now a tight thing going whoosh around my arm and squeeze squeeze squeeze. It makes me have to bite my teeth together and squeeze my hands.

She says yes. She says nurse again and something something *hospital*.

I'm thinking *hospital*, of course. But I still can't remember. Stupid head. Stupid brain. Did I run into a car? Did I have a G&T and vodka, and did I run into the road and forget about the car? But I look down and there is no big, hard bandage on my arm, just the scratchy, touchy plastic band, and the other arm is being squeezed by the tight pressure thing, but not quite so much now. And where is my mum?

Because even then, with the car and the broken arm, my mum was there with me in the hospital, sleeping in the chair beside me.

'Where is my mum?' This is me. 'Do you know where she is?'

'I see you.'

'No. Not me. My mum. Her name is Jenny Nicely. Where is she?'

'I see you.'

I don't think the nurse can be very clever. And, really, that's not good for a nurse because when I was little, like twelve or fourteen, I used to say about when I was grown up that's what I would be. Because of liking plasters and uniforms and because of nurses being nice to me when I was doing games and being measured. But it wasn't such a good idea, in the end. Because of having a brain a bit like a jumble sale. And because of the forgetting. And because of not liking needles or blood. And because of walking dogs being a much better job for me, in fact, because of liking animals more than anything, and especially Tinie and all the puppies. And maybe this nurse has a brain which is a bit of a jumble too. So I try again, talking slowly.

'My mum is called Jenny Nicely. She's a poet and she works in the bookshop. Do you know where she is please?' And I look at her and I'm making my face that says this is important. And I say please again, because of that being polite.

'I see you.' Again. Silly woman. I'm right here. Of course she sees me. She's just been putting her plastic thing in my ear and holding my wrist. And I even have my name written on it just there, on the plastic thing.

'Doctor here soon. Talk to you. Know more about then.'

And then she's gone. And she's talking to someone else. And it's only now I'm really thinking about being in a room with other people and other beds. I don't know any of them. I don't want to be here. I don't want this thing on my wrist, this touchy thing, but when I try to pull it, it's too tight to come off, so I keep my fingers under it, so it's not touching my skin. And when another nurse, but with a different colour uniform, brings me some toast, she doesn't put the butter on and anyway the butter isn't butter, it's margarine, and it's in a little tub that is tiny and the margarine is too yellow. If I was showing it and not telling it, I would say it is the same colour as a daffodil. Or a buttercup, or a dandelion. And it is hard to spread it with one hand, and with my fingers underneath the plastic band. And the margarine doesn't melt and there is jam but it's strawberry so I don't want it. And the toast is not nice. It's cold and brown, not white – which is telling, not showing and I don't even care. I want Nutella. I want my mum.

'Bathroom?' This is not the same nurse although she's wearing the same uniform, which is blue too, just with different hair and different skin and a different face and long hair not short hair. 'You've come too far. Here darling. It's back here.'

I wasn't looking for the loo because of mostly wanting to go away and not be here anymore, but I do need a wee, actually. In fact, a lot. I can't even shut the door because of it being confusing how to do it, and because of being in a hurry. And then, after my wee, I try to go away again, but I can't because of the door not opening and because of another nurse telling me, come on, sweetheart, let's get you back to bed and saying, what's happened to your wrist, and it's because of the loo paper, which is inside the touchy band, to stop it touching my skin, which was a very bingo idea, actually. And the nurse is telling me, the doctors will be along soon and do I want another cup of tea because, look, mine's gone cold and I haven't even drunk it.

'I don't understand. Why are you here? Where's my mum?' This is me.

There is a box of chocolates on the plastic table over my bed. It's Roses. And I like Roses, the strawberry ones mostly, despite not liking strawberry jam or even strawberries in real life. And the ones like Dairy Milks but teeny-tiny. Or maybe that's the different ones which are even more purple. But not the coffee ones. Not ever. But I'm not even opening it. I'm not even saying thank you. Because of my brain being a bit stuck in thinking, 'Where is my mum?'

'Surely you remember?' That's Danny Flynn. And I don't understand. Remember what? Why is he here? Is he my boyfriend now, maybe? Maybe he is, because of walking me home and bringing me chocolates? There was another thing? Yesterday, maybe. A thing . . . Something happened. He held my hand. Bingo! So maybe he is my boyfriend now. And I've never had a boyfriend before. But I can't remember. Because of the jumble sale. And still the fog. And Julie Clarke is with him and that is making my brain even more stuck. Because Julie is my social worker, or not anymore because of being quite old. And Danny Flynn is in my writing group. So why are they even together? And now it's Julie Clarke talking and she's asking don't I remember, and saying about my mum and an emergency and me being in the park in the night and it being cold and wet.

I'm looking at her. I'm even forgetting to count. Because I don't remember, and I should. She's saying it was an emergency – and that's an important thing. But my stupid brain can't even remember. I know it's not a lie, because of it being Julie and my mum who used to do the role plays with me, and the rules, and the one about lying being bad, and because of Julie being one of my core workers, but not anymore because of me being grown up now and her being so old. But in my head there is a feeling now, and I'm thinking I would like to throw my pillow – which isn't my real pillow because of not being soft like my real one – right at them and shout at them to go right away. And I would like to go right away too.

13

Now I am going to try very hard to show and not to tell. And what I am not going to tell is about my mum, who is Jenny Nicely, and about her being here in front of me and all these tubes and big boxes making beeps and things. And I am not going to *tell* about me crying, or me saying wake up Mum and shouting a bit too. But I'm going to show that there are lovely long eyelashes, because my mum, Jenny, has really long eyelashes that don't even need any make-up, they're just natural, but they are not moving, not up and down at all. Her eyes are not open and looking at me.

If they were open they would be big and very dark, like coffee with only the tiniest bit of milk in it. And they would be kind and always looking at me to make sure I am smiling and nothing is wrong.

My mum, Jenny Nicely, says that when we're sad

or we're scared or when people are being mean to us, sometimes those are the times when it helps to smile, even if we don't feel like doing it. Smile brightly, Hope Nicely, that's what she says. And maybe I should smile now. Maybe this is one of those times. But I can't do it. I can't smile. And I know it is my mum, with her lovely eyelashes, even with her eyes still closed, but on her nose and mouth it's a bit like an elephant, because of it being covered with a thing and a long tube like a trunk.

All around her are televisions on feet, but not with the news or *EastEnders* or *Coronation Street* but just with numbers and lines like graphs. And her pyjamas are not the ones with the squares and colours which are Scottish, like on men's skirts called tartan kilts, but it's a nightie that's not a nightie because of it not having any buttons. Like mine that I wore until I was allowed to put my clothes back on again, my real dry ones that Julie Clarke and Danny Flynn brought me, which are my white hoodie and my leggings that don't have my bottom showing. But her arms are wrapped in blue wrappers. And the doctor is saying, sshh, you can't be so noisy in here. Not in I See You. Because of me telling my mum that I love her and that I want her to wake up.

And I'm trying not to shout but then it's time for me to go, because I have to talk to the doctor outside. Julie Clarke and Danny Flynn are saying, come on then, your mum's in the best hands. But in the room there is a sound like a scream – and I can't say it's me making the noise, because of not telling, only showing, but my mouth is open and my hand is on my mum's arm, but not on the bit with the needle going in. And she is cold, like when you take a cucumber out from the fridge.

The doctor is saying, I'm very sorry but we really must leave. And I don't understand. Because my mum loves me, and adopting me was the best thing she ever did in her whole entire life, better than all her poems put together. So why won't she wake up to talk to me? I'm telling her and telling her and telling her to wake up, but still she keeps her eyes closed.

'You do understand, Hope?' This is the doctor. We're in the different room now, with no beds, only a desk and some chairs and tissues on the desk. I wasn't allowed to stay in the other room. Because of the patients needing it to be calm and quiet when they're so poorly.

'My mum's not awake because of being kept asleep, and being kept really cold to look after her brain. So she's having a long sleep. Then she'll wake up. But when will . . . ?'

'Hope.' Like he thinks I don't know my name already. I'm sitting on my hands and I'm telling my brain to listen. I'm not humming. I'm not shouting. Not anymore. I'm listening so hard it's giving me a headache. 'That's what everybody hopes will happen. That your mother will wake up. Unfortunately, we can't know yet that she *will* wake up and, if she does, we don't know what long-term effects there will be. When somebody's heart stops and they stop breathing, the brain is starved of oxygen and that can cause damage which can be permanent. It's impossible to predict what sort of recovery that person will make, if indeed they do recover . . .'

Sometimes people talk to me as if I am a very little girl and as if I don't understand anything. They talk like I'm stupid, like I'm a Nicely No-Brain, rather than grown up now, with a real job and writing a book, which is a Big Achievement. This doctor is talking to me now, but he's talking very slowly, and he's asking do I understand, and I'm thinking he's saying to himself in his head that I don't really understand. And I do understand. Because I know about brains that get damaged. But what I say is, and I say it slowly, too, and not even shouting at all, just very quiet: 'In fact, I think my mum will recover.

Actually. I think she will wake up and her brain will be good as new.'

'Do you understand what I'm asking you, Hope, darling?' Julie Clarke is saying this to me, and leaning towards me with her hands out and a big expecting smile, and this because of me still not replying to her question, which is because I'm thinking about it in my head still. But her big smiling and big nodding is like a cue, and with her looking at me too. And I'm thinking it's because of her wanting me to say something.

'You're asking me if I want to go to a place like a hotel or like a hospital but nicer, and with my own room and people for making food and taking me in a minibus to work and also there's a television in the room where all the other people sit.'

She's nodding and she's telling me, exactly, yes. It's a lovely centre and also has a pool table and video games and it . . .

I don't want to go there. Because of not knowing it or where it is. And never having been before. And because of not knowing the other people or whether they will call me No-Brain or Spaz, or whether they will wee in their trousers or want to talk all the time when I don't want to. Or they might want to watch *Question Time* or football. Then Julie says, OK, well if I'm not so keen on the respite centre, she might be able to find out about if there's a foster family. And then I would . . . But I don't want a foster family. I say no and I think it's quite loud because the old woman on the table next to me stops eating her soup and turns her head to look at me when I say it.

We are not in the room with the doctor anymore. We are in the café downstairs, and it smells like carrots and maybe curry and washing-up. And also a bit like ice cream though I think that's in my head. And all around us are old people and nurses, or maybe doctors, who are wearing the uniforms a bit like pyjamas, but in all different colours. Some are light blue and some are blue but more dark, and some are green. And the light above me is doing a funny thing where it keeps going lighter, and not so light, and lighter again, and I wish someone would turn it off. It's making my head buzz.

I haven't finished my pizza and that's maybe because of eating my whole box of Roses, except for the coffee ones, because yuck yuck yuck. But it's also because of the pizza not being like the ones my mum buys, which have cheese on the top and cheese inside the crust, and also pepperoni, but this one is only cheese on top and it's not so nice. It's more prickly, in my mouth. And ham. But I have picked off all the ham and I'm eating the very last bit of it, I'm still chewing, and I'm saying to Julie that I don't want to live with a family that I don't even know and haven't even met before. And fostering is for children, not grown-up people like me who have real jobs and who are even writing a book. Not even if they're a very nice family. And I'm saying no thank you, not even live with them for one night or two nights. And I'm saying that I can live in my home, even without my mum there. Because of me being grown up now, and independent. And it would be perfectly fine, actually. And anyway, she'll be back home very soon. My mum, Jenny. Just as soon as she wakes up.

And while I'm saying this, Danny Flynn is walking up to the table and he's carrying a tray and he's saying one latte for Julie and a white tea for Hope – although actually it's a brown tea, just one with milk in it, and no sugar – and this one's his. And he's putting the cups in front of us and he's listening to Julie saying, yes, Hope, she knows I'm very independent and of course she understands about me not wanting to stay with strangers, but let's think about the practicalities, and have I ever actually lived – even just for a night – on my own. And she's saying that it's a shame that her grandson is staying with her right now as it means that her sofa's already taken at the moment, and that Katya – that's another social worker, but one who is younger and not retired – is away on her honeymoon this week, because she might have had other suggestions. But, seriously, Hope, do I really think that being alone would be such a . . .

The light is still doing the thing, of going bright and then not bright, like it's shouting and then doing quiet talking, but in light not in talking. And my head is saying stop it. And I put my hand in front of my eyes because of not liking the light. And it's like it's making my brain blink.

Danny Flynn says actually he has a suggestion and it's about his home, which is with his mother and his brother. They have a spare room, and I'd be very welcome to it. And it's only round the corner from my place, so it wouldn't feel like I was miles away and it would be easy as anything to nip home whenever there was something I needed. I'm looking at him through my fingers. Because of the light, going bright, not bright, bright. When he smiles there are little dips in his cheeks, just on the side of his mouth. And I know there's a name for them. It's not pimples. It's something . . .

'. . . not sure what the regulations are.' This is Danny. 'But my mum is a trained paediatric nurse, although she's not working right now, and she's also registered as my brother's carer, because of his Asperger's. And, I mean, I'm CRB-checked, we have to be if we work in the children's library at any point, but I'm not sure if we even meet your . . .'

And Julie is saying, well, that's extremely kind, and actually, no, there are no official regulations because of my age and the unusual situation, but what does he think his mother would say. And Danny Flynn is saying, oh, actually, he already asked her, because he'd been thinking about what would happen to me when I came out of hospital. He says his mum would be delighted to have me there. And he's saying that I could have my own en suite shower room. And I ask what that means – my silly head, I'm thinking they're talking about a *sweet* shower room, not like chocolate and sweeties sweet, of course, but like it's very little and pretty and like a maybe very furry pink carpet and pictures of puppies and baby rabbits everywhere. But actually in fact it means that it's in the same room as the bedroom and just for me and nobody else, with my own door, so you don't have to go out into the corridor in the middle of the night for a wee. And there's a desk, for writing my book, and, in fact, there's a telly in the bedroom too. So even if Danny Flynn or his mum or his brother wanted to watch *Question Time* or football, that would be OK. Because it would be my own space, only there would be somebody there to make food and give me some company if I wanted it. And Danny Flynn could even . . .

He stops talking now but that's only because of me shouting out the word, because of remembering it, because of course they are dimples, not pimples. And it's a bit funny, because pimples are spots, like they're also called zits and crater face. But then I say sorry for interrupting. I say my silly mouth. And he smiles some more dimples into his face, and it's a little bit pink in his cheeks like he's warm in here, and he says that's OK. Anyway, as he was saying, he could even walk me to work in the morning, on his way to the station, and he's sure I'd like his mum's cooking because she's amazing, and his brother is funny, once you get to know . . .

'Flip a pancake.' This is me. Not shouting but a bit loud, well, really quite loud, and maybe even shouting in fact, but only a little bit, I think, not properly yell, yell, yell, and the old lady on the next table looks at me again. And Julie and Danny Flynn say what's wrong, and I say I think I am meant to be at work because of it being . . . and I'm trying to think which day it is, and I'm angry with my muddled old jumble head, because when you have a real job like I do, it's important to be reliable, and to know which days and not to forget to go.

But I don't need to think very long because of Danny Flynn saying it's Thursday, so I'm not meant to be at work today anyway, and not to worry, he's spoken to Karen and she knows all about Jenny and about me being in hospital, because remember, Hope, that it was Karen who guessed I would be in the park last night, when nobody could find me. And he says that Karen says only to go back to work when I'm good and ready, and that she said to make sure to give me her love and say she's thinking about me. And I'm a bit confused, because of not thinking that Karen, my boss, and Danny Flynn knew each other, but in fact it's not a big mystery at all, that's what he says, because of me going away from my house, running without my phone, and because of my mum, Jenny, falling on the floor, and her phone was there too in the kitchen, and Danny used both of our phones to find the numbers of the people who might be able to help. And it wasn't stealing because my phone is right here, see – and he takes it out of his pocket and puts it on the table – and my mum's phone is safe and sound, at his house to give her back when she wakes up.

And the light is still doing the thing that is making my head feel funny: bright light, bright, and then not bright. And it's doing a little buzz, too. And in my head, I'm thinking about being on my own in my home, and I'm thinking that I can do it because of being independent and all the practice and the rules and clocks and locks and brushing my hair and cleaning my teeth . . . But I'm thinking too about the making a cup of tea and forgetting about what goes in where – even if I do know about the teabags and the cups and the kettle, and even if I'm very good at making it usually – because sometimes my brain doesn't want to remember what to do. I'm thinking about my mum saying: oh, Hope, did you really do that?

And I'm thinking about a time when all the lights went out, because of a cut, and even when I pressed the switches they didn't come on, and I'm thinking about my shouting and shouting and not liking the dark and my mum, Jenny, saying not to worry and look, here are candles, and look, isn't this cosy. And I'm thinking about a box of Roses and a hand holding mine. And the light is going up, down, up, up, down. And I'm putting my hand in front of my eyes, because of the light hurting my brain. But I can still see Danny Flynn. And I say: 'Can I get my get my special blanket? And my golden notebook. And also my pillow? From my bed? If I come to your house, please, with the sweet bath and the telly in my room? But can I have my real own pillow from my real own bed? Because I like my pillow best.'

5

RESEARCH

14

It is very good that I am staying at Danny Flynn's house and that is because of a really important reason. I didn't even know it before I came. It's not just because of having my own pillow – and also my own pyjamas, because we collected them too, from my house, from under my pillow. They're trousers, not just open with a tie, so nobody can see my bottom when I walk around – although because of the sweet bathroom that's OK, because that's just my space, with nobody in there too. The very, very good reason for coming to Danny Flynn's house, is because of Barry. I think Barry is happy to have me here too, because he follows me everywhere and when I sit down, he sits down too, and he looks at me with his big eyes. And when we're having our cup of tea with a nice slice of fruit cake, he sits right under my chair and, if I put my hand down, he licks my fingers. Danny Flynn's mum says he's a Yorkie Shit-Poo because of being a cross between a Yorkshire terrier and a poodle and also a Shih Tzu, but Danny Flynn says what she means is Barry's a little rescue mutt. And I'm still laughing and laughing because of his mum saying the dog was a Shit-Poo, because of that being so funny and very rude.

And Danny Flynn's mum says she can see how much Barry likes me, and that Danny told her about me working as a dog walker, and what a nice job. But I can't answer her because of still laughing, and some of the tea has gone on my white hoodie, on the sleeve, because of me spitting it out from my mouth with all the laughing.

Danny Flynn's mum is called Bridget and her hair is like the colour of horseradish sauce – this is me showing, not telling, and anyway it is not white, not like snow or paper, and it is not grey, like the sky – and her skin is a little bit more pinky-white than Danny Flynn's, but I don't know how to show that, because of it not really looking like anything else, except maybe a nail polish that Veronica Ptitsky was wearing in the last writing class, but with a white line at the end of her nails.

She has freckles, Bridget does, which are more like the colour of tea with milk in or maybe those biscuits which are for dipping in your tea which is called dunking. Those ones are called Rich Tea biscuits, like they are biscuits with lots of money. But mostly they are only on her nose and on her arms, the freckles. And she has a big gap between her front teeth which makes a little whistle when she says sh . . . She has an accent, too, much more than Danny Flynn does, which makes it sound like she is always in a good mood. She talks quite a lot. Not as much as me – although I'm not talking so much right now, because of the laughing. And she says what a shame it is, about my mum being poorly, but she's sure that she will be right as rain in no time, and in any case, it's nice for them to have me staying for a little while. It will make a change to have a bit of female company, when it's usually just her and her boys. She means Danny and Connor and Barry.

'You shouldn't really say that a recovery is something you're *sure* about. Particularly as statistics would suggest a higher chance of Hope's mother not making . . .' This is Connor Flynn now, and it's the first time he's said anything apart from hello, Hope. But he doesn't finish what he's saying because of Bridget saying, not right now Connor.

Their kitchen table is square but a bit longer on two sides, and made out of wood, with six chairs around it. And Bridget is in one chair and I am in one chair, with Barry just under it, by my feet. And Danny Flynn is in one chair and beside him is Connor

Flynn. Connor looks like Danny quite a lot, with hair that is a bit brown and a little bit orange, just with more of it on the top of his forehead, where Danny doesn't have quite so much, and it's curly too but not so long. Connor has a face which is thinner. In fact all of his body is a little bit thinner too. And his eyes don't look at me when he's talking, which is a bit funny, because of Danny always looking at me and Bridget looking at me too when she's saying, with her nice accent, more tea, and can I fit in another slice of cake?

Connor is looking out of the side of his eyes, and it's like there is someone else standing beside me that is more interesting to talk to than me. Or something in the corner of the room maybe. But in fact there isn't anybody else there. I checked. And when he talks he does a thing with his fingers like he's stretching them or maybe playing the piano with them, except for maybe one finger on each hand. But I'm thinking this is not an exercise for his fingers, but maybe it's because of his being on the rainbow, which is the one for autism, because of Danny Flynn saying that and also because when I was at school there was a boy in one of the classes, but not in my class, and his name was Edward and he did a thing with his hand, which was like waving it all the time, even when there was nobody there to wave at, and it was because of the autism. Some of the other children in school said that he was my boyfriend but really I didn't even know him or talk to him. It was only because of thinking we both had rainbow brains and thinking we were both a Stupid Spaz. They said that it was true love, but it wasn't really any sort of love at all.

In my head, I'm thinking about my rules, the ones that are important and golden, and I'm thinking about the rule that we don't ask other people personal questions, like how much they weigh or how much money they have or if they're a Tory or a . . . the other one. And maybe asking about the autism is like that. And there was a thing, that Danny Flynn said, a special thing, actually, about a special vegetable rainbow, which name I can't find in my head right now. I'm thinking that his brother, that's Connor Flynn, might not want to talk about it. So instead of asking about that, now that I'm not laughing at the Shit-Poo thing anymore, I talk about me and about the dogs and the walking. I tell them the names of all the dogs and which ones are the best at coming back and which ones have to stay on the leads and which ones are always going away into the trees.

'In fact only between eight percent and forty-one percent of out-of-hospital cardiac arrest cases will make a recovery, depending on which research sources you're trusting. Cardiopulmonary resuscitation can double, or some sources say triple, survival rates but only if it is administered correctly and within the first minutes following arrest. Outside of that, the chances of death or of hypoxia resulting in life-affecting—'

'Connor. Hope really does not want to hear . . .' This is Bridget.

At the same time I'm saying: 'Are you a doctor?'

'I'm not a doctor.' This is Connor and although he's answering my question his eyes are looking off to the side, like into the corner of the room. But he's laughing with his mouth although not with any sound. 'But I do like to read *The Lancet* and *The British Medical Journal* to keep up with the latest studies and research. Danny says I'm a walking encyclopaedia, though he says most of it is useless information. But this is how I come to know a lot about cardio . . .'

'Connor is studying biochemistry. He's doing a distance . . .' This is Danny Flynn.

'*Clinical* biochemistry, and it's an online post-graduate diploma.' This is Connor. 'I'm studying the links between metabolic factors and incidence of autism spectrum disorders. My underlying . . .'

'I have a disorder. Me too. A *spectrum* disorder too.' I'm shouting, only a little bit, and maybe it's interrupting but I think that's all right because of it being a conversation and because of it being the same subject and not just something from my head. And because of Connor Flynn talking a lot, so maybe it's OK for it to be my turn now. 'It's a spectrum too. But mostly I call it a rainbow instead because of sometimes forgetting and because of a rainbow being like a spectrum with all the colours spread out in the sky.'

I'm saying the word *spectrum* again and it feels nice in my mouth because of usually forgetting it and now I know it's the right word. 'I'm just a little bit blue or maybe a bit indigo, like the colours, but not red or orange, which is when you maybe can't have a real job or go—'

'. . . theory is that an individual's personal endocrine and environmental make-up have a pivotal role in determining whether or not . . .' This is Connor Flynn. And this is a bit like interrupting, even though he was talking first, because even with me telling him about the rainbow, he is still telling me about his studying. Maybe Danny Flynn thinks it's a little bit interrupting too, because he's looking at his mother and she's looking at him. And they're both smiling, and they're shaking their heads, just a little bit, too.

I'm thinking maybe Connor Flynn didn't hear

me. So I tell him again, with my hand up to show it's not really interrupting, and, actually, it's more like still my turn.

'*My* spectrum is because of my birth mother, because of her drinking vodka and beer and wine when I was in her tummy, and because of it going into my brain and making—'

'Foetal Alcohol Spectrum Disorder.'

Connor Flynn must be very clever because that is exactly right. And I'm opening my mouth to tell him that, but he's still talking, so I don't say anything.

'FASD being the umbrella term for the range of effects caused by prenatal alcohol consumption and the leading non-genetic cause of learning disability in the UK. The term recognises the broad spectrum of manifestations. The fact that alcohol in utero could have repercussions on the gestating baby has been acknowledged for centuries, of course, however it was only in, I'm thinking 1971 or '72, maybe 1973, that Foetal Alcohol Syndrome, the first diagnosable form to be discovered, was named, recognising the physical and neurological effects of prenatal alcohol consumption on the gestating child. Estimates generally range from affected population being between nought point nine and five percent although a more recent study suggested up to seventeen percent of UK babies.'

I'm still not saying anything. I'm just looking at him with my mouth a little bit open, because I do want to tell him something – that labels don't matter, it's only people that matter – and it's important to tell him, but I'm also listening to all the numbers and trying to think what they mean. And it's a bit like it's blocked in my brain and so I don't say anything.

Connor Flynn really does seem to know a lot of things. His diploma must be a very good one, I think. Because, actually, he's very clever.

'Until recently, diagnosis has largely relied on the facial characteristics of thin upper lip, smooth philtrum and small palpebral fissures, as well as small stature and reduced intellectual ability. However most individuals on the broader FASD spectrum have no craniofacial effects and IQ will often be within average parameters. Individuals will have a unique presentation of symptoms, of varying severity, while wider manifestations may include difficulties with memory, motor and cognitive skills, language, attention, executive function, emotional regulation, allied with impulsiveness and lack of risk-awareness, difficulties in social interaction and difficulties with attention. Studies have identified 428 other conditions which may co-occur with FASD. Multiple similarities and crossovers with ADHD and autism spectrum disorders, though, in FASD the cause is evident, whereas with ADHD and autism spectrum disorders there are vastly differing theories.'

I think he's finished talking. I'm thinking maybe now I'll tell him about labels not mattering. Only people. But, actually, he hasn't finished.

'FASD correlates to lifelong brain damage caused by the consumption of alcohol, a teratogenic compound, during pregnancy, due to the placenta's inability to stop it passing through to the foetus. The varying manifestations can be attributed to the point in gestation at which—'

'Connor, *please* . . .' This is Danny Flynn.

Connor Flynn looks at him, or more sort of past him. It is a moment before he talks again. 'Back in my box?'

'Back in your box.' When they smile they both have the dimples. Danny Flynn is looking at me and he's doing a thing with his eyes like making them go round in a circle, but Connor Flynn is still looking into the corner of the room, like there is a thing he needs to watch there. For a little bit I'm looking into the corner too, because maybe that's where the box is. But then I'm thinking that, in fact, it's not a real box, and it's only a joke one that they're pretending about.

On the wall is a picture and it's with both of

them except they're not grown-up men, they're boys with curly hair, and even Danny Flynn has it all over his head, at the front too, and they are standing on the sand and wearing swimming trunks, even though it's not very sunny. Danny Flynn is taller than Connor Flynn – that's just in the picture, because now it is Connor who is taller than Danny. Next to them is Bridget except with hair that is more the colour of mustard than horseradish, and longer, not short like now, and with a floppy hat on top. And there is a man, too, who has hair like leaves when they're red not green, and he has a smile with dimples too, and shorts and a shirt, but with short sleeves not long ones. And I know who he is because Danny Flynn showed me the photograph already when he was telling me about all the rooms and the house. He is Fergus Flynn, who was Danny and Connor's father although not now because of being no longer with us, sadly, because of cancer.

'You'll have to excuse my brother.' This is Danny Flynn, and he's talking to me. 'Connor sometimes forgets not all of us are as fascinated by every fact and statistic and piece of trivia as he is.'

Connor Flynn is smiling into his chest and looking out of the corner of his eyes and he says: 'That's because you're not clever enough to understand them.' Danny Flynn punches him on the arm, but it's not very hard, not like boxers, more like he's really doing it very gently, maybe not even touching him at all, but still with his fingers folded up to pretend it's a proper hit.

Connor Flynn is twenty-eight years old, which is older than me, because I'm twenty-five. And he has lots of certificates already, like one in maths and one in chemistry but that one's not *bio*chemistry, only the normal kind. And he did have a job when he was younger and he liked it when he was making tables, but ones on computers, not real ones for eating. They were tables that would measure things that were called probable outcomes and were all about families and their money and their salaries and their buying behaviours, and it was in a bank, but he didn't like it when other people didn't understand about his outcomes and said about him not being good at explaining and about it not being obvious what it meant. He has four A Levels and even *two* in maths, because of one being an even harder maths. And what he likes most is research, because of it being a process. And he does some different work now, not the same job. Because of wanting a change.

Now it is research, which is called academic, and that helps him to have money to do more studying, but mostly he doesn't do it with other people, because of finding it better to work just with evidence and numbers. He has eleven GCSEs and that is four more than his brother. I don't know how many more it is than me because of not being able to remember how many I have. I know I do have some. I think I do, because of having to make a cushion about me, which I put a dog picture and some buttons on, and an apron, which I gave to my mum, and also some other tests, like maths, but I think that was different letters to GCSE, because of not being with the other children. I can't remember what letters it was. Maybe it wasn't GCSEs.

I tell Connor Flynn that I like research too, because of having to do it for my book. And I tell him about my book and about how it is going to change my life and find my birth mother. And he asks what research I am doing, he says what is my methodology but I don't know that word so I just tell him about doing my research in the library and what I'm doing is writing about what I know and where my cardboard box was found and writing down all the questions that I want to ask my birth mother, like why did she put me there. This is what my mum, Jenny Nicely, does when she writes a poem. She writes down lots of words on a page. She says after a while they start to talk to her.

'Yes, but in terms of *actual research* what sources have you consulted? Have you spoken directly to the police officers or the doctors involved in your case? I presume you'd have had to approach the newspapers for the original articles, or are the archives now available online? Or perhaps they were saved for you? With your adoption history. That's likely, of course. Do you have a file of all the paperwork? I imagine your adoptive mother must do so. And, then, it would be interesting to know what happened to the actual cardboard box. It would be interesting to know what clues it offered. DNA testing was not so widely used at the end of the twentieth century as it is now, of course, but still I imagine it was a valuable piece of primary evidence. Would the police have kept the box? My guess is . . .'

'I . . .' I'm looking at him and my mouth is open but my head is feeling like it's been emptied by all the questions. I don't know any of the answers because of not having thought of them at all, but only thinking about why my birth mother left me at the church, and if she knew how she'd made my brain, and not thinking at all about who kept the cardboard box or any of the other stuff. Now I'm worrying that Connor Flynn will think I'm stupid if I tell him about not having done any of these things for my research, and he'll think no wonder I don't even know if I have a GCSE or not.

I say: 'It was only a cardboard box. But I have

the blanket. That is evidence. It's pink and it was in the box with me and it's still mine now.'

'Has the blanket ever been washed?'

And I tell him, oh yes, because of it going in the washing machine when it's time to change sheets, which is every week or maybe every day but I think it's every week, because of needing our homes and bodies to be clean. So it's a very clean blanket even though it's as old as me.

'Unfortunate. Washing the blanket will certainly have compromised the DNA evidence, though of course there are a number of variables such as temperature of the wash and the detergent you're using which would need to be taken into account. Deoxyribonucleic acid, that is DNA, is found in all living cells and contains genetic information, which is why it's so useful in genetic fingerprinting, such as identifying parentage. But putting this blanket through a wash over that amount of time will invariably mean that any DNA that there might have once been will no longer be intact enough for examination.'

I think about telling him that, in fact, I have the blanket right here in my bag in my room – not really my room, but where I can stay for a few nights, with a sweet bathroom and a white duvet with stars embroidered on it – and hopefully not too long because I'm sure my mum is going to be right as rain very soon. It's my blanket, which is not big enough to be my real blanket, because of me having grown so much bigger than a baby, of course, but my blanket is still big enough and soft enough to snuggle when I'm going to sleep. It's not just pink but it's pink with green flowers. But I decide not to say anything about the blanket because of Connor Flynn telling me that it's compromised. I'm not quite sure what that means but it sounds bad, and so Connor Flynn wouldn't be able to do research with it. Also I don't tell him because I don't want him to think I'm a baby boo boo who needs a blanket to go to sleep. But anyway I don't need to say anything else, and that's because of Barry barking. It's a very funny bark. It's quite high but not as high as a chihuahua, and Bridget says it's him telling us he wants to go out in the garden. I say can I go out with him please.

There's a ball in the garden and Barry is very good at bringing it back to me when I throw it and each time he drops it right at my feet and looks up at me with big eyes. I play with him for ages and I'm still laughing a bit because of remembering in my head about him being a Yorkie Poo-Shit. And when he's brought back the ball like maybe a hundred or a thousand times, I sit on the step and he comes straight to me and puts his head onto my leg with his eyes looking up. And that's why dogs are so special, and I'm thinking I like Barry even as much as I like Tinie Tempah. Dogs are much better than friends, because they care about you. And I tell him it's nice to be staying with him, and I tell him about my mum, who is called Jenny Nicely, and about her being in the hospital because of having an arrest and I think it's a cardio one, and not a police one at all, like on the telly when you have to right to remain, although they did come and get me, the police. I tell him about the doctors saying they don't know if she'll wake up but that I know she'll be right as rain because the doctors don't know my mum and how strong and clever she is and how unique.

Barry doesn't say anything of course, because of him being a dog, but I think he's listening to me, and his fur is soft and nice when I stroke him. I think he agrees too and thinks that everything will be right as rain.

15

Danny Flynn was not fibbing when he said that his mum was a good cook and even before I've tasted my dinner I've been smelling it, and thinking about it, even when I was in my sweet bedroom, having a little nap. But it wasn't a real one, a nap I mean, because of just having my eyes closed but my head not wanting to sleep, and that's because of thinking so hard about if things will be right as rain. But even then, it was like smelling toasty and roasty, like sausages, like when my mum, Jenny, does them with fried potatoes and peppers for special breakfast, and a little bit like pancakes. And it was like in the advert which was on telly when I was little, maybe ten years old, and isn't on the telly anymore, because of being old-fashioned maybe, and it was of a pot for putting gravy in, and the gravy is making a big line of smell that you can see on the telly that's stretching and stretching. It's a smell but you can actually see it, and it's going into the children's noses and they're going *mmmmm*. And that's like me now, with the toasty, roasty sausage smell and even though nobody's told me time for tea, I'm coming out of my sweet bedroom and I'm in my pyjamas and I've even got my slippers on, because they're soft and Danny Flynn's house only has carpet in the bedrooms and not in the kitchen, which is wood. My slippers are very funny because of looking like dog feet, which are very much bigger than my feet, and they're shaped like a foot of maybe Barry, which is paw and that's what my slippers are.

Bridget says, 'Look at you in your funny slippers.'

And I say, 'They're paws.'

'I can see that.' This is her. 'They look very snug.'

I say I'm very hungry and is that tea because it smells very nice. And I say mmmmm, like in the advert with the smell you can see. And Bridget laughs and says good, good, and it's nearly ready and do I like toad-in-the-hole. And I think this is a question that must be a joke or else it is really a big problem, because even if it smells as mmmm as with the smell you can see, and even if it smells just like pancakes and sausages, eating toad is not a thing I want to do. Not ever. And my brain is telling me about being polite but it's too late because my mouth is already saying that eating toads is yucky disgusting.

Danny Flynn is laughing and I didn't even know he was here in the room, but he's in the armchair, watching the news, and he's turning round now and he says don't I know what toad-in-the-hole is, and he says don't worry, it won't be slimy or have warts on it. He promises. And Bridget is laughing too and saying, it's OK, they don't eat toads in this house either and toad-in-the-hole is just a funny name and, in fact, what it is, is sausages in Yorkshire pudding, with her very special gravy, and she's certain I'll like it very much. Danny Flynn says Hope Nicely, you're priceless.

The toad-in-the-hole is very delicious and the knife and fork have handles which are plastic, but they're not thin and hard, and that's good, because I don't like it when the handles are thin and hard or when they're only silver. And Bridget and Danny Flynn tell Connor Flynn the story about my muddle, and about me thinking we were going to eat a toad. Connor Flynn doesn't have his sausages inside his Yorkshire pudding like Danny Flynn and Bridget and me. He has a plate with his sausages on one side and his Yorkshire pudding on the other side, because he likes it best that way. And no gravy. But Connor Flynn knows lots of things about toads, like they are part of the same family as frogs and it is called Bufonidae and that there are toads in all corners of the world, but not in the continent of Antarctica. And I ask him if he knows any facts about sausages and he's thinking for a while before he says, actually, not very many, except of course that the name for a sausage comes from the Latin word salsisium which means something that is salted, with salt.

Barry sits under my chair and, when nobody is looking, I give him a little bit of the salsisium-in-the-hole, but only a tiny little bit because of it being so delicious and me wanting to eat it all. And pudding is treacle tart and it's with custard. It's so nice that I have seconds and then even more seconds. And Bridget says how good to see that I have an appetite and she's glad I like it because she can't bear food going to waste.

There is coffee at the end of the meal, but not for me, because coffee is yucky, even if it's without the caff. But I have a tea and it's a mint tea. It's like hot water, but with a bit more taste and it's a bit green. Danny Flynn is telling me about who he's been speaking to on the telephone. He's been speaking to the hospital about my mum and everything is the same, that's what he says: no change. But they say that's to be expected because of my mother being sedated and Danny Flynn has to go to work tomorrow but the hospital has the number for the house and the number for him, and my number too, so if there's any change at all, they will let us know straight away. And if I want to go and see Jenny tomorrow, Julie said she can pick me up about two, and he's sorry about leaving me but he has to work, and Mum and Connor will be here and, actually, Marnie Shale phoned to ask after me and see how Jenny was, and said she'd love to call in to see me. Also Karen, my boss, called and everyone sends their love.

Bridget says she's sure my mum will be better soon, then Connor Flynn says, statistically, unless CPR was instigated within the first couple of minutes, the likelihood of brain damage or—

'Thank you, Connor. Enough.' This is Bridget and she's putting a hand on his arm, but he pulls his arm away. Connor says, or fatality or persistent vegetative, and Bridget says, enough, a bit louder this time, and it's interrupting but he stops talking. I'm not sure what he's talking about or why he's stopped. But maybe it's something to do with his special vegetable. It sounds a bit like it.

'I thought maybe you'd like to take Barry for a walk tomorrow?' Bridget is saying it to me and I can even feel my mouth smiling and my face feeling a bit warm, because I'd like it very much.

The bed is very comfortable and nice to sleep in and I have my own pillow, from my own bed at my own home, and that's good because of it being so much better than the hospital one and not flat and because of it smelling of the right washing machine. I have a nice night, apart from the bit where Bridget is there and saying shh, it's OK, you're just having a bad dream, and my head not knowing where I am or who she is for a bit, not just because of the big old muddle but because of being a sleepyhead too.

It takes me a little while to stop screaming and she's cuddling me, just like my mum, Jenny, would do too, if she was here instead of being in I See You. I'm sitting up, with my hands in front of me and they're made into balls and squeezing my fingers tight, tight, tight. And my neck and my back feel wet, and like sweaty hot, and in my mouth it's a bit salty like a toad. And Bridget is there with her arms around me, saying everything's OK now, and she's saying, louder, don't worry, boys, it's just Hope having a bad dream. She brings me a glass of water and asks if I want the little light left on. And I say no, because I'm not a baby boo boo. She says OK then and she says sleep tight now. And that's nice but it's not goodnight, Hope Nicely, sweet dreams and see you in the morning, which is what my mum, Jenny, always says. After Bridget has gone and she's shut the door very quietly, I take out my pink blanket from under my pillow and I hold it tight with it soft against my cheek and my eyes still open, even in the dark.

16

I am five foot tall. That is what Connor Flynn tells me and I think he's probably right. He says it because of me not knowing how tall I am, and I want to say an answer like thirty or twenty-three, so that he doesn't think I'm a stupid No-Brain, but I don't even know what to say, like is it metres or inches or something else, actually. So I just say I don't know, and I say it in my quiet voice, because of not being very proud of not having the right answer. He says well, he's very good at estimating and in his estimation I am five foot zero, which is the same as 152.4 centimetres because 2.54 centimetres makes one inch.

He says, of course it is one of the signature characteristics, to have short stature and a small head, although I don't appear to have any of the facial abnormalities that often accompany the condition. I don't really know what to answer, so I just look at my Rice Krispies, and eat some of them, and Bridget says not to ask personal questions and Connor Flynn says he's not asking personal questions, he's simply assessing height, which is nothing more than objective data, and he is five foot eleven and that is three inches taller than Danny Flynn because of Danny Flynn being a short arse. And he does the dimple smile thing, even though he's looking into the corner, but Danny isn't really listening because of eating toast and mostly reading the paper.

Danny Flynn says it's time for him to go because of not being able to take today off work, he's afraid, and not wanting to be late, and he says but Mum will take care of you, and Barry will too – look at him there by your feet again, looks like he's forgotten who the rest of us are. Danny Flynn says, and be sure to tell Connor to get back in his box if he's annoying you. He says, oh yes, and Marnie Shale's going to pop by this morning, isn't that kind of her. He says he'll be in touch if he hears anything from the hospital and, remember, Julie said she can take me in later. And she said to call her any time as she's around all day. And not to worry about Karen, she's not expecting me at work today. And if there's anything I need . . .

When he leaves he says ta-ra then, everyone, and he gives his mum, that's Bridget, a kiss on her cheek and he gives me one too, but not Connor Flynn. I'm wondering if maybe Danny Flynn really *is* my boyfriend now because of the kissing, but I'm not sure because of never having had a boyfriend ever before and not really knowing how you can tell if someone is one. I'm not sure if it is something I can ask.

After my Rice Krispies I have some Honey Nut Cornflakes, too, because of not being able to make up my mind, and because of wanting both. At home we have Cornflakes sometimes but not ever Honey Nut ones because my mum, Jenny, doesn't like them, and never ever Rice Krispies. Mostly, at home, we have porridge and sometimes sausages, but real ones not salty-toads, with spicy potatoes or maybe peppers, but not on a workday, only on a Sunday or other days that are not when we go to work.

I have real tea for drinking this morning, not mint tea, but a nice real cup. And I'm trying to listen to Bridget, who is Danny Flynn's mum, talking and talking about chores like the garden and paying the gas bill and going to see her dad who's in a home, but in my head I'm doing a little walk, like in the trees with a dog. It's not a real dog, like Barry or Tinie Tempah, just an in-my-head one who doesn't even need a lead because it's just walking along with me, not going away and running into where it shouldn't be. It's not a bad fog or a big jumble in my head today, it's just a place where I'm a bit stuck, but quite nice stuck, like it's good to be going for a walk in my head. But maybe I'm a bit too much in my own walk, because when my head tells me that my name is being said, it's like it's by someone a long way away and it's been said quite a lot of times.

'Hope. Hey, daydreamer. Look, you have a guest.'

It takes my head quite a long time to work out what's happening and even to remember where I am. My cup of tea and my bowl with the Honey Nuts isn't on the table anymore and I'm still in my pyjamas and my paws but now there is someone else in front of me and she's . . .

Inside my head I'm looking for the answer, because of still being in there walking around, and now trying to remember who this is. I'm looking at hair which is a bit bouncy, and a big smile, and hearing an accent that sounds like laughing. For just a little moment I'm thinking whose home is this and where is my mum, Jenny? And I know who this person is but, just for a little bit, her name isn't coming.

'. . . that lovely. Look what Miss Shale has brought you.'

'Marnie, please.'

And it's a face that I know, and an accent, which is going up and down like a wave, saying Hope, you poor thing, how are you coping? And I know who it is, because it's Marnie Shale, because of her saying it. But my brain is still coming out of its walk.

Marnie Shale is holding out some flowers. They are yellow and white, and the other woman is saying she'll put them in water and pop the kettle on. And, *of course*, she's Bridget. She's Danny Flynn's mother and – bingo – of course, I know exactly who Marnie Shale is. What a silly jumble head I am to take so long.

It's not just flowers that she's brought, but chocolates too, and these are ones that look like little seashells or maybe snails, and they're not just brown chocolate but yellow chocolate too, not properly mixed in so there are two different colours. They're very delicious though, so when I've had my first one just to try them, I have another one just because of wanting to.

'How are you coping, you poor thing? It must be so distressing. Danny said you were with Jenny when she collapsed?'

I nod without saying any words and it's because of the chocolate snail in my mouth.

'You must have been so scared. All on your own. Such a terrible shock.'

My head doesn't really want to think about it. I'm thinking about putting my hands over my ears but I can't because of having another chocolate in my hand and needing to put it into my mouth and I have to eat it quickly so that I can say a reply. 'Danny Flynn came. He was there too.'

Marnie Shale nods, like big up-and-downing with her head, and she says, yes, yes, of course, and wasn't that so lucky. And what about Jenny, she says, how is my mum doing? Is there any change?

And I'm thinking, of course there's a change. It's a big, huge, ginormous change because of my mum not being awake anymore and being in the hospital and not talking or saying sweet dreams or let's have a nice cup of tea, and just being asleep and in the bed with the elephant nose and the noises all around and the screens. But I'm also thinking that this is not what Marnie Shale means, actually, because of what Danny said, about his phone call to the hospital, which was *no change*. He said that they would definitely let me know if there was any change. And that was a promise. So I shake my head and I say, no, no change.

Bridget is back now, with a big smile, and she's bringing a tray and on it are the flowers and a teapot and two mugs, and she says, Hope, aren't you going to offer your guest one of your chocolates? I think this is because of me having the box by my hand on the table and with a chocolate in my mouth. But

Marnie Shale laughs and says no thanks, they're all for Hope. She's brought a book for my mum too. And she takes it out of her bag and it's called *Infinity Sister* and it's by Marnie Shale with her name on the cover and she opens it to show me what she's written inside, which is *Dearest Jenny. The hardest times are when we find the greatest strength – wishing you better. Love always, Marnie x*

Bridget says how very special, and do please excuse her but there are a ton of jobs she needs to be getting on with in the house, and please don't think she's rude if she leaves us to it. Marnie says, of course, but is she sure she won't join us for a cuppa and she hopes she's not in the way, and Bridget says no quite the opposite, and it's lovely to meet her because Danny loves her books and says how interesting her classes are. Bridget says how kind of her to come and see Hope – that's me – but honestly, she has a hundred things to be doing, so please, do excuse her . . .

While they're talking I'm looking at Marnie's book and the writing which is pretty and looping in a black pen – and there's a chocolate fingerprint, too, but not a big one and only in the very bottom corner of the page, and I think maybe it's from my fingers, so I close it again. I say: 'What's your book about?'

Marnie Shale says, well, I suppose it's about

friendships and expectations and disappointments, but ultimately, hope. And I say Hope like me, and she laughs a bouncing laugh and says no, the other type of hope which is really wanting something to happen and not knowing if it will or not. By the way, she says, never ever repeat what she's just said when she comes to talk about elevator pitches in the writing group.

I'm very confused by this and I don't even mind if she thinks I'm stupid, because I don't even know what an elevator is or a pitch, except for a football pitch. But in fact, this pitch is a bit like a sport too because of it being a throw that you do in baseball, which is like rounders for Americans, but it's a word that can mean trying to sell something in a quick way, like you're throwing it really fast to try and make someone want it. And an elevator is also American because it's a lift, like the one at the writing group which goes down to the bottom floor which is the library and up to the third floor which is the room with the almost round table. An elevator pitch is the way that you would describe your book if you only had the time it took to be in the elevator, which is the lift, and you can't press any buttons to make it stop. That's just three floors. So it has to be fast and it has to be exciting.

'So really the complete opposite of what I just

said.' That's Marnie Shale and she's always laughing. But I say I thought her elevator pitch was perfect, and is it OK if I go and get my notebook from my bag to write it in? And so that's what I do. I write, in my neatest letters, *Infinity Sister by Marnie Shale. This book is about friendships and expectations and disappointments, but ultimately, hope.*

Marnie Shale says that you know a real writer because they always have their notebook with them. And it makes my cheeks feel a bit warm, like having a silver star put onto my star chart, or like Barry choosing my feet to sit by. And she says, Marnie Shale, how am I getting on with the writing, and am I managing to do much. And I say no, not really very much, because mostly I'm just thinking about it. And then I stop for a moment, then I say, which is doing research.

Marnie Shale thinks research is vitally important because a book is much more than just all the words inside it. A book is nothing without authenticity and voice. And for this we need research and also planning. This is what Marnie Shale says: research is like the brain and planning is where we bring in the heart. She says that we will talk about this later in our writers' group sessions, and that research and planning are just as necessary in non-fiction as they are in a novel.

She says it ties in with what she's asked us to think about during the week, do I remember, which is about what is at stake in our stories, which is what really, really matters. Because, she says, the best writer in the world can write a book and we will not be interested if there is nothing at stake. There needs to be something that can be lost or can be found, there need to be elements of risk and redemption, and profound change. I like the way she says profound. It sounds like she should be singing it. I have to put my hand over my mouth because I want to sing it out too – *profound, profound, profound* – but I think it might look stupid, because of it being her word. Also there is a chocolate snail in my mouth and we should not sing with our mouth full. There has to be a journey – Marnie Shale says this with her accent that is up and down like a wave, and with also doing the funny thing with her fingers like she's making little rabbit ears beside her head – a book needs to show that there has been a journey (rabbit ears) or the reader just won't care.

'The reader must care, Hope. If you make them care, everything else will follow. And when it comes down to it, what we all care about is not words, or things, it's *people*.'

I'm listening to Marnie Shale but I'm also looking at the box of chocolates because of there not being very many left, like only two or maybe three, and sort of wanting one but sort of not wanting one because of feeling a little bit like I might be sick if I do. And so I don't take another one but I'm licking my fingers, where they're a bit chocolatey, and she's talking about journeys still, and characters, and our planning seeing them in one place and then taking them to another place, and we see what is at stake. And it's not like the steak which you can have with chips or in a pie with mushrooms – even if you have to pick the mushrooms out if you don't like them very much because of them being a bit slimy – it is what really, really matters, and then, in the end, there has to have been a change. And I say: 'A profound change,' and it feels really good in my mouth, especially when Marnie does a smile.

I have a sip of my tea but it's a bit cold now because of forgetting about it while I was eating all the chocolates. Marnie says that this is what we call a character arc, and I think she means like in Noah's Ark, which is a story about a big boat in the rain which was a flood. It is about Noah and God. And I say: 'The animals came in two by two, hurrah!' but it's not even that sort of ark, it's an arc like a shape which goes up in the air and then comes down again, like an arrow being shot up high and then reaching the top and coming back to the earth. Like a tragic something, but I don't really know what the word is. Like a change. That's why it's a journey.

I'm trying to think about arcs and journeys, but it's a bit difficult and I'm thinking about my book. My book is just about me and I think maybe people like me don't have an arc, maybe because of having brains that are unique but a bit of a jumble, and that's what I say to Marnie Shale. I say I don't think I have an arc. But she looks at me, like she's trying very hard with her eyes, and she says, she has a feeling that my arc will be exactly like a perfect rainbow.

Now it's me who's looking at her really hard, because I'm thinking how did Marnie Shale even know about that? Because I thought that was just for me and my mum, Jenny. I don't know what to say so I just keep sipping my tea even if it's cold now.

'Hope.' Marnie Shale's eyes are very dark and very open and looking at me without looking anywhere else, like I'm the best thing in the room to look at.

I say yes. She has her mouth open like she's going to talk but then she doesn't say anything. So I say yes again, in case she didn't hear me. And she says sorry. She says do I mind if she asks me a question. And I say, no. And, of course, I don't mind it. Because that is how you do a conversation. One person asks you a question and then you answer it, but you try not to talk and talk and just say everything that is in your head. Instead of that, you should try to ask them a question, too, because of it being polite and not just about you.

So now I'm waiting for my question, but Marnie just looks at me for a bit. And I'm looking at her too, and sort of smiling because of her being nice, and also because of waiting. And I'm thinking maybe Marnie Shale has gone for a walk in her head, and then she says what made me decide to write a book. And I say, well, to find my mother and change my life, and she says yes but why – when was it that I had the thought of a book? What was my spark?

A spark is like a little tiny bit of fire, and that is what I can see in my head. Like it's red and orange and yellow and dancing inside my brain. And I'm thinking about the question and I'm thinking about the answer, and what the answer is. But I can't remember.

I'm squeezing my brain very tight to make it think better but it still doesn't want to tell me. I remember my mum, Jenny Nicely, saying oh, a book, yes wouldn't that be an achievement. I can remember her talking about the writing group and Marnie Shale, and how nice she was, and would I be OK, being there, just me and not her, not Jenny. I remember

buying the notebook, from WH Smith, and I
remember, in my head, seeing what my book would
look like one day, with my name on the cover. But,
flip a pancake, I can't remember the moment when
my brain said, here you go, Hope, here's a very good
idea. I can only remember the idea being there already.
And so I'm not saying anything, just thinking with
my mouth open and no words coming out, only in
my head. And now I'm thinking too that Marnie
Shale will think I'm stupid because of not having an
answer and because of it being a conversation but
with me saying no words. So I say: 'I just thought it
would be a good idea.' And then I say, 'And why did
you write your book?' And that is very good
conversation because of not just talking and talking
but asking a question too.

Marnie Shale must be going because she has a busy
day ahead of her, but I have to promise to let her
know if there's anything she can do. Anything at all.
Bridget is with us now, and she's had a cup of tea
too, and she and Marnie have talked about libraries,
and how it's not fair how they don't get enough
money and some are even closing, and they've talked
about doctors' waiting times and the lights at the

crossing by the main road which never give you time for crossing. And Connor Flynn is in the same room too, although he is reading a book called *Peptides and Proteins* and not talking about anything.

Bridget is saying well, how very nice of Miss Shale to have come round, and to have brought the flowers and the chocolates and the book for Jenny. And she looks at me and doesn't say anything for a moment, and I'm not sure what to say so I just look back. Marnie Shale says it was lovely to see me and to meet Bridget and Connor and she just wishes there was something that she could do, but that she's sure that Jenny will come through this and that . . .

Connor Flynn looks up from his book, which is called *Peptides and Proteins*, and he says that, actually, the chance of that is not particularly—

Bridget says, Connor, please, not now, but then she says yes of course, they'll let Marnie Shale know how everything is going. And Marnie Shale says well, Hope, it would be lovely to see me at the group later, but of course she'll understand if . . .

'Let me see you to the door, then, Miss Shale. Hope, love, why don't you get yourself ready? Julie's taking you to visit your mum this afternoon, but maybe you'd like to take Barry for a little walk before lunch.' That's Bridget.

I'm shouting yes, yes, yes, because I really do

want to walk him. And while Bridget is out in the hallway, with her voice and Marnie's having a conversation but not loud enough for me to hear what they're saying, I'm looking for Barry's lead, and it is on a hook by the door to the garden. I've found it even without having to ask Connor Flynn where it is. And there is a packet of poo bags on the windowsill above it so I take them because that is very important and only bad dog walkers don't pick up the poos, which is poop-scooping. When Bridget comes back in, I already have Barry on his lead and I have three poo bags in my hand, because he might need more than one poo and I don't want to run out of them. And I'm really looking forward to walking him. I can't wait. But Bridget looks at me and then she starts laughing. She says, am I off for my walk like that, and I say yes I am. She laughs a bit more, and Connor Flynn looks up from his book, and he laughs too. It's a funny laugh because it's like ha-ha-ha and then it goes up high, and more like a hiccup.

Bridget says haven't I forgotten something. But I have Barry's lead and the three poo bags, one two three, and I'm thinking hard, so I say: 'Treats?' because some dogs only come back to you if you have a tasty bite or a piece of cheese and otherwise they just look at you or they run off into the trees. But Bridget points at my feet and says, *seriously*, am I planning to go out like *that*? And I look down. Connor Flynn is doing a bit more of his hiccup laugh, like it doesn't know if it wants to go out or in. And it's because I still have my slippers on. I'm still in my pyjamas and I haven't even got dressed yet today. And now I'm laughing too, because of me standing here in my big furry paws and my toasty dressing gown over my jim-jams, with Barry's lead and the poo bags still in my hand.

17

'. . . every time they pull, even if it makes it very slow. And then you don't start walking again until they stop and wait for you. And if they pull again, you stop walking again. And then you have to stop, even another time, and another, and do it again, until they've stopped pulling and they're standing still. And if they bark you should turn around and walk them in the way that they don't want to go, until they stop barking.'

This is me and I'm telling Connor Flynn about the best way to teach a dog. And in fact, it's not so necessary because Barry is being mostly a very good dog who is not pulling at all, except for wanting to do a bit of sniffing and sometimes a wee with his leg in the air, against a tree or on a bit of long grass, which is like all dogs because of them liking to show where they have been with the smell of their wee, which they can smell even if we can't.

Connor Flynn doesn't say anything about the dogs. He's still talking about the thing that he was telling me before, which is about peptides and proteins. I don't even know what peptides and proteins are, which is why I started saying about the dogs instead. Bridget says I am very honoured to have Connor come on the walk with me, because of him mostly liking to stay in his home with his books and not wanting to be out with other people. Because of his routine. But she said, good for me, and, actually that could be very useful for her because of her being able to get out and do a food shop while we're out, so yes, why don't I go with Connor instead.

'And when they see another dog and they wag their tail, sometimes it means they want to play with them but it's not always because of that, because dogs wag their tails too sometimes when they are thinking about other things, even fighting, not just when they're happy. And . . .'

'. . . secretion from neuroendocrine cells facilitates the pathway to tissue elsewhere in the body. But what is interesting is that the neuropeptide Y and the receptor . . .'

'. . . the fur on their necks stands up and also when they lift up their lips on their mouths and do this with their teeth – *rrrrrrr* – with them shut, and growl, and they're looking at you with their eyes like . . .'

'. . . human peptide bond formation is dependent on a number of neurophysiological factors, and we have to think about its involvement in central and peripheral nervous system processes before we can begin to . . .'

It's sort of a conversation but a little bit not one too, because of Connor Flynn and me talking at the same time and not really asking any questions. I'm sort of trying to listen to his words, like the peptides and the molly cools, and Connor Flynn is not looking at me but sort of out of his eyes and sometimes at his fingers, which are doing the long stretchy thing and sort of moving like he's playing the piano. But then he stops moving his fingers and stops talking about peptides. And he makes a noise. Like a moaning noise, like maybe sad or maybe hurt, and he puts his arms over the top of his head.

I say what's wrong, and he says he doesn't like it. I say don't like what. And he says the dog. And he's still there with his hands over his head and not walking, and his head down and rocking. I say what dog? I say, Barry? But he just keeps on making the noise.

And I look down. Barry is just by a bit of grass which is longer than the grass around it, and in a position that is a dog poo position, which is with his back all round and his bottom down near the ground. And he is doing a poo. I can even see a bit of the poo landing on the ground and curling around into like a round thing or maybe an oval. And it's OK, because of having the poo bags in my pocket, so I take out one of the poo bags and I bend down and Connor Flynn makes an even louder noise, like something is really hurting him, and he is rocking even more and I ask him is he all right and he says noooo, nooooo, nooooo.

Barry has finished his poo now and he's just waiting. And it smells a little bit yucky but not as bad as when it's Tinie Tempah, because of him having a tummy that can be a bit funny. And I have the poo bag on my hand and it's OK because none of the poo goes on your fingers if you do it right and I know exactly what I'm doing so no poo ever goes on mine. Even though I'm not very good at tying knots, it's OK with the poo bag because it's just cross it over once and then cross it over again and it's really lucky because there is a red poo bin very near and so I put it in and come back and I ask Connor Flynn what's wrong.

He's still doing the noise, but he stops a little bit, and looks around, not really at me, just more all around with his eyes that go to one corner and to another corner and he is doing a bit less rocking and then a bit less and he even takes his hands off from his head and puts them in front of him again. He says he has issues and I think he's telling me that they are about an old factory and I ask him what old factory. He says no, not old factory, and then he says it again, and it still sounds the same and so I have to ask again. And then he says olfactory – o-l-f-a-c-t-o-r-y, pertaining to the sense of smell, and that sensory hypersensitivity and overload are common as a characteristic feature of Asperger Syndrome.

I don't really know what he's talking about but then he says he believes it can equally be the case in Foetal Alcohol Spectrum Disorders and do I not experience any sensorially triggered reactions. I don't say anything because of still not understanding, and mostly I'm just looking at him without any words in my mouth, but not wanting him to think I'm a stupid No-Brain Nicely. He says: 'Being affected by sound or smell or taste or touch or visual stimulus. Hypersensitivities? Such as clothing labels against your skin or loud noises or certain sounds or . . .'

'Flipping lights.' This is me. Because I think I've understood, and also I've remembered about me. I hate lights that go on and off and on and off. Which is flipping and flashing. And they make me want to hum and bang my head. And even now, just thinking about it, even without the lights doing the on and off thing, just remembering the way it feels, it makes me want to do a bit of shouting. And I don't like labels very much, only nice clothes that are soft. And my mum, Jenny Nicely, buys my clothes from charity shops mostly, because they're softer than the ones from the new shops. And she cuts out all the labels, too, so Connor Flynn was right about that, and very clever.

I say, and nothing scratchy. And Connor Flynn says no, he can't wear wool jumpers and how also if he has different coloured food on his plate they can't be touching. A pea can touch a French bean, because of both being green, but not a French bean and a carrot, because of that being an aggravating stimulus and making him have a meltdown. He's still doing a bit of rocking with his hands on his head, but it's while we're walking now, so I don't ask if there's anything wrong, I just let him do it, and Barry is barking and wagging his tail, looking at another dog, which is a border terrier and still a puppy. I let Barry go off the lead for a play, which is very funny because of all the chasing and the happy noises and Barry even rolls over in a whole circle. But when I call his name he comes right back to me.

'. . . if for example it was a box with printing in a certain language, that might tell you something important, or the barcode could contain salient information. It might even pinpoint a particular warehouse or . . .'

I'm listening very hard and I'm having to walk very fast, because of Barry stopping for a sniff by a rubbish bin, and Connor Flynn not waiting for Barry to have his sniff, so now I have to hurry to reach him again, with Barry on his lead and hurrying fast with me too.

Connor Flynn finds it strange that I don't know anything about the box which was left, which was the box with me in it. I've been trying to tell him that it was just a box and so it doesn't really matter, and that what was important was the thing that was inside it, which was a baby, and that was me. But he mostly wants to talk about was it a box for food or for industry or for something else and he mostly wants to know why it has not been a part of the investigation, which was for the police who wanted to find the mummy of the baby, which is me, or of the research, which is me thinking about my book in my head. And it's better than him talking about the protein things and the other pepper things but it still makes me feel a bit like not talking at all, because of not wanting to seem stupid, because of not even knowing about the box I was left in even though it was me who was left and not Connor Flynn. And now, even though Barry is being very sweet with his walking, like jumping and looking up at me, and being a very good boy on his lead and not even pulling at all, in my head there is a feeling that is not very happy.

'. . . freedom of information request regarding the police investigation, of course. But it's also only logical to assume that interested parties would originally have been sent communications at each step of the proceedings. It would have been disclosed to social services, most certainly, and it is highly unlikely that your mother would not have been given all relevant information as part of the adoption process and she's certain to have kept a file. I imagine you have already studied all the documentation?'

The funny thing about Connor Flynn is that although I know he's talking real words to me, they don't go straight into my head, but they sort of get lost in the way from my ears to my brain. Like they're stuck in the jumble and I can't find them when I'm looking. And I know that he's asking me a question, but I don't really know what it is.

But I don't want to say that though. And so I just say yes.

He is doing the piano thing with his fingers, and

his eyes are not looking at me, but sort of towards me and away into a different place. And he says perhaps there was evidence whose importance I overlooked. And I say yes again, because of Connor Flynn waiting for me to say something and because of not knowing what else to say. Hs fingers are moving and moving and it's a bit of time before he speaks and then he says, it's Station Close where I live, isn't it. I say yes, number 23a, and he says and that's just round the corner from his house, just the other side of the park, out of that gate over there . . .

18

Even though my brain knows about my mum, Jenny, being in a hospital with an elephant trunk on her face and all the noises and no change, it is like I don't *really* know it, because after I've unlocked the door, I'm hurrying into the kitchen because I want to introduce Barry the dog to my mum.

'Come on, Barry.' This is me. And I'm walking as fast as I can with him on the lead with his legs moving quickly because of them being so little.

I want to tell her about him being a Yorkie Poo-Shit, and about how good he is, and him walking very well. I don't even slow down in the hallway, just walk very fast and into the kitchen, and smiling. And, flip a pancake, even when I see that there's no Mum there, just the chair and it's empty, apart from a yellow cardigan on the back, and the table, and the cooker with no saucepan, even then I'm thinking that she should be here, saying, hello my Hope. And a bit of my brain is wondering why she's not. I'm looking around and in my throat it's a bit like squeezing and my breath is a bit noisy and feeling-it-in-my-lungs like running up the stairs.

It smells just normal. There's the cardigan on the chair and it's my mum's. It's her big yellow cardigan and it smells like tangerines and cinnamon. It smells like Jenny Nicely, my mum. And even though it's babyish to cry, that's what I'm doing.

Connor Flynn is standing just inside the kitchen door, leaning on the door frame. He's saying, where do we keep our important papers, and about reports and adoption certificates and archives. I can't really say anything back to him because of the crying. So he waits for me and I'm counting – one, two, three – one, two, three – but it's not working because I'm crying even harder, with my nose all runny and having to wipe it on the back of my hand because of Mum not being here to give me a tissue. I'm not shouting or banging my head, just doing the sobbing and the history thing, the . . . historics – and Connor Flynn is staying where he is and just doing the flicking-moving with his fingers and not talking, just eyes going left, right, up, down and everywhere but not at me.

'Maybe in the study, if you have one?' This is him.

We don't have a study because of it being just a little flat and because of working in a bookshop not paying millions of pounds, more's the pity. And I don't mean to shout but I do shout, quite loud. 'No, we don't.' And I shout even louder. 'Can't you see I'm crying?' Because it's not very nice to just keep on flicking your fingers and moving your eyes and asking about having a study when someone else is crying. I'm moaning now and rocking. Backwards. Forwards.

Connor Flynn turns his head so it's towards me now, even his eyes, although they still look like they want to be in all the corners instead. He says, I'm very sorry you're crying.

For a little bit, neither of us says anything else. I'm holding the yellow cardigan and I'm cuddling it in my arms, with it up to my nose so I can smell its Mum-ness. And Connor Flynn and I are looking at each other a bit. His eyes are like his brother, Danny Flynn's eyes, which is a colour that is a little bit green and a little bit grey, and eyelashes and eyebrows that are a colour like sand, or maybe Rich Tea biscuits or just a little bit Ginger Nuts.

He does a thing with his mouth that is a bit like a smile but not turning up at the sides enough to be a real one. And he's still looking at me. Except not quite so much with his eyes.

'Maybe I should make us a nice cup of tea.' This is me. I'm starting to say it because I'm very good at making tea, that's what my mum says – Hope, my darling, you do make a *lovely* cuppa, except for one time when I forgot about the milk not going in the kettle, but that was a long time ago, and we have a new kettle now. Really I am still very good at making it, and it's because of squeezing the teabag against the side of the cup before I take it out – and a nice cup of tea makes everything better. But just as I'm starting to say this, Connor Flynn is talking too, with his eyes gone away.

'Perhaps there are filing cabinets in one of the other rooms . . . ?'

On my mum's desk there is a pile of books. One is a ginormous dictionary and its name is Collins. And there's another book called *Roget's Thesaurus*, which is not quite so big. It's yellow. I don't know what it's about but maybe a dinosaur. And there's poetry and poetry and poetry and poetry, by people called Maya Angelou and Seamus Heaney and *An Anthology* and Grace Nichols and Rupi Kaur and also called Jenny Nicely who is my mum. There's a bowl too, with big hoopy earrings and bracelets and keys. There's also a photograph in a silver frame and it's Jenny Nicely, with a big smile on her face and the bluest dress in the world, which is at Oxfam now, because of putting on a few pounds, and there's me, standing in front of her, with her hands on my shoulders. My hair is in bunches and I'm holding an ice cream which has sprinkles and a flake and we're on holiday but I can't remember what the place is called. There were sandcastles – although not for me because of sand making my fingers and toes feel scratchy – and fish-n-chips, and kites and a pony and a seagull that stole a doughnut out of my hand, and a house with a maze. In the photo, I'm staring up at my mum and at the sky, and I'm laughing.

I want her to be here so much. It's like tummy ache.

'This looks right.' This is Connor Flynn.

On one side of the desk, its legs are just legs, like a table or chair, but not a person or a dog. On the other side there are no legs underneath at all, but a cupboard instead and it has three drawers. The top one has a postcard taped on it, with my mum's writing, saying *Poems, etc.* The bottom one says *Finances, etc.* The one in the middle says *Personal, etc.*, and this is the one that Connor Flynn is pulling open now and looking through with his fingers. He's talking, but not really to me, I don't think, because of it being so quiet, like he's whispering it to himself really: employment contract, marriage certificate, decree nisi, absolute, passport, rental agreement . . .

On my lap, Barry is wriggling, because I think he wants to be on the floor running around. But I don't let him jump down. I'm holding him, with my arms tight, and in my head I'm counting – one, two, three – one, two, three.

I don't know if it's a rule, but in my brain I'm thinking that it should be my mum, Jenny Nicely, who is sitting at her desk and saying, ah, yes, this is more like it, *Adoption file* and *Hope's stuff*. And even if it's not a rule, being in my mum's room without her in here too, and Connor Flynn putting all her papers on the desk and turning them over as he's reading, going, interesting, interesting, ah, I see, it is making my head itch. It's making me feel squeezed and tight. I'm thinking a thing which is not very good, because it's that I want to hit Connor Flynn. I want to bang his head down against the desk and yell and shout and scream and maybe even punch and kick. But I mustn't do it, because of keeping our hands and feet to ourselves and hurting other people being bad. And also because of research being valuable. But I'm thinking how he should not be here, and how rude that he did not even want a cup of tea.

One-two-three, one-two-three. I'm humming a little bit, too.

'Adoption, adoption, adoption, adoption, Interesting. Social workers' report. Original newspaper cuttings. Preliminary . . . adoption ruling, and . . . Ah, look, a box of stuff for you, called: *Hope Nicely, My Life*. Mostly photographs.'

Barry is moving his paws now, pressing against my arms, with his claws digging. They're scratching me. And it's like I want to shout, and the claws are going scratch, scratch, scratch, and in my brain, it's like there's scratching there too. Scratch, scratch, scratch on my arms and in my head, but the shout is still not coming.

'Letter from caseworker; letter from lawyer; results from . . . that's curious . . .'

Connor Flynn has his back to me and he's not even talking to me. He's not even turning round to say, guess what, Hope, this is research and it's all about you – about you and not about me, so really I should be telling you and not just mumbling to myself, like it's my own life and my own story and my own book.

One-two . . . Barry is pushing and wriggling and whining a bit. I don't think he wants me holding him anymore but *I* want to hold him. His claws are making scratches on me. I'm going to scream. And

I'm going to kick Connor Flynn. I can't help it. I *need* to scream. And I *need* to kick. But just as I'm standing up, and getting ready to run at him, yelling, yelling, yelling, he says a thing, and the kicky anger inside is gone.

'Were you aware of communications from somebody claiming to be your biological parent? Or of a request for contact?'

I'm on my feet, with my mouth open for the yell, and even with one foot ready for giving him a big kick. I'm holding Barry so tight, with my arms hugging him, even though he's moving and scratching a lot, because I don't want him to be hurt. But now I'm just standing. And still my mouth is open, but the noise is gone out of it and it's just a silent mouth now, with my eyes even wider. And in my brain it's like when you're listening to a language of people on the bus, like French or Spanish or the other one, which is what all the builders talk, and you're trying so hard to understand but it's not making real sense.

'Of a meeting arranged? Let me see, is there a date here . . . ?'

There is a place in the woods where I walk with the dogs on my dog-walking days, and it's a very funny place, because when you call one of their names – like Humpty or Tinie or Scooby – you can hear your voice shouting, like it's saying it back to you. And that's called an echo. So when I shout out Humpty, there's another shout *Humpty* straight after, and it's really an echo which is me, coming back. And now in my head, it's like an echo. *Biological parent . . . biological parent . . . biological parent; contact . . . contact . . . contact.*

19

Even in my dumb old jumble head, I know that this is important. I know I should be asking a question now, but it's like there are so *many* questions and they're all fighting because they all want to be the first one to come out. And so I'm saying nothing, but with my mouth open, and Barry in my arms going whine, scratch, whine, wriggle, because of wanting to be down on the floor and running around. And I say, shh, because I'm trying to make my head think and to make the echo and all the questions be quiet.

'. . . interesting that this is here because your recollection is of there being no connection whatsoever between you and . . .'

Like pressure in my head. Like noise. All the questions and Barry yelping and Connor Flynn with his talking that doesn't quite make sense. I want to put my hands around my ears but I can't because of having to hold Barry tight to stop him scratching and pushing. There is a thing. Like something in a deep hole. In my brain. And the echoes. There is a thing. A big, big thing. But I don't know what.

'I don't think we should do any more research now.' This is me. I'm shouting, over the barking and the noise in my head. 'I want to go now. I think we need to wait. My mum will tell us about it. My mum, Jenny Nicely, when she's better. Because she'll know all . . .'

'But, as I keep saying, statistically, the chances of your mother recovering with full mental capacity, following an out-of-hospital cardiac arrest without immediate resuscitation are small. Death or a vegetative state are the more probable outcomes because of—'

The yell is back. In my mouth. The big angry yell that went away is right back. There's a thud, which is Barry landing on the floor as I let him go. I'm squeezing my hands into balls. And I'm yelling and I'm jumping onto Connor Flynn with my hands punching and my feet kicking and my mouth yelling and yelling and yelling. And, although I'm not very big, I don't think he was expecting it, because he's knocked forward off the chair – which is one on wheels and made out of leather – and his head is banging onto my mum, Jenny's, desk. And all the books – all the poems and the dictionary and the dinosaur one – are falling onto the floor, going crash, crash, crash.

I'm screaming – *you don't know anything. You're a stupid man, you're a rotten No-Brain.* And I'm yelling. *I hate you.* And I'm screaming. *My mum is going to be right as rain.* And I'm shouting *shit, fuck, liar, cunt* and all the things that are golden rules to never say. I'm kicking with my feet and pushing my hands onto Connor Flynn's head, and it's going knock, knock, knock against the desk. But the photograph is still standing up, with me smiling up at my mum with my ice cream, just the frame shaking, each time I hit him. For a while, Connor Flynn doesn't even move or do anything. He just stays very still while I punch and kick, and knock, knock, knock.

After a bit I stop hitting so much, but he's still not doing anything so I just stand there, waiting, for quite a long time, until Connor Flynn tries to stand up. But maybe he hasn't noticed about the chair which has fallen over and is just one wheel sticking up behind his leg, because he sort of does a stumble-trip over the wheel and he's falling backwards and knocking me back down too.

The bed is just behind the desk and that is where I land, with my hands still in balls and with Connor Flynn landing on top of me, with his legs pressing down on my legs and then his body on me, and he's taller than me so his shoulders are on my head. My head is squashed on the side, with my nose in his T-shirt, and I can hear his heart going bumbum bumbum bumbum bumbum right in my ear. Connor Flynn smells of washing powder and soap, which is quite clean and fresh, like in the adverts, and he's too heavy for me to do anything, but not so heavy that it hurts. It's quite comfortable and warm, really, with him on top of me now. And – I don't know why I'm doing this, maybe because of my arms being the only bit of me that I can move – I put my arms around Connor Flynn, so that I'm holding onto him. I keep them there, not really squeezing him, just around him until my hands are touching each other on his chest, a bit like a hug, although I don't always like hugs, even from my mum, but I want to do this now, I don't know why, and in my ear I can hear bumbum bumbum bumbum bumbum and a whoosh noise which is him breathing, and on my cheek is his T-shirt and in my nose is the clean washing smell.

But then he jumps up, like he's in a hurry to be not lying on me anymore. And he nearly falls over the chair again, because of it being on the floor, but he manages to put his hand down on the desk, and stay standing. He's facing away, not at me, and he puts his hands over his ears and I think he's talking to himself. He's rocking a little bit, like with his shoulders and head going up and down.

'Are you OK?' This is me, because I don't know what he's doing. I don't think I've hurt him because I'm not really very big. But he doesn't reply to me so I say it again.

It's a little while before he says anything. Maybe he has to stop rocking first or maybe, in his head, he's trying to find the thing to say, and maybe it's a bit of a muddle like a jumble sale. So I wait, except for asking him again one or two or three times.

'I . . .' He's still doing a little bit of rocking but very slowly now, like he's standing up more straight. And he's facing me, but not with his eyes quite looking at me. '. . . do not like being touched. It makes me anxious.'

In my head I want to shout at him that it was his fault because of it being him who fell onto me, but I'm telling myself that it's good not to shout, and it's good not to tell people when they do bad things, which is not really a golden rule but it's a good thing to know and I've practised it with my mum, Jenny Nicely. And she would be proud of me now, because I don't even tell him it at all, not even whispering very quietly. I don't say anything. Nothing.

'Why did you hit me?' This is Connor Flynn and I'm a bit surprised by him asking, because I'm not thinking about hitting and kicking anymore. I've sort of forgotten about doing it at all, even if it wasn't very long ago, like just a minute or two maybe. I don't really know what to say to him, but he asks me again.

'Why did you hit me?'

'I don't know. I just wanted to.'

He's stopped rocking now. He's looking at his fingers. He says he understands. And then he's quiet.

'What do you understand?'

'A typical psychophysiological response pattern. Excitatory neurotransmitters responding to emotional stimulus and creating aggression through hormone secretion and muscle contraction. Neuropeptides facilitate the pathway between mind and body. We should go home now.'

I'm still just looking at him with his words in my head being more like French or Spanish or one of the other languages that I don't understand.

Barry puts his nose between my knees, with his tail wagging, like he thinks it's time to go.

'It's 11.56 and it will take us two minutes to walk back. Lunch is at twelve o'clock. We need to leave now.'

6

COMMON PITFALLS

20

'Hope Nicely! Good to see you. G&T later?' This is
Veronica Ptitsky. She is the first person waiting outside
the room, in the reception, and me and Danny Flynn
are the next ones to come in. She's doing a big smile
and waving one hand at me, like she's very happy
that I'm here. In her other hand she's holding a coffee
which says *Starbucks* and there's a red splodge on the
white plastic cover over the hole. I think it's because
of lipstick. Her hair is yellower than it was last time,
and shorter. But still frizzy.

'G&T is gin and tonic?'

'Yes, of course.'

'I don't drink gin and tonic.'

'No, of course you don't. So, just the tonic like
before, T and no G, remember? Or a Coke perhaps.
Or a Sprite. Or whatever you'd like to drink. Will
you come?'

'If Danny Flynn does.'

Now she's doing a funny face, like a surprised one, maybe, with her eyes very wide and her eyebrows going high into her forehead and her mouth a bit open like it's saying, Oh. And she's looking at Danny Flynn and saying to him, well that *is* a surprise and so much for her intuitions, because she'd rather assumed that . . .

And he's saying, no, no, it's just that Hope's mum has been poorly so she's been staying with his family. And Veronica Ptitsky says she's sorry to hear it and she hopes it's nothing too serious. And I say there's been no change but not to worry. I don't say about her maybe being vegetive, maybe. That means like being asleep, except without the ever waking up. Connor Flynn told me, although with different words, like maybe neuro and activity, and maybe about electric. But I don't say it to Veronica Ptitsky anyway, with any words. I say not to worry, she'll be right as rain soon.

Then it's silent, with Veronica Ptitsky drinking her coffee, until Susan Ford – I still remember her name, easy-peasy, because it's like my teaching assistant and like my car too – comes in. She doesn't have a coffee, just a handbag and a shopping bag, which is from Marks and Spencer, and she says hello everyone, how have we been. And the next one to come is Peter Potter with his nice voice which is saying, hello again, folks, and he's carrying a book by John le Carré, and then Jamal – not Jam Al – whose other name I can't remember, but who is writing a book about a vampire, and then maybe Stephen, maybe Simon, who wrote about a party in the dark and who is wearing a hospital uniform, like the pyjama ones, and carrying a big bag with a strap over his shoulder. And I'm looking at him hard.

'Do you work at the hospital?' This is me, asking. It's because of the uniform. He has to turn his head because he had gone past me already when I said it.

'Sometimes.' He doesn't look very sure. His eyes are looking all round, like he's being Connor Flynn and doesn't want to look at me.

And I'm still looking at him very hard, but still he doesn't look back. He just says: 'Better go and get changed out of this quickly before we start. Excuse me.'

I don't really want him to go because I want to ask him if he's been with my mum – Jenny Nicely – because of her being in the hospital too, and if he knows when there's going to be any change so that she can be right as rain again and come home quickly. But I can't ask because he's gone too fast and because Peter Potter's talking to me now, and saying Danny's been explaining about my difficult week and he hopes

I'm coping all right, and if there's anything he can do . . . And then the other woman is coming in, and she has a coffee too, but not a Starbucks, hers is in a cup which has a leaf pattern on it and no name. And her hair is *so* long. Almost at her bottom. Kelly Shell-y Bell-y. That's it.

Now the lift doors are opening again and the man with all the neck scarves and the funny name is coming out. I can't see if he has a new one on his neck or not, because of his big coat, which goes down to his knees and has big black buttons. He has a hat, too, which he takes off now, as he's saying hello all. And he says hello Peter and hello Daniel and hello Veronica and Susan and Kelly, hello Jamal, but not the hospital man, who is maybe Stephen and maybe Simon, because of him being in the toilets now, changing out of his uniform, and not me. He just gives me a little nod that is almost not moving his head at all. So I think maybe he doesn't remember what my name is.

'My name is Hope.'

He's talking to Susan Ford now, asking her if that concert was good and he saw it had good reviews, and such a marvellous conductor, and I don't think he's heard me so I tell him again and this time louder, to make sure.

'My name is Hope.'

And he turns his head to me and says: 'I think we *all* know what your name is.'

It's lucky, really, me living with Danny Flynn this week, with my mum in the hospital, otherwise I'd just be watching *Coronation Street* or *Pets' Hospital* and would have forgotten all about the writing group. Me and my jumble head. We were eating tea, which was shepherd's pie, or mince and mash for those that like that best, which was Connor Flynn, and it was very nice, except when Connor Flynn did a bit of moaning because of some peas being in the wrong place which was in the mince and not with the other peas, and his mum Bridget had to say, look no harm done I'm taking them out now, and then Danny Flynn said, sorry, Mum, but Hope and I will have to skip pud, because we have a writing group meeting tonight. And Bridget said, oh, she thought that was Wednesdays – which is what I thought too, except not really remembering which day – and he said yes, it is Wednesdays, but this is a special session because an editor is coming to talk to us about what she looks for in a book. And he said, oh Hope, had I forgotten because Marnie Shale had told us about it in the last group. I didn't remember at all but when

I looked in my blue notebook it was written in my own writing, not joined-up but quite neat, *Extra group. Friday 7.30pm. Patsy Blake from*

I haven't finished writing where Patsy Blake is from, so maybe my brain was going for a little walk or I didn't hear it right. But now it is Friday and it is 7.30 p.m. and I'm sitting at the table which is round but a bit longer, and Marnie Shale is telling us that this is Patsy Blake, and we're all saying hello. She's quite old with hair that is white on the inside, and more yellow on the outside, and lipstick that is going into the lines around her mouth and when she talks her voice is deep and like sore throats. She tells us what she does, which is being an editor at a publisher, and I write down the name of it – and it is Marnie Shale's publisher and she is Marnie Shale's editor – and she's also talking to us about all the other places where she has worked. And she's talking about the other side of the coin, and us having to think about the story and the writing and the art and her having to think about the sales and the bottom line and the commercial potential.

'The next bestseller.' This is her. 'That's what we're searching for.'

And then the scarf man – except this week it's like a fat tie, but still with a big knot and squares on it which are yellow and orange – he's saying, well, in his personal experience his own editor always says that publishing is a game of . . .

I might have to count. To stop me shouting. Because of his voice. Because of the way he talks. But I'm not going to shout. No way, no way, no way. I'm sitting on my hands.

When my mum, Jenny Nicely, took me to the zoo, in the place where there were seagulls who stole doughnuts and a huge house with a maze, we went to the zoo-house which was full of the animals which are a name I've forgotten but it's mostly got lots and lots of snakes. I don't like snakes, because of them being slippery and killing people, but I looked at them and watched them moving, with their bodies all long and slithering. His voice makes me feel like the snakes made me feel. This is why I have to sit on my hands and tell myself no shouting, not even a little bit.

'. . . of course we all appreciate sales are key, but what is one to do if the publicity side is . . . ?'

I'm not rocking, or banging my head or shouting, but I'm having to squeeze my hands shut, even with them being under my legs. I'm squeezing them so tight that I'm squashing my thumbs. But the snake feeling is getting worse. I might have to shout now. But then there is a hand on my arm, and it's Danny Flynn. And I look to the side, and his eyes, which are a bit green and a bit grey and very like his brother's eyes, are looking back at me and he does a little smile. And it's like the snakes are gone and now it's a nice animal feeling, maybe one of those monkeys with tiny hands and big eyes, or maybe a panda or a rabbit, but that's in a different zoo. I smile back at him and I let my hands be not so tight and bring them out from under my legs, and write some things in my notebook again.

Danny Flynn's hand and his smile did that.

When he came back from work today he gave a kiss to Bridget and said, evening Mum, and then one to me too – on my cheek – and said, and good evening to you, Miss Nicely. He didn't give a kiss to Connor Flynn, just a sort of pat on his shoulder, but hardly at all because Connor Flynn doesn't like other people touching him, and said, all right you?

I've never had a boyfriend before – only the vodka ones with their hands under my clothes, and that doesn't count and if it ever happens again, I have to tell my mum and even the police – so I don't know how you are supposed to know if somebody is one. A boyfriend, I mean. Maybe they have to tell you, but maybe not: maybe you're meant to already know. I don't know about all the other things either, like the dates in restaurants and maybe flowers and having some rows but then making up and being in the rain but saying is it raining, you didn't notice it was raining. And having a song which is called our tune and which is special. And also doing you-know-what, which is fucking.

Maybe Danny Flynn will ask me to marry him and give me a diamond ring, and then I would be Mrs Flynn. Except that's not even right, only in olden times like *Downton Abbey*. Because now women aren't anybody's thing – that word, there's a word which is wrong – so I could be Ms and still be Nicely. I think that's what I will do. Or maybe Danny could be Mr Danny Nicely, because that would be a good name and maybe he'd like it. Or we could be double bubbles like my boss Karen – because of having married Darren Jones and now she is Karen Jennings-Jones and not just Karen Jennings anymore. If Danny Flynn and I were double bubble I'd be Ms Nicely-Flynn.

Possessions. Bingo! That's what women aren't. Not anymore. When my mum was married, before she had to tell him to sling his hook because of him being a bad news bear, she was still Jenny Nicely. That's because of being a feminist, which is the best thing to be, and because who'd want to be called Jenny Pratt anyway?

'. . . keep sight of the bestseller potential, though of course we have to genuinely love the work.

However, from the writer's point of view, the only focus can be . . .'

While the woman with the throaty voice, Patsy Blake, talks, she is looking around with her eyes and watching very hard and while she is saying this, she is looking right at me so now I'm making a face which is serious, like I'm thinking only about writing and books and not at all about marrying Danny Flynn. I'm writing in my notebook, although not real sentences, just words like *work* and *focus*. I'm even nodding my head to show that I'm listening very hard.

'. . . through an agent, which generally will iron out some of the most common pitfalls that authors tend to fall into.'

'What are the most common pitfalls?' This is the man called Jamal. He's tapping his pen on the desk, like a woodpecker going peck peck peck, and I'm glad when he stops because it annoys my ears.

'Well, as I say, most publishers will only look at work submitted by agents, so, really, this will generally have been remedied before it reaches our desks, but I would say the mistake made the most frequently by writers is to not understand what your book is really *about*. What I need is the one-line sell that will have me so intrigued I just have to read on, but I also want a glimpse of what is at the very heart of your story, and too often, in my experience, the author has a complicated, intricate plot, but no real sense of what it's working for – of what the book is, at its essence, *about*.'

'Sorry. Can you give us examples of what you mean?' This is Veronica Ptitsky.

'OK. So. Your book. Pitch it to me.'

'Oh God. Put me on the spot.' Veronica Ptitsky is laughing and putting her hand to her forehead. 'Right. *Champing* is accessible LGBTQ erotica, set across the class divides of the world of stables and horse racing.'

'Perfect.' This is Patsy Blake. 'So you've given me the environment and I can see a definite commercial potential. That's the pitch. But you've not told me what the actual—'

'There's no Q.' It's not proper interrupting because I need to tell Veronica Ptitsky that she's made a mistake, so it's helping in fact, though really she should know it better than me, as it's where she comes from. And I should have my hand up really, to show that I have something to say, but I always forget that.

Everybody's looking at me now and the knot man is doing a thing with his eyes, like they're looking at the ceiling, and I think his mouth is saying *for heaven's sake* but not with noise.

'I'm sorry.' Patsy Blake is looking at me too, but doing a different thing with her eyes, like the eyebrows are coming down to try to touch them. 'What queue? I was merely asking your classmate . . .'

'Lgbt. There's no Q. *Lgbt*. It's only spelt LGBT.'

'Hope.' It's Veronica Ptitsky and she's reaching across the desk and putting a hand on my arm, with nails that are painted red, except sparkly. 'Q means queer. Lesbian, Gay, Bisexual, Trans – and Queer. LGBT. LGBTQ. It doesn't really matter. It's just . . .'

Lesbian is when women like to do you-know-what with other women. Gay is when men like to do it with other men, but lesbians can be gay too, although men-gays aren't lesbians, only women-gays. I'm not sure about bisexual but I think it's being gay and lesbian at the same time so you can do you-know-what with everybody. Trans is what they're always talking about on the news, and when my mum Jenny Nicely's listening to *Women's Hour*, they're always saying about it, and it's what Hayley Cropper was in *Coronation Street* but that was a very long time ago, when not so many people wanted to do it. I think queer is just like gay, but maybe ruder because it's what the boys at school used to shout to other boys when they were being not very polite to them.

I'm still thinking about this, and I'm wondering what it's like in Lgbt with all the community doing you-know-what, all the men with the men, and the women with the women, and the bisexuals with all of them. Maybe they have to wear big fluffy hats with flaps on their ears, because of it being so cold. But maybe I've got that wrong, because Veronica Ptitsky is from America, too, not just Russia, only her name, so maybe they're wearing bikinis and eating ginormous burgers in Lgbt. I don't think I could live there, because of not being a real lesbian, just only once, and that wasn't a proper one, just because of me wanting to touch her big boobies to see what they felt like, and her – Tessa in class 10C – calling me a sick lezza, and pulling my hair and punching me until I cried. But now I know we have to keep our hands and our feet to ourselves. It's a golden rule which I've practised zillions of times with my mum, Jenny Nicely, so I'm definitely not a lesbian anymore.

'. . . when you boil it right down is about identity and belonging.'

'And there was me thinking it was because of the sex.'

'Sex sells, absolutely. But why was this book – this trilogy – such a runaway sensation, why did all those millions of women connect with this book in such a fashion when, traditionally, this is such a difficult genre? It's not the dialogue or the characters and the plot. What every reader identified with was that sense of a search for belonging. That's the universal that hooked them . . .'

'Along with the multiple orgasms?'

'Well, yes.' They're both laughing.

'Who else?' The woman called Patsy Blake is looking at me again. 'What about your book?'

'It's about me. It's my autobiography. It's non-fiction.'

'OK. And what's it *really* about?'

'It's *really* about me. It's going to find my birth mother and then she'll have to tell me why she made me like this, by drinking lots of G&Ts with me in her tummy. And why she left me in a cardboard box. It will change my life and give me closure.'

'*Interesting!*' She's leaning forward towards me as she says this, with a big smile and showing her teeth, which are not as white as snow. And her eyes are watching me and so are everyone else's – except for Stephen, or maybe Simon, and he's looking out of the window, with a hand over his mouth like he's maybe yawning – and the man with the knots, and he's looking up at the ceiling with his mouth in a straight line and his arms crossed.

'That sounds a *fascinating* book. Again, what this sounds like to me, though, if you don't mind my saying so, is a search for truth and identity. I'd be genuinely eager to read the submission if that landed on my desk. Anyone else?'

And now it's Lu-do-vic-knot-man and he's talking about his emperor and all the murders and how it's Dan Brown meets Virgil, which he's said before, and how he's been published before, though only ac-a-de-mia, which he's said before too, actually, and the Patsy Blake woman is saying 'Interesting' again, but it's not as loud as when she said it to me and she's not leaning right over the desk, but just sitting back, with a pen in her fingers, like a wand or a fork. 'But we all experience coincidences. They do really happen.'

This is the first time Stephen/Simon has said anything in the whole class. And it's about pitfalls, which mean mistakes that writers make and that make their books not so good. And I've been listening very hard, with my brain being sharp and focused, taking in almost everything, and I think it's because of being so happy about my book being *interesting* and also remembering the word closure. But I'm wondering if I should have put my hand on Danny Flynn's arm when Patsy Blake was talking to him and saying she wasn't sure he'd quite communicated what his book was actually *about*, beyond the setting and the characters and their actions – what it was that gave the dystopian plot a real sense of meaning.

Where is the love? That's what she asked him. *Where's the pain? The life, the death, the driving force? An aching quest not just for a move up to the sunshine, but for what? Where is the beating heart of your book?* He's been sitting there ever since, with his elbow on the table, and his chin on his hand.

But now it's Simon Taylor who's talking, or Stephen maybe, and it's about coincidences, and that they really do happen. And it's funny, because I'm remembering about his story, about being in the room, in the dark, with the person, who had the same name as the girl in my school, who was sent away because of throwing a chair, and also the social worker, who only came once and who brought me a teddy that was actually a monkey. And that's two coincidences, but I don't say it. Because the woman – Patsy Blake – is already answering, so it would be interrupting. So maybe I'll say it to him another time.

'Of course they do. You're right. My husband's parents moved to England from South Africa in the 1960s when he was little, and they lost contact with the rest of their family. So, fast-forward sixty-odd years and when my daughter was backpacking in America a few years ago, she ended up sitting next to another young woman on a Greyhound bus and they started chatting. This woman was South African, and on holiday, and my daughter told her that she had South African blood and the other woman asked what her name was, and then this other woman said, oh, Blake, that was her mother's maiden name. It turned out that her grandfather was the brother of my father-in-law, and so these two women on the bus, these strangers, were actually second cousins. Here they were, both thousands of miles away from home. What are the odds of that, do you think? So yes, coincidences do happen in real life. But you know what they say – *you couldn't make it up*? Well, that's the thing. In literature, coincidences come across as contrived and, as writers, you must beware that they don't give your reader cause to question. The thing is, fiction must be more believable, more *real* than life.'

'But what about . . . ?' This is Susan Ford now. She's not interrupting because Patsy Blake has finished what she was saying. Susan Ford is talking about Dickens, who is the writer who wrote *A Christmas Carol*, which is about not being mean or making people stay at work late and not ever giving them more money, and also *Great Expectations*, which is what she is talking about now. And Patsy Blake is replying, and it's yes, yes, but in her whispery, croaky voice and I'm trying to keep on concentrating, but it's like my head has been working so hard and now it wants to slow down and have a little bit of time on its own, without all the thinking. And so while all the words and the names, like Pip and Magwitch and Miss Havisham and stretched and implausible, are coming into my ears, my brain is not wanting them to come all the way in, just to leave them outside in my ears.

For a little while, I'm just looking at the faces: at Marnie Shale's nodding, like it's so important, with her hair bouncing, and at Veronica Ptitsky who's writing very fast with a pen that's pink and shiny, and sometimes putting it in her mouth, and at Simon/Stephen who is not in his nurse uniform anymore, but in a T-shirt which has a picture of a soldier in a helmet, and on the helmet it says *Meat Is Murder.* And when I look at him, he is already looking at me and then hurries his eyes away as soon as he sees that I've seen him. But especially I'm looking at Patsy Blake, with her not very white teeth and her eyes which make lots of wrinkles when she's about to say something else. But inside my head, it's not really worrying about the Dickens and the Hardy and the bringing it into our own writing, it's just having a bit of a well-earned rest and listening to all the voices, without caring what they mean.

For a little while, there are no proper thoughts inside my head, just the noise without the meaning. But then the thoughts are coming, without me even wanting them, and they're my memories, from earlier, which are back in my brain. It's Julie Clarke's voice – that's the accent from the place, and she's my social worker, except not anymore because she's retired now, and it's in Jamaica, with long stretchy words – and her voice is asking how is everything and how am I, and am I finding it OK being with Danny Flynn's family. I'm saying fine, fine, fine, and not saying about punching and kicking Connor Flynn or even about the filing cabinet. That's not really a lie, it's just a not-telling because she didn't ask anyway. And I didn't say about Danny Flynn being maybe my boyfriend because I'd forgotten about that.

And in my head, I'm hearing Julie Clarke – Kingston, that's where her voice is from – and it's her saying maybe if I'd rather, about how her grandson could stay with friends, or about the other social worker whose name will come to me any minute, and being able to sort something out, or about finding other families, and nobody's forcing me to do anything. And – this is still in my head, because outside of it are all the writing group people talking about what makes the reader *truly connect*, but inside my head are the memories and it was earlier today, like about three or four in the a.m. or the p.m., the afternoon one, not the morning one – I'm thinking about me telling Julie Clarke that I liked being with Danny Flynn's family, and telling her about Barry and what a very good dog he is, and about Danny Flynn's mum being a good cook and very kind too and about Connor Flynn being very clever but not liking to smell dog poo.

And then there are other things that she was saying, but my memory, oh my goodness . . . It's about my mum and about the doctors and about them using cooling to make her head colder because of it being better for her brain. And something about oxygen and about what the doctors hope, but I can't quite remember what.

We saw my mum, Jenny, and I sort of forgot. I wanted her to be sitting up in bed with a cup of tea, saying hello my Hope, look, here I am, right as rain again. But she wasn't. And there was a doctor and his name . . . I can't quite remember but his accent was from maybe India, because of not sounding like Harpenden at all, and because of him having a bit of that sort of skin, too.

I think maybe I yelled. I don't think I did any kicking, so that's good. But I remember Julie saying, it's OK, Hope. And saying, I don't want to worry you, it's just something we need to think about. And saying did I understand. And asking about if my mum, if Jenny Nicely, had any other family, and saying it won't come to that, but . . . And saying about not having to even consider any of this yet.

She doesn't have any other family, my mum, Jenny. Just me. Her parents are dead – they were hippies with itchy feet – and she doesn't have any brothers or sisters. And she married a bad news bear and the day she divorced him was a joyful day. But now she has me and adopting me was the best thing she ever did and I am everything she needs.

'. . . one of the greatest pieces of European literature of all time, but to say you have to suspend your disbelief when Prince Andrei ends up in a hospital bed next to . . .'

In my head, I can see my mum, Jenny Nicely, and she's in her hospital bed with the elephant mask, and it's not where she should be. She should be at home, in our flat in Station Close, with her yellow cardigan on, and making something nice for tea, which is smelling yummy and ready for me to come home to eat, and with her arms wide and ready and open.

And in my head I can hear more voices, like they're all saying something to me. I can hear Connor Flynn, and he's saying, *likely that if she survives, she will be in a vegetative* . . . I can hear the doctor, with the Indian name, and he's saying, *lack of oxygen before the commencement of CPR is a concern but until* . . . I can hear Julie Clarke and she's saying, *sure it won't come to that, but* . . . And, in my head, it's like I'm trying to shout over them, saying, *she's going to be right – as – rain.* And it's like in my head I'm putting my hands over my ears because I don't want to listen to them. But I can still hear it and now I'm putting my real hands over my real ears. But it's all still there: *vegetative . . . lack of oxygen . . . come to that . . .*

There is a word that I know, because of poems, and having been to school, and having a teacher in RE which is religious education, who liked to make us know things. The teacher was Mrs McMurchy and the word is revelation. It means when there's a thing that you understand but only suddenly, and you haven't done before, and it's just, like, all in one moment and then it's there, and you can see it, even though you didn't think you could. It's like a big fat bingo. And this is what is happening to me. A revelation. All of a sudden, it's in my head, and it's obvious and I can't make it go away.

My mum might not ever be right as rain again.

It hurts inside my body, in the bit where my heart is. And my tummy.

She might not ever wake up, with her big smile and her arms open and wide. She might just stay there, with the elephant mask and the noises. She might be vegetive or she might be dead.

'Hope? Are you OK?'

The chair makes a big bang on the floor. I have to push past Danny Flynn and then past the next person, who is called maybe Kelly. Kelly Shell-y Bell-y. My chest hurts. It wants to breathe but it can't. I don't say sorry or excuse me, and I don't shut the door behind me. And now I'm kneeling on the floor, in the reception outside, not even under the desk. And I'm banging my head on the floor. I'm crying and it's so noisy, but I can't make it stop.

Now, here are Marnie Shale and Danny Flynn and Veronica Ptitsky, and they're asking what's wrong, what is it – and I can't say anything for a little while, because of all the sobs in my mouth, and my chest not wanting to breathe, but eventually I manage to tell them.

'I want my mum.' My words are all wobbly and not quite right, but I think they can hear them because they're saying, of course, and, oh, poor Hope, and it was a bad idea for me to come, because I must be so worried and confused. Danny Flynn is saying it's his fault, he thought it might be good for me to keep busy. And I'm saying yes, yes, yes, but . . . And I can't manage to say anything more, even though I really want to tell him about it not being his fault at all, because the revelation could have come anywhere, not just here. And now it's not hard to breathe anymore, but it's like I can't stop myself from breathing, but I'm doing it so fast, and it's making so much noise. Marnie Shale has her arm around my shoulder and Veronica Ptitsky is rubbing my other shoulder with her sparkly fingers. And she smells like the bit in Superdrug where all the perfumes are, the test ones which you can spray on your hands, which is nicer than the carpet smell of the floor which is still in my nose from banging my head on it.

'Let's get you home.' This is Danny Flynn. He means his home.

I'm trying to say no. I'm trying to say he should stay for the rest of the group. I'm trying to say sorry. But I can't stop breathing, breathing, breathing, like one of the dogs, when it's hot and they've been running and they have their tongues out going pant, pant, pant.

'I'll take notes of the rest of the class.' This is Veronica Ptitsky. 'I'll record it, too. You won't miss a word. I have your email, Danny, I'll send it over later.'

Veronica Ptitsky likes recording things. She told us in the first writing class about how she records herself talking about her ideas and thoughts, which is her audio notebook, and she records other people, things they're saying that she thinks are interesting or characterful or that might give her inspiration.

She's always pressing buttons on her phone. She takes photos, too. And videos.

'But . . .' I don't want to go home, to Danny Flynn's home. I want to do the writing class and have Patsy Blake tell me again how *interesting* my book sounds, and then go downstairs and see my lovely mum, Jenny Nicely, sitting outside, waiting for me. But Danny Flynn is saying thanks, Veronica, that's very kind, and so is Marnie Shale, and they're giving me hugs and saying I should look after myself, while Danny Flynn is going to collect our bags and coats.

7

THE STILL POINT

21

Barry is snoring, with his head and front paws on the pillow, and I'm pressing my cheek into his fur. He smells like dirty puddles, but I don't mind. I can feel his body going up and down and up and down, and hear his noises and it's tickling my nose. And if I was in a mood for laughing, I would think it was very funny to listen to him, because it's such a very loud noise for a dog who's so little. But in my head it's not a mood for laughing. It's a very sad mood.

Usually Barry sleeps in his basket in the lounge, and isn't allowed in the bedrooms, but Bridget said it was OK, because I'd had a hard day and maybe it would cheer me up a bit, and she could see how devoted Barry was to me and just this once wouldn't hurt. She did say, only in his basket, though, and put it on the floor at the end of the bed, but I don't think Barry wanted to stay in it.

I'm telling my research to Barry. Really I want to

be telling it to my telephone, like Veronica Ptitsky, with her audible notebook. But my phone is not an iPhone like hers is, because of me having had lots of telephones and because of putting them down and forgetting them, and so it's best if they're just old ones from eBay, without a lot of data for doing things like the searching which is called surfing, and no audible notebook at all, just a camera, which is mostly for pictures of dogs. Anyway, my phone is on the desk by the window, and so is my notebook which is a real one, and I don't want to get them, because if I get up then Barry might jump out of the bed, and I like having him with me, like a snoring teddy bear. So I'm just telling him my research instead, and very quietly, because it's very late at night, in fact so late it's the morning, because of being 2.17 which is what it says on the clock by my bed, which is also a radio if I want it to be. But the radio is off now and the light is off and the only noise is me, telling Barry my research, but really whispering because I don't want anyone else to hear.

'I'm not very good at tying knots, so that probably wouldn't work.' This is what I'm telling him. 'Like when my rope came undone last time, and I just hit my knees and hurt my head and I had to talk to Camilla da Silva for months and months, and take all the pills. So that's not the best way, unless I find out how to do the knot better.' I'm thinking about it. Maybe Connor Flynn knows how to tie knots because he seems to know lots of things. He's very clever.

If I had my notebook, I would write it down: *ask Connor Flynn how to tie a knot in a rope that won't come undone.* But instead I just whisper it to Barry and he snores back at me.

This is not research for my book. It is research for something that is very bad. It is so bad that we don't say that it's something you *do*, we say it's something you *commit*. Committing is bad. Like crime and murder. You don't commit good things. You don't commit jobs or love or helping. You don't commit golden rules.

I don't want to commit anything. But now that I've had my revelation, it won't go from my head. Because what if my mum, Jenny, is not right as rain soon? What if she's dead in a box, or vegetive with a brain that's damaged, like mine but not so lucky? What if she's asleep without ever waking up, and what if she can't talk and cook and tell me, hello my Hope, and sweet dreams, and tell me she loves me, and tell me smile brightly, Hope Nicely?

And what I'm thinking is that I wish I didn't have to always be me, stuck in this stupid old jumble head. Because if I wasn't such a No-Brain Nicely, then I would have known how to put air into my mum

Jenny's nose to make it go into her brain. I would have known about the number to call, and it would have been the right one.

Everything would have been all right if I hadn't been such a rubbish person. This is why I'm doing my research – though it's not even proper because it's not from surfing, or books or filing cabinets. And because of not getting out of bed to fetch my notebook or my phone. It's No-Brain research, but I'm doing it because it's important, to help me think. It's called focus. It's planning, which is valuable.

'There is shooting with a gun, where you put it in your mouth.' This is me whispering to Barry. But I don't know anyone who has a gun, and I don't know where they sell them. Or there's poison, like Hayley, who was the letter T, in *Coronation Street*. But that was a long time ago and I'm not sure what sort of poison it was or if you can buy it in normal shops. I don't think you can just go into Superdrug and say please can I have some poison. There's also an overdose, which is a bit the same, and that's just taking pills, so maybe I could do that instead. There are pills in Danny Flynn's bathroom and in my bathroom at home and even in my washbag in the sweet bathroom right here, which are my pills for taking every night, except when I forget because of my mum not being here to tell me.

Maybe Connor Flynn would know how many pills you need to take. Is there a right number, like fifty or a hundred or a hundred and seventy-three?

Now I'm thinking very hard and also trying to remember what I've already said. It's like making a list, which is a good way to focus. There are knots and guns and poison and pills. And I'm thinking, though my brain is feeling a bit tired now, and the radio which is a clock says it is 2.24.

Barry is snoring and I'm feeling like my breathing is wanting to join him. Grrr. Grrr. Grrr. And my eyes are finding it a bit difficult not to be shut. And the words in my head feel like going for a long walk. But I'm remembering another way too. To commit *it*. When I was on the train with my mum, Jenny Nicely, after we'd been to London to go to the museum where there were dinosaur bones and real ones that moved and watched you, we were waiting in the train, without moving, for hours and hours. But the train had to wait for a very sad reason. 'Person on the track,' I tell Barry.

In the morning, I'll write all this down in my blue notebook, with numbers 1, 2, 3, 4, 5.

22

As they came in for the jump, Alissia leant forward, arching her back and raising her body up from the saddle. Her heart galloped in time with Sappho's beating hooves and her breaths came fast, chest rising and falling beneath her tight jacket. Rain pelted down. Alissia could feel it whipping against the skin of her face, the wind tugging her long auburn hair from under her helmet.

Too wet for riding really. She was soaked to the skin. She should turn back. But the blood was pumping through her and she yearned to run Sappho faster still. This was always when she felt most alive, feet in the stirrups, every nerve tingling with adrenalin.

Sappho leapt the fence. In those seconds of effortless motion, Alissia's mind flew free, remembering the vision that had greeted her as she had strode into the stables that morning: long legs and shapely buttocks in tight denim, bending across a hay bale. Then the stranger had straightened and turned and stared right at her. Alissia was used to gazes quickly diverting as people recognised her – she was, after all, the local celebrity: champion jockey, holder of three gold cups. But those eyes had fixed on her own – shining dark irises, framed by long lashes below a jet-black fringe.

'Hello.' Lips pink against smooth, dark skin. 'I'm Devinder. The new stable manager.'

Devinder. Sappho landed. Alissia sat back into the saddle, feeling the pulsating of the mare's rhythm between her thighs. The voice had been soft yet self-assured.

Back in the dry of the stable, Alissia tied up the horse and unbuttoned her jacket. Beneath it, her shirt was soaked transparent. Better get this wet stuff off before she caught cold. The stable hands all knew she liked to be alone after finishing a ride. They knew to wait until the star jockey called them in to see to Sappho. There was a towel on the peg in the corner, for when she arrived back sweaty and needed to rub herself down.

She removed her riding hat, shaking her damp hair free, and then unpeeled herself from her shirt and unclipped her rain-soaked bra, dropping both onto the straw-covered earth beneath her. Bending over, she clasped her boots and pulled at first one, then the other, slipping her feet free from inside the hard leather. She unzipped her jodhpurs, tugging them away from the skin they clung to and easing them off.

I'm still holding a spoon of porridge in my hand, in front of my mouth, and my mouth is open but the porridge is cold because of me forgetting to eat it, while I've been too busy reading the story. Danny Flynn printed it out for me, with all the notes about the end of the class yesterday. It was a shame we didn't stay at the class because it was very interesting with the woman called Patsy talking about what mistakes we should try not to make. I can't even remember why we didn't stay until the end but it was very nice of Veronica Ptitsky to do the notes for us – and they were very good and in order, with a, b, c on different lines. Maybe that's what I'll do with my research, instead of 1, 2, 3, 4.

Marnie said we'll be discussing my book in the next class, Veronica has written at the bottom of her notes. *Extract attached. Warning: may contain dirty stable scene . . . enjoy! Vx*

There's a big surprise in Veronica's story, because even though all the staff at the stables are not meant to go in when Alissia is in there, after riding her

horse, she's not all on her own. The woman called
Devinder, who has the pink lips against the dark
skin, doesn't know about this and it being a rule,
because she's new and hasn't been the stable manager
for very long, so people must have forgotten to tell
her. And she's coming into the stable right now, and
Alissia doesn't realise it until she hears a husky cough
and by that point she's completely naked, even
having let her silky knickers drop onto the straw-
covered floor, which is going to make them a bit
mucky. Maybe that's why it is a dirty stable scene.
Maybe she doesn't even care about the dirt because
of being so wet. But then – flip a pancake – there
she is, all naked, apart from a diamond on the chain
around her neck, and she's hearing a cough and
turning round, and she's seeing Devinder, but
Devinder isn't saying sorry and going away, which
is what would be polite. Instead, she's keeping her
dark, shining eyes on Alissia, and she's saying, good
ride? And Alissia is glancing at the towel on the peg,
and about to reach for it to cover herself but, oh
flip a pancake, she's not doing that. No, she's shaking
the water from her long, auburn hair, and she's
standing there with her thin, muscular legs slightly
parted, and she's letting Devinder's gaze wander
hungrily from her face down to her pert breasts and
her – oh flip a pancake.

I still haven't taken a mouthful of my porridge, even though I love porridge. I'm still holding the spoon in one of my hands – the right one, I think – but with my other hand, I'm slipping my fingers inside my pyjama trousers so that I can stroke my little fanny button. There is a golden rule which is about not touching ourselves when there are other people with you, and I haven't forgotten. My brain is not that jumbled. I am twenty-five years old and I know about these things, because of practising hundreds of times. I am not really a fanny wanker, but I think it's OK, because there is only Connor Flynn in the room with me and he is reading his book, *Peptides and Proteins*, and not looking at me or talking to me, just mumbling to himself a little bit about neuro-something. And he is in the armchair and he can't even see my hand in my pyjama trousers because of me being on the other side of the table. And maybe it is breaking the golden rule a bit, but it's because of the story making me *really* want to. It's because it's a bit rude, even though it's dirty, and even though it's breaking a rule that Devinder has come in the stable when she's not meant to, but I don't think Alissia is really cross, because she's letting Devinder put her soft, moist lips on hers and her fingers too.

Veronica Ptitsky is a very good writer because

even though I'm not a real lesbian and I've never even been horse riding, I can really see what is happening in my head and when she's writing about Alissia and Devinder and the sighing and shuddering, that's what I'm doing too. I don't think Connor Flynn notices, or not very much because he only looks up from his book a little bit and I don't say anything, I just eat my porridge now. Even though it's completely cold, it's still very nice.

'Hope. We need to go.'

Danny Flynn has his coat on and his bag, which is a backpack, over his shoulder. I'm still in my pyjamas with my paw slippers, but now I remember, he did say we had to hurry up so as to go to the hospital, but I must have forgotten, because of Alissia and Devinder and my porridge. Now Danny Flynn's shaking his head and saying we need to be quick, because of going to talk to the doctor at the hospital who is only there until ten, so could I please go and put on some clothes as fast as possible please. I'm not very good at hurrying but I say I will.

I'm still feeling a bit funny, because of the reading and the rubbing, and Danny Flynn is standing by the door, with his arms folded. And as I'm walking past, I have a thought in my head, which is that I'd really like to put my arms around him and press myself against him really tight. I'm not quite sure why I think it, but I don't have time to tell myself about the golden rule and about keeping our hands and feet to ourselves. And I have done practising with my mum, Jenny, about not just doing the first thing that comes into my brain, but I sort of forget about this. Instead, I grab Danny Flynn with my arms and I press my body against his, with a little bit of a rub of my tummy and my chest up against him. Mostly my chest.

'For heaven's sake, Hope.' He puts his hands on my shoulders and pushes me away. And even though I'm holding onto him, he's stronger than me. And even Connor Flynn has looked up from his book, to watch.

'What do you think you're doing?' This is Danny Flynn. And I don't answer him because I don't really know the answer. I just wanted to do it. And maybe it's OK anyway, because of us maybe getting married, maybe. But he's giving me a look like it wasn't a very good idea, actually. And he's shaking his head and saying, go on, hurry up, *please*, don't I realise we should have left already. And he's saying, for heaven's sake, again, but only mumbled, not really to me.

I hurry as much as I can, but it's not very fast, because of having to sing the whole of my brushing song, which is to make sure my teeth are clean, and because of having to write my research, and doing it a, b, c, d and then having to think for a long time about which is e, which is person on the track. And by then Danny Flynn is knocking on my door and saying am I coming because we're late. So I come, but I'm still holding my notebook and my toothbrush is still in my mouth. I only realise when I'm in the dining room and I say I'll take them back to my room but Danny says just leave them on the table, he's sure Connor won't mind popping them in my room. Connor says not until he's finished this chapter because Danny knows that he *never* leaves a half-read chapter, and Danny says *clearly*, Connor, and *heaven forbid* that he should have suggested otherwise. He shakes his head with his eyebrows low. But then he does a sort of smile with his mouth and says he doesn't know why Connor Flynn wastes his time reading that rubbish anyway, and Connor says, well, that's because he doesn't have the IQ to understand it, and Danny Flynn tells him to get back in his box.

Bridget drives us. Danny Flynn says thanks Mum, and sorry Mum, and she says no really, it's no problem. He's looking at his watch and talking about how we should have been at the hospital by now because Mr Kephalopolis will . . .

'What's funny, Hope?'

I'm putting my hand over my mouth and I manage to stop myself laughing, because of trying really hard. I don't know why, but my brain just thinks that it is a funny name.

'Hope. Don't you ever . . . ?' He doesn't finish what he's saying, maybe because he's turned to look out of the window. Bridget starts saying how it's turned out nicer than she thought it would but the forecast has rain later.

I'm in the back of the car. Danny Flynn is in front and there's a bit that's for resting your head, so I can't see all of him. But because he's looking out at the street, I can see the side of his face and his head, with the hair that's a little bit red, and it's quite curly and long over his ears and on his neck, but on the top there's not quite so much. It would be nice to know if he is my boyfriend or not, but, really, I don't want to ask him. Maybe this is why in those films and on telly, people say, oh I wish he would just give me a *sign*.

Bridget doesn't drive into the hospital because she'd have to pay for the car park, but she's just dropping us off, so she pulls up and says here we are. Danny Flynn is getting out and Bridget says, I really hope it's all OK.

'What's OK?' This is me, because I've forgotten

about my mum and the elephant nose, because of thinking about Danny Flynn and waiting to see if there's a sign and now I'm like, flip a pancake, how could I have forgotten? Now, I don't want to come out of the car, because of feeling not very nice, but Danny Flynn is opening the door for me and he's not saying hurry up, or for heaven's sake, but he's holding out his hand and doing a sort of smile.

He doesn't keep holding my hand when I'm out of the car though, so I don't know if it's a proper sign, but he does say he's sorry if he was a little bit short. And I'm confused because he's not really short. He's shorter than Connor Flynn but he's much taller than me. But that's not the sort of short he means.

'You know. Snappy.' This is him. 'I didn't mean to snap at you, I just didn't want us to be too late. Mr Kephalopolis' secretary said he was only in until ten.' I don't laugh about the Kepaphopolis this time, because I'm walking so fast it's nearly running and it's making me breathe too hard. But Danny Flynn isn't slowing down to make it easy, he's just doing long legs, walk, walk, walk, and looking up at the signs, which are like flat boxes with writing, and lit up, and going, *hmm*. And there are lots of people going in both ways, and some have arms in bandages, or some are in wheelchairs and being pushed. And

I'm thinking that would be nice, because of my breath going so fast, but then we're in the right room and there are lots of people sitting on chairs and one of them is Julie, who is my social worker, except not properly anymore, because of being retired now.

I'm about to say what a . . . and I'm looking for the word, which is when you're sitting on a coach in America and there's a person next to you who is a stranger, but also they're the granddaughter of your grandfather or, maybe, your uncle. Or a cousin maybe. It's a bit of a jumble, thinking about it, but in fact it's not one anyway. Julie is saying she wondered if we'd been held up and Danny Flynn is saying sorry we were so long, and they're talking to a man behind a desk, who has a beard, but not on his cheeks, just on his chin, and he's saying yes, Mr Kephalopolis, yes, just wait there. And then there's a woman in a nurse top who's saying, follow me please, and then, in here please. I'm expecting Mr Kephalololis to be in there waiting for us, but in fact there is just a desk with one chair behind it and two chairs on the other side and also a sort of bed, which is blue and plastic, and like when I walked into a car and they needed to look at my arm and to see if I could move it and then they said I had to go for an X-ray because of it being probably broken. There's also a computer on the desk, and a telephone.

'Hello. Thank you for coming.' He's coming in from a different door. He says his name but it's so quick it doesn't even sound like what everybody has been saying. He has a real beard, on all of his face, where a beard should be, not just on the bottom, and it's a really big beard. He's wearing a white shirt and it's tucked into grey trousers, and there's a button that is open, and a bit of hair is poking out there too. But it's rude to stare, so I'm trying really, really hard not to.

'Please, do sit down.' I'm going to sit on the plastic bed, but Julie says no, no, Hope, you have a chair, and Danny Flynn says he'll stand and, please Julie. And for a little bit we're sort of swapping places and waiting for each other.

'So . . .' This is Mr Kepaphoplis. He's on the other side of the desk and he's looking through lots of papers, and at the computer screen. 'So . . .' He's already said this, and I'm waiting for him to say something else, with my hands under my bottom, and *one, two, three.*

'Jennifer Nicely.' He looks up from the papers, and he's putting his fingers together, so that just the ends are touching the fingers on the other hand. It's like a finger game that I used to play when I was little and it was called this is the church and this is the steeple, except with his fingers, he's not making the steeple, only the church, and he's looking at me. 'You're her daughter?'

I say yes. I'm about to say, but not her birth daughter who was made by her, but actually her adopted daughter and the best thing that ever happened to her, because of my birth mother leaving me in a cardboard box. But I tell myself, no, Hope. With my hands under my bottom still. Because, I've practised this. I don't need to tell everybody everything about me or everything that is in my brain. So I just don't say anything. Only, yes.

Mr Kephapolis nods, looking at me, and says, well, Hope, you understand what has happened to your mother?

I'm not sure what to say back, because I think I've been told what happened, but I don't really remember now, only a little bit. I'm trying to think about what Connor Flynn said, because he knows everything. But I can't remember his words.

'I didn't do the right thing. CRP . . . The blowing thing. So now she's in . . .' I'm thinking so hard, and it's not coming and then it does, like when I was having my breakfast. 'I See You.'

'Sweetheart. It wasn't your fault. All of us panic at times like that.' This is Julie Clarke, with her accent, which sounds like she's happy about it, even though I don't think she is really. 'It's just lucky Danny was there.' She looks at the doctor. 'It was Danny here who performed CPR until the ambulance came.'

Mr Kephalopolis nods and says good stuff, and looks at me again, with his fingers still making the church. If he was doing the finger game, he would need to make the steeple now, and then he'd need to turn his hands inside out, because if you look inside then here are the people. But he doesn't do that. He's just touching his fingers together, that's all.

'So, what we need to understand is that when someone stops breathing and their heart stops, it means there is no oxygen going to their brain, and if a brain is without oxygen for any time, the brain cells begin to die, which is when damage will be caused. Now . . .' He is tapping his church fingers together a little bit, while still looking straight at me. 'As I believe has already been explained to you, there is some evidence that lowering the body's temperature may help minimise brain injury, and this is what was done with your mother when she was brought in. But over the past twenty-four hours, we have gradually brought her temperature back up to normal.'

'So is she better now?'

'No, Hope.' His fingers are still touching – the ends of his fingers on one hand, touching the ends on the other hand – but now he's brought his hand up to near his face so that both of his thumbs are also touching his big beard. And then he puts his fingers between each other. But it's not the right way to do the people, because of it being on the outside, not the inside, so maybe he doesn't know that game. 'Your mother remains unconscious.'

'But will she be better soon? Now that she's not cold?'

'I'm afraid I can't give you the answer to that. We all hope that she will be, of course. I have had patients who have spent weeks or even months in a coma, and have subsequently regained consciousness and gone on to make good recoveries. But equally, many people who have been through what your mother has never wake up at all.'

He's looking at me again, as if he's waiting for me to ask a question. But I don't do that. I just look back at him. He puts on his glasses again. 'One of her nurses has reported your mother's eyelids twitching. That might be encouraging. But equally, what I'm trying to tell you, I suppose, is that we should be aware of the possibility that she may never recover. Do you understand what I'm saying?'

I nod, because he's telling me about maybe death. And I know it, too, because Julie Clarke has put her hand on my shoulder, like that might make me feel better.

'Is my mum sleeping now?'

'A person in a coma does look very much as though they are asleep, but they have none of the normal sleep patterns, and, unlike somebody in deep sleep, they will not react to any stimuli. But patients who have emerged from a comatose state sometimes do recall dreams and also an awareness of the world around them. And I always encourage family to talk as much as they can, hold hands, keep on acting normally.'

'I should talk to my mum? Even with her being in the coma?'

'Well, yes, I think it's good to do. There have been cases where patients have clearly remembered conversations that have happened around them while they were still unconscious. However, it is important . . .' Mr Popolis looks quickly towards Julie and up at Danny then back at me, 'to remain very calm. It is fine to talk or sing even, or chat about your day. But *calmly*. You understand, Hope, everybody finds it difficult to see someone they love in this state, but it is very important not to become agitated or to touch the machines. And it is also very important not to try to take your mother's mask off.'

297

I'm a bit surprised by how hard he is looking at me, with his thumbs against his beard and his fingers holding each other. And Julie Clarke says in a quiet voice that she's quite certain that won't happen again, and that's a bit funny because *again* means something has already happened, and I don't know what she means. Maybe she's feeling a bit confused.

'Do you understand, Hope?' It's the doctor, with his fingers apart now and just pointing towards me, and his eyes even harder on mine, like it's very important. And I say yes, I understand. And of course I do, because I'm not stupid.

'. . . but he doesn't like it when his peas go into his macaroni cheese, or especially when Barry does a poo in the park because of not wanting to smell it. That's because of the asparagus spectrum. And normally he doesn't even like going for a dog walk in the morning, because of always wanting to do the same things in the morning, and that is reading his book and doing research about science and brain things and pep . . .' I'm thinking hard but the word won't come '. . . things. And it's because of his routine. That's what he really likes most. But he did come for a walk with me, because of it being a nice morning and because of him showing me the way and because of Bridget saying what a nice thing that would be. But most of the time he's doing his research. And Danny Flynn is always telling him he doesn't know why he even reads all his books and it's very funny because Connor Flynn says that that is because Danny Flynn isn't even clever enough to read them.'

It is very quiet in the room apart from a sound that is like breathing but it's not coming from my mum, it's coming from a machine. And when I take a sip of my tea, it is very cold.

'Danny Flynn had to go to work at the library today, that's where he is now, even though it's Saturday, because that's when most people go there to get their books. He likes it best when he works in the children's library. And if I want, one day, I can go in with him, and I can help him put the books back on the shelves, but only if I'm ready quickly in the morning and not still eating porridge when it's time to leave.'

I don't really like my tea but I keep on drinking it, because my mouth is a bit thirsty with all the talking. 'And I still don't know if Danny Flynn is my boyfriend because he hasn't told me and he hasn't even given me a sign. But maybe he is now, actually, because he gave me another kiss when it was time for him to go, but it was on my cheek, not like, you know . . .' I take another sip, 'that one . . . the one with the rain, when she didn't realise it was raining. And at the end they're on the bench. Or in Veronica Ptitsky's horse book which is with two women because it's BLT . . . No, I mean LGB . . . T. You know. The community.

'It's quite exciting if he is because I've never had a boyfriend before, but I don't really want to ask him, because if he's not really he might think I'm stupid, and he might not even want to let Barry sleep in my bedroom, who is meant to be on the floor but mostly . . .'

There's a knock and, for a moment, I'm not even sure what it is, because I've sort of forgotten where I am, because of being so busy talking. I've been in my head, just talking, talking, talking and not thinking about hospitals or elephant masks or my mum, Jenny, who is just lying there and not saying anything at all. But now Julie Clarke is coming in, with her head first, looking round the door, and saying is it OK . . . ? And she's coming in and putting her hand on my mum's arm, and looking at her and then at me and she's saying am I OK – but not really saying it because it's only her lips moving and not any sound from them.

I say I am OK. But I'm a bit tired from talking so much. And it's a bit boring because nobody is listening or saying anything back to me, and maybe it's time for me to go back to see Barry now because probably he wants someone to throw his squeaky ball for him.

8

CONFLICT AND RESOLUTION

23

'. . . best practice therefore, that I would never choose to present my findings until all evidence had been collated and I had made a full analysis of all available data and information. And there are still too many areas of conjecture and theory for me to do that, although already there are most certainly a number of inferences that can be made with absolute confidence. And already it is clear to me that in your approach to ascertaining the full picture of your origins, you have limited yourself to only those few . . .'

All I said was that I'd been thinking about my book and that maybe Connor Flynn was right that the cardboard box could be important or that maybe my blanket is. And now he's talking and talking, about proof and methodologies, and also about restricted memories and self-protective filtering of facts, but I stop, and I put my hand out, like a cue, and I say: 'Close your eyes and hold your nose and turn around.'

This is because I can see Tinie Tempah is crouching in the position, with his back in a curve that means he's about to do a poo. Connor Flynn turns around, with his eyes shut and his fingers pressing his nose, so he's not looking and he's not smelling, and when I've scooped it into the bag and put it away in the bin for poo, I tell Connor Flynn that it's OK and he can carry on walking now.

This is the second time that I've done my job again, since my mum, Jenny, has been in the hospital. It's not unsupervised because of Karen, that's my boss, being on the other side of the park, with the other dogs, but it is a little bit unsupervised, because it is just me and Tinie and Sallie and also Barry, and Connor Flynn is walking with me, and he's going to make sure I remember when to bring the dogs back at the right time, but only with me doing all the business with the poos, and also holding the leads and being in charge.

I like talking to Connor Flynn because of him being so clever. And now I'm wondering if it's a good idea to ask him a thing, and that's the thing about Danny Flynn. But I don't want to ask, because of being worried that Connor Flynn will tell me I'm stupid and that he will think how on earth did I even think that. But, flip a pancake, I *really* want to know. And in my head, I'm trying really hard to think of a way to ask the question, without really asking it, like being a sly and secret person with a plan.

I have an idea. And it is a little bit sly and secret. I say: 'I wonder if Danny Flynn has a girlfriend.'

The reason that it's being a bit sly is because I'm not saying about the girlfriend being *me*. But I have to say it three times before Connor Flynn seems to hear me and then he just says, highly unlikely, and nothing else.

We carry on walking a bit and I say, why, and he says what do I mean why – and I say just why, that's what I mean. And he says why what. I say why is it highly unlikely about Danny Flynn having a girlfriend? He puts his eyebrows together for a moment, and says that, well, objectively, to give me a simple answer to that would be conjecture and theorem since science has thus far failed to identify any single contributing factor, and although there have been multiple studies into particular gene variants, a recent study, encapsulating genome-wide association studies on data from more than 470,000 genetic databases, suggested that there were thousands of genetic . . .

I'm listening, with my mouth a little bit open. And Connor Flynn is still talking and it's about regions on chromosomes and chromosome 8 and other ones too, and cultural considerations and preferences and complexity . . .

I don't understand what he's talking about. I don't even think it has anything to do with Danny Flynn. It's just about DNA and orientation and sequences. And I'm thinking maybe Connor Flynn wasn't the best person to ask about this. I'm thinking maybe I should even change the subject. But then it just comes out of my mouth without me telling it to.

'Don't you think Danny Flynn is my boyfriend?' And it's not quite shouting.

He stops talking about entire genomes and he stops walking, Connor Flynn does, right there in the middle of the path. And he looks at me. And he says: 'You are asking me if my brother, Danny, is romantically or sexually interested in you? That's correct? That is the question? Whether I believe that Danny might choose to be in an intimate relationship with you?'

My cheeks are feeling a bit warm, but not like when I've been given a silver star. I'm cross with the question now, because maybe I shouldn't have asked it. But it's too late and I nod and I say, yes: does he think maybe Danny Flynn wants to be my boyfriend?

And Connor Flynn is giving me a look, with his eyebrows going up nearly to his hair. And then he's laughing and laughing and laughing, like it's the funniest thing he's ever heard and like he can't stop. And his laugh is like a hiccup which goes up at the end.

And I don't know why he's laughing. I think maybe he's laughing at me. Maybe he thinks it was such a silly thing, for me to think that Danny Flynn would want to be my boyfriend at all. Maybe it's because of my muddle brain and maybe he's thinking why would *anyone* want to be *my* boyfriend. Not likely, Hope Nicely. And I'm thinking it's not very nice, actually, to be laughing this much. And I'm thinking, actually, Connor Flynn has his own rainbow, even if he calls it a vegetable and a spectrum instead. He's not an ordinary drop of light. And so maybe, he should think about not laughing at people just because they ask about someone being their boyfriend. Maybe, actually, he should think about hurting someone's feelings.

I say what's so funny, but he just laughs even more.

'Hope, it's OK. Shh, darling, everything's all right.'

I don't know what is happening. I was just here, walking, with my mum, and she was wearing her dress, the one that is the bluest dress ever, and we were walking in the park with a puggle called Pepper, which is funny, because Pepper doesn't even come for walks anymore because of moving to Yorkshire. And it was very sunny and with a big rainbow in the sky, and there was an ice cream van, except it was huge like a house. And my mum, Jenny, was saying let's run as fast as the wind and we can have a nice ice cream. But then there was a big hole, just suddenly, which wasn't there before, in the middle of the park, and everything was falling into it, and now there's no ice cream van and no Pepper and no sun and no mum.

I'm in a bedroom but it's not my bedroom and I'm sitting up in my bed and the woman is saying, it's OK, and calm now, calm down darling. And she's saying everything's all right now, it was only a dream. I don't even know who she is, except I sort of do, because she's Bridget, but in my head I can't find the reason why she's here, in my bedroom, and why it's her talking to me and not my mum. And I can't stop crying, until I'm too tired to cry anymore and my eyes don't want to be open.

The dice make a noise like drums when I'm shaking them between my two hands and then it's tap, tap, tap as they're rolling, before they stop, on the table, which isn't really a table but more like a tray with wheels underneath it and long legs.

It's a two-dots and a four-dots and that's no good.

'. . . which was very kind and she even sent an email to Danny Flynn to ask if I was feeling OK, and to say that if I want to go for a . . .'

Shake, shake, shake. Tap, tap, tap. One-dot and one-two-three-four-five-dots, and that's no good.

'. . . T and that's like a G and T but with no G in it which is gin, then we could do a girls' night out and she could come and get me. But I don't like pubs, not even the White Hart, and I don't even like the T very much.'

It's not really a conversation, because of my mum not replying. Because of the coma. So it's just me talking, talking, talking. But very quietly, because it is best to be calm and quiet when you are in the hospital. So that's what I'm being.

Shake, shake, shake. Tap, tap, tap. Three-dots and two-dots, and that's no good.

'But still, it's very nice. To want to do the girls' night with me, and she says it doesn't even have to be a pub and maybe we could go for a pizza instead, or whatever I want to do. And she's writing a very good book. It's about horses and also about the community, you know the one, for the women and for the men and, you know, and everyone . . .'

Shake, shake, shake. Tap, tap, tap. One-dot and another one-dot. No good.

'LGBT. And sometimes Q. But it doesn't really matter because it means the same thing. And she puts all her thoughts on her phone, which is called her special notebook, by recording them. And sometimes she records other things too, like people talking, in the class, or just in her life. She even sent a bit in her email and it was like an arrow in a box, but you could press it, like for real – on Danny Flynn's laptop, you could – and guess what, it was me, going, my name is Hope Nicely. Hope as in hope. And Nicely like nicely.'

It was from when I'd said it to her. Because of her recording me without me even knowing it.

'And, guess what else, Marnie Shale brought me some more chocolates. Well, sort of they were for you, because of her visiting you at the hospital, but maybe more for me, really, because of you being still with no conscience. And I saved some for you, but then I forgot and I ate those ones too, so now there aren't any left. But when you're right as rain again, we can buy some more. Because they were from Marks and Spencer's and I know which ones they are.

'And Karen has sent you a card and it's really nice, with a picture of a basset hound with his ears in the air, and it's a really good one because of most of them just having flowers on them. And . . .'

Shake, shake, shake. Tap, tap, tap. And it's a six-dots. And I'm really excited. Because that is right. And the other one is still turning. And I'm telling it, be another six-dot, *please* be another six-dot. But then it stops, and, flip a pancake, it's only a three-dot. And that's no good.

There's a knocking. 'Hello, Hope, OK if I . . . ?' It's Julie Clarke and she's opening the door and doing a sort of wave with her fingers all taking turns. 'Ooh, you're playing dice. What a nice idea. I thought maybe you'd like a sandwich . . .'

There's a nurse coming in too, and she needs to look at my mum's temperature and her pressure thing, and to empty the wee bag, and Julie says we'll get out of your way, and no, really, no problem, we were just thinking about a spot of lunch anyway.

The other one is back now, from her wedding holiday, the one who isn't Julie Clarke but is the social worker after her, the one whose name I can't remember. But Julie's still coming to the hospital, and I think that's best. Because of the other one talking to me a bit like I'm stupid, and because of her calling my mum Jen.

'So what's the game you're playing? Yahtzee? Or craps?'

I stop myself laughing because of craps being not a game at all but another word for poo.

'It's not a game.' This is me.

It was Connor Flynn who told me about it, and he knows because of being very clever. It's a thing called probably-ty and that is how probably it is that something is going to happen. That's what it's called. It's a bit like statistics. And he told me about it because of talking about all the numbers, which are percents and chances of if my mum will be right as rain. But when he told me about it being a ten percent or maybe it was twelve or seven, or whatever number it was, that my mum would be alive still and then there's another one, another percent number, of her brain being all right and not damaged too, I think maybe he knew that I didn't understand it. Because of my brain being a jumble that doesn't like numbers. And he said, look, and he said, imagine that the chances of your mum surviving the out-of-hospital arrest, which means her not being dead – he said, think of that as being the same probably-ty as throwing a die and the number is a six-spot. So that's a one in six chance. And then the probably-ty of her not having the brain damage is like throwing another die and it's at the same time, and it's another six-spot. So it's like throwing two six-spots both at the same time. And that is how probably-ty works.

But I don't tell Julie about this now, because of it being difficult for me to explain it, even though I do understand it now, mostly. And I think maybe she's going to ask me more about it but she doesn't because something happens now. We are in the corridor, with the smell like hospital, and not so much like ice cream anymore, with the signs in the boxes saying *Radiology* and *Outpatients* and *Orthopaedics* and all the people walking, and some with their arm in plaster or in a nightie with no back. But then I see Simon Taylor from the writing group. Or maybe he's Stephen. And I shout both the names, just in case. And I'm running to him, and I'm nearly falling into an old man in a wheelchair, and the old man says watch where I'm effing going, but I don't have time to say sorry, because of hurrying.

And it's funny because Simon Taylor has turned round and he's looked right towards me, and I think he's seen me and I'm waving my arms, but then he's turned and he's walking away. And I'm running and I'm shouting, Simon, and then Stephen, and then Simon again. But he hasn't stopped. Except then there is a girl and she's in a wheelchair too, and being pushed by maybe her mum, and they're right in front of him. And Simon Taylor, I think maybe it is Simon, stops to wait for them to go past, and I'm running my fastest until I've reached him and I say, hello,

315

and I say I was shouting at you, didn't you hear me. And now he's looking at me and saying, oh, hello, Hope, fancy seeing you here, and no, didn't hear you at all. And it's funny, because of how loud I was shouting. And he's looking around him, but not really at me. And he's playing with his collar.

'I knew it was you.' This is me. And it's a little bit loud again. 'Because of you working here. I knew it was you, straight away.'

'Well, yes. I don't work here every day but . . .'

There are a lot of people around us. But not Julie. She's still behind me. Because of me running when she was still walking.

'I knew it was you. And I think you can tell me all about my mum. I think you know if . . . ?'

'Sorry, but I don't know what you're talking about . . .' He's got his eyebrows pushing together and his mouth is pressed in. I'm trying to tell what his face means, by thinking about the pictures in the magazines and the sides of buses. And it's a bit like the man who is saying to his wife, what biscuits, but behind his back, he's holding the packet of biscuits.

And then Julie is there, asking why did I run off, and then saying hello to Simon and putting out her hand to shake his, and saying haven't they met somewhere – so I'm even more sure that he does know something about my mum – but at the same time Simon is saying he'd better shoot, actually, because he's late for seeing someone. When he says shoot he doesn't mean shoot with a gun. He means he has to go quickly. My mum, Jenny, has a friend called Brenda Pollard, who sometimes comes round for tea and a natter and she always says it. *Goodness me. Is that the time? I really must shoot.* So I know what Simon means. Or maybe it's Stephen. But then he's gone and I don't understand why he doesn't want to tell me about my mum if he works here, even if it's not every day.

My sandwich is tuna and sweetcorn, which is nice, except that it's in brown bread and that's not my favourite. My favourite is white bread, or especially a white roll, but not the hard ones, the nice soft ones, and it doesn't matter if they're long or if they're round. But they didn't have any tuna in rolls, only cheese and pickle, or chicken, and they didn't have it in white bread either. Tuna. Only brown bread. And it's not even cut very thick so it's a bit bendy and some of the sweetcorns have fallen out.

I'm telling Julie Clarke about all the dogs, and especially about Barry, but also about Tinie Tempah, and about which ones like to play and which ones don't really want to, and which ones can only be on the lead, and which ones growl at the others when they're in a bad mood. And Julie isn't saying very much, just a little bit of nodding and, oh I see, and oh, really, but mostly she's just drinking her coffee and eating her sandwich, which is a long roll, and a soft one, but it's chicken, which I don't like so much.

And Julie's asking me about who that man in the corridor was, and I'm telling her about him being Simon – or maybe Stephen but I'm thinking now it really is Simon. And I'm telling her about him being in my writing group, and about how he's writing a book which is non-fiction and an autobiography, just like me. And I'm telling her that although he looks quite old, and like a person in a nurse's uniform who probably wouldn't go to any parties, in his book he talks about being at a party and sitting in a room with a woman, even though it's dark and he doesn't even know her, and that maybe it was also about falling in love. And there's a thing, about the woman, a what's-it-called. The word. Which is like being in a coach with your cousin, even though you don't know that's what they are. But I can't remember what it is.

And Julie is doing a thing with her head, which is shaking it, and saying that she's really quite sure that she's seen him before, somewhere, but she can't quite place him and, darn it, it must be her age. I think she's probably right, because Julie Clarke is really quite old.

And then there's music, and it's 'Yellow Submarine', which is a song I know, because it's very famous. But I don't know where the music is coming from until Julie has opened her bag and taken out her telephone and is answering it, saying, hello, and yes, yes, she's with her here now, and oh, right, yes, she sees, of course, we'll be right there. She puts her phone back in her bag and she looks at me.

'It's Jenny. She's opened her eyes.'

24

'But still, it does have to be a good thing, doesn't it?'
This is Bridget, with a big pile of mashed potato on
her fork, but not eating it, just looking at me. 'I
mean, if she's opening her eyes, then hopefully soon
your mum will . . .'

'Actually, strictly speaking, no, there's no objective
reason to call this good news as the move from the
state of coma to the vegetative state does not
necessarily imply further improvement. And even if
the patient moves on from a vegetative to a minimally
conscious state, if damage to the brain stem has
been—'

'Connor. Please.' The potato is still there on her
fork.

'But, medically, if the damage has—'

'Connor. Enough. Hope, love, can I pass you
more vegetables? Another lamb chop maybe?'

'. . . but even from the perspective of mortality

rates, the high risk of infection or pneumonia or of a recurrence of—'

'*Connor, enough!*'

Connor Flynn looks down at his plate and, at last, Bridget puts the potato into her mouth.

It's quiet tonight. Danny Flynn isn't here because of a date in the diary which has been there already for weeks. Bridget says it's because he's having dinner with his friend. I say which friend, and she says, oh just his friend. She has her mouth a bit open like she's going to say something else, but she doesn't say anything else. Also, it's quiet because I don't have my chatty head on. Maybe because of all the talking, and all the having to ask my mum why she wasn't looking at me, even with her eyes open now, or why she still wasn't speaking to me.

I'm not as hungry as usual, even though the tea is really nice. And I don't have another lamb chop or any more vegetables, and only one bowl of apple crumble, even when Bridget tells me, go on, Hope, she's sure I can squeeze in a little bit more, and even though it's with ice cream, which isn't just vanilla but has bits of chocolate and nuts in it. And when Bridget is taking all the dishes through to the kitchen, I say I think I'm going to go to bed. And she says, oh Hope, really, it's still early, don't I want to stay up a bit with her, because it's one of her favourite films on telly and it's the one about Harry meeting Sally. I say I've seen it already and Bridget says so has she, lots of times, and Connor Flynn does a groan and says, oh not that again, it's so-o boring, and Bridget says just because there aren't any aliens wanting to blow up the earth or zombies or evil robots shooting people. She says it's a lovely film and so romantic.

When Bridget says film, it's like she's saying fill-em. At first that's what I think she's saying. One of her favourite fill-ems. And I don't know what she means, except for maybe it's the same as 'fill them', but I don't know what would be the 'them' that would be filled. But when she says what its name is, that's when I realise. It's not a fill-em, it's a film. And it's only Bridget's accent that makes it sound different.

It is quite a good film, even with me having seen it before, because of all the bits I've forgotten, like the bit where Sally is pretending to be a fanny wanker in the café, and there's an old woman who wants one of what she's having. That's very funny. And when it's that point, Bridget says, oh, Hope, that's a bit naughty, isn't it, and she does a giggle. And Connor Flynn doesn't say anything because he's reading *Peptides and Proteins* again, in the armchair, not on the sofa with us, but Bridget says we're honoured because normally he wouldn't even stay in the same room when she's watching one of her movies, and it must be my presence.

When it's nearly the end of the film, with the man called Harry running and running to be in the right place, and then with the people being older and talking about just knowing, I hear a noise, and I think maybe it's Barry because it's a bit like snuffling. But it's not Barry because he's not even in this room, he's gone to my room and he's already on my bed. The noise is Bridget and, when I look at her, I see she's crying.

'Don't mind me.' She's doing a smile, and crying at the same time. 'It's just it's so . . .' She makes her face all squeezed up. 'And I don't know why I . . . It's not as if my Fergus had a romantic bone in his whole body. But still . . .'

I don't say anything, because the film hasn't finished yet and I'm still watching it until the end, and when it finishes, I say, righty-ho, off to bed now.

Bridget says, OK, love, and thanks for watching with her. She says it's nice to have a bit of female company round here for once.

'. . . interesting question, though not an area in which I'm especially well read.' Connor Flynn gets a wrinkle above his nose and I think maybe it's because of concentrating.

I'm looking at him, but I'm also looking at Scrappy, the bearded collie, who is having a sniff on the grass, because of it being important to always watch the dogs when you're a dog walker. So I'm looking at Connor Flynn, then at Scrappy, then at Connor Flynn again, with my head going one way then the other.

'Of course, there have been studies analysing how the methods employed differ between the categories broadly defined as attempters and completers, and in terms of *effectiveness* then, yes, one would certainly conclude, as I suppose you would expect, that jumping in front of a train is far more *effective* as a method than pharmaceutical means or asphyxiation. But I'm not sure that any could be described as *best*. First, really, you would have to define that notion of *best*.

'I did read an article about the relatively high rates amongst doctors, compared to the general population, though the actual percentages elude me, and the method of choice for them was self-poisoning. But then of course, you would have to take into account the fact that—'

'Turn around and hold your nose.' And I'm reaching into my pocket for the poo bag.

'And it's like every single day, he wakes up and it's not tomorrow, it's just like yesterday again. Like every day is the same yesterday, because of it being the same song on the radio, which is . . .' I'm trying really hard to remember the song, and I almost can, like in my head there's one note or maybe two notes, but the rest of it isn't coming. But still I can see his face, with his hair all messy, and he's looking out from under his duvet, and at the alarm clock which is also a radio, and a bit like my one in Danny Flynn's house, in my own bedroom, with the sweet toilet. And he's throwing the alarm clock at the wall, because of it never being tomorrow.

Shake, shake, shake. Tap, tap, tap. A five-spot and a four-spot.

'And he learns to speak Italian and to play the piano and even to teach it to other people because he's so good, even though he couldn't play it at all before. And also how to make a beautiful picture in the ice, which is a statue. And it's a statue of her. And they go dancing. And they make angels in the snow. And even though she doesn't like him in the beginning . . .'

Shake, shake, shake. Tap, tap, tap. A two-spot and another two-spot.

She doesn't have her eyes open today. Just closed and like sleeping. Like yesterday and the other day, the ones before. But not with the elephant nose. That has gone away and now it's just a tube that goes underneath her nostrils. And the nurse was in here, just a little bit, putting things in her ears to see about the temperature, because of being a bit hot, and being a bit worried about an infection.

'But it was very romantic, and better than the other one. Not the Harry one, that one was really good too, but the one on the other night, which was a bit old-fashioned, with them going to the top of the Empire Tower. But that was Bridget's favourite, and she was crying so much, I didn't think she would stop. I only cried a little bit. And Danny Flynn said we were as soft as each other.'

Shake, shake, shake. Tap, tap, tap. A one-spot and a five-spot.

'And tonight it's his turn to talk about his book when we go to the writing group, and it's called *Up-World*, or maybe *Down-World*, and it's very sad, with all the babies living under the ground. They have to collect the water for all of the people who live in the real world, which is up at the top. He says maybe I shouldn't come this week, because of not being up to it, because of being too sad and maybe wanting to go away again, but I told him, not likely, I told him definitely, I'm coming because . . .'

Shake, shake, shake. Tap, tap, tap. A six-spot and a six-spot.

'. . . of wanting to . . .'

A six-spot and a six-spot.

On my face, I can feel the biggest smile coming. It's ginormous, stretching into my cheeks. And I'm jumping up, out of my chair and onto my feet. Because I've done it. *A six-spot and another six-spot.* And it's the best thing in the whole wide world. It's fan-tanty-tastic. Because I've made the probably-ty. And now I'm looking at my mum, Jenny, and I'm waiting for her to open her eyes and say, hello my Hope, and to be right as rain.

Danny Flynn doesn't have any shoes on and I'm thinking maybe his feet are cold because he's standing on the doorstep with his toes out. Maybe, if he wanted, he could borrow my slippers, the ones which are the paws, but only when I'm not wearing them. He has the door open, and he's saying to Katya, who is the other social worker who isn't Julie Clarke, does she not want to come in. And she's saying, no, really, she has to get going, she's just dropping off Hope and she wanted a quick word.

And he's saying, seriously, they've suggested no more visits for . . . ?

She's saying, well yes, they said it might be best all round, just for a while, if . . .

I think it's because of the machines, and the punching them, and the chair that fell on the floor. And maybe a bit the shouting when the nurse said about not doing that. And then the banging my head on the wall. Maybe because of that too.

And she, Katya, is saying perhaps it's better for a few days anyway, and that the doctors are quite concerned about Jenny's temperature, and they were running a few more tests, because of worrying about an infection. And she's saying Julie's going in to have a talk to them later. And she's sure in another day or two . . . And the hospital have promised they will give us updates on every single thing that happens.

I wish it had been Julie Clarke who had brought me back. I like her accent better than Katya's. And she doesn't do the thing with her mouth, which is like making it into a little tiny hole.

'But Hope, love, wouldn't you rather stay here with me? You've had such a tiring day. I thought maybe we could watch *Pretty Woman*. I don't know if you've . . .'

'I want to go with Danny. To the group.'

Bridget and Danny Flynn look at each other. And it's spaghetti bolognese, but earlier than normal, because of Danny Flynn having to be there an hour before to talk to Marnie Shale, because of his one-to-one. And Bridget is holding the cheese, which is in a round pot, and Danny Flynn is putting the pepper back on the table. Connor Flynn isn't looking at anybody. He's just eating his spaghetti, which is on one side of his plate with the bolognese on the other side. I think maybe he's still cross because this isn't the time we normally have tea.

'But, you do realise you'll have to wait outside for me while I'm in with Marnie? It's a whole hour. Won't you be a bit . . . ?'

'I want to go with you.'

'And I *want* you to come. I'm just not sure it's the best thing. Remember last time? I'm worried that—'

'I want to go to the writing group.'

It's a bit boring, just me and the chair and the desk. And on the other side of the room there are some benches, except nice ones, not just wood but puffy ones, with comfortable seats, but not quite sofas, because of having no back. The bins are empty because of the cleaner coming and emptying them, but now she's gone. She didn't talk English anyway.

I'm trying hard to concentrate. This week's class is about conflict and resolution and, as well as talking about that, we're going to look at Danny Flynn's bit of his book. He's left me with the printouts, which is his bit called *Up-World (extract)*, and also some quotes which were sent from Marnie for us to think about. And one quote is about every character in our book having to want something – even if it's only a glass of water. And that's by somebody called Kurt Vonnegut, which is a very funny name. Marnie Shale has put in some notes saying to us to think about our characters and how they are being stopped from getting the thing they want. This is conflict. And even though my book is not fiction, but non-fiction, because it's an autobiography, I'm thinking about what I want. Because my main character is me. And, actually, I do want a glass of water, because I'm a bit thirsty, but also I want to write my book and persevere and . . .

I'm not looking down at the words on the paper,

but I'm looking into the room, which is the reception, but not really at the benches that are like sofas, or even at the poster on the wall, which is about saving our libraries, but mostly I'm just looking at nothing. I'm thinking about my mum, Jenny, and about her eyes just being open – like mine now, but without her saying anything or maybe even thinking anything, and without turning to look at me. And I'm wondering what is happening in her head, and if it's a big jumble or a fog or just a nothing. I'm wondering what it is like inside a head if there's nothing in there. Because in my head, there are words and words and words, all trying to say themselves at once. But what if they weren't there? What if it was just empty? Would I still be me? Would I be Hope Nicely? Or would I be someone else? Or would I not even be that, because of there being nothing in there?

I'm trying to stop thinking about this, because it is making me want to hum. I need to be thinking about the conflict instead, and what it is that I can't have but I really want.

Also I need to be reading the extract bit of Danny Flynn's book, because of not having remembered to do it earlier, and he said it's not even a sad bit, it's an exciting bit with rocket-cars and an explosion and lots of tension, but still I'm not really wanting to read it, because of the poor babies. And I'm thinking about maybe getting a glass of water. But not a make-it-up one in a book or a quote, a real one for real drinking.

There's a machine in the corner, which isn't a silver machine, like a coffee one. It's a square, which is plastic and clear, and I think it has water in. It has a tap, which is blue, and there are even some glasses. They're not glass ones, they're plastic too – and when I take one out it goes crunch in my hand, and pops in a little bit, but not all the way. It's a little bit difficult because the tap doesn't turn, like the one in my kitchen does, and it takes me a long time to work it out. It doesn't pull and it doesn't twist. There's a special way which is to make it point down and it does a little click. But then when I take my hand away it stops. And I have to do it again. And again. But each time it's just a little tiny squirt, so my glass of water isn't very full, and I've drunk it really quickly and I'm still thirsty. I'm trying to put more water into my crinkly glass, but it's just a teeny bit, and maybe it's because of the big square bubble having just a little bit of water in the bottom and mostly being empty. So then I have an idea, and I take the crunchy cup into the Ladies, and there is a normal tap with normal water, it just turns and it doesn't just go drip, drip, and it's much better, because now I have a real cup of water to drink, even if it's not so cold. Now I can go back to my printouts and not be thirsty.

I'm swinging open the door of the Ladies and seeing that the reception is not empty anymore. There is a back. It's a person and he's sitting on one of the puffy bench sofas and taking off a coat, which is a leather one. The hair is black, but just a little bit white, and I know who it is except I still don't know definitely if his name is Simon or Stephen. He's pulling his arm out of his jacket and now he's opening his bag, which has straps and, for a moment, I'm just watching him undoing them, and I'm thinking about him being in the hospital, and hurrying away in the corridor, even with me shouting both his names at him. I'm thinking about me not being allowed to visit my mum, Jenny, for a little bit, because of it being for the best if I don't. And I'm thinking about how I want her to look at me, with her lovely eyes like coffee with just a tiny bit of milk, and I'm thinking about Connor Flynn saying statistically and probably-ty, and I'm thinking about the doctors saying infection and concern. And I'm thinking about two dice with two sixes.

Simon Taylor is taking out a telephone and looking at it. I'm thinking about him saying he doesn't know what I'm talking about, about my mum, and I'm thinking again, about him hurrying down the corridor, even with me shouting very loud. I'm thinking maybe he does know about my mum. I'm thinking that's probably-ty. I think he really does. And maybe he's being sly and secret, because of not wanting to tell me, because of it being best for me. But I'm thinking it's *not* best for me. Because, flip a flipping pancake, Jenny Nicely is my mum and why won't anyone just tell me why she's not looking at me or why I'm not even allowed to be with her?

Why won't anyone tell me if there's even still something in her head or if there's nothing left? Or if maybe she's dead with the infection, and that's why I can't see her anymore.

I'm remembering to tell myself all the golden rules, about not shouting and not telling everyone everything and not correcting people or doing the other thing about . . . And keeping our hands and feet to ourselves and . . . Accusing, that's the word. And I'm telling myself all the things I must not do, but it's like my brain has another idea. My brain's idea is to grab Simon's shoulders, or maybe it's Stephen, but very hard with my hands and to shout very loud: 'What is it you don't want to tell me?'

I don't think Simon Taylor, or Stephen maybe, had even known there was anybody else there, because of it being his back that I could see, with him facing the other way, because now he's jumping up and he's shouting too. And what he's shouting is fuck. And he's turning round, so that it's his face looking at me now, not his back. His eyes are very wide and his mouth is sort of open, sort of like a big 'O'. And he's saying fuck a few more times, but not so loud now, and what the fuck am I doing.

I look into his eyes and I say I want to know what the thing is he's not been saying to me. In his face, it's like a twitch, like his eyes just closing shut but his cheeks doing it too, before he looks at me again. With his face still now.

'I'm sorry, but I don't know what you're talking about.'

'You do.' I'm not shouting now. It's just talking but it's like I'm trying so hard to make him do it, with my eyes and with my voice. 'Tell me what you know. The thing you think I shouldn't know. Because of it being for the best. Because I do need to know it. And I *know* you can tell me about my mum.'

He does a sort of sigh. It's silent. With his mouth like it's blowing.

'Hope, I'm sorry. I just can't. I'm not sure I know anything. I don't know why you think I do.'

Now I know I'm right. Even with my jumble brain. Even with my memory like a flitty thing. I know that he can tell me. Because of his face being like biscuits behind his back. That's why he was running, with me shouting at him, in the hospital. Being sly and secret. Julie Clarke said that just because

335

he was dressed in the nurse clothes, it didn't mean that he knew my mum. She told me it was a very big hospital with lots of different departments, and him being there was just a – it was a . . . the thing, like being on the coach, and finding out you're sitting next to your cousin when you don't even know them. One of those things. But I know it wasn't one.

And Simon Taylor is doing an upside-down mouth like he's very sorry, or like he doesn't know what I'm talking about. But I do. It's not a . . . the thing . . . a co-in thing. The coach thing. And the name thing. The two Susans, one Ford and one not-Ford, or two Ellies. Or not even two, *three*. I don't believe it can be one of those at all. The word. A . . . The word. I think he does know.

And I'm shouting. 'You do know. You know all about her. I know it's not a . . .' And my brain is working so hard. I'm squeezing it and squeezing it to make the word come. And it's nearly there, but not quite.

'Like two Susans. Or like you knowing Ellie and me knowing Ellie too. That thing. The Ellie thing. Or like the being in America thing. Everybody thinks I'm stupid. But I'm not stupid. And I know you can tell me if she's even alive. You do know. And I want you to tell me if she's ever going to be right as rain, or if she's . . .' I don't want to say the word. I don't want to say it about my mum, about Jenny Nicely. I don't even like the word. I hate it. But I do say it. 'Dead.'

And Simon Taylor is very quiet now and he's shaking his head. And he's sort of talking to himself and not really to me, but just saying: I don't understand, I didn't think, and, but how on earth . . .

He looks at me and says: 'How do you even know about Ellie? I don't understand. I thought . . . ? How do you know . . . ?'

And I want to shout, because he's being very stupid. Because he must know that's not the thing that is important. It's just the word. The two Ellies, or three in fact, because of his Ellie in the party room, and the other Ellie in my school and also the one who brought me a monkey. That is not what's important. It's only for the word, because I don't care about any of the Ellies. Or about the Susans either. Only about my mum. Only about Jenny Nicely. Because that is what we are really talking about. But I'm not shouting. I'm not even counting, one, two, three. I'm just looking at him very, very hard. Because this is like the emergency. Except this time I have to make my brain be clever. Because he does know about my mum. I'm sure as sure that he does. And I'm not a baby boo boo. And I'm not stupid. I need to know the truth.

'Stop thinking about the consequence,' I tell him. I don't think this is the right word, maybe. It doesn't feel like bingo. Just a nearly-bingo. But it's not important. What is important is my mum, Jenny. Only that.

I look at him and, with my words very slow, I say, I just need him to tell me. But still he's just making a face with his mouth all upside down, and very quiet, and shaking his head. So I make myself say the word again. 'Is she dead? Tell me.'

'I can't talk about it.' This is him. 'I don't even know how you know. I swore to myself I wouldn't say anything. Not yet. I don't want to . . .'

But now I know. I am right. And in my body, where my heart is, it's tight and taking my breath out of my mouth. And I can feel *bumbum bumbum*. Because it means it's real and it's so, so bad. It means a horrible thing.

I say, I want you to tell me. And I think a bit, and I say, it's important. And then I say, please.

'Oh, Hope.' He puts his head down, like he's holding his hands by his tummy, and he's looking at them, with his mouth doing a bit more blowing with no noise. Then he looks at me again, with his eyes which are blue, but not very blue, just like the sea when it's not a very nice day. And then there's a bit of his mouth which you can't see because it's under the other lip, with maybe him biting it. And then he says my name again.

'I'm so sorry.' And then he does another sigh and he mumbles a bit of swearing, and sort of crunches up his face and he does more swearing but not so mumbled.

I make myself say it again. 'Is she dead?'

His voice is very quiet. 'Yes, she's dead.'

I can hear the words. It's one, two, three words. That's all. Three words. One, two, three. And they've gone into my ears, but it's like my brain is a door and it's not going to open to let them in. It's saying keep them out. Keep the door shut.

Simon Taylor, or maybe Stephen, is saying something else but there is no sound coming in. My head is too busy pushing, pushing, pushing at the brain doors to keep them shut. My hands are over my ears, with a bit of rocking. But still I can hear the screaming in my head. And it's from me. It's me screaming. Maybe in my head or maybe in my mouth too.

And I think he's saying something else, and maybe something about Ellie again. But I don't even care about that. Why would I care about that? I only care about my mum. And I'm still screaming. And I have to go. Right now.

I have to go away.

I'm looking at the lift and I'm wanting to be in it, but Simon or Stephen Taylor has his hand on my arm, with his fingers gripping, and it's stopping me from moving. So I'm pulling his hand, to try and take it off me, so I can go away. I have to go. Right now. I don't want him to stop me. I won't let him stop me. I have to go *now*. But he's holding onto me and trying to keep me there. The words, like explain, and talk and wait, are outside my head and his mouth is moving and his arms too, but I just want him to let me go. I want to go now. I'm pushing at him with my fists, to make him let go, but still he's holding onto me too tight and saying I can't go, because I need to listen to him.

And then there is a noise, like a ping. The lift doors are opening and the man who's coming out is the one with the scarf-knot. There are no patterns today, just purple, and it's inside a big coat. And he's saying: 'What is that little savage doing to you?'

He doesn't need to run very far, because we're so close to the lift, just between the puffy bench and the desk. Just a couple of steps away.

'Get off him this minute, you vicious little beast.' This is what he says, and he's pulling me away from Simon who is maybe Stephen, because maybe he doesn't know that it was me who was trying to go away anyway.

He's pulling me really hard, with his fingers digging into my shoulders. And now it's him who's holding me. It hurts.

And I need to go away. My mum is dead. It's the worst thing in the world. And it's real. I need to go.

I lift up my knee very hard and it goes whack, right between Lu-do-vic's legs which is where his goolies are, but inside his coat and his trousers. And he's making a noise which is a bit like the soft corduroy cushion in my kitchen, when I sit on it very hard. Like bphhh. His fingers have stopped pressing into me.

There's another noise which is like a crack or a bang, and it's because of him bending over so quickly, with his hands between his knees, and his head hitting the desk as he bends down. And the other man, called Stephen or Simon, is saying, oh God, is he OK. The lift doors are still open. I'm running into them. The buttons say 1, 2, 3, and at the bottom there's one that says G. I press that one because of G being ground, which is the library. And it's still open, the library, with people in it. There's an old lady who drops her books. I say sorry but in my head, only, because of my mouth not saying anything much, except for some noises, which aren't crying, just like little sounds like maybe an animal.

My mum is dead.

I don't have to think about where to go. Sometimes, I forget about the ways, the which ways to go, even if it's to my house, but not now. Now it's like my brain doesn't even need to try to remember, it's just taking me. It's quite noisy with the car horns and the people shouting about watching where I'm going and also it's noisy in my mouth, which is the sounds, like an animal, and the big breathing, because of not liking to run so fast.

Three words. One. Two. Three. Yes, she's dead.

I don't have my notebook. It is still in my bag, the one which is a backpack, and it's still on the back of the chair, by the desk, in the reception of the writing class, on the third floor above the library. It's in there with also some biscuits and some old knickers, which are a bit smelly, because of me forgetting them. And I'll have to remember to take them out next time. And wash them to make them clean.

Except, that's wrong. There isn't going to be a next time. Silly me.

Even without my notebook, I'm thinking that I can remember my research, because of it not being very much anyway, and because of Connor Flynn helping me, too. Because of him saying the thing about throwing oneself into a train being maybe not the *best* way but being another type which is with the most probably-ty maybe. It's not how doctors want to do it mostly, because of that being with poisoning. But that's OK because I'm not a doctor. And, even without my notebook, I think it can't be that difficult, not even for me, just when the train is coming, that's when I have to do the throwing.

I think it's probably easy-peasy.

The station is very close to my home. That's why it's called 23a Station Close: because of the station. It's just on the left, like if you lift up your hand, with your thumb out and a space and your next finger out too, it makes a letter L. And L is for left, like G is for ground.

I can't buy a ticket, because of my purse being in my bag, with the notebook and the knickers and the biscuits. But luckily, the gates are open, I don't know why. So I don't need a ticket to make the gates open. I'm thinking maybe I just need one because of it being the law. But I think it's OK for me to not have one for the law, actually, because anyway I'm not going *on* the train. As I'm coming past the bit where the ticket machines are, there's a noise, like whoosh, whoosh, rattle, and it's the train which is leaving right now, so – flip a pancake, I'm missing it. And I'm running and running, in case I'm just in time. But when I get to the top of the stairs and then down again, which is the platform, it's empty, with no people and no train.

There is a sign which says when the next one is coming and it's at 18.16, then another one at 18.23, and the first one is to Gatwick Airport and the second one is to Rainham (Kent). For a moment I'm wondering which one is my train, which is very silly, but then I'm thinking how long is that, because of not having a watch and not being very good at the time. There is a big clock that is hanging up, with its letters very straight and red, and it says 18.07 and, as I'm looking at it, it changes to 18.08. I'm thinking it's maybe not a very long wait, not like an hour, so I sit on a bench, which is a real bench, made out of wood which is hard. There are empty crisp packets on it, which are Prawn Cocktail and Barbecue Beef and a newspaper which is the *Sun*. And it smells a little bit like wee.

In my ears and in my body I can hear a sort of banging, which is bumbum bumbum, and that's my heart, because of running. And I'm thirsty again, like Kurt Vongut says, because of wanting another glass of water. And I'm wondering how long the train will be.

I'm thinking about the throwing. I'm thinking probably it should be like a jump, like when I was at school and we did the long jump and the high jump. And I'm thinking this should be most like a long jump, really, but maybe I don't need to count the one, two, three steps first. But then I'm thinking maybe one, two, three would be good, because of already counting it in my head, with my hands under my bottom, because of not feeling very calm, and because of my chest being too fast. And I'm really very thirsty now, and I'm humming a bit and I'm thinking about the three words.

Yes, she's dead.

I don't really want to be a person on the track. But I don't want to be a Hope Nicely without a Jenny Nicely. I just want to be the old way, like before, with my mum who had her big arms and her nice smell and wasn't open eyes with no words and wasn't dead. But now she is. She's dead and in a box.

Now I have to rub my hands over my face, because of all the tears, and because of my nose being snotty. I'm crying very hard. And I'm wishing I had my bag, because of having some tissues in there, because of my mum, Jenny Nicely, always saying to me, have you got your phone, and have you got your purse, and have you got some tissues. And now my fingers are wet with the snot and the tears and I can only wipe them on my leggings.

I'm thinking about a squirrel. I saw it one time, when I was going into the park. And the squirrel was lying in the road, with its tail still all fluffy and its arms and legs straight out, like maybe it was reaching for a nut. And its eyes were open and black. And it was dead. But when I came out of the park, after doing my walks, where the squirrel had been, it was more like a pile of goo. It was red and pink and bits of purple. And if there hadn't still been the tail, it wouldn't even have looked like anything.

18.10. I'm thinking that after this it will be 18.11 and then 18.12, then 18.13 then a few more and then 18.16 and then it will be the train to Gatwick Airport and I can do the long jump.

I'm shaking now. When I wipe the snot away from my nose, it's like my hand is banging against my face, because it's shaking so hard.

One, two, three.

There is someone else coming down the stairs onto the platform. And it's a person who's walking towards me.

'Hello, Hope.'

25

It's a way of walking that isn't like most other people. It's quite straight with arms swinging, and it's a way that I've seen when I've been walking Barry in the park on – not yesterday but maybe the day before – with Tinie Tempah too. And I'm confused. Because what is *he* doing here?

I'm looking at him without really knowing what to say, but thinking he really is the cleverest person in the whole wide world, and thinking how, how, how did he know. But he's putting his hands to his ears and putting his head down. For a moment, I don't even understand why, but then I do. It's bingo in my head. It's because of it smelling like wee and crisps, so I say does he want to go to another bench maybe? He says yes.

I say OK. I say, but not for very long. Because of the train coming.

He looks at the sign and says, what, the Gatwick Airport train in five minutes, and I say yes.

'How did you know about me being here?' We're walking to the next bench up the platform, which is one that doesn't smell, but it has a plastic bag which is from Tesco at one end, and I pick it up and put it in the bin, because Connor Flynn doesn't like it being there.

'I assessed it to be the most probable location. Danny called to say that you had run away from the library and to enquire whether you might have returned to our house. He said that he believed you to be in a state of distress. He seemed to feel that you would most likely be in the park. I believe your employer Karen is there now looking for you. But having seen the list of suicide methods in your notebook, with "beneath a train" underlined, coupled with your recent evident interest in the subject, I felt it was more logical to make this my first destination in trying to locate you.'

'I . . .' I'm looking at him and I don't really know what to say. 'You thought I'd be here because you read my notebook?'

'That was one consideration, yes. You left it on the dining table, with your toothbrush, and Danny asked me to return it to your room. But, your recent fascination with the success rates of suicide methods was a more influential factor in my hypothesis, as well as Danny's report of your state of mind.'

Connor Flynn is so clever. I'm quiet for a moment and then I ask: 'Did you come here to stop me throwing myself?'

He puts his eyebrows close together and then says: 'As I have already explained, I came because Danny asked me to find you and a process of deduction led me to think that this was where the probability of me doing so was highest. I'm assuming it's the emotional response to a neuro . . .'

I'm trying to bring his words together in my head. I ask him, so doesn't he care about me throwing myself?

He puts his head to one side, with his eyes not looking at me, but like they're looking for other people over my shoulder. He says, yes. Evidently. It seems an entirely illogical course of action for me to take, stemming from an over-responsive emotional state. And he can only suppose that the neurological impulses—

'My mum is dead.' This is me, and when I say it, I'm having to make my hand wet with more wiping of my nose and eyes.

'Your mother? Jenny Nicely? Is dead?'

I say yes, and I'm crying harder than ever.

'Highly unlikely.'

And now I'm stopping wiping. Because I'm looking at him.

'But you said the probably-ty . . .'

'I mean not that the probability of her dying, per se, is unlikely. Merely that of her being dead at this actual moment. The probability of her making a full recovery is still relatively small, and there is still a chance of death. So, granted, death itself is not improbable. However, it seems highly unlikely that she should be dead at this precise moment, given that Danny had a phone call from the hospital twenty-one minutes ago, at which point she was certainly still alive. And on this basis, your suicidal intentions seem particularly illogical.'

When he says twenty-one minutes, he's looking up at the clock, with the straight red numbers, and they're saying 18.14, and I'm thinking that that means I will need to do my throwing soon, but also in my brain it's like there's just a sudden jumble – like one huge pile of clothes and toys and old spoons and things has just been dropped in it. Because why is Connor Flynn telling me that my mum, that's Jenny Nicely, is alive, when the other man, who's Simon I think, and probably not really Stephen at all, was telling me that she was dead?

Maybe it is a trick. Maybe Connor Flynn is being secret and sly to stop me jumping. Because soon I'm going to have to do the jump. And then I will be dead, like squirrel goo. Maybe that's why he's lying about my mum being alive.

'Are you telling me a fib?' This is me. 'Is it to stop me throwing myself? Is it just a big trick?'

Now he's really squeezing his face up, with his eyebrows nearly touching.

'I find it almost impossible to lie. My brother would tell you that. He says it's a character fault. So no, certainly not. I'm merely saying I believe your mother, Jenny Nicely, to be alive. And that if you are planning to take your life because you believe that she is dead, then it would seem a logical prerequisite that you should be certain that this fact is correct first.'

There are some other people on the platform now, a woman with a pushchair and a coat that looks like it's a furry animal, and a man with a hoodie, and he's moving his head, with headphones on his ears. They are standing on the platform and going a bit nearer to the edge, and there's a sound, and it's a train, even though I can't see it yet.

'It is correct. This fact. She really is dead.' I'm feeling tight in my chest and jumbled in my head and inside me it's going bumbum bumbum, so fast, because if I'm going to throw myself, I have to hurry up now. And I don't want to do it. But I have to do it. And I don't even want to think about how it will be. Maybe hurting and maybe screaming with the train hitting me. I'm looking to where the train will be coming, and up to the clock, which is 18.15, and back to Connor Flynn. 'It *is*. Because otherwise why would Stephen Taylor say it? Simon Taylor. He works at the hospital – he *really* does – so he must know.'

'Simon Taylor?' It's like Connor Flynn is sitting up, with a bit of a jerk, making himself taller on the bench. But now I can see the train and it will be here quite soon. And really I need to go and do my jump.

'Who is Simon Taylor?' This is Connor Flynn.

And I don't know what to do. Because he's asking all these questions but the train will be here so soon. I say, he's just a man and he's called Simon Taylor. I met him, at the writing group, because he's one of them. But also he's at the hospital sometimes because of working there.

'Let's consider this.' This is Connor Flynn. And he's being quiet. He's looking at his fingers, doing the straight piano thing.

'The train's coming.' This is me telling him. And inside me it's bumbum bumbum bumbum and it's so fast. I'm crying and I can hear myself breathing with big noisy breaths. 'I have to get up . . . I have to go now.'

I'm standing up. The train is nearly coming into the station now. I take a step away from the bench, because I have to go to the edge now. *Right now.*

'I have to go. I have to do it now.'

'Technically not, since there's another train in five minutes.' He's pointing to the clock. So now I'm looking there, when I should be making myself ready.

'The one to Rainham (Kent)?'

'Yes.'

I don't understand why he's saying this. Why is he talking about trains to Rainham (Kent)? I'm about to be dead, and he's thinking about the thing – the word – about trains and the times and the tables.

'I *need* to go *now*. Simon Taylor knows, he knows it even better, because of working at the hospital. It's not just a phone call, it's a real person. He *knows* and he says my mother is dead . . .'

I can see the front of the train. It says Gatwick Airport. I take one more step towards the edge.

'But, objectively, I fail to see why you would believe his report of your mother's death above that of the hospital worker who told Danny specifically that your mother was not dead. In fact, conversely, that she was positively alive. This must at least put into doubt the reliability of Simon Taylor's information. The more natural assumption would surely be that it is Simon Taylor who is either mistaken or lying and the person calling from the hospital who is correct.'

And now it's me looking at him, and my face

feels like it's a big open-mouth 'O'. And I don't have any words coming. Because I don't even understand. And then there's the train, and it's already come and it's stopping. And I'm not on the track. So, flip a pancake, now I will have to do the throwing when it's the Rainham (Kent) train instead. But I'm not even thinking about that. I'm thinking about the jumble. And not knowing what it all means. In my head, it's all the questions. I'm such a jumble head I can't even throw myself right.

And I'm just looking at Connor Flynn, and the train is going away again, with the woman with the pram and the man with the headphones and the whoosh and the rattle and the click on the tracks.

I'm putting my lips together, trying to make a word. But I don't know what word. And then at last one comes and it's just *don't . . . ?*

I'm not even sure what else I want to say.

Connor Flynn is looking at his hands, with the finger-piano-playing thing, and he's murmuring a bit to himself, like, *most likely assumption* and *interesting*. And *perhaps another Simon Taylor*. And most probable explanation. And then it's like he remembers that I'm there.

'Simon Taylor is one of the members of the writing group that you and Danny both attend? That's correct?'

I nod to tell him yes.

'And is your mother – Jenny Nicely, I mean – aware of this? Of him being one of your classmates?'

I don't know. I tell him, I don't think she knows him.

I don't know why he's asking it. Because, even though he's really so clever, he doesn't seem to understand about Simon Taylor, who maybe isn't Stephen at all and only ever Simon, being the one who works in the hospital, and that being why he knows these things. And that's what is important, not about him being in my writing group. That's just a thing. The word . . .

'. . . possibility that it would be a coincidence.' This is like he's talking to himself again. And that's the word I was looking for. About coaches and meeting people that you don't know but who are your cousin really. And about the Ellies too. He looks at me again, but in his way that's not really looking at me, but only at my ear or my shoulder. 'This is very interesting, because Simon Taylor – Taylor is the name of the person named on the DNA paternity test in your mother's paperwork.'

I don't even know what he's saying now. And I say I don't understand. 'What test . . . ?'

'Paternity. To confirm or disprove his biological fatherhood. DNA is the most reliable method of ascertaining paternity using the analysis of patterns of Short Tandem Repeats or microsatellites. These are highly repetitive sections of DNA and consist of a number of nucleotide repeating . . .'

Fatherhood? I'm looking at Connor Flynn and I'm trying to understand. Because there's a thing that I think he's saying. About Simon Taylor. About him being . . .

'He's my . . .' I can't say the word. There is no air in me. It's not even a jumble. It's like my brain is too surprised to even do any thinking anymore. Because all my life, I've thought about having a birth mother who threw me away, but I never ever even thought about having a father. Or hardly at all.

I say I don't understand, but Connor Flynn is still talking. And it's about tracts of repetitive DNA and bi, tri and tetra nucleotides and polymorphic regions and forensic certainty.

I say I don't understand again and Connor Flynn says: 'Investigations of short tandem repeats based on the mutations of—'

'I don't care about short tandems.' This is me. I'm shouting. 'Why is Simon Taylor a test in my mum's papers? What test did he do? I don't even understand.'

'The DNA results were with your mother's papers, along with all the adoption documentation. I didn't have time to read them fully, but they were in fact irrelevant. However, I do recall the name. Although both Simon and Taylor are common enough names, so it's not beyond the realms of probability that it would be a different . . .'

'Why didn't you tell me?' My brain is still trying to understand but, flip a pancake, it's like this has to be a big make-it-up fib. A ginormous one. Because how can it be true? It's like my brain is on a merry-go-round, and everything is turning too fast for me to see it properly.

'Tell you what?'

'About the DNA. About me having a father who was Simon Taylor.'

'Unnecessary. The forensic analysis proved objectively that he was *not* your father. And a negative DNA result must be accepted as conclusive beyond doubt since in ninety-nine point—'

'Simon Taylor did a test to see if he was my father . . .'

I still don't understand. Not about the ninety-nine point nines or the negative DNA or about Simon Taylor doing the test. And I need to understand. But the train must be coming soon. The one to Rainham (Kent). And then it will be too late.

'Yes. It proved that he was not. Conclusively. The probability of a false result is so small as to be

357

negligible. Of course, without full knowledge of the precise methods used in testing it is impossible to say quite how small the chance of a wrong result is. But assuming competent geneticists, approved conventional methods and aseptic technique in a laboratory environment, the likelihood of an inaccurate result is between one in two million and—'

'But . . .' My head is so tired. It wants all the questions and the ginormous muddle to go away, and just to leave it. Because I'm not even meant to be thinking about this.

'My mum would have told me. About the DNA. And Simon Taylor. And the being my father. Or the not being. Conclusively. She would have done.'

Connor Flynn isn't saying anything more to me, really. He's just looking into the air with his fingers moving. And he's talking only to himself, about the accuracy to nine decimal points. Or maybe ninety. And about one to six or more base points, and about variable numbers and more about short tandems and genetic linkage. But I'm here too. I'm on the platform. And I don't even know what I should be thinking about. Because if the train comes, the Rainham (Kent) one, which is coming in maybe just a minute or two, maybe I should still be doing the throwing myself, because that is what I've come here for. Only for that. But my brain is so full.

I want to ask my mum – Jenny Nicely – what all these things mean. But I can't ask her. And now I don't even know if I can ever ask her again.

Connor Flynn is still sitting on the bench. He is still moving his fingers and still looking at a place that is not quite on my shoulders. And he is still looking like he has all the answers in the world and that he is the cleverest person I have ever met. But most of all, there is only one thing that I really want to know.

'And she's not dead? Really not?'

Connor Flynn doesn't reply, because of still saying mutation rates and homologous chromosomes. So I say it louder. A bit shouting.

'My mum is alive? Really, really really? She is alive? She's not dead?'

'It is most probable that your adoptive mother is alive based on the fact that Danny Flynn received a call . . .' he looks up at the red light clock, 'twenty-seven minutes ago asking for you to go to the hospital as soon as possible. Jenny Nicely has regained consciousness.'

26

In the taxi, I'm staring out of the window and we're going past the shops that say bookmakers and off-licence and hardware and post office. And underneath the streetlights there are people, doing the things that people do, like walking, and standing at the bus stops, and wrapping their scarves around their necks. And I don't know what I'm feeling inside, because of it being almost like there have been too many feelings and now there are none left.

My hands are in my lap, one on top of the other, and I can't stop them shaking.

And – I don't know why I'm doing it – I hold out my hand, and put my fingers around Connor Flynn's fingers.

He pulls his hand away, fast as anything, like I've burned him and says: 'I don't like being touched.'

I lift up my hand, to show him how much it's

shaking. I say can't he hold it. I say, I need him to do it. I say please.

'But I don't like anybody touching me.'

'Please can you. Just for one minute. Please.'

He makes a sound, a bit like humming, but he takes my hand, holding it inside his. It is stiff and tight, with his fingers just holding onto mine on the outside, not in between them. He's also lifting his other hand up to in front of his face. I think he's looking at his watch, because he's mumbling the numbers to himself. And when he gets to sixty, he takes his hand away again.

'Where have you been? We've been worried sick. Hope, what were you thinking, running off again? Nobody had any idea where you'd . . .' Julie Clarke's accent is like somebody singing in my ears but she's looking at me with her mouth down, and a bit like the man with no cereal left. But then she stops, and shakes her head. And she says: 'Oh, sweetheart, thank goodness you're OK. And you heard, about your mum, that she's been trying to talk . . . ?'

Julie doesn't want me to be overexcited. She says the doctors told her we should keep our expectations realistic, and of course, Julie says, she's so disorientated

– Jenny is – and it's not even real words. I shouldn't expect a miracle.

'She didn't seem to recognise me at all. And she didn't seem to understand what I was saying. So I wouldn't want you to think . . .'

Connor waits outside while I go in. Julie Clarke stays in the corridor with him too, because she has to send lots of messages to tell people I'm safe, but a nurse comes into the room with me. Her name is Zehra.

My mum, Jenny Nicely, is sort of sitting up, because of the bed being higher where it can lift her up at her head. And the mask isn't on her, just the little tube under her nose – and that's good because I can see her face. Her eyes are closed, and I'm thinking that this is what she's been like all the time, but then she opens them. And she looks up towards the light on the ceiling and then she looks towards the window.

I say, hello Mum. And in my body, it's like bumbum bumbum, really hard and really fast, because it's not very nice to think that I was going to throw myself and be squirrel goo, but also because she's moving her head, and she hasn't done that for all the time since she had the thing, which was the emergency.

She doesn't say hello back, and she doesn't open

her arms for a big, lovely hug. But she does make a noise. And it's not a word, I don't think, but it's like a few letters, like maybe A and O and maybe U. And then she blinks, and it's a big blink, like her eyelids are hard to move and like she's having to try really hard.

I walk to beside her bed and I put my hand onto her hand. I put my fingers into hers, and I do a little squeeze, gentle as I can. I say, hello Mum, again.

She turns her head. Away from the window and slowly, slowly, slowly until it's towards me. And her eyes are on mine, but it's like they're not really looking at them. And they're closing again. I think maybe she's falling asleep.

I say, please don't be gone. I say, come back to me. I say, I love you. I don't just say it once. I say it twice and then again more times, many times. I keep saying it. I love you, Mum, I love you, I love you.

And she makes another sound. It's still not a word. It's still more just like a letter. Like a letter O. And then again. O – o – O.

I stay beside her, with her hand in my hand. I'm listening. And I'm crying, but silent, with just tears and no noise. And then my mum makes another sound, like two letters together. Like O and then p. Like O-p. O-p. Like she's trying to do the alphabet.

And her eyes are opening again, and they're looking towards me, and they're black and brown, like coffee, but with just a little tiny bit of milk. And they're looking, not up to the ceiling or not to the window, or not like it's into nothing. They're looking at me. Right into my eyes.

I say, 'I love you, Mum. I love you so much. Please come back to me.'

And she says it again, and this time I know what she's saying.

'Hope.'

9

CONCLUSIONS

27

'And how do you feel about this?'

This is Camilla da Silva. She's the one who asks all the questions, but there are no right answers, just me talking and talking and talking. And mostly it's about how did I feel about this thing, or what did I think about that thing. She has a candle on the table by her chair, it's a big one, with not just one burning string, but one-two-three, in a glass pot, and it smells really nice, like our tree in the front garden when all the bees come buzzing. And the burning bit is called a wick. One, two, three wicks.

She has a notebook. Camilla da Silva does. But it's not as nice as my notebook. It's blue too but it's not so big and not quite so blue. Her pen is really nice though. It's shiny and silver, almost as nice as my special pen, but not quite.

'I feel . . .' I'm thinking hard, to give the right answer. But in my head, I'm hearing a word. And the word is silver. Maybe because of the pen. And also because of her name being da Silva too. But I have to stop thinking about the word and think about how I feel about the things I know now.

'I feel . . .' *Silver. Silver. Silver.* 'I feel . . .' I'm telling myself not to stare at the pen. Julie Clarke says it's important for me to say the truth to Camilla so I'm trying really hard to do that. I'm squeezing my brain and I'm telling all the *silvers* to be quiet. And I'm thinking Camilla's question in my head again. *How do you feel?*

But it's not easy to know the answer, because of my memory, maybe, and the jumble and forgetting lots of things, even if they're feelings and even if they're important. And really because of not understanding quite everything still, although it's been explained a lot of times. Because of it being such a lot to take in.

We're going to talk about it a bit more later. Julie Clarke and Simon Taylor and me. They're going to take me to the hospital to see my mum, Jenny Nicely. But now I'm concentrating, and trying to think about feelings, and all the practising and all the magazines and buses. But I can't find the right answer.

'I don't know what I feel?'

Camilla da Silva doesn't say anything. Her chair is the same as my chair – which is brown and I think it's leather – except that my chair has arms and hers doesn't. And also my chair can spin. I'm holding the arms with my hands and going a little bit from side to side. And still Camilla da Silva isn't saying anything. She's just looking at me. I think maybe she wants me to say something else.

'It's a lot to take in.' This is me. And Camilla da Silva is nodding so I think this was a good answer.

'You *have* had a lot to take in. How do you think you *should* feel?'

Her eyes are very wide, and I really want to give her a better answer instead of just 'I don't know' again. I put my thumbs inside my fingers and squeeze, like maybe that will help me think. *How do I think I should feel?*

And I'm thinking about adverts in magazines, and role playing with my mum Jenny, and pictures on buses, and cereal and biscuits, and Simon Taylor crying when he came to the hospital with Danny Flynn. And him saying he was so sorry.

'A bit sad, and maybe a bit angry. And mostly sad . . .'

'Sad. Why do you say that?'

'Because of never saying thank you for the monkey. And because of Simon Taylor, too, and him wanting to be my father and not being my father, because of the DNA and the test showing that it was

ninety-ninety-nine at least probably-ty that he wasn't
. . . And him saying everything was his fault, even
though I don't think it was really.'

'Why do you say it wasn't his fault?'

'I don't know. Julie Clarke says my mum had
tried to tell me before.'

'About your birth mother?'

'Yes. But I don't remember it.'

'You don't remember her telling you?'

'No. Julie Clarke says it made me do not very
good things. Like maybe drinking vodka or running
into a car.'

'So when your mum, Jenny, tried to talk to you
about your biological mother, it made you do harmful
things to yourself?'

'Julie Clarke says it did. I don't remember.'

'You don't remember drinking alcohol or being
hit by a car?' This is Camilla with her big eyes looking
at me.

My head is a bit tired now, like maybe it's time
to stop talking. But Camilla is still looking at me.
She's still waiting for an answer.

'I do remember *that*, of course. I remember the
vodka because of the boys from school saying it was
fun to do it. From class 11E. And they had vodka
in bottles that were for water, Because of the bottles
saying Highland Spring, except when you drink it,

then yuck. They said I should drink it with them, because if I didn't, I would be a lame Spaz. And that's not a nice word. It's a horrible word. And I didn't want them to call me it. I didn't think they should even say it at all. So I do remember it, actually. And I remember drinking the vodka mostly in the playground. Because of us being friends and having fun. I remember the car too. Because of it hurting.'

'You say they were your friends? The boys you drank with?'

'Yes. That was why we had to drink the vodka together. Because of being friends and it being fun. They said that was why.'

'Did you think it was fun?'

I'm looking at Camilla da Silva. And I'm thinking about the boys saying, look, Spaz Nicely's drunk, and about them saying your mum threw you away in a cardboard box like you were rubbish, and about them saying, come on, Spaz, you know you want to. And about the car. And my arm pointing the wrong way. And screaming for my mum.

Camilla is still looking at me like she's waiting for an answer. But I can't remember what her question was until she says it again. 'Did you think it was fun?'

And I shake my head and I say, no, not very fun. I've talked and talked already and now my head is feeling not so chatty anymore. Really I'd like to close my eyes and not answer any more questions and not have to think about what I remember and what I don't remember and how did I feel. But I'm not closing my eyes. I'm looking at the three burning bits of string. One, two, three. Wicks, actually. And I'm smelling the nice smell from the wicks, which is me using a word which is like an old factory. And I'm spinning a bit in my chair, one way and then the other way.

'Hope?' It's Camilla. She's asked me a question but I haven't listened properly, so she has to ask it again.

'You don't remember your mum trying to tell you about your birth mother?'

'No.'

'You've been told that you attempted to do harmful things to yourself after she talked to you about your birth mother. But you don't remember it yourself?'

'No.'

'And how do you feel about that?'

She's looking at me with her eyes wanting me to talk. I don't want to even talk. But it is *very* important, that's what Julie Clarke says, and it will help me. So even though I don't want to talk, that's what I have to do.

'I don't know how I feel. Julie says that was why my mum thought it might be good for me to write my book.'

'It might help you to know how you feel about your birth mother?'

'Yes.'

'And why do you think you can talk about it now, when it was so hard for you before?'

'I don't know. I just can. I don't know why. Maybe because of my book. Maybe because of writing it to find her now.'

'OK. So, your book is helping. You've talked about being part of a writing group. How's that going?'

But I don't want to tell her that. And now in my tummy it's a bit like something squeezing, like it's making everything inside me feel heavy and tight. And I say I don't want to talk anymore. I say thank you. I say I think it's time to stop.

I'm not going to *tell* that it's poached eggs for lunch, because of the number one rule, but I'm going to *show* that there are one, two, three pieces of toast on my plate, and it's white bread, but a little bit brown because of being toast now, and on one of them are baked beans and on the other pieces of toast there are white circles – except more oval really. They're my favourite sort of eggs, much better than scrambled, and even better than fried ones, actually. Because of not being so flat. When I put my knife into my egg, the yellow runs out onto the toast and onto the plate too. And it's the yummiest bit. But when Connor Flynn puts his knife into his egg, none of the yellow runs out, because of Bridget making it not so runny for him.

'Marnie Shale says it's still all right to put it in my book. Even if it is a little tiny coincidence. She says it's still all right.'

I didn't even have to look for the word in my brain one tiny bit. *Coincidence*. Not even bingo. It was just there.

'What coincidence? Him working at the hospital? Or being in your writing group?' Bridget Flynn means Simon Taylor. I know that's his only name now, and not Stephen at all. I'll always remember it now. Because of talking to him on the telephone, and also because of him coming to Danny Flynn's house with Julie Clarke. I think that was yesterday, maybe. And soon he'll be coming again, actually, and Julie Clarke too, because of them and me going to the hospital later.

I've done so much talking today, it's been talk, talk, talk. In the morning, there was Marnie Shale, popping by for a little word with me, with Danny Flynn here too, not going to work in the morning, because of a half day. Marnie Shale brought some chocolates, which were like the snails, but I didn't eat very many at all, because of not feeling very hungry, actually.

And then there was more talking with Camilla da Silva. And after that a little nap, because of all the talking, talking, talking making my head so sleepy. And now Bridget Flynn is looking at me, with her eyebrows close together, and asking about what coincidence.

'Only a *tiny* bit of a coincidence. Not one like sitting in a bus with your cousin who you don't even know. Because of Simon Taylor wanting to find me anyway, so it wasn't a ginormous one.'

'Hang on, so this Simon joined the writing group to find you?'

'No. Because he didn't know that I was going to be doing the lessons too. He didn't know that I even wanted to write a book. But he did want to find me and that was why he wanted to talk to my mum, and he did go to the bookshop too. But my mum wasn't even there. Because it was her day off, maybe. Maybe it was a Sunday, when he went, and my mum doesn't work on Sunday.'

'Still, sounds like quite a coincidence to me.' This

is Bridget again, with her eyes wide and her mouth too. 'Let alone him working at the—'

'Not really . . .' It's Danny Flynn speaking really quickly. I'm dipping my toast into the egg, and pressing it down with my fork, because of that being the yummiest bit. So I'm looking at my plate now. But with a bit of my eyes, I'm seeing Danny Flynn looking at Bridget and shaking his head. But he stops when I look at him. And he smiles at me, even though he's still talking to Bridget.

'Lots of people want to write books, Mum. And the NHS is the biggest employer in the country. As you should know. And—'

'It *wasn't* a gigantic coincidence about him working in the hospital, actually.' I'm only interrupting a little bit because of it being important. 'Actually it was as far away from a coincidence as anything.'

'But . . .' I think maybe Bridget is going to say something else but Danny Flynn is putting his finger to his mouth. Connor Flynn is cutting his egg into slices. He's already eaten all his beans.

'He really *really* didn't know about my mum being in the hospital.' I'm explaining it to Bridget Flynn. And I know because of Simon telling it to me, and Marnie too. And that's why it's not such a gigantic coincidence so I can still write it in my book. 'He didn't even have any idea that she was there.

Julie Clarke was right about it being a ginormous hospital and him being in a different part of it. And that's because of him being a special sort of nurse. An alcohol nurse. For alcoholics. The disease for people who can't stop drinking vodka and gin – I mean G. And beer and wine. And that's not a coincidence at all, about him being that sort of nurse, because he even decided to do that job because of my birth mother and me, maybe, too. That's why he decided not to be a computer programmer anymore, but to become an alcohol nurse. But mostly he works with people in their homes, and only sometimes in the hospital, like maybe once a week, and he didn't even know that my mum – Jenny Nicely – was there. So that is really not a coincidence like one person going to America and meeting their cousin in a bus, even without knowing who they are. That's much more ginormous. That's a real couldn't-make-it-up coincidence.'

Connor Flynn has stopped cutting his egg and he's looking at me now, except not really at me, but more past my shoulder.

'The comparison is of the probability of one individual encountering a previously unknown family member on a random form of transport in a random town and, one could perhaps assume, a random country, with what, a separate individual from a known area working in the hospital that another individual is being treated in?'

I say yes, because I think that's what I'm doing, maybe.

Connor Flynn is still looking past my shoulder, with his fingers doing the piano thing.

'It is impossible to assess the variables for each situation, of course, and there are too many unknowns to establish an approximate probability to any degree of certainty. However, my assumption would be that the probability of scenario A would be vastly less than scenario B, taking into account both geographical and—'

'It's a more gigantic coincidence being on the bus. Being in the hospital is only a little bit of one. That's what Marnie Shale says.' This is me. It's only a little bit interrupting because I don't understand what Connor Flynn is saying.

'Well, yes, of course. The degrees of differentiation are impossible to calculate reliably but without doubt the greater coincidence would be the meeting of an unknown family member in a random state in . . .'

I'm smiling really hard now. Because Connor Flynn is so clever. And because I was right about the coincidence. And Danny Flynn is saying Julie and Simon will be here soon to take me to the hospital.

This is my box. That's what Julie is saying. And she's saying it with a big smile. We used to look at it a lot together when I was younger – it's my very own box, but not the box I was left in, which was a cardboard one. This is the same size as the one which my trainers came in, except it doesn't say *Nike*, of course, it says *Hope Nicely* and it says *My Life* and it is white and it is wooden and not big enough to put a baby in, unless it was a very tiny baby. It is on my knees and it has a photograph on the lid, which is me, but when I was very little. Julie is saying: 'Look at you in your cute little Baby Grow.'

A Baby Grow is not for growing a baby, even if that's what it's called. It's like pyjamas, actually, but only one pyjama, not a pyjama top and a pyjama bottom, just one whole pyjama. And my Baby Grow has pictures of dogs all over it. I'm not sure what type of dogs they are, but maybe Yorkie Poo-Shits, just like Barry. My hair is sticking up on my head and I'm smiling but without any teeth, except for tiny ones at the front. I'm standing up with both my hands on a sort of trolley, not like a supermarket trolley, like a little one with lots of wooden bricks, and some of them are blue and some are red and some are yellow and some are green.

'You remember this box? From when you were very little, looking at it with your mum, and with me sometimes too. I don't know if you remember but . . .'

'I do remember.' This is me, and I sort of do. Remember. But sort of I don't a bit too, because my memory – well the least said about that – and when I look at the box, even now, even with knowing what is inside it, mostly, I can feel my heart doing a bit of *bumbum bumbum*.

The box is on my lap and I am opening it. I am sitting in a chair, which is a proper one with arms, but not as comfortable as Camilla da Silva's chair, which is leather, and it doesn't turn from one side to the other, more's the pity. And I am in the corner, not the corner next to my mum, Jenny – that's Julie Clarke who is there on that side of the room. There is Simon Taylor too. He's sitting next to me, so he's in between Julie and me, on his own chair, but it's not one with padding or arms. It's just plastic.

Inside the box is a book. Not a buy-it-from-a-bookshop book. Not a book like my mum's poem books. Not like my lovely blue notebook or my book of golden rules. Not my book, which is an autobiography, because I haven't written it yet of course, but one which is like a schoolbook for lessons, like biology and spellings and maths. It's an exercise book, actually, and it is a bit messy at the corners, but with writing on it, which is mostly Julie's writing, she says, but also another social worker's from when I was even littler. This writing is not so loopy and neat as Julie's is. It leans to the side more.

And it says: *My story*. And it says, *When I was very tiny, my mother wasn't able to look after me, but a kind woman called Anne found me outside her church, and then a lovely person called Jenny said she wanted to be my new mummy and she would always love me very much. And so I went to live with her.* There is a photograph, stuck in with Sellotape – except the Sellotape is more brown than normal Sellotape, and it's lifting up a little bit and not all stuck down anymore, and when I touch the lifted-up bit it goes crinkle under my finger. The photograph is of me, when I'm a baby, an even littler one, with a white hat and a dummy in my mouth, and there is a picture too of my mum holding me, of Jenny Nicely, but when she was not so old and before she'd put on a few pounds, even before the blue dress, but still with her big silver earrings which are hoops and lots of bracelets.

And there is a photograph of the church, which is called St Magdalene's, even though that wasn't the name of the vicar, which was Anne Bentley. And the book says other things, like how I went to Cherry Tree nursery and then to my school, and about me liking to eat chocolate mousse and Gummy Bears, and my favourite song being 'Zoom Zoom Zoom' and the 'Grand Old Duke of York'. I don't think that was ever my favourite song so I don't know why it says it. But I do remember Gummy Bears. They were yummy.

There are lots of photographs in the box too – under the book, but not stuck in. There's me in the park, and me with Julie playing with a wooden car. On one it's a picture of me, when I was little. It's when I was six years old, and I know this because of Simon Taylor showing me the date on the back, and saying, so you would have been six when this was taken, and because of remembering it now. Maybe. And I'm looking at this picture and at me, with my hair in two ponytails, which is bunches. I'm sitting on a chair, in the picture, and the chair must be quite big because my feet are in the air and not down to the floor. I don't remember my red shoes, so it must have been a very long time ago. And I'm wearing a T-shirt that is Angelina Ballerina and I'm holding up a monkey and I'm smiling, with all my teeth, except for one, which is on the top and must have been a wobbly-fall-out one. Beside me, it's like it's another me there too, except not me who is six years old in the photo, with frilly socks, but more like me now, me all grown up.

But this me is not me at all, actually. It is Ellie,

who is the social worker, who bought me a monkey – the monkey that I'm holding in the picture. *That* monkey. And in the photograph I'm looking at the monkey. But now, in the real world, not the photo one, in the hospital, now, what I'm looking at is mostly the Ellie in the photo.

I'm looking really hard at her face, because of it being so interesting – and that is because it is really so much like my face.

If I was going to show it, not tell it, maybe I would say about her skin being a bit like a yoghurt that is peach, or maybe more like apricot, which is like mine too, and with black hair too. And having a mouth that is quite a lot like my mouth too. It is just a mouth, but with the lip maybe a bit bigger on the bottom than the top. And both of our mouths are smiling. I think I do remember the monkey – in a little bit of my brain – because of it having a plastic face and a thumb that went into its mouth and having a name, which was Monkey. I don't know where it is now. The monkey.

'Wasn't she pretty?' This is Simon Taylor, and he's looking at my photograph too. And he's not talking about the monkey. He's talking about Ellie, because she was his girlfriend once, a long time ago.

There are more photographs too, in the box. There's one of me with my teaching assistant who was called Susan, but not Ford. That's someone else. And there are some old pages from newspapers, which say *The Mystery of the Christmas Box Baby* and *Abandoned Newborn Found on Church Steps on Christmas Eve.* And also there is a necklace which has a glass circle on it, and inside is a tiny bit of hair, and I think maybe it's mine because of it being black too.

There is one other picture, but it's not in the box – except now it can be if I want to keep it. Because it's from Simon Taylor's pocket in his leather jacket, but now I can have it forever if I want to. He's giving it to me.

'I guess I've changed a tiny bit.' He's taking the photograph out and he's passing it to me. He's laughing a bit and he's rubbing his head with his hand. 'God, time flies.'

I'm not looking at the photograph yet, because I'm still looking at Simon Taylor because he's saying about time flying, which makes me think of a clock going across the sky like an aeroplane, or maybe a bird. And I'm trying to remember what the word is that is like feeling like money, or time being in the sky, which is not real. But it's a . . .

It's a . . .

And he's shaking his head and saying one day I'll understand about it feeling like only yesterday.

Analogy! I'm smiling because of that being such

a good bingo. And now I'm lifting up the photograph to look at it, with Simon Taylor still talking about it being unbelievable, and where do the years go.

'It's not a tiny change at all.' This is me. And I'm shouting a bit because of how very big the change is. 'It's gi-nor-mous. It's a gigantic change.'

Because in the picture, it's Simon Taylor with a face that is very young, and with hair that is long and yellow instead of black and a little bit white. And he's wearing a T-shirt which is Bart Simpson saying *Cowabunga* and also long shorts with flowers on them and he's holding a cigarette which is a rolled-up one and in the other hand a beer, which is a Lite. And she's next to him, with his arm – the one with the beer – around her shoulder. Eliana, who is also Ellie. And she is also the social worker, who wasn't a real one, in fact, who gave me a monkey, and also my birth mother, but not yet in this photograph, that's what Simon Taylor says, because of not even knowing that I was in her tummy, and because of her tummy being quite little even though I must have been in there already. And she's not wearing a smart skirt and a shirt, like in the other picture, the monkey one, but shorts which are very, very short, like *teeny-tiny* and made out of jeans, and tights which have lots of holes, like maybe hundreds, like so many that it's more holes and rips than tights.

And a pair of boots, which are DMs, like Julie Clarke wears sometimes, which are also called Docs. And she has a shirt which is tied around her waist.

'I wish you could have known her.' This is Simon Taylor again. 'She was always laughing and always singing. Suzanne Vega and Tracy Chapman. Joni Mitchell too. She loved all that stuff. I used to tease her about being an old hippy. And wherever we went, I never really cared about making friends, but she just seemed to attract them. People. She had this warmth. She talked to anyone. She never stopped chatting away.' He does a funny little laugh. 'A bit like you, actually.'

He's stopped talking now, and he's looking at me, with his eyes so big, and so like they're telling me something. And I nod, because I think that must be what he wants.

'She was a good person, Hope. You need to understand that. And all the drinking and the . . . other stuff. It wasn't really who she *was*. She was happy just to get on the bus, and find new places, and sing her songs and meet her people. It wasn't just the getting wasted. But it was just . . . That summer. It just all went a bit . . . crazy. I don't quite know what happened. None of it was really her fault. It was just a thing. It wasn't *her*. None of it. Do you understand? Tell me you do understand.'

He's looking at me with his eyes so big, and his whole body leaning towards me. And I'm thinking that what he really, really wants me to say is that, yes, I do understand, and I'm thinking about all the practice with my mum, and all the pictures on the buses, and the thinking about people's feelings, because of being grown up now. So that is what I say. I say yes I do understand, with my voice like it's really important to me. But, really, I don't understand.

'I think maybe we've discussed this enough now, Hope.' This is Julie Clarke. She has a look on her face that is a sort of smile, but with her lips together and her head on one side. 'You've had so much to take in already, darling. Maybe we should stop talking about all of this until another day. I wouldn't want to upset you. Maybe we should wait until Jenny's fitter.'

We both look at my mum, Jenny. She's asleep.

And I'm thinking Julie Clarke is saying about waiting and not talking anymore now because of the other times when my mum, Jenny Nicely, tried to talk to me about my birth mother, about her being dead. And it's a very strange thing, because I don't even remember those times. But it must be true because I don't think Julie Clarke would tell me a lie, and my memory, well . . .

'It's just that in the past, this has been an issue

for you, Hope my darling. And I'm concerned that you're in a very vulnerable . . .'

I'm trying to listen to her talking and it's lots of words like issues and loss and vulnerable. But in my head I'm thinking more about why I can't remember. If the Ellie who brought me the monkey was my birth mother, why can't I remember? And why can't I remember about her being dead, too? If my mum, Jenny Nicely, has told me about it, why can't I remember?

I think Julie Clarke wants to stop talking because she thinks maybe I will do not-so-clever things like breaking the window, or taking all the drawers in the kitchen and throwing all the knives and forks and spoons and plates on the floor, or screaming. That's what Julie Clarke says I did before. And the rope with the knot that came undone. Julie Clarke says that all those things happened around the times when Jenny tried to talk to me about my birth mother, whose name was Ellie and also Eliana. And the car. The running into the car. That happened too.

But I don't remember my mum, Jenny Nicely, *ever* talking about it. I do remember the monkey. And I remember the vodka and the friends, who were not very good friends, actually, because of not keeping their hands and feet to themselves.

And I remember the car and screaming and

screaming, and not being able to move my arm. And I remember my mum, Jenny Nicely, cuddling me and saying she loved me and that everything was going to be OK.

The rope was a different time. When I was already grown up with a real job. It was when I used to walk back from the park to my home, which is 23a Station Close. After walking the dogs, Karen, my boss, gave me my money and I walked back and my mum was there. Now, Karen always comes back with me to the house now, or else my mum picks me up or Karen, my boss, takes me to my writing group, except now it's a bit different, with me walking more with Connor Flynn or Bridget or Danny Flynn because of living in their house now, but then, before, the pub time, I walked back on my own. And sometimes, when my mum wasn't there because of working in the bookshop, I had my key and it was all right, because of just watching TV, until my mum was home too. And one day, I met some of my friends from school – even though they weren't really friends anymore, because of being not very good ones, and also because of not being at school anymore – and they said, oh look, it's Hope Nicely. They said fancy meeting me there, and what was I doing now and I told them I had a real job, actually, with real dogs and real money. And they said I should go to the pub with them. And I said I didn't like pubs but they said I should go with them anyway. It was because of being like a school . . . what's the word? Like a party. And that was why it was OK. It was like a school party. For old friends.

A celebration. Because of meeting them again.

And the pub was not the White Hart. I can't remember its name, maybe another animal one. And it wasn't very nice because of being noisy and smelly too. And my friends didn't have any money, but it was all right because of me having some money. And it was enough money for some beer for them, and for me too, and for some other people, who I didn't know, but who were their friends from the pub.

But it wasn't a very good celebration. My friends told the other people in the pub about me being a pissy knickers and always shouting in school and being a Spaz. And also about me drinking vodka and running into a car. And I think it was maybe funny, because of them laughing a lot. But I wasn't laughing so much. It made me think that maybe, actually, it would be good to be just an ordinary drop of light, even if it didn't make a rainbow. Maybe it would be good to be a person who was not me at all. And it made me think that maybe adopting me wasn't the best thing my mum, Jenny Nicely, ever did. Maybe it was not all for the best, actually.

It made me think about the rope.

But Julie Clarke says it was because of all the words like issues and loss and susceptible and vulnerable. And about there being so much to take in and about it being a low point. She thinks it was about my birth mother being dead. *Triggered*, she says. Because of my mum, Jenny Nicely, trying to tell me, even if I don't remember it.

And Julie Clarke thinks that now there is so much to take in again. She means about my birth mother. About Ellie.

'We really don't have to talk about all this now, Hope.' This is what she's saying. 'Maybe it's best to leave it until another time.'

But now I do think I want to talk about it. And there is a lot to take in, maybe. But maybe now it's different. Maybe because of my book. Because I'm writing my book now, and it is a Big Achievement. And the book is because of wanting to find my birth mother, and now I have found her. Sort of I have. So I do want to talk about it, actually.

I'm not shouting. I'm not throwing toys or knives or spoons. I'm not *even* counting. Not even one, two, three. I'm not sitting on my hands. I'm not humming. I'm only looking at my mum, Jenny Nicely, with her eyes closed still, but now it's only called sleeping, now she's got her conscious back, and it will help her to be right as rain.

'I do want to talk about it actually.' This is me. I'm talking to Julie Clarke. And I'm looking at her hard to show it really is OK. 'Even if it's a lot to take in, I do want to know about it.'

Julie Clarke does a noise with her nose, which is a bit like a sigh. And she looks at Simon Taylor and she moves her shoulders up a bit. And then she does another sort of sigh, but with her mouth. And she asks me if I'm quite sure, sweetheart, that it's not going to make me upset, because, honestly, we can always carry on this conversation another time. It might be easier for me. She gives me a very long look. But I tell her I am sure, actually.

I still have the photograph in my hand. And he really has changed a lot, because of looking so much older now, with lines around his eyes and around his mouth and his hair with white in it. And when he smiles there are even more lines around his eyes.

'OK, Hope. Well, I met Ellie at a party in . . .'

'The party in your book. In the dark room with the coats?'

Because of course I know *that*. It's from his extract.

'Of course. Yes. Exactly. In the dark room.' Simon Taylor smiles again and he says, well, it was very much love at first sight for both of them. And I say, doesn't he mean hear. And he says, not right here, but not far away – it was in Hatfield, which is where he was a student and . . . And I say, no, *hear.* Love at first *hear.* Because of it being dark and him not seeing her in the room, except a little bit with the cigarettes. So it wasn't love at first sight. It was love at first *hear.* And Simon Taylor says, oh, oh yes. It was love at first hear.

'She was the most spontaneous person I ever met.' This is him. And he tells me that spontaneous means not just sitting around and thinking about doing things, but going right ahead and doing them – seizing the day. And when he told her his real dream was to travel to America, which is where they did grunge, which was music with guitars, and dirty clothes, she said, OK, go for it. He didn't have a real job and she had a holiday which was going to be months and months, because of being a student. And they both had an overdraft, which is making money from the future come to you now. And so that is what they did. Five days after meeting each other in a dark room in a party, they bought two tickets to go to America with their overdrafts.

'What neither of us knew is that she must have already been pregnant.' Simon Taylor is telling me this now and it is a bit difficult to understand, but it's because of Eliana having had other boyfriends before Simon Taylor, because of being very spontaneous. And also that's why Simon Taylor thought he was my father except in fact he wasn't. Because of DNA. But Ellie didn't even know that she had me in her tummy. And this is because of always having had problems with you-know-what girl stuff, which is periods, and also because of them partying too hard, and thinking that is why she was being sick so much. And although it was fun in America, they also had lots of fights and the biggest fight was right on the day when they were going to the airport to fly back to England and, in the end, it was such a bad fight that Simon Taylor said, right, just fuck it – 'Oh, God, I'm so sorry, Hope. Do excuse me, Julie' – why didn't she just fuck off back to England on her own and he'd stay right there in America because there sure as hell wasn't any other reason for him to go home if she was going to be like that.

And, afterwards, when she had gone back and he was still in America, he wanted to phone Ellie straight away, because of missing her so much, and also to write to her, but he didn't even have her new address because of her being a student and not having one yet. And he didn't have her phone number because of it being different then, with phone boxes not mobile phones. It was in the old days when there wasn't even the internet, for looking on Twitter and Facebook. So it was impossible. And he couldn't get on another aeroplane, because of not having any more of his overdraft, so he needed to work before he could buy another ticket. But he didn't have a thing called a visa for it even. And it ended up being more years, and a very wild time, and when he did come home in the end, nobody even knew where Ellie was and nobody knew about the baby, which was me, because of her doing that all by herself, in a bedsit, not even with any nurses, and being so scared and just putting me in a box because of being in a panic and with her brain so confused that she didn't even know what she was doing. And it made her so sad that for a long time, she wasn't even a student anymore, only a dropped-out one, and very messed up.

'She was only nineteen, Hope. Six years younger than you are now. Still a kid, really. She never forgave herself for abandoning you.'

There is a happy bit and a sad bit in the story that is about Ellie. And the happy bit is that she met a very nice man, who was a Kiwi – which is not the furry fruit, but a person who comes from the country of New Zealand. And Simon Taylor is not sure if it was love at first sight, or love at first hear, or what sort of love it was. But it was some sort of love probably, and this very nice Kiwi man helped her to get herself happy again, which is also called getting her shit together, which meant going back to university, and also coming to meet me with Monkey the monkey, because she would never be able to have a nice life ever, if she did not see me just once. And she saw that I was with a lovely new mummy and a nice home and a nice life for me too. And that is the happy bit and the moving to New Zealand and becoming a Kiwi too, and also a teacher.

But then there is the sad bit, and this is the bit that Simon Taylor knows, because of Ellie finding him on a computer when they were much older and he was not doing grunge in America anymore, but was back in England and being a computer programmer. And there still wasn't Facebook or Twitter, so it wasn't easy as anything, but there was something called Friends Reunited, which is how she found him. And it was good because she could tell him all about me, and it being the worst thing that she had ever done, and also about maybe him being my father. But it was not good too, because of her also telling him another very, very sad thing which was about her having a bad cancer which was very serious and the doctors said that probably she would die.

Julie Clarke is saying – and it's a little bit

interrupting, but I think it's OK, because she's leaning towards us, with her hand up like a cue: 'What you have to realise, Hope, is that we all wanted what was best for you. And Jenny and I were aware that you had issues regarding loss. It's one of the reasons that she felt writing your book might be such a helpful . . .'

In my brain, somewhere, not right at the front, I do remember, perhaps. Maybe I remember my mum, Jenny Nicely, saying how would I feel if one day I learned my birth mother had died. Would I want to know? I remember a little tiny bit – but not in the front bit of my brain so I'm having to look very hard like it's hiding. And I don't like death. I don't like people being in a box and gone forever. And I'm sitting on my hands because of thinking about it. I'm even humming, but only a little bit. And Julie is saying, Hope, Hope, sweetheart, are you all right?

And in my head, I'm doing a little bit of counting. One, two, three. Just a little bit. Because I think I do remember. I think I remember talking to Camilla da Silva. And her saying, *what were your feelings?*

'I'm so sorry.' This is Simon Taylor and he's putting his hand onto his head and shaking his head too. 'This is all my fault.'

'Your fault that Ellie is dead?'

'No. My fault that it's all ended up coming out like

this. It must be such a shock to you. I should have listened to Jenny. I should have talked to her first.'

'My mum Jenny?'

'Yes.'

'Jenny Nicely.'

'Yes.'

'How could you listen to her if you haven't talked to her first?'

'I . . .' He's shaking his head.

'Simon first approached us – social services – thirteen years ago about the DNA test to see if he was your biological father, and that was because your birth mother had been in contact with him to say that she was poorly. And in fact, Eliana had already contacted us too. She thought Jenny should know. But whenever Jenny tried to talk to you about her, you would become very upset. And that's why, even though Jenny said she thought it was the right thing to do the DNA test – and she tried very hard to discuss it with you too, to make sure it was something you wanted – afterwards, when the results came back, she said she thought it was best for you if we didn't try to talk to you about Eliana again too soon. She was very sorry for her, of course, and I believe she wrote to her, but she didn't think it would be good for you to have to deal with all the emotions of confronting your birth mother's existence knowing that you would then have to deal with her being gone again. She said her priority had to be your mental well-being. You do understand, don't you, darling Hope? Your mother would never hide anything from you.'

And I'm thinking about if I remember or not. But my brain, it's such a jumble. And my memory . . . I'm thinking maybe my mum did ask me. About would I want to know if somebody was related to me, or would I not want to know. And asking my mum if related was family, and about putting an earbud into my mouth, like cleaning my ear, but in my cheek. And me saying, a test to see if my mouth was clean? I don't remember her saying about a father but maybe she did. Probably she would have done.

Julie and Simon are both looking at me with their eyes watching very hard. I think they're worrying about me maybe shouting or screaming or going away. But I'm looking at my mum, Jenny, now. Because of course she would never hide anything from me. I'm more precious than all her poems put together. And her eyes are still closed, because of still needing lots of rest before she can be right as rain. But I think her head has moved a bit now.

'Before Ellie died she wrote to me.' This is Simon Taylor now. 'We knew I wasn't your father by then, but she sent me a card for you, in case I ever had the chance to meet you and give it to you. When you were ready.'

'Like now, maybe?'

'Well, yes. Except I never meant it to be like this. I'd been working in Manchester, for a few years, but when I moved back here, I got in touch with Jenny through Facebook. I told her who I was and asked if maybe I could meet you and tell you a bit about Ellie.'

'And give me the card?'

'Maybe that too. I think your mum tried to talk to you, and I think it upset you. So she said she didn't think it was a good idea and, of course, I had to respect that. But then a month or two ago, I was a bit early for a train and I went into the bookshop by the station, to fill some time. There was a book of poems by Jenny Nicely on the table at the front, and I remembered from her Facebook page that it was where she worked. I asked the woman at the cash desk if Jenny was there, and she said no – your mum wasn't working that day, so I was just going to leave again. But on the same table as the poetry book, there were some flyers for the writing group. And I'd been thinking for a long time how I'd like to write down some of my experiences – like a memoir – about my time in America. I thought it might help me put it all to rest. Anyway, I emailed Marnie to sign up. I didn't have the slightest idea that you would be in the group. That was quite a shock, actually. I couldn't believe it on that first day, when you introduced yourself. Especially as you look so much like Ellie. But then I thought that it could be a really good thing, because it would give me a chance to get to know you a bit, without upsetting you by telling you who I was or anything about the connection with Ellie. I thought maybe it would be best that way.'

'But it's definitely not a coincidence.' I am looking at him very hard, with my brain a bit worried. 'Not a ginormous one?'

'No. Because I wouldn't have been looking at that table, and have taken the flyer, if I hadn't realised the link between the bookshop and Jenny, would I? So, no, not a complete coincidence. But then when you started asking me about whether I worked at the hospital and what I knew about your mum, I thought you'd worked out who I was. When you left that session with the editor, and were so upset, Marnie mentioned a family issue and I was worried it might be my fault in some way. I didn't know about Jenny being ill. I just thought you'd rumbled me, and that it might be bad for you and that Jenny might be angry because she'd think I'd gone behind her back.'

And now I'm thinking about my mum, Jenny Nicely. And I'm looking in my box, and taking out the necklace with the hair, and the book with the not-very-straight corners, and the monkey photo. And I'm saying to Simon does he still have the card from Ellie. He says yes, he has it here and he's putting his hand in his pocket. And Julie says maybe we should wait until Jenny . . .

'Don't worry.' This is me talking. 'I'm not going to drink vodka and run under a car. I'm not a baby boo boo anymore.'

And now Julie and Simon Taylor are both looking at me, with their eyes wide. It's a little bit like the advert that was on telly yesterday. In the advert there's a woman who is talking to her dog and he's just being a dog lying on the floor, but then the dog talks to her too, and he says isn't it time for tea. And their faces are like the woman's face, with her wide eyes too. It's a surprised look.

And then there is a noise, and it's my mum, Jenny Nicely, maybe because of hearing Julie say her name. Or maybe she's been listening all this time. And now she's opening her eyes – and they're lovely eyes, which are very big, with long lashes, and they're the colour of coffee with just a tiny bit of milk. And I say to her does she want anything. I say does she want some water, maybe, like the man who wanted

402

a glass of water in the quote. Konnigurt something. She nods. So I go to her, and I give her the glass of water from her table, and I help her drink it, because she's not very strong yet, even though she's doing lots of resting and the doctors say we can try to have her out of bed maybe later today. And that would be fan-tanty-tastic because it's very boring, with her just lying down. I put her cup back down and I sit on the bed, beside her, even though I'm meant to really sit on the chair.

I hold her hand, and I say, look. A card for me. I say it's OK, I'm not going to do any silly things. And in my head, I'm sure it's true. Because it's all very calm. I'm not even thinking about humming. The envelope has my name, but no stamp. I'm thinking this is a shame because it would have been nice to have a stamp from New Zealand. Maybe even one with a kiwi on it. Maybe a furry kiwi fruit with a crown like the Queen. But I open the envelope, with my finger going ss-hh-ipp and holding the card in the other hand, with also my mum's hand. It's a card, with a picture on the outside and writing on the inside on both of the sides, but not on the back. The writing is joined-up. The 'e's aren't like my 'e's. They're like '3's but the wrong way round. and the 'i's have hearts instead of dots above them. Maybe I should do my 'i's like this too.

My dear Hope,

We met once when you were very little, but I was too scared to tell you who I was. My name is Eliana. I am the person who left you on a church doorstep when you were one hour old. I will not call myself your mother as I do not deserve that name and because you have a lovely proper mummy now.

I always hoped that one day I would meet you again but the sad thing is that I am ill now and I don't think that can happen. I think about you very often, though, and I suppose I have always had a dream that one day I would tell you how sorry I was, and that you would be able to forgive me. That is not something that I would expect though. You have every right to hate me, not just because I left you all alone in the world, but because even before you were born, I was doing you harm. All I can say is I didn't know then what I was doing. For most of my pregnancy I truly did not realise, and for the rest I was in terrible, stupid denial.

Now I am a teacher in a special school in Christchurch, which is in New Zealand. It is beautiful here and I think you would like it. Since living here, I have worked with quite a few children whose mummies drank before they were born, and I have seen the challenges these awesome little people have had to face. I was so happy to meet your lovely mummy, Jenny, because I know that she loves you and that she will help you take on the world and win. You are lucky to have her.

There are a lot of things I wish I could have told you. But mostly this. I am so sorry for what I did. And also this, from the moment you were born, I never once stopped loving you.

Goodbye, Hope. Be safe. Be awesome. Be whatever you want to be.

Love,

E. x

It's a funny thing because the 'a' on 'awesome' is a bit of a splodge. It's because a tear has just fallen onto the card. And Julie is saying, here, sweetheart, have a tissue. And it's a funny thing too because of what the picture on the card is. I'm looking at it now. It is of a green field with trees and a house, like one in the country, with a roof made out of straw, and also there's a lake. And in the sky there is a big, gigantic coincidence. Because it's a rainbow. With all the drops of lights showing all their colours. And how could she know about that? And it's all of the colours, up into the sky and round and down again. I'm holding my mum, Jenny Nicely's, hand, and her hand is giving mine a bit of a squeeze and I show her the picture.

And I think maybe there's a tear on her eyelashes too. And I think she's going to say something. But she just does a little smile and I say does she want some more water.

28

I'm looking at my plate and I'm wondering if the sausages are the toad or the Yorkshire pudding is the toad. But I think the Yorkshire pudding must be the hole, really, because that's what the sausages are in. And you put things in a hole, you don't put them in a toad. And this time I know about what it's called, and I even know about sausages having a name which is in Latin, but I can't remember what it is. I could ask Connor Flynn. He would definitely know which bit is the hole and which bit is the toad, but I don't feel like asking.

Bridget is doing most of the talking, about what a frost there was this morning, and about the weatherman on the telly saying there is going to be a storm at the weekend and really she might have to think about bringing the geraniums in. Connor Flynn is eating all his baked beans first. Danny Flynn is mostly looking at the table, and occasionally at me, but maybe when he thinks I'm not seeing it.

'I was thinking I won't go tonight either.' This is him, and it's while Bridget is taking the plates away for the washing-up, and then it's going to be jelly and chocolate pudding. He's talking about the writers' group. And I know that he's saying it because of me being not allowed to go anymore. Even with my scholarship, I'm not in the group anymore. The writing group. Because of it being very unfortunate. Because of kicking the man in the goolies. His name is Lu-do-vic.

Marnie Shale came round to tell me. Maybe yesterday. She said she was so sad. She said that if it was up to her, she'd have me in her class and tell him to get stuffed any day. But she said her hands were tied. That wasn't a real thing – not real hands and really tied. It was an analogy. Because of me having kicked Ludovic with the knotty scarves, and because of him saying that it was not acceptable and that I had to be excluded from all the other classes. And especially because of him saying that if Marnie Shale didn't agree, he was going to go to the police, which is called pressing charges. And that, surely, wasn't in anyone's interests.

Marnie Shale said it was probably the saddest she'd been about anything in her professional life, but that there was nothing she could do. It was out of her control and she was very, very sorry. She said, if there was any other way she could help me with my book, and she said how proud she was of me, and of my scholarship. And how proud Jenny was too.

She said she'd been to see Jenny in the hospital, and what a miracle, even if she didn't seem to recognise Marnie completely yet. And she said did I understand, about the classes, and how if there was anything she could do about it, she would. But there wasn't. And this shouldn't stop me writing my book, and it was still a very Big Achievement for me. And I said yes.

'I was thinking maybe I'd just stay here and we could watch a film, or something. Or maybe go to the cinema . . .'

I'm looking at Danny Flynn but he's not looking at me. Only at the table.

Going to the cinema is what you do with boyfriends – but in the films, they call it 'going to the movies', but I'm wondering if Danny Flynn is only saying it because of me being not allowed to go to the writing group. Because of being sorry for me. I'm thinking about him with his laptop, even when I'm watching *Coronation Street* or *Pretty Woman* with his mum, and him with his whole face all scrunched up, because he's concentrating so hard about his babies in a cave.

I say, I don't want to watch a film. I say it's fine. I say I want him to go to the writing class.

A little bit later, when I'm sitting on my bed, with Barry beside me, and my slipper-paws on top of the duvet, there's a knock on the door and it's Danny Flynn again. He sits on the side of the bed and says am I really sure I don't mind? Because there's a movie on at the cinema about three women and one's a queen and the other two are her friends, and am I sure I wouldn't . . . ?

'Are you my boyfriend?' I didn't ask the question to come. It just came. I didn't even know I was thinking it. But now I'm looking at him, and I'm waiting. Because really, I do want to know. I think, actually, I need to know. Because sometimes I think probably he is, because of holding my hand or giving me a kiss, or asking me to go to the movies. But when I said it to Connor Flynn, he just laughed and laughed. So maybe it's because Danny Flynn would never want to be my boyfriend, no way Jose. But what if Connor Flynn was laughing for a different reason, like maybe just thinking of something very funny at that moment? Just a joke in his head. Maybe Danny Flynn *is* my boyfriend, actually, but maybe he will not be very happy about Connor Flynn holding my hand too, after the train that went to Rainham (Kent), and the other train too. Because even if Connor Flynn didn't like it very much, I did like it quite a lot. And maybe Danny Flynn will think that is a lot for him to take in.

Danny Flynn looks at me and he's doing a thing with his eyebrows that makes him look like Connor Flynn, just with a bit less hair above. And I'm looking at him too. And I'm waiting. I can feel it in my tummy.

'Am I your boyfriend?' He's squeezing them together now, his eyebrows, which gives him a funny face. He puts his hand near my hand, but not touching it. I nod. But also I'm wishing I hadn't asked, because, flip a pancake, maybe he's going to laugh now, just like Connor Flynn did. Maybe he's going to think I must be a stupid No-Brain to even think it. Probably I shouldn't have asked. And I'm looking at his face, and I'm thinking he's going to laugh now. He's going to say he'd never want to be *my* boyfriend. Not likely Hope Nicely. Because who'd want that?

But he doesn't do that. He just does a strange sort of smile.

'No, Hope. No, I'm not. I am your friend. At least, I'd like to think I am. But I don't think I will ever be your boyfriend. I hope that's all right.'

I'm still thinking about Connor Flynn laughing when I said it to him, with his hiccupy laugh, like it was the funniest thing in the world. And I'm thinking what a baby boo boo I am. Who would want to be my boyfriend?

'Because I'm too stupid?' And it's another question that I don't want to ask, but my mouth is doing it anyway.

He lifts his hand up and puts it down, so it's right on top of mine now. 'No, not at all. I have never ever thought you're stupid.' He looks at me, and it's not a smile really, but sort of, and there are the dimples in his cheek. 'Primarily, Hope, I can't be your boyfriend because I'm gay.'

'You're . . . ?' In my head this is a big surprise. A ginormous surprise. 'But you never told me. I didn't think that you were BGLT . . . You never even gave me a sign.'

He's doing a bigger sort of smile now, with proper dimples, and he really looks like Connor Flynn. 'LGBT? No, I don't suppose I ever did. Well, I have done now. Why? Do you mind?'

And that's a very silly question because why would I mind?

He's still sitting on the side of the bed, with his hand on my hand, not saying anything else for a little bit. But then he says, 'I do think there might be someone who would really like to be your boyfriend though.'

I say Barry, and I pick him up and give him a big squeeze and he's all furry and gives my neck a lick. That makes Danny Flynn laugh quite a lot. But he says, no, Barry wasn't who he was thinking of. And his dimples are even more dimply. Then he stands up.

'And you're sure you don't mind about me going to the writing group? I feel so awful about going without you.'

I tell him I don't mind about not going, actually. But it's a bit of a lie, because really I do mind a lot.

'Hope, love, there's someone here for you.'

It's not very long since Danny said goodbye, like five minutes or three minutes or anyway not very many minutes. When I'm opening my door, I'm wondering if maybe it's him and he's come back to say he's not really going to the writers' group and we're going to go to the cinema after all, whether I want to or not. But it's Bridget who's knocking on the door saying this and, in the dining room, sitting on the sofa, is Veronica Ptitsky. She has a jacket which looks like a zebra and her lipstick is the pinkest pink ever and she has boots which are black and very shiny and up to her knees. I ask her what she's doing here, because she should be at the writers' group and she says yes, she's come to pick me up so hurry up, let's not be late.

'I can't go. I did a bad thing.' This is me, because probably she doesn't know about it. 'I kicked Lu-do-vic in the goolies.'

'Yes. I just spoke to Danny. He told me. Good for you. If ever someone deserved a kick in the nuts, it's that man. Coming?' She's holding her arm out like she's waiting. And I really want to go but, flip a pancake, I can't, because of Marnie's hands being tied.

'I *can't* come. Because of him pressing the charges if I do. I'm not allowed anymore.' She doesn't say anything for a moment, so I say, 'More's the pity.'

'Come on, Hope. Just trust me.'

I look at Bridget. She shrugs and nods, with a smile.

'You do want to come, don't you?' This is Veronica Ptitsky. And I say, yes, I do. I really, really do.

'Good. So let's go.'

And I'm about to go with her, but Bridget is laughing and saying haven't you forgotten something. And my paws are still on my feet.

All of the group are still in the reception and haven't gone in yet. Some of them, like Susan Ford and Shelly Bell-y Kell-y with her long hair in a plait to her bottom, are sitting on the puffy benches, and some of them, like Peter Potter, are standing up. Danny Flynn and Simon Taylor are in the corner, near the water machine. And Malcolm with his orange face and Jamal, who's not a real vampire. Ludovic is between the lift and the desk but with his back towards us, so we can just see his big coat and his hat, which is like an old-fashioned one, like maybe Frank Sinatra or Mr Wormwood from *Matilda*.

But he turns round when we come out of the lift, maybe because of it going ping. And it's like his face goes from being just a still face which isn't feeling any sort of feeling, to a mouth-down and eyes-wide face, which does not look happy at all. His face makes me want to go right back into the lift and press G to go back down to the library, and to walk out of the doors and far away. But Veronica Ptitsky has her arm through my arm, like the women with the long dresses on the telly. And she gives my arm a squeeze.

'Well.' This is him, and it's with his not-happy mouth, and his hands on his hips. 'Hope Nicely, I was given to believe that you were aware of the discussions between Miss Shale and myself.' When he says Miss Shale, it's Miss with a hissing sound, like he's pretending to be a snake. 'I was under the impression that you would no longer be inflicting your presence upon us.'

He is leaning forward, towards me. His cheeks are a bit red. I'm pressing my mouth tight, with my lips together. I'm telling myself not to cry but, flip a pancake, I can feel my eyes itching like they really want to. I can't even think of a thing to say. And I think maybe I am going to have to cry.

'Actually it was me who asked Hope to come back.' This is Veronica Ptitsky. She has taken her arm out from mine, and she's stepping forward, until she's right in front of Ludovic.

He's saying, oh, was it indeed, dear Veronica – and perhaps, in that case, she had not fully understood the seriousness of the situation. Let him enlighten her. Perhaps she did not appreciate how hard he had had to consider whether he should report my act of assault, of actual bodily harm lest we forget, to the powers that be. He lifts his hat up, like he's saying how do you do, and on his forehead there is a mark which is a bit blue and a bit purple and also there's a bit of a big lump, and I'm thinking maybe that's where he hit his head on the desk. Probably it is. Because it did make quite a loud noise.

Veronica Ptitsky takes another step forward, so now she's almost touching him. Now she's putting her hand in the pocket of her zebra coat and, when it comes out again, she's holding her telephone which is the one that is pink and also gold and with the glitter on it.

'There was something here that I was looking at earlier. Now what was it?' This is Veronica. And she's looking at the phone and then lifting it up to show it to Ludovic. 'Oh yes, this. Here it is. This is the homepage for the university where you lecture?'

He's giving her a funny look with his eyebrows close together. 'Well yes. But surely that's of no . . .'

'But I'm right? This one?'

'I fail to . . .'

'Bear with me please . . . this page here . . . about their guidance on diversity and inclusion.'

'Miss Ptitsky. I simply do not see . . .'

'Just let me find what I was looking at earlier, ah yes . . . *positive action* . . . *equality assessment* . . . *tackling discrimination* . . .'

'I trust you're not suggesting that . . .'

'*We have a full commitment to creating a community for all staff and students where each individual is valued for their unique strengths and given the opportunity to* . . .'

'This is irrelevant. I have never . . .'

'. . . *irrespective of gender, religious beliefs, age, ethnic background, sexual orientation, personal circumstances and to* . . .'

'I do not see . . .'

'. . . *full respect for different abilities at all times.*'

He is leaning towards Veronica with his mouth not quite over his teeth and his eyes very wide. 'Miss Nicely's behaviour has *nothing* to do with my workplace's equal opportunities policies. I don't think you're quite comprehending that this . . . person . . .' he is looking at me with a not very nice face, 'attacked me, very violently and without the slightest provocation on my part. She'd already accosted Simon here. She is clearly incapable of . . .'

'It was not an attack, though, was it?' It's Simon Taylor now. And I'm turning my head from Ludovic, with his eyebrows down and his hard looks, to Simon, and he's doing a little smile. I think the smile is to me. 'In fact, it was me who was restraining her. Hope was trying to get free from me. Then you came up and grabbed her too. Her kicking out was just self-defence.'

'Self-defence? Rubbish. It was no accident, and she kicked me with considerable force. For heaven's sake, it was a blatant physical assault.'

'Come on, Ludovic.' This is Peter Potter with his big white eyebrows. I've only just turned my head back from Simon to Ludovic, and now I'm having to turn it again. 'Hope is hardly Mike Tyson, is she? Can you really imagine her wanting to hurt a fly?'

Everybody is looking at me now. Even me. I'm looking down at my hands because it's a bit odd to be looking at all the eyes. I don't know who Mike Tyson is but even I know I'm definitely not him. For a little while nobody says anything, but then Danny Flynn does.

'This is clearly all a misunderstanding. Hope didn't mean to hurt you. It's just cruel to stop her from coming back to the group. She's really sorry about everything that happened. Can't you just shake hands and make up?' Danny Flynn has a big smile, with all his dimples, and his hands held out. But I don't think Ludovic, with his red face and wide eyes, is very happy about it.

'I have no intention of either shaking hands or making up. And I would suggest the misunderstanding is entirely yours. You seem to be forgetting the victim in this—'

'It's not his fault.' I'm a bit surprised by who is talking now because it is me. And I didn't even think I was going to speak until I realised I was speaking. And it is interrupting, maybe, but it's because of not wanting to look at Ludovic's cross face anymore. 'The kicking. It was my fault. It was all my fault.'

And it's true. I should have kept my hands and feet to myself. And I didn't do that, more's the pity. And maybe now it is for the best if I'm not in the group anymore. Because it was a golden rule and I broke it. But now everybody is looking at me again, like they're waiting for me to say something else. So I say, 'And it's OK. I can maybe write my book on my own, actually. Even without the lessons.'

'But Hope, *none* of us *want* you to leave.' Kelly Shell-y Bell-y isn't interrupting because I'd stopped talking. 'I certainly don't. We *like* having you here. You're one of—'

'Oh please!' This is definitely interrupting actually, because Shell-y Bell-y Kell-y was being so kind and Ludovic did not even let her finish. 'She's one of us? Do me a favour. Just listen to yourself. So damned *woke*.' His mouth is turning down. 'It's political correctness gone mad. She's rude and she's stupid and she's disruptive and she's dangerous and it's a disgrace that she was ever allowed to join in the first place, when normal, intelligent people like us have paid good money to—'

'. . . *It's political correctness gone mad. She's rude and she's stupid and she's disruptive and she's dangerous and it's a disgrace that she was ever allowed to join in the first place, when normal, intelligent people like us . . .*'

This is the most confusing thing ever, because Ludovic, with his eyes so round and wide, is still talking but then there's another voice, and it's talking too, and it's another Ludovic too, saying the same thing but a little bit later. It's like Ludovic interrupting Ludovic. And this new Ludovic voice is coming from Veronica Ptitsky's phone. The one with the glitter. She's holding it up and it's saying the thing that he just said.

He – the real Ludovic, with his mouth still open – stops talking and looks at her very hard. I think maybe he is angry but he doesn't say anything else.

'Just about to tweet this video to your university, then, Ludovic.' This is Veronica Ptitsky with a gigantic smile. She has very white teeth. 'I'm sure they'll be very impressed with your attitudes.'

'You would not dare.' His face is sort of red and sort of white at the same time.

Veronica Ptitsky has her head a little bit on one side, and puts her finger to her telephone like maybe she's going to press it or swipe it. 'Oh really?' She is smiling such a very big smile, but not him. He's not doing it at all.

'Don't blackmail me, you stupid little . . .' I think the next word that Ludovic Sawyer is starting to say is one which begins with a 'b' or a 'p' maybe, because of that being the shape of his mouth now. But he doesn't say the rest of the word. Maybe because he's thinking that, actually, it's not nice at all to call somebody stupid so he shouldn't have done that. Maybe he's feeling sorry. But Veronica doesn't seem to mind at all, because she's still smiling at him, and she's still holding up her telephone. And I think what he is, actually, is really very angry, actually, because of his face being such a funny colour.

'Come on, somebody.' He is looking at all the group, except not very much at me, actually, mostly at the others. 'You all know it. Hope Nicely should not be in our classes at all. She doesn't belong here.'

He's pointing with his finger when he says this, but not really at anyone, just into the air. And he's looking at Malcolm, who has the orange face and the big gold watch. But Malcolm is just doing the thing with his shoulders which is called shrugging and also shaking his head.

'Actually, mate, hate to tell you but I think Hope's fantastic.' This is Jamal who's not a personal trainer, really, at all. And not a vampire either. 'If I had to pick somebody to leave the class, it would not be Hope, that's for bloody sure.'

It's very nice to be called fantastic, although bloody is swearing but only a little tiny one, so it's all right. I'm smiling a bit now, although not when Ludovic gives me a look.

'I don't believe this.' Ludovic's voice makes the 's' very long. 'Not one of you is willing to admit she should never have been on the course in the first place. Back me up, Sue.' He's looking at Susan now.

Her last name is Ford, like my car. Susan Ford. But he's calling her Sue, so maybe that's her name too, and saying, surely she'll agree that it makes a travesty of the entire course to have people like 'her' on it. I don't know which 'her' he means but then I think maybe the 'her' person is me.

'Shame on you, Ludovic Sawyer.' It's Susan Ford who's saying this.

Susan Ford has her hands on her hips. That's what my mum, Jenny Nicely, does, sometimes, when she needs to have a serious word. 'I think you owe Hope an apology. I think you need to tell her you're sorry, and I'm sure she'll be sweet enough to accept it, without any hard feelings.'

He's looking at Susan Ford and his mouth is open. I'm looking at Susan Ford too. Everybody is.

'*Me* apologise to *her*?' This is Ludovic saying this. And we all look at him now.

Susan Ford is looking at him and I am too. And now Danny Flynn is, with no dimples, and Simon Taylor too. And Veronica Ptitsky, with her telephone still held out in her hand, and she's giving a very hard look. And Jamal who is not a vampire. He has his arms folded. Malcolm, with his very orange face, is looking too, and Kelly Shell-y Bell-y. Peter Potter is shaking his head, but very slowly.

'I . . .' It's Ludovic Sawyer. And he doesn't say

anything else. And in my chest it's a not very nice feeling. It's tight and I can feel bumbum bumbum bumbum. And I don't want the feeling to be there. I want it to stop.

'You don't have to.' I'm shouting it a bit, because I want to say it so much, to stop everyone looking at him with their hard faces. 'I'm sorry. Me. I'm the one who did the kicking. I'm very very very sorry. And you're right about me not coming back. I'll just go now. I think that's what I should do.'

I'm turning towards the lift, because I *really* do think it's for the best if that's what I do. Because it's not very nice for Ludovic Sawyer to have to say sorry when it's me who broke the golden rules.

'Wait, Hope.' It's Veronica Ptitsky. She puts her hand on my arm, then she looks at Ludovic again. 'One moment. Give Mr Sawyer the chance to accept your gracious apology and agree to put this silly misunderstanding behind us.'

Everybody is still looking at Ludovic but he's not saying anything. And I can't show or even tell what the expression on his face is, because it's a bit like lots of different faces all at once. Like maybe angry, but also maybe being the person with the biscuits behind his back.

'Won't you, Ludovic? You were upset. It's understandable. But you wouldn't want Hope to be excluded from the class. Surely. People might think you actually believe that she does not *belong* here.'

And her eyebrows are very high. 'I think we can all see the only reasonable thing is for you to accept Hope's apology, and to move on.'

When I was little, my mum, Jenny Nicely, and I sometimes played a game. It was called blink. And it was about looking at each other with our eyes wide open and trying very hard not to close our eyes for a blink. And the first person who did the blink lost the game. And it's very funny, because I think maybe Veronica Ptitsky and Ludovic Sawyer are playing that game now. He's looking at her and she's looking at him. And I'm looking at both of them, and even I am not doing very much blinking, actually, just mostly watching them play.

'You . . .' And I think maybe Ludovic Sawyer is going to shout at her or maybe even run at her, because he does look a bit like Sallie the whippet when she wants to run at a squirrel or a crow. And Veronica Ptitsky is doing her biggest smile again, with her phone in her hand.

And then it's like he makes a puff sound and his shoulders go less high. And he stops playing blink and he looks at his feet. And he says something, but it's not very loud, so Veronica Ptitsky says maybe he should say it again. Maybe he should say it to Hope so that she can hear it.

And he looks at me, but a bit like Connor Flynn without his eyes really looking at my eyes.

'I accept your apology.'

Veronica Ptitsky's smile is even bigger. And her teeth are very white. My toothpaste box says *instantly whiter smile*, as well as *minty breath* but even with my toothpaste I don't think my teeth are as white as Veronica's.

'Perfect.' This is Veronica. 'And was there anything else . . . ?'

I do a little smile too. Just a tiny one because I don't know what else to do with my face. And Ludovic Sawyer is still looking at me but not really. I think maybe he's counting to three in his head, because he has his thumbs in his hands, with his fingers squeezing them, and that's what I do sometimes when I'm counting to three.

And then he does look at me. And I think maybe he's taking a big breath.

'I am sorry for the misunderstanding.'

And then he looks away. And Jamal, who's not a vampire, is giving him a pat on his shoulder and saying *good stuff*, and Peter Potter is giving a big grin and also looking at me and doing a wink. And Veronica Ptitsky is saying, marvellous, all sorted then, and there's a ping, a bit like a . . . wooden instrument, and it's Marnie Shale and she's coming out of the lift and saying, oh hello everybody, what's going on, and did she miss anything?

And it's a xylophone. Bingo!

Marnie Shale is very surprised when she sees me there, but she says she's thrilled that everything has been cleared up. Ludovic doesn't say very much for the whole of the class, just a little bit of yes and no, and not really putting his hand up at all, which he usually does a lot. And at the end Marnie Shale says well, next time, it's Hope's turn to submit an extract. But of course, only if I want to. She knows I've been through a lot recently, so no pressure. But I do want to. I really do. I'm going to try my very hardest to write it. I am going to persevere really hard. And when Veronica Ptitsky says who's coming for a drink, everybody says yes, except Ludovic, because of him having a headache. Even I say yes, but for just a T, even if I don't like pubs. And *even* Marnie Shale says, oh go on then, just this once.

10

CLOSING TIME

29

My Book (working title)
(extract) By Hope Nicely

My name is Hope Nicely.
Hope as in hope, and Nicely like nicely.

Why am I writing this book? Well, that's a bit of a
long story in fact. But mostly a good one too.
Because of having an arc, like an arrow going into
the air and flying for a while, before coming down
in a different place. Or like a rainbow, a big one
across the sky. And when I first thought about it,
about writing my non-fiction book called an
autobiography, it was because of wanting to find
the mother who made me the way that I am, and
because of it maybe changing my life. Now I'm still
writing my book except now it's different, because
of her being found, and also being dead. So now

there's another reason for it, for my book. But I don't want to tell it, I want to show it, with a picture that is of me, but the picture is made from words.

In my picture there is Danny Flynn, who is not my boyfriend because of being from the community which is LGBT and sometimes Q as well, but only if you want, because of everyone being unique. And there's Veronica Ptitsky, and she says I can't pretend I don't have any friends now, and she's going to teach me how to make a notebook on my telephone, because she knows how to do it, even if it's not an iPhone. And she's going to give me a cover too, with glitter in, and stars. And there's Marnie Shale, who thinks I deserve the scholarship more than anyone she knows. And there are all the other people in the group, even the ones whose names I can't remember, except maybe not so much Ludovic, even if he's back in his box and Veronica says he deserved a good kick in the nuts. And there's Simon Taylor, and he's not my dad because of DNA, but he says he would have been proud to be it. And in my showing picture, there's Bridget and Barry, and Barry's on my bed, even though his basket is on the floor. And I can still share him, even when I don't live here anymore. And Bridget says when she goes to visit her sister in Ireland for her niece's wedding, which is quite soon, please could Barry come and stay with me, maybe, for a few days, if it's no bother. And of course it's no bother, because I really want him to. And Karen, my boss, is in my picture too, and when she's not walking all the dogs with me, in the woods or the park, sometimes she's doing something else, which is helping other dogs, who have lost their homes and lost their owners, to find new homes and new owners. It's called rehoming. And she says maybe I can do some helping there too, in the kennels, and maybe, maybe, maybe, one day, when my mum is a bit stronger, we can see if there's a dog who might come and find a rehome with me. Not a puppy – because of all the poos and the chewing, and the chaos – but a nice older dog, who is calm, with good manners, who can be Barry's best friend, and mine too. But only if it's OK with my mum.

Because, of course, in my showing picture there's my mum, my real, real mum, Jenny Nicely, and even if sometimes she forgets things now, like who is the prime minister and what happened with the pizza menu before she came into hospital, the doctors think it will come back, actually. Her memory will. And even if it doesn't come back in every single bit of her brain, it doesn't even matter, because of her already remembering that adopting me was the best thing that ever happened to her. Anyway, I'll be able to help her, because of knowing what it's like to have a head that's a bit of a jumble sale. And I tell her, smile brightly, Jenny Nicely. My mum can walk all the way to the window now, without any stick at all, and she can come home soon, which is fan-tanty-tastic, because Julie's going to sort out a person to come and make our tea for a little while, and do the shopping and the housework and the caring.

And in my picture too there is Connor Flynn. He's the cleverest person I've ever met and the dimpliest, apart from maybe his brother. He doesn't like going to restaurants or to the cinema or pubs or dancing, which is what boyfriends usually do. But I don't like those things very much either, and especially not the pub, except just a little bit for a T sometimes, just this once. But Connor Flynn comes with me, almost every time now when I walk the dogs. Although it's not his real job, only mine, and I always tell him when one of the dogs is doing a poo, so he can turn around and hold his nose and close his eyes. He even held my hand once, for a whole minute. He didn't want to do it but still, it was very romantic. And he doesn't think I'm stupid. He says it's just my spectrum, which is my rainbow that is in my head. He says it's not intellectual, it's another word. It will come to me. And anyway, it's what makes me unique.

I used to think I was blue or a little bit indigo. Now I know that I'm not even a colour like anyone else's. I'm one that is just me. And I'm very lucky. I'm the luckiest person I know.

My name is Hope Nicely. Hope as in hope, and Nicely like nicely. And this is my very own book. It's going to be a Big Achievement, when I've finished persevering, but I'm not writing it to change my life anymore. I don't need to do that. Because, I'm going to show not tell you my story, and when I do, you'll see that everything is right as rain . . .

Acknowledgements

When I began writing *Hope Nicely's Lessons for Life*, it was only as an exercise (not the press-up kind, as Hope would wish me to stipulate) and it would have felt very presumptuous – publication being such a distant dream – to have compiled a bibliography of references as I went along. So I now find myself unable to acknowledge every source which I have consulted. This may be a good thing, as the list would probably have been longer than the novel itself, but I would like to make a blanket thank you to every writer, blogger, academic, campaigner or web editor who has popped up during my trawls through the internet's vast oceans.

While I've strived for accuracy in what I've written, I ask the inhabitants of Harpenden to pardon a slightly abstract depiction of their town, with its quiet railway station and third-floor library office space where the writing group happens. Once I'd written Hope's Harpenden, I could not bring myself to move her into a more faithfully-accurate version.

The world of writing groups and 'golden rules' is one that I am very familiar with, however. Every writer should work at their craft and Stephen King's *On Writing*, which crops up in the novel, is the ideal starting point. Writing a novel is daunting and, like Hope, I have benefitted from being part of a group. In 2016–17, I took a three-month novel-writing course with Curtis Brown Creative, where I was helped to find my identity as a novelist by Anna Davis, who heads up the initiative, and by Charlotte Mendelson – a fabulous tutor (and author) – as well as by my wonderful band of 'classmates'. Writing is a solitary activity, and sharing it – with honest feedback – is a good workout for anybody's writerly muscles. On this front, thanks also to Chris Brosnahan's super-supportive writers' group at North London's All Good Bookshop (previously Big Green Bookshop) with whom I shared fresh extracts of my book as a work in progress.

Hope's earliest cheerleader was my husband, Ben, who read the first page almost as it was written – and he has been Hope's biggest supporter ever since. A massive thank you too for their sensitive readings and encouragement to Anne S and Anne T, to Belinda and Emma (medical guru), Mike, Nicole and Tim.

Acknowledgements

Thanks to Edward, Grant and Ben D for their time and their wisdom, and to Jonathan for his great (subject matter allowing) photographs.

I must also thank the Romantic Novelists' Association's New Writers' Scheme, which offers manuscript assessment by published members to unpublished ones. Thank you to Jane Corry for introducing me and to the RNA's tireless team who make it such a great organisation, and in particular to the anonymous reader whose stunningly positive manuscript appraisal gave me the confidence to send Hope Nicely straight out on her next stages of the journey to publication.

Thank you to all those who have shared their professional or real-life experience of FASD, particularly to Tracy Allen of FASD Awareness for such generosity with her time and expertise, to her team for being so welcoming and to Dr Adesoja Abiona for his enlightening presentation on the condition. Thank you to Lydia Jones of Vibrance (also Channel 4's *The Undateables*) for taking the time to read *Hope Nicely's Lessons for Life*. And thank you to Steven – Hope's golden rules owe so much to you and your saying that her feelings reflected your own was the best review I could ever have had.

Thank you to the team at Lutyens & Rubinstein: Susannah, Hana and Fran, and to the finest fairy godmother of the literary agenting world, Sarah Lutyens. Thank you for believing in me! Thank you to the awesome team at Bonnier Books UK: to Sarah Bauer, my editor – I don't think either of us expected to be editing *Hope Nicely's Lessons for Life* during a pandemic, but despite coronavirus, I have loved working with you on this book – and also to Katie and to Clare and to everybody there who has put so much energy into bringing Hope Nicely onto bookshelves. As Hope might say, I am the luckiest writer I know.

Where Hope Comes From

As a journalist of twenty-plus years, I'd written extensively for national newspapers and magazines, telling the stories of thousands of real people. They had entrusted their pains and joys to me. And as my job was to tell *their* story and I owed it to them to do it right, the writing had always come easily. But when it came to creating my own characters and plot lines, it felt much less intuitive.

So, my focus was to find a character I believed in. A driving voice and a story that knew what it wanted to say. To learn from this exercise, I decided, I needed a protagonist who felt distinctive enough to lead the way. But . . . where to start?

For me, one of the hardest aspects of writing is always the infinity of possibility. But you do have to start somewhere. And if there was one unifying thread in the hundreds upon hundreds of stories that I had written on other people's behalf, it was that I had always believed, however joyful or tragic, that no story should be bereft of hope.

Hope. A noun and a verb, but also a name. The sort of name that is charged with meaning.

So, Hope. But why was Hope writing this book? And why would a reader *care*? Well, Hope was writing a book because it was going to change her life. Bingo!

Hope needed a last name. I tried a few for size. And Hope Nicely came my way. Hope as in hope. And Nicely like nicely. Why? Because it felt right. Because in just that name – Hope Nicely, who was writing her book to change her life – there was already a story forming.

Hope as in hope. And Nicely like nicely. Why am I writing this book? That's easy . . .

As for the decision to locate the action in a writers' group, it felt like a situation I could recreate authentically. I had previously taken a novel-writing course and I regularly attend a local writers' group. It felt fun to create my own fictional group, and I relished the idea of writing about writing.

So there was Hope Nicely. She was writing her book to change her life. Except, of course, she still needed a little help from me.

I wanted Hope to have a voice that was all her own. And, as a writer – and the most freeing thing from my point of view – I was simply going to write as many words as possible as fast as I could. This was because *Hope Nicely's Lessons for Life* started out as an exercise for National Novel Writing Month, a yearly challenge to write a 50,000-word novel in the space of just 30 days. So no agonising over what was the *ideal* word to use, the *ideal* plot line. Just words. Hope Nicely started life as an exercise without any agenda. The name came first. It fed into the first line, which fed into the next. Those lines led into the character.

Why would writing a book be such a challenge? Well, Hope was a person that nobody would ever have expected to do this.

OK. But *why not?*

In all those years of writing other people's true stories, the important thing had been to ask the questions and listen to the answers. That is what I started doing with Hope. *Why* are you writing the book? *Why* did nobody ever believe you would be capable of it?

From the questions came the answers. From the answers came Hope.

Honest and endearing and impulsive. Hope had a brain that was a bit of a muddle. But *why* . . . ?

I myself have some small notion of how it feels to have a jumble sale brain. In 2010, a condition called primary hyperparathyroidism sent my calcium levels soaring. As calcium has a role in carrying messages to your brain, high levels can do unexpected things. Confusion, memory problems and anxiety were symptoms which I experienced. For me, chemotherapy and surgery corrected the problem, but the experience gave me a respect for how small fluctuations in the body's delicate balance can impact emotions, reasoning and behaviour. It was humbling to experience how a person can be fully aware that their brain isn't firing as it should, yet powerless to do anything.

Years before I had written about a mother whose child was born with Foetal Alcohol Syndrome (as it was termed before FASD was recognised as a broader spectrum of conditions) and I had been particularly moved by her story. But until Hope's voice was already in my head, I didn't realise that I was going to write about a character who had FASD. It felt rather as though I was discovering this about her, even as she grew into existence. It meant that I had to educate myself.

I did research to reassure myself that I was reflecting the condition accurately. But Hope's voice was what came first.

On 30th November I hit my 50,000-word target. Coincidentally it was the day that Bristol University released its study suggesting that FASD was more prevalent in the UK than previously thought.

I put out feelers to various groups and was reassured by the positive feedback. But my biggest debt of gratitude is to Tracy Allen. Tracy is a busy woman who has been more than generous with her time. She runs FASD Awareness, a charity for families affected by the condition. Tracy and her husband Paul have fostered many young people with disabilities, some with FASD. After I sent her my first draft to look at, she told me how much Hope reminded her of one of the children they'd previously fostered, who was now an amazing young woman living successfully with FASD.

Since writing *Hope Nicely's Lessons for Life*, I have met up with Tracy for coffees and lunches (recently Zoom ones, thanks to the coronavirus pandemic) and she invited my husband and myself to the group's recent activity day. I feel privileged to have been given this glimpse into the dedication that goes into trying to bring about a better understanding for young people with FASD. It is a condition believed to affect more than autism does, yet many people have never even heard of it.

Tracy and I first met in person in September 2019, when the group's trustee, Dr Adesoji Abiona, gave a talk about the medical aspects of FASD. It was an enlightening presentation for me.

In the late 1990s, when I was in my twenties,

the magazine at which I worked had their summer sports day in Regent's Park. As well as the statutory three-legged races and rounders, there was a great deal of beer and wine and, after a hugely boozy afternoon, everybody headed to the pub.

I was utterly unaware that I was pregnant at the time. The first I knew about it was when I had a miscarriage in the early hours of the next morning. The doctors at Middlesex Hospital estimated that I'd been about nine weeks along, and said that it looked as if I had been carrying twins. Though nobody said it, I felt sure that the drinking that day had contributed to – or caused – my miscarriage. I'll never know for sure if that was the case, of course, but it is something I think about to this day.

Bizarrely, it had not registered during the writing of *Hope Nicely* that this experience had any specific bearing on my own novel. I'd even talked to Tracy about the miscarriage in terms of how damaging drinking in pregnancy could be. I wasn't ashamed of it. I hadn't known about the pregnancy and I'd become pregnant again just a few months later. By the time I came to write *Hope Nicely's Lessons for Life*, I had two teenage children. In fact, Dr Abiona's talk was on my son's twentieth birthday.

The doctor talked about how alcohol drunk during pregnancy crosses unobstructed into the foetus through the blood stream, about the different stages in gestation and the lack of understanding as to why one mother drinking heavily for nine months may have no discernible effect on the baby, while in another case, even light occasional drinking might lead to a severely affected child.

My motivations for writing this particular book began to feel less random. I had written an entire novel about a young woman who had FASD. I had let her voice guide the story. I'd freed my brain to go with the flow, and the result was Hope Nicely, writing her own story to find the birth mother she had never known. What a strange thing the subconscious is.

Hope Nicely could have been my child. As it turns out, she is only a fictional one. But, nevertheless, she has taught me a lot.

Read on for more from Caroline Day, including Hope Nicely's Golden Rules, a poem by Jenny Nicely and questions for your reading group

HOPE NICELY'S GOLDEN RULES

By Hope and Jenny Nicely

Rules are important. They tell us how to behave. Everybody needs rules to live by and we must try our hardest to remember them. Sometimes we might forget a rule – and that is OK, because everybody forgets things sometimes. But we should try even harder to remember next time.

Rules help us to understand the world. They help us to respect other people and ourselves too. They are very valuable. They are our lessons for life.

1) KNOW WHO I CAN TRUST

Hope, I promise that I will always, always, always love you and nothing you can do or say will ever change this. There are other people who you can trust, too. I will help you to know who they are. Mum x

I listen to the people I trust.

I don't trust everyone.

Most people are good people, and safe to be with. But not everybody is.

If I do not know somebody, they are a stranger.

I don't trust a stranger just because they say I can.

I ask myself: Why do I trust this person? What is my reason?

I should not go with a person or do what they ask me to do just because they want me to.

If I am scared or sad or confused, I talk to the people I know I can trust.

In an emergency, I can call 999.

I know how to say no.

2) ONLY I AM ME

Hope, I love you for who you are and there is nothing about you that I would change. If anybody ever makes you feel that you should be different, then that person does not deserve to be with you. Love yourself, my darling. x

I am proud of me.

I am not afraid to be me.

I am not afraid to cry or to laugh.

I am as good as everyone else.

Making mistakes is OK. It helps me to learn.

I am unique. There is nobody like me.

We are ALL unique. Nobody has the very same body or the very same skin or has the very same feelings or the very same brain. Inside we are all different too.

I make my own choices.

I will try not to say yes just because I want to please you and to not look silly (but please check I really understand).

I am complicated. I am capable.

3) THINK BEFORE DOING

Hope, my love, we all speak or act without thinking first sometimes. And I believe it is that little bit harder for you. I am so proud of you for trying. x

I listen to myself.

When I'm angry, step away.

Sometimes only I can make my brain be still again.

I find my calm. I count to three.

Think about consequences. Consequences are what happen because of something I do – even if I don't want them to happen.

Little things can have big consequences. A little tap can make a big flood.

If I think about consequences, I am looking after myself and the people around me.

Being sad is not bad. It is not bad to cry. But if I can, I smile too.

When I can, I smile brightly. But only if I can.

4) KEEP OUR HANDS
AND FEET TO OURSELVES

Hope, it is not only our brains which have feelings – our bodies do, too. We should never be ashamed of our bodies, but we have to think about other people. This is called respecting each other. It is very important. x

My body belongs to me.

Other people's bodies belong to them.

We keep our hands and feet to ourselves.

We do not touch each other unless we both agree.

Other people's bodies can make people feel uncomfortable or embarrassed.

Keeping a space of an arm away can help people feel more comfortable together.

Some parts of my body are private. They are not bad, they are just private.

They are private because they are not for showing or touching when other people are with me.

If somebody I trust needs to see or touch a part of my body to help me, then that is OK.

In relationships, too, people see and touch each other's bodies sometimes. But only if they agree they both want to, and only if they trust each other. Otherwise, they should say no.

Hitting or kicking other people is wrong, unless they are trying to hurt me.

A hug is good, but only if I want one.

5) REMEMBER RULES
AND PLANS

Hope, my love, we can't always know what is going to happen to us, but life is easier when we try to know what is coming next. Having a plan helps us to feel more in control. A plan helps to make our brain feel clear and it helps us not to make so many mistakes. x

Keep to rules, laws and plans.

If I forget sometimes, I will try extra hard next time.

It is OK to make changes, but good to know the routines for our day.

Planning is good for my body and my brain. Routines make life less stressful.

I eat at the right times. I drink water and go to the loo before my body really needs to. I keep my body clean and fresh.

I write my appointments on my planner. I set alarms so that I don't forget.

Being on time is important.

Life will not always follow my plan.

There will be some surprises and shocks. Try to find my calm. Remember my golden rules.

I am capable. I am calm. I am brave.

6) CARE ABOUT WORDS AND PEOPLE

Hope, you know you can share everything with me, always. You are more precious than any poem I will ever write. Poems are only words – but words are how you tell the world about yourself. They do matter. When you talk, listen to what your words are saying. xxx

Sometimes there is so much in my head but I do not have to say it all at once.

Take a breath. Find my calm.

Talking is not just words in my mouth – talking is about knowing what I'm saying.

Don't tell people everything that is in my head.

I am real. I am important. I do not need to shout.

Sometimes I feel outside. Sometimes I feel hidden. But I do make a difference.

A conversation is about more than one person.

Ask questions. Listen. Don't interrupt.

Not lying does not mean I have to tell everybody all of the truth.

Some things are personal. People do not need to know everything about my life or my body or my money. I do not have to tell them everything even if they ask.

Swearing is not a clever way to say something. I can find a better word.

It's OK to say sorry. And sorry. And sorry.

Sorry does not make me bad. It makes me want to grow.

It is OK for me to laugh at myself. You can laugh at myself too.

My words matter.

I matter.

Caroline Day

MARNIE SHALE'S NUMBER 1
VERY IMPORTANT GOLDEN RULE
OF WRITING

Show, don't tell.

Extraordinary Drop of Light
by Jenny Nicely

i
am
not
you
not
able
– me,
to see
as you
see nor
to feel as
you feel. i
am ordinary,
see. me, plain
rain-drop which
light eschews and
passes through. i am
not like you. clear, am i
a mere bystander to you
extraordinary drop of light,
rain on whom sun alights, who
causes it to pause and to deflect
this is divergence – the spectacular
emergence of colours as light comes
through and bounces askew from the
dispersive prism of your mirror mind
refracting into red indigo and blue
… and you – you do not see that
you are bright in the sky, you
do not know that you are
extraordinary too,
indigo, blue.

Reading Group Questions

1. What is the significance of the novel's title? What do you think Hope learns in this book, and what did you learn from it?

2. In what ways is the novel a coming-of-age story?

3. How does the novel explore friendship? How does it explore family?

4. What is the significance of names in this novel?

5. What did you like about the writing style?

6. To what extent is Hope an unreliable narrator? Have you read any other novels with unreliable narrators, and what did you think of this new take on narrative perspective?

7. What do you think of the central relationships in this book? How does Hope move from relying solely on her mum to also relying on her friends?

8. Had you heard of Foetal Alcohol Spectrum Disorders before reading this novel?

9. Have you read any other books with neuroatypical narrators?

10. Who was your favourite minor character and why?

11. This book covers many difficult topics, including that of depression and suicide. Did Hope's first person narrative help make it more personal for you? Have you read any other novels that have made you think about mental health in a new way?

12. How does writing become therapeutic for Hope?

13. How are the elements and devices of novel-writing that Hope learns – dialogue, conflict, upping the stakes, narrative arc, and even 'show, don't tell' – reflected within the novel itself?

14. The visiting editor, Patsy Blake, asks Hope what her book is *really* about, and adds that she thinks it's about identity and belonging. What do you think the book Hope is writing, and indeed this novel, are *really* about?

15. If you could set six 'golden rules' for everyone to live by, what would they be?